This Time Last Year

This Time
Last Year

Douglas Hobbie

A John Macrae Book

Henry Holt and Company New York

Henry Holt and Company, Inc.
Publishers since 1866
115 West 18th Street
New York, New York 10011

Henry Holt® is a registered trademark
of Henry Holt and Company, Inc.

Published in Canada by Fitzhenry & Whiteside Ltd.,
195 Allstate Parkway, Markham, Ontario L3R 4T8.

The author wishes to express grateful acknowledgment to the John Simon
Guggenheim Memorial Foundation for support during the writing of this book.

Library of Congress Cataloging-in-Publication Data
Hobbie, Douglas.
This time last year : a novel / Douglas Hobbie.—1st ed.
p. cm.
"A John Macrae book."
ISBN 0-8050-5492-8 (HB : acid-free paper)
I. Title.
PS3558.03364P57   1998
813'.54—DC21   97-28237

Henry Holt books are available for special promotions
and premiums. For details contact: Director, Special Markets.

First Edition 1998

Designed by Michelle McMillian

Printed in the United States of America
All first editions are printed on acid-free paper. ∞

1   3   5   7   9   10   8   6   4   2

The darkness
keeps us near you.

—Wendell Berry
from "To the Unseeable Animal"

'Twas just this time, last year, I died.
—Emily Dickinson

CONTENTS

This Time Last Year

1 *The Project*

The Gore on Queen's Gate, small and quiet, and only steps from Kensington Gardens, turned out to be better than expected. The hotel had been her sister's suggestion, a place Mary and Fitz had stayed more than once. The corner room she shared with Lynn on the third floor was almost spacious, with elaborate draperies, worn Oriental rugs, a pink love seat, and two double beds. There was a youth hostel next door and the Royal College of Art next to that. At the other end of the tree-lined street, past the mute façade of Imperial College, stood the Natural History Museum and the Victoria and Albert Museum, two sights Elizabeth was inclined to skip for the present. In half an hour, she had showered and impatiently attempted to get her hair right with the blow-dryer, she'd done her makeup routine and pulled on the same clothes she'd worn yesterday, a relaxed all-purpose outfit by Eileen Fisher. She felt better and maybe looked better when she threw herself together. Too much fussing made her feel uptight.

"Okay, how's this?"

Lynn, practicing stretching exercises in her underwear on

the threadbare Persian carpet, didn't look up. "Are you eating breakfast?"

"Let's meet back here at five or so. We'll freshen up and go out to dinner. No, I don't want breakfast."

"Maybe you'll end up with a date," Lynn said.

"I'll see you back here." She paused at the door. "Be honest, is this too sloppy?"

"You know how you look."

"A woman on the verge?"

"An adventuress."

"Be careful crossing the streets, all right?" Lynn hadn't been to London before, and Elizabeth tended to be protective toward her, the responsible older sister, a role her own older sister had never quite assumed where she was concerned.

"I know, everyone's going the wrong way."

A blond young man chaining his bicycle to the wrought-iron fence outside the youth hostel glanced up as she came down the stairs, and again as she walked toward him, adjusting the strap of her shoulder bag, tracing the edge of the outside pocket with her fingers, yes, her pocket guide there with good reliable maps, excellent. The cool air was a tonic, her planned morning's walk all the exercise she would need today. The boy reminded her of David, his smooth serious face, sturdy shoulders, the faded knapsack, so she smiled as she walked by him.

Cutting through a corner of the gardens, skirting the Albert memorial to her right, Elizabeth entered the park, following a path along the Serpentine. Three horsemen cantered toward her on so-called Rotten Row, posting on their saddles, fresh balls of horse manure steaming on the track. There was something stirring, sexual, as they thundered past—two men and a woman—but everything was tinged that color this morning, as though she couldn't help herself. Ridiculous. Never ridden a horse, to name one thing

4

she'd never done, never known what all that thunderous commotion between your knees was about. The woman was actually a girl, she saw, whose pink face pouted with concentration. Two dogs raced alongside in the grass, manic and feisty, those rat-catchers, Jack Russells was what they called them. The English were a bad movie with their horses and dogs, their damn boots and black caps, a little desperate somehow, carrying on with mortifying pastimes like the bloody fox hunt, for crying out loud. They came down behind her at a gallop as she crossed the riding area, causing her to dart into damp grass, laughing, giddily alarmed. Oh not smart, Elizabeth.

Tourists armed with cameras already swarmed before Buckingham Palace, posing themselves before the Victoria memorial and the tall forbidding front gates. Striding along purposefully under an arching canopy of plane trees, Elizabeth was not one of them. In St. James's Park a stout squat man stood at the center of a circle of birds—St. Francis at the Frick, she thought—feeding them from his open palms, half a dozen sparrows perched on his balding head. Wasn't that awfully unsanitary, their dirt and feathers and bird shit? From the bridge that crossed the pond she stopped to take in the resident waterfowl and the distant view of Whitehall. She checked her watch: hours to kill. A tall man she was sure she'd noticed observing her in the pedestrian subway when she left Hyde Park now passed behind her on the bridge and stopped a few yards away. Stonewashed jeans and bulky running shoes made him American to her, although he wasn't toting a tourist's typical paraphernalia. He looked in her direction, daring himself to speak, Elizabeth imagined, and she proceeded toward the east end of the park at her aerobic pace. The inflamed outside edge of her left big toe, the cost of stupidly traipsing all day yesterday in espadrilles that pinched, had begun to throb despite the comfortable and roomy lace-up shoes she was wearing today. At the corner of the park she surveyed the scene as though getting her bearings. Sure enough, this clown was on the path behind her. Damn it all. She wanted to force his hand, if that's what was going on here, and get it over with. Like a person who'd just remembered something important, she headed back the way she'd come. Predictably the man raised his head attempting to catch her eye as she approached. A bland handsome face with large teeth in it. Maybe fortyish. He wasn't menacing, he was one of those self-assured dopes.

"Excuse me," he said.

She stopped, heart racing.

"We've been headed in the same direction since about Hyde Park. I was wondering, are you from the States? Just a hunch."

"No," she said emphatically, mustering a British accent. "The answer is no."

He raised both hands. "That's all right."

She hadn't intended to enter Westminster Abbey until she saw the twin towers sticking up there, someone's incongruous eighteenth-century addition, she recalled, but then it seemed lazy and cavalier of her to walk right by—*the* shrine to Anglo-Saxon civilization, for God's sake, and when would she return to this city. Maybe never. The soaring feeling as she cast her eyes upward to the vaulted ceiling was a sensation remembered from her first visit here almost ten years before. The clamorous intention of the architecture almost seemed corny—transcendence—yet it worked. You wanted to believe there was more to man's existence than life on earth. A moment later that intimation escaped her in a sigh, a breath of resignation, as she stood over the Tomb of the Unknown Warrior and read the magniloquent inscription imbedded in stone with letters made from brass bullet casings. Gave the most that man can give life itself for God for King and Country, that was a mouthful. Buried among kings because he had done good toward God . . . Warrior! More like a child. Somebody's precious expendable flesh and blood.

No one would want to know it was their boy whose corpse stood in for the countless nameless faceless casualties of the Great War. Unknown meant nobody, a body.

Her memory of the convoluted interior was remarkably intact, enabling her to anticipate the Abbey's grandeurs as she walked through, naming various notable details as they appeared. She had no patience for the heaps of upright statuary, while the tombs with their recumbent effigies provoked a more real sense of the dead. Elizabeth I's visage looked grim. Her sister was in there with her: buried under her. The elaborate ornamentation of Henry VII's chapel seemed overboard. In the midst of all this stone and marble the wooden bridge to St. Edward's shrine was a crude anomaly. She didn't know the first thing about Edward the Confessor, except that he was somehow at the bottom of all this history. Her ignorance, which had seemed remediable ten years ago, was now permanent. She'd never known any more about Edward the Confessor or Henry VII than she knew about the Unknown Warrior. Less really. That was just too bad.

The ancient Coronation Chair with its legendary stone made her think of her mother, who was ten when she sailed to the United States from Scotland with parents hoping to better their lot, who would pine for their beloved country the rest of their lives. One souvenir from the Old World, a miniature brass Coronation Chair with a tiny removable Stone of Scone, had made the journey with her. The souvenir had survived into Elizabeth's childhood, although she never knew what had eventually become of it. The initial sighting of the real thing ten years before had had the force of a revelation and made her laugh out loud. Now the sight of the vacant chair unexpectedly moved her, a symbol of her mother's innocence and of her own irrecoverable loss.

Her mother, Henry's father, and then, impossibly, his daughter. It was as if their marriage had been oppressed by illness and death almost from the beginning. Her stomach felt empty, and she steadied herself against a massive pillar, cool to the touch, until the nauseating wave of dizziness passed. She had not been with her mother at the moment of her death and her regret was a wound, a burn, that wouldn't heal. She'd left the hospital in the afternoon, promising to return that night with Mary. Regarding her with the kindest eyes in the world, her thin fragile mother had said, Oh, I'll be here, you go have a good dinner. She died an hour before the sisters returned, she'd been alone. That memory was linked to another, her last visit with Henry's daughter, two days before her death. The young woman had been entirely alert and astonishingly calm. The room was full of late afternoon light. Take care of my dad, she'd said, and the girl's smile as she said the words, affectionate, trusting, even peaceful, was like a blessing.

Oh God, she thought. Not here, Elizabeth. Now come on. Stop it.

A dozen people obediently shuffled into the Confessor's shrine and gathered before the royal chair. In a showy British voice, intrusive and irritating enough to stop her tears, the male guide regaled them with lore about the Stone of Scone, which had surely been used at Macbeth's coronation, he said, captured by Edward I at the end of the thirteenth century, temporarily seized by Scottish nationals six hundred and fifty years later. She fled, walking quickly, and soon found herself treading on memorial plaques—Byron, Tennyson, Henry James—poets tucked into their out-of-the-way corner, a far cry from real power and glory. She continued down the south choir aisle, ignoring the cloisters, and returned to the Abbey's vast nave. She couldn't get her breath. I will, she thought, I'll take good care of him, I promise. When she tipped her head back, the arched ceiling blurred, the faraway height of it dizzying, suffocating. You can't pass out in Westminster Abbey, for God's sake, it's just nerves, you're fine. She slipped into the end seat of the nearest pew and bent her head to her knees as though in ardent prayer.

Moments later, hurrying outside, the sunshine surprised her. She'd forgotten it was a beautiful day.

She stepped into the street, the Houses of Parliament just across the way, and seemed to set off a shriek of alarms. Before she understood, two black cabs were past, miraculously missing her, the tires inches, she imagined, from her forwardmost foot. She'd looked the wrong way. I'm going to get killed, she thought, that's why I'm here. Her legs were weak with fright as she walked along the river, the damn toe burning. She refused to favor it. She glanced at her map, yes, the bridge before her was Lambeth.

The Tate was welcoming, yet she had lost her desire to look at art. She drifted through the galleries, feeling unfocused and edgy. She decided the title *The Cholmondeley Sisters*, circa 1600, referred to the two almost identical women in the painting, not the identical infants they were holding. Gainsborough's sumptuous portrait of his daughter Mary stopped her for a minute. She went past Reynolds and Hogarth and those Stubbs horses quickly. Couldn't stand still for Constable or British landscapes in general. Blake was too much work. The Pre-Raphaelites had always repelled her. Almost the whole of the modern collection seemed familiar, movements and individual vocabularies so instantly recognizable from decades of museum-going in New York that she went through naming names without stopping to pay attention. There were three exceptions. The leering cruelty and deforming vengefulness portrayed in Bacon's *Three Studies for Figures at the Base of a Crucifixion* disturbed her. If you believed people were grotesque, did it mean you viewed yourself that way? The woman in Lucian Freud's *Naked Portrait* was contorted at the lower end of a brass bed, her right knee drawn to her chest while the left foot seemed to clutch the corner of the bed for support, legs parted, exposing her crotch. Her cunt, she thought. The eyes of the figure stared, one hand in a fist, as if stricken by a daydream. The nakedness Freud captured, a leveling intimacy, prevented you from assessing the woman's mundane appeal. The painting didn't invite you to imagine a person or contemplate any reality beyond the painting itself. The actual person was probably pretty beautiful, Elizabeth imagined, as a woman crossing a room, for example, but the painter's truth about her, her vulnerability and sadness and discomfort, her nakedness, made any question about her looks absurd. It was the painting that was beautiful. If Elizabeth couldn't see herself in Bacon's ferocious distortions, she couldn't help identifying with the figure in Freud's portrait.

Standing before one of Rothko's black and maroon paintings, she almost started crying again, Jesus, Elizabeth, you're a freaking wreck. You disappeared into these paintings, the room went silent, and here was her mother's death again and Henry's daughter dying so young, disappearing. Everyone died, and until you died you went around anguishing, making yourself sick. A trip to England made you feel like a criminal. She didn't want to go around sentenced to misery because terrible things happened, which no one could control. Because living meant dying. What was she so anxious about? She wasn't committing a crime. Meeting someone for a drink or whatever wasn't a fucking crime. How old are you, she thought. She'd felt smarter and more together ten or twenty years ago.

She carefully dripped Visine into her eyes in the rest room, she freshened her lipstick and neatened up her hair a little. There was nothing wrong with the way she looked. She got a warm roll and a watercress salad and a glass of white wine downstairs, which took the edge off her appetite and maybe her nerves. The place was busy enough so that she felt invisible rather than conspicuous. People seemed cheerful, amiable, happy to be here. A thin elderly man wearing a coarse wool suit and red shoes made her smile. A second glass of wine was a temptation, but risky; let's not be stupid. She still had an hour. She'd been anticipating the Turner paintings, hoping to repeat the exalted feeling they'd inspired the first time she'd seen them, saving them today, but now when she entered the Clore Gallery she realized she'd had enough, she couldn't look anymore.

They'd run into one another in May at Gourmet Garage on Wooster, of all places, near the cheeses. He was only in Manhattan overnight—he'd spent the school year at RISD—just then getting a gift for the people who were putting him up, leaving for Paris the next morning. Early in June he would be staying with a friend in London before going on to Northern Ireland to follow up a project that he'd begun the summer before. I'll call you, he said when she told him, laughing, that she planned to be in London about the same time with a friend. That coincidence, informed by the very unlikelihood of running into him on the eve of his departure, seemed like fate or something. By the following morning she made up her mind to forget about it. To her surprise, a message— Welcome to London, As ever, Gustavo—along with a number where he could be reached, awaited her arrival at the Gore two weeks later. As ever, Gustavo! Ignore it, Elizabeth. But when he phoned later that night she agreed to join him for a drink the next day. I suppose I can spare an hour, she said. She and Lynn were leaving London the following day. He suggested a pub in Chelsea, conveniently not far from Queen's Gate, three o'clock.

The sight of him alone at a table outside the pub, his hunched unmistakable profile, momentarily gave her cold feet and she told the cab driver to continue to the end of the block. It was ten past three. The smart thing would be not to show up at all. Except he knew where she was staying, he was persistent. No, the smart thing was to spend a harmless hour talking about nothing of consequence, and to leave after one drink.

Gustavo Lacaz. Flashes of the year they'd been together more than ten years before kept intruding. Sexual stuff almost embarrassing, it was so one-dimensional. They'd met at an opening, photographs he'd done as a United Nations photographer in Bangladesh in 1984. Elizabeth's friend Annabelle, the manager of the gallery, had frankly set them up. He was born in Buenos Aires, but his father, a mathematician, had moved them to Berkeley following a decade of teaching posts at European universities. Gus had graduated from Berkeley and then taken an M.F.A. at Yale. Two years younger than she was, dark with large dark eyes, he was confident, determined, and his aggression was sexually exotic to her. She was used to tamer, more deferring men. Fucking was the drug and both of them, early- to mid-thirties then, wanted to be addicted. He continued to see other, usually younger women, an irresistible philanderer, and that became the insurmountable problem. Then he was out of the country for a time. She eventually received a copy of the book *Portrait of Tibet*, which resulted from his stint there as a photography instructor with an outfit called Journeys International. She got hung up with him again for several months the year she was getting to know Henry—another matchmaking setup—as if testing her new romance against the Gustavo heat. Their weekly encounters ended when he went off on another project, South Africa this time, funded by a Guggenheim Fellowship. The year he taught at the School of Visual Arts, he would invite her out for lunch or a drink every two or three weeks, it seemed—he'd gotten her number from Annabelle—and she almost never refused. She was married then, but she liked being a friend to whom he could confide his ambitions and frustrations, and she enjoyed the sexual innuendo between them, the slight rush. His work, an ongoing documentary of his personal odyssey through some public calamity, largely pictures of people, was gaining recognition. *Granta* published his photographs of Bucharest, though they were more like art than photojournalism. One year he was part of a group show at MOMA, and another year three large pieces were chosen for the Whitney Biennial. Their last meeting had followed the death of Henry's daughter. She contacted him at Princeton, another of his one-year teaching posts, feeling confused and angry and shut out by her husband and his former wife, and she'd come close to a bad mistake. She wanted to be comforted, they both got tipsy, he stuffed his hand down her pants in the cab, and she practically made a scene outside her apartment building in order to get away from him. That seemed to have finished them for good. Yet bumping into him at Gourmet Garage over two years later still carried a charge, an unmistakable current arcing between them over the pyramid of goat cheese. They both seemed to acknowledge that the initial exchange all those years ago, while lasting little more than a year, had burned deep.

He stood up as she approached his table and now, unlike their chance meeting in New York, he leaned toward her mouth with his big face, half smiling. She turned her cheek to him. They were the same height, so their face-to-face encounters fluctuated, so to speak, with what each of them had on their feet. Today she seemed to have the edge on him, thanks to her thick-soled walking shoes.

She began recounting highlights of her day so far—horses in the park, the coveted miniature Coronation Chair of her childhood—too eagerly. The way he listened, observing her, made her tense. She didn't want to perform. When their pints of bitter arrived, she took a long swallow—"God, I'm thirsty"—and went on about her scare crossing Millbank—"I should be dead"—and the way a Lucian Freud painting had made her feel stripped bare. How he was making her feel at the moment, letting her babble on as though he had no obligation to contribute to the conversation here. He was thick, bearish. His large square hands were paws spread out palm down on the wood table on either side of his beer mug as though she was meant to draw their outline on the table with a pencil. He could almost encircle her upper arm with one of those hands and he could easily encircle her upper thigh with both of them. He sat back, his palms pressed together as in prayer, the beer before him still untouched, while she talked about how exhausting museums were. He was enormously vain about his hands, he was a vain man.

"I seldom go to museums in foreign cities," he said. "I want to be out on the street."

She wanted to know what he would be doing in Ireland and he told her he'd discovered a neighborhood in Belfast, "visually dynamite," faces like you rarely saw anymore. He was eager to return to Bosnia—he'd been there once, only to Sarajevo—but that was impossible for the time being. In the fall he would be part of a group exhibit at the Corcoran—stuff he'd shot in New York's Chinatown a while ago. He was wearing a black T-shirt under his linen jacket, and she thought she'd like him to take off the jacket. His facial tics as he talked about his work, his pouting seriousness, an almost glowering frown, the dark mobile eyebrows, were remarkably familiar to her, as if little time had passed since they'd last talked. His hair, which stood off his skull in a dense uncombable shock, was grayer, she thought, and she could see signs of aging around the eyes, although his skin was very good, firm and smooth. He unbuckled his watchband, rubbing the top of his wrist with his thumb before rebuckling it. His natural bulk and his bright health were part of his beauty. The way an ape was beautiful. Or an inflamed penis in the palm of your hand, against your cheek, was beautiful. She touched the pendant that hung against her chest, a piece of amber in silver, rotating its dense smoothness between her fingers. Her focus alternated between his eyes and his mouth. She was aware of that. She looked toward the street: white buildings, wrought-iron gates, flower boxes. She didn't know a soul in this city, she was anonymous, she might be anyone.

Every year was a struggle, he was saying, hustling jobs, shows, funding, while trying to get the work done and make it good. The implicit plea for sympathy or admiration, the implicit boasting and self-regard, disappointed her.

"Poor you," she said.

When she brought up the photographic work she'd seen at a recent Whitney Biennial, he let her talk without offering his opinion, bound to be unimpressed by the heralded stars of his generation, and then simply changed the subject—"What's happening with you these days?"—which was like a slap. Unlike Henry, who was always at pains to explain and persuade, unwilling to let a difference of opinion pass, Gustavo didn't care what you thought about Nan Goldin or Cindy Sherman, and he didn't have the patience to argue or enlighten. You could think what you pleased. She tipped up the last of her beer. She didn't want to feel irritated, she wanted to enjoy herself for five minutes.

"Are you still doing the same work?" he asked.

She stood up. "I'll be right back." Her anger was visible to her in the bathroom mirror; he had surely seen it. She slipped her hand down the front of her skirt into her underpants, touching herself precisely. Viscous. His presence and her nutty daydreaming, following all the anticipation, had aroused her. Where is your head, Elizabeth? She rinsed her hands and reapplied her lipstick. What's happening with you these days? Oh fuck off, Gus.

There were two fresh pints on the table when she returned. "I can't drink another beer, I'll be drunk."

"Drink what you want. You never answered my question."

Her own artistic aspirations, pathetically encouraged for four deluded years as a painting student at Parsons (a phrase that had become rote as a summary of her youth), had found their practical outcome, following a decade of frustration and disappointment, in designing window displays for retailers like Bloomingdale's, Saks, Bergdorf Goodman. A temporary job taken to see her through one Christmas season had stumbled her into a so-called career. She had persevered through most of her twenties as a pauper on the Lower East Side. A regular paycheck, which increased substantially as she assumed greater responsibilities, proved irresistible. By the time she began to feel like a bona fide grownup—car, decent apartment, furniture, clothes, travel—there was no going backwards. She preferred working with people, playing her part, to working alone. She liked appointed tasks, clear goals, getting the job done, and getting paid for it. She wasn't an artist was the conclusion she'd come to. Letting go of the illusion was a relief.

"I'm still doing windows, but I'm between jobs right now. It was time to make a move. Up, I hope. I want to be the boss now, I'm old enough."

"You look well, Iz." He added, "You don't age, do you?"

"Oh never. Wouldn't dream of it." His old name for her surprised her. She sipped from the stout glass. No, she was not going to drink it all. She wanted to change the subject. "I saw a sort of Serrano retrospective at the New Museum. His morgue pictures are something, aren't they?"

Gustavo grunted skeptically.

"What's your problem with his work? I thought it was strong stuff."

He reached into his jacket pocket and handed her a small faded blue box. "My Paris aunt, my mother's sister, gave it to me the other day. She was cleaning out her drawers, she thinks she's dying."

The box contained a graduated necklace of brilliant deep blue beads, only sparingly gold-flecked, with a gold clasp.

"A gift to my mother when she was a teenager. My aunt claims they'd belonged to their mother. I don't think I believe her. You must have it, she said, you must have it, Gustavo."

She knew that his mother had died in Paris when he was a boy, the only child, and his father had never remarried. "How nice of her," she said. "Lapis lazuli, don't you love that name. It's beautiful." She placed the necklace in the box and handed it back to him.

"That's for you," he said. "Keep it."

She set the box down on his side of the table. "It was your mother's, you should keep it."

"What am I going to do with a necklace? I want you to have it."

"I can't accept it, Gus." She lightly touched the top of his hand. "But I'm touched. Thanks."

He turned his hand, snaring hers, and leaned toward her across the table. "Let's go to your hotel and fuck like we used to." He said this matter-of-factly. "It would be awfully good, wouldn't it, a present to us from London."

She was already ahead of him, waiting, and she didn't flinch. Smiling rather sadly she said, "I'm enjoying this. Don't spoil it."

He sat back. They drank. The silence was full, pleasant to her, not awkward or uncomfortable. It was more interesting to have the proposal out on the table, the unmistakable point of their get-together.

In a moment he said, "You're here with a friend, you said. Henry permits you to go off on your own?"

"We decided a little distance would do us good. He's holed up in an inspiring pastoral setting, working."

"That sounds deadly." He added, "Was it his daughter who died? Has he gotten over it?"

This was a wrong turn. "That's not something you get over, Gus."

"I've seen my share of corpses."

"That's not the same thing." She didn't want him to be stupid.

"Isn't it?"

17

She was exasperated that he was blowing it. "Of course not. It wasn't your child."

"I've seen a lot of suffering children, Iz."

"And their parents feel the same way Henry feels. In Bosnia or Rwanda or anywhere else. You've never had a child, Gus. Please don't call me that. I'm not Iz."

"Not Romania." He had photographed hundreds of dark-eyed children who had essentially become prisoners of the state-run orphanages of Romania—abandoned children whose brains had been destroyed by deprivation. "What do you know about how parents feel?" he asked her.

"I've seen what Henry's been through." A moment before, she'd wanted to touch him. He was ignorant, his arrogance was cruel. "You have no idea," she said. "What time is it? I told Lynn I'd meet her at four-thirty."

"I've made a dinner reservation for us at a very nice place nearby. You have plenty of time to freshen up at the hotel. I'll get you around seven. What's your friend's name?"

"Lynn."

"Lynn can come. I'd rather she didn't, of course."

She didn't want her anger to show. "It's not possible, Gus. We have tickets for the theater."

"This is better than the theater, believe me. What show is it?"

"Lynn's arranged it. I'm not sure where we're going."

He knew she was lying. "Don't leave." He placed his hand on her shoulder as he stood. "Time to drain the monster," a quip that may have gone back to the first time they'd met.

She picked up a yellow piece of folded paper from the floor by his chair. It was a receipt from a Chelsea antique shop for a necklace of lapis lazuli, which had cost, she calculated, about three hundred dollars. It must have fallen from his jacket pocket when he removed the piece of jewelry. She placed the slip of paper on the top of the pale blue box, which still sat in the middle of the table. Gustavo Lacaz. They used to screw their brains out, but that's all there was to it. Drain the monster, she thought.

She made a point of not looking at him as he returned to their table.

"Do you mean you would have let me think that was your mother's necklace if I'd taken it from you?" She wanted to give him an out.

He smiled, noticing the yellow receipt. "Of course not. I wanted to get you something. The embellishment was an afterthought. My confession would have been the punch line."

"When was I due to get the punch line?"

"I didn't have it precisely planned." He placed the box directly before her. "Anyway, it really is for you."

She came to her feet. "I don't want it." Smiling, she added, "You must have it, Gustavo."

He caught her wrist. "What about dinner?"

"I told you that's impossible." She waited until he released her. "This was fun. Let's make it Sarajevo next time."

"I'll call you when I'm back in New York."

She knew where she was and decided the walk back to Queen's Gate would wake her up after the beer. She was both disappointed and relieved that he'd made it so easy for her to walk away from him. I've seen lots of corpses. He had nerve, but lacked curiosity and sympathy. He had never pestered her with questions, wanting to know her. Unlike Henry, she thought. Gustavo's work suddenly irritated her. His compassionate portraits could look like revelations, souls laid bare, but he was concerned with the surface, the effect, he looked no further than the camera did. Half the work was random accident. He was pathetic, she decided, walking briskly toward the Gore, with his be-all career. Mere tragic loss could never hold him up. Did Henry grasp something the likes of Gus failed to grasp, or was it just the other way around? She didn't know the answer, and she would never know it. But who did know the answer to such questions? How to live was like asking what life meant. The pain in her toe had mysteriously subsided just then, which was a considerable improvement for the moment.

A medium-sized, well-dressed couple in their forties—fellow countrymen, she thought—stood at the top of the stairs leading into the Gore. The man was fair with flushed coloring and a mottled reddish beard trimmed close. Elizabeth recognized the inflamed patches on the woman's cheeks as acne rosacea because Henry's ex-wife, Sally, coped with the same condition. But what made the woman's face look painfully sore was emotion, not a skin problem, and her husband's face likewise looked grim. Yes, it had to be her husband. They appeared removed from their surroundings, oblivious to the woman ascending the stairs. As Elizabeth excused herself, edging between them, the woman said, "I can't bear it," and the man replied, "We have to bear it."

The small cheerful lobby was quiet the blond girl at the desk didn't look up as Elizabeth passed. She'd done plenty of hiking for one day, and decided to forgo the stairs. She anticipated having the room to herself for an hour, hoping Lynn wasn't back yet. A bath would be heaven. She stepped into the elevator. The person who rushed in behind her from the bar, where he'd evidently been lurking, was Gustavo.

"Oh Christ, Gus." The instant she pressed the button for her floor she realized her mistake.

He wasn't talking. She recognized the solemn, agog expression on his face. His heavy hot-blooded mode had often amused her—until she let herself be swept up in his self-dramatization. At the moment, standing there like he'd been struck dumb, his large eyes doomed-looking, he was a nutcase. Don't start, she thought. When they reached the third floor, she hit Lobby again.

"What are you doing, Gustavo? I don't want you here. Come on, out," she said as the doors switched open.

An elderly woman with a dog stepped into the elevator. Gustavo punched three again.

"Kindly press five please," the woman said. Oh so British.

Elizabeth didn't move when the elevator stopped at her floor. After the lady with the dog stepped out at five—"Come along, little man"—Gustavo hit three again and she thought, no, she wasn't taking his bullshit. She marched down the corridor, ignoring him, although he was right behind her. At the door to her room, she turned to get the nonsense over with.

"I'm tired, I'm not inviting you in. You have to go." She rapped on the door. "Lynn, it's me."

His hands were at her, flattening her breasts, clutching her ass, shoving her skirt up. He slumped against her, his mouth burrowing at her neck, inhaling her smell. "Elizabeth," he said. He was ridiculous.

"No. Don't do this. What's the matter with you?" His force and weight made her feel flimsy, ineffectual. His hands were under her skirt, plowing over her skin, and as he reached for her crotch from behind, her feet momentarily left the floor. "You're hurting me. Stop it."

"I want you," he said. "Don't fight me."

She hammered his shoulders with narrow fists, a flurry of harmless blows. "You're scaring me," she pleaded, and he let go. "I've never seen you like this," she said. That wasn't true. But for a second there she didn't know what he was capable of. She could lose her power to control him, was the feeling; he could lose himself.

"I know what you want," he told her. "I smell it."

"I want you to go. The beer was fun. Now you're really fucking it up."

"I know you," he said. "I know you inside out. You're greedy."

"Oh please. For God's sake." She was rummaging in her pocket-book for the key and it dawned on her that opening the door to her room would be asking for it. Come on, Elizabeth. Think.

He was on her again, coercing her balled hand—he had her by the wrist—to press against his penis, for God's sake. "Feel it," he said. "Do you feel that?"

As if relenting she closed her hand around him, thick, enormous, and he seemed to relax. When she pulled away this time, she sidestepped him and slipped through the door opposite, which led to the staircase. In a moment she was back in the lobby. She entered the large front room where breakfast and afternoon tea were served and went to a table by the window. No one else was present. Her chest was constricted, breath cut off at the top of her windpipe, maybe more frightened, she thought, than she should have been. The girl from the front desk approached the table to say teatime had ended for the day, but she could certainly get whatever she might like at the bar.

"I'm waiting for a friend," she said. "I thought I'd watch for her coming down Queen's Gate."

She continued staring out the window when Gustavo sat down across from her. Outside, an older man in tank top, shorts, and running shoes walked by at a brisk pace with a spunky Scottish terrier on a leash.

"I'm sorry," he said. "I assumed we wanted the same thing. I thought you understood that when you agreed to see me."

"That's not what I understood."

"I thought we were playing upstairs—hide and seek. I didn't really frighten you, did I?"

She turned from the window. "You dope." She added, "Yes, you frightened me."

"I apologize." He put the pale blue box on the table between them, a replay of that gesture at the pub.

"I told you I don't want that damn thing." His sentimentality repelled her. "You're ridiculous. Good-bye. Go."

"You're leaving tomorrow?"

"Yes."

"I plan to call you when I'm back in the city."

She shook her head, discouraged. "I wish you wouldn't."

She watched him walk down the sidewalk toward Cromwell. He was a pretty sad case. Deluded. The artist and world traveler. His work was a cynical fraud. Pain and suffering represented his opportunity to make his mark. She would have felt sorry for him if she wasn't so furious.

For a low moment in the bathtub she was lonely and regretted driving him away. A girl could do worse than get ravished in the Gore on a sunny afternoon. The stupid bastard, she thought, regulating the hot water with her left foot, the sore toe so slightly swollen and reddened you wondered how it could hurt so much. She was no girl. Her days of Gustavos were numbered, if not kaput.

Lynn stuck her head into the humid room. "Pregnant?"

A bad joke. She said, "Just nauseated."

I came to Speedwell, population about fifteen hundred, not a soul in sight, because I believed that a period of self-imposed isolation would provoke me to become productive again, to embark on some *new project* that would ferry me to the rest of my life. The property in southern Vermont belonged to my wife Elizabeth's older sister, Mary, who had only been back to it once since her husband had suffered a fatal heart attack there the year before, age fifty-five. He'd been picking string beans in the garden, I think it was, when he keeled over. Mary had acquired the property back in the halcyon days of her first marriage and while she had no intention of revisiting Vermont in the foreseeable future, she insisted, her sentimental attachment to the place prevented her from doing anything hasty. She viewed the land, over a hundred largely wooded acres, as something substantial to pass on to her children one day, although for the time being her two grown children were too taken up with their *various agendas*, Mary said, to be bothered with an isolated and distant summerhouse surrounded by nothing but woods. A local dairy farmer inspected the premises every so often and maintained the adjacent mowing, manuring the field each fall and cutting it twice during the summer. When Elizabeth mentioned my proposal to her sister, Mary was enthusiastic, grateful to have someone temporarily remove the stigma of abandonment, she said, from the small house that had been a beloved getaway for many years.

Stigma of abandonment!

The third week in May, the same day I wrapped up my duties at the New School, I made the over-four-hour drive from the city, pulling into Mary's long private road just in time to send a dozen startled turkeys scuttling across the green field west of the house like a flock of indignant old ladies, I thought, racing to their tour bus. I was in a good mood, intoxicated by my drive through all that new green of Vermont, and it was a cheerful thought. The clapboard house was a small center-chimney cape with a one-story ell. There was a fireplace in the living room, and a wood-burning stove, a Vermont Castings Vigilant, in the kitchen; two bedrooms and bath upstairs. Mary's second husband, Fitz, had been handy—Fitz the straightedge, Fitz the hammer, Fitz the table saw—and had built the addition off the living room to be his study. The perfectly square room contained a bookcase, an old rocker with a caned back and seat, a built-in workstation for his computer, and an antique refectory table of dark oak piled with books and journals and newspapers. I moved the table and the adjustable desk chair into the larger living room, set them in the middle of the pine floor, and shut the study door. I decided to sleep in the smaller bedroom on one of the twin beds, rather than use their bed.

I hadn't anticipated the edginess I felt as I first walked through the house, the excitement almost of trespassing. Mary had only returned here that once following her husband's death—Elizabeth had accompanied her—to collect her most personal and valuable belongings and close the house up, and to me, as I passed through the low-ceilinged rooms, it seemed like a place people had very recently left and were bound to return to soon. I'd only been here twice before—a spontaneous visit soon after Elizabeth and I were married, a get-acquainted occasion for me, plus an October week-end a few years later. We'd planned to reciprocate by putting them up when they traveled from Boston to New York, but Fitz preferred staying in his hotel. *My* hotel, he called the Westbury on Madison and Sixty-sixth Street. Fitz's hotel! We tried halfheartedly to catch up with them for an evening during the holiday season each year, although even that became iffy once Elizabeth's mother died. If I put my mind to it I could probably name each and every time I'd been with the Underhills in the last seven years. On the one hand Fitz could be irresistible, a tall man with a beautiful smile, and yet even while he was charming the pants off you, you weren't sure you believed a word he said. I thought of the country house as Mary's, and even before I arrived I knew I wouldn't be working in Fitz's study and I wasn't going to sleep in his bed, no, absolutely not.

Lilacs and narcissus, apple blossoms and viburnum, birds, silence, the air—all that was plenty for the first few days. Hanging out in the yard each morning with a cup of coffee and my pal the song sparrow, sniffing blossoms like an intoxicated, overly appreciative halfwit, a walk in the afternoon, a drink in the evening with the unseeable wood thrush before I prepared my solo pasta and salad, bread and wine meal, that was all I needed for the first few days, relax, go with it. Nightfall. I could get two stations on the small television I moved downstairs from their bedroom, and I'd sit there after dark watching whatever was on those stations, flicking back and forth—from *Frontline* to *Day One*, from *Nature* to *Funniest Home Videos*—like a senseless animal mesmerized by the play of light until finally, a week after my arrival, and just as Charlie Rose was becoming infatuated with an awful author of popular novels, I pulled the plug on the tube and stashed it upstairs in Mary's closet. The radio was enough: *Fresh Air, All Things Considered, Jazz A La Mode.*

My new project was to be a freewheeling meditation on the three great loners of American literature, as they've been called: Walt Whitman, Herman Melville, Emily Dickinson. A meditation on the staggering originality of nineteenth-century American genius sprung from obscurity and appetite, isolation and repression, eccentricity and reclusiveness. The darkness and light of that genius, Melville contrasted to Whitman, with Dickinson achieving the all-encompassing vision. A meditation on three inspired misfits who sat down in modest rooms in the midst of busy households (if you were Dickinson or Melville) and took it upon themselves, driven by a mysterious and wonderful compulsion—a kind of disorder—and with almost no encouragement (excepting Melville's early success), to create the heart and soul of American literature. I was returning to three heroes of my youth, I imagined, hoping to experience as much as possible the heat and glow of my first literary passion, the fire that had persuaded me, age twenty, that I knew what was important in life.

I sat at Fitz's table in the center of the living room, leafing through the books that surrounded me, shuffling my mounting stack of index cards, or staring at the small blank screen of my computer, every morning for some interval of time, contemplating my project, before I decisively came to my feet and fled to the outdoors.

With bow saw, pruning shears, and ax, reluctant to fiddle with Fitz's chain saw, I cut back brush encroaching upon the yard from the encircling woods, I mowed the small lawn, mostly clover, dandelions, ground ivy, and moss, with Fitz's manual reel-type lawn mower, I cleared brush from the perimeter of the hay field as well— unwanted birch and poplar saplings, sumac, grapevine, assorted briars—a regular pioneer, and spent a solid five days picking up a section of stone wall that bordered the field on one side, walking out to marvel at my work each evening with two or three fingers of scotch until the blackflies drove me inside, in bed by nine or so, exhausted but wide-awake, absorbed as ever with my daughter, assailed by thoughts and images that automatically came up the moment I wanted my mind to shut down, like the screen saver on my Mac.

"I don't think this is working," I'd told Elizabeth during our last phone call, "this change of scene idea. I feel like the caretaker. Fitz's ghost is all over the place. I keep the door to his study closed, and it's like he's in there with his computer. Not Mary, but Fitz. I haven't spoken to a human being since I got here. I go into town for milk and the Sunday *Times*, and they look up at me, silent dour faces propped over cups of coffee, like a doomed man has just walked through the door."

"Come home then," she said. "You don't sound good."

"No, the isolation takes adjusting to, that's all." She was bound for over a month in the old British Isles with her sidekick Lynn, a holiday drummed up as her consolation prize while I was cooped up in Speedwell with my project. I'd called to say good-bye. "I expect you to call once a week. Agreed?"

"I'm not going to call unless I have to. I'll send postcards."

"What if I have to get hold of you?"

"You'll be out of luck." Their plan was to seek out B-and-Bs on a daily basis, nothing prearranged, all options open. "You won't need to get hold of me, especially if you get into something. Four weeks go by in no time."

"Fitz died picking beans, isn't that what Mary said?"

"Something like that. She found him in the garden, anyway."

"Maybe I'll plant a garden, so by the time you get here we'll have kale or something. Swiss chard."

"I told you, I'm not going up there, it's too lonely for me."

"I'll be here."

"You're going to be working, which makes it even lonelier. I want to try the original plan. I'll have my big escape with Lynn and you can come home when you've accomplished something. Just get busy."

"Take care of yourself. Some of those roads are scary. The rotaries . . ."

"We'll be fine. Lynn is a great driver."

"You have the number here, of course. Just in case."

"Of course."

"I'll be thinking of you."

"Don't worry about Fitz. He's no longer with us."

The next morning, awakening to the realization that you could not be reached caused me to bolt from the bed, as though I'd just learned you'd been involved in a terrible accident.

Index card #57:

Elizabeth Melville to Catherine Lansing (M's cousin), 1876 (*Clarel*):

The fact is, that Herman, poor fellow, is in such a frightfully nervous state, and particularly now with such an added strain on his mind, that I am actually afraid *to have any one here for fear that he will be upset entirely, and not be able to go on with the printing . . .*

If ever this dreadful incubus *of a book (I call it so because it has undermined all our happiness) gets off Herman's shoulders I do*

*hope he may be in better mental health—but at present I have reason
to feel the gravest concern and anxiety about it—to put it in a mild
phrase—please do not speak of it—you know how such things are
exaggerated—and I will tell you more when I see you.*

Did the author of *Moby Dick* throw Lizzie down the stairs? I
asked myself, pushing back from Fitz's oak table and coming to my
feet. I hoped not.

For three fair days the first week of June, Graves, whose desperate
farm was a mile away, the nearest neighbor, mowed and tethered
and raked and baled the hay on Mary's field. When I walked out to
have a word with him, possibly grinning and waving a bit too
eagerly, he gave me a nod—a sturdy, handsome man in his sixties,
green hat and blue denim overalls, whose severe mouth and strong
straight nose made him seem the direct descendant of Saint-
Gaudens's *The Puritan*—but he didn't stop the tractor.

The vegetable garden, twenty feet square, was enclosed by a
crude, unpainted picket fence. Johnny-jump-ups had ecstatically
self-seeded, along with various unnameable grasses and weeds,
and I allowed patches of them to survive when I turned over the
soil with the long-handled shovel, warm sun on my back. Andrews's
nursery in the neighboring town had everything you could want
in the way of plants: kale, yes, collards, Swiss chard, onions, tomatoes, spinach, mustard greens, squash. Everything! I planted seeds
for arugula, carrots, bush beans. I watered with Miracle-Gro, I
top-dressed my mounded beds with black-brown processed cow
manure, and for the next few days I could hardly take my eyes off
the garden, repeatedly walking out to see it, a welcome addition to
the Vermont scene, inherently worthwhile.

I entered Fitz's study thinking there might be books on gardening, possibly a garden journal, for Fitz had been fastidious and

orderly in everything he undertook. Mary had left his study exactly as it was at the time of his death. The study door had been closed when she and Elizabeth had come here last September to collect Mary's stuff, and Mary had left it closed. Elizabeth assumed her sister couldn't bear to look at his things, the lost private world of Fitz, she assumed it was a sentimental revulsion, although if it had been her, Elizabeth said, she would have taken everything from her husband's study, hoarded every suddenly precious and irreplaceable scrap of his personal life. Mary said, I never went into that room while he was alive, and I'm not going into it now, maybe someday, she said, not now. Except for the table and chair that I'd already removed, everything was as it had been the year before, the computer, laser printer, fax machine, the books and photographs, stacks of stapled articles, his pocketknife, for example, a pair of binoculars, sunglasses, his geological specimens, his computerized chess game. Mary had left all this just as it was the day she found him sitting up in the garden, slumped against the fence with one hand inside his shirt and the other holding a fistful of string beans. The poor guy! There were books on birds and trees, wildflowers and butterflies, edible wild plants; there were books of popular nonfiction that Fitz would have called his summer reading. No books on gardening. Mary had told me to use the house as I wished, including Fitz's study, but as I glanced around the room, I decided, no, I'm not coming in here again. I knew all I wished to know about Fitz.

I knew he'd taught biology for many years, first at BU and eventually at Harvard, a lifetime goal of his, all the while ambitiously cranking out his esoteric research papers. That general job description—*research*—was all I knew about the presumably unfathomable investigations Fitz pursued. We had never discussed work, his or mine. The one and only time I mentioned my daughter's ongoing ordeal to him, he raised his eyebrows, he nodded gravely, pouting, and said nothing, a silence that was enormously discouraging and offensive to me. I had been seeking reassurance. I knew he delivered papers at professional meetings here and even in Europe once or twice a year and was highly regarded in those circles. Fitz is in Paris, Elizabeth would report after getting off the phone with her sister, Fitz is in San Francisco, Fitz is in Hawaii. I knew he had been a bachelor until, forty-something, he married Mary, his Cambridge neighbor, which was puzzling. Why would you marry the likes of Mary, who had come with two teenage children at the time, at that advanced stage of your blazing career and diehard bachelorhood? Money was the best reason Elizabeth could think of and Mary had come into plenty of money with Ted's death. Ted: Mary's first husband, father of their two children, a botanist of independent means, thanks to an enterprising grandfather; he had died in a climbing accident on a plant-finding expedition in Ecuador while still in his thirties. According to Elizabeth, Fitz and Mary had been involved with one another for years, beginning some time after Ted's accident, and they'd finally decided to make their arrangement legal for the most practical reasons. Elizabeth had loved Ted, she said, and had never liked Fitz the unreadable, Fitz the aloof, Fitz the unfriendly.

I hadn't foreseen that marrying a second time would embroil me with another entire family, its dead as well as its living. I'd imagined it would just be Elizabeth and me. My divorce from my first wife, Sally, was motivated by a desire to free myself from her long-lived parents, her constant brothers, her complaining aunt, as much as it was motivated by the unhappy state of our marriage. And yet I didn't quite realize that marrying Elizabeth would mean marrying her mother, marrying her sister, marrying Fitz to some extent. I knew he ate oatmeal for breakfast, I knew he dosed himself with vitamins, cod-liver oil, and ginseng every day of the week. I knew he was a quasi-vegetarian, who enjoyed preparing quasi-vegetarian meals with his chef's knife. I knew he exercised on his NordicTrack with the same fanatic discipline that governed most aspects of his affluent, productive, and orderly life. I knew he liked to take himself off to weekend retreats, despite his ordinarily busy schedule, where he'd meditate for hours at a stretch, tortuously cultivating his spiritual side. That was how Mary had first introduced Fitz: a brilliant scientist with a spiritual side. There had been over three hundred people at the memorial service in Wellesley, people from everywhere presumably. I knew that Fitz had never read one of my books, or expressed the slightest curiosity about my work. I knew he had a nifty BMW to dart about the city and a Land Rover to take him safely to the country. I knew he liked good cigars and expensive wines. I had only entered the study in search of a book on gardening. This room is exactly as he left it the day he died, I thought. There had been no opportunity for Fitz to set his affairs in order, to sort through his papers and what-have-you for the last time, to save or discard. . . . No, I would not set foot in the study again, I decided as I left the room and shut the door behind me. I knew all I wished to know about Fitz.

Index card # 36:
George Whitman on his brother's 1st self-published edition of *Leaves of Grass*, 1855:
I saw the book—didn't read it at all—didn't think it worth reading—fingered it a little.

I'd brought the answering machine from my office at the New School and hooked it up to the phone in the kitchen. My rudimentary Phone Mate. *Please leave a message,* that was my succinct recorded greeting, so unlike Elizabeth's eager, aggressively friendly version at home. Although I didn't really expect to hear from anyone—my son, for one, was also out of the country—I left the machine on in order to screen unwanted calls, I was in the habit of screening phone calls, and I didn't want to miss Elizabeth if she tried to reach me while I was out of the house. I rarely entered my office at the New School without being greeted, more like accosted, by the small red blinking light, letting me know I had a message, so here in the sticks the unblinking red light became a bit of a downer, rather emphatically announcing each time I passed it that there had been no call, no message. No, no one has tried to reach you in the last hour, the last day, the last week. Being alone in a pastoral setting, a serene isolated sylvan setting, you noticed the silence was filled with sounds. A little paranoia was natural in the sticks, I told myself. Easy does it. But the constant unblinking red light exerted a pressure, it began to feel personal. Harmless electronic convenience! The first thing I did when I came downstairs in the morning was check the Phone Mate for messages. I couldn't help irrationally glancing toward the old oak icebox that now served as a telephone table to see if the red light was flashing or not, as though the phone could have rung in the middle of the night without my hearing it. I rarely entered the kitchen from the other room, for that matter, without checking out the Phone Mate to see what was up with the light. When I came in from outdoors, my glance fell on the small machine with even more eagerness. And if I left the premises, went off in the car for groceries or beer or my *Times*, I returned convinced that I'd find the light earnestly blinking, certain someone must have called while I was away from the phone.

One afternoon quite spontaneously I called the house from the pay phone outside Baker's store in town and listened to my recorded answer—*Please leave a message*—and then actually left a message for myself. And it was a relief, momentarily, to walk into Mary's kitchen and find the little red light blinking, a satisfaction that evaporated as soon as I pressed the button, beep, and listened to my message. *Hello, testing, this is to verify that the answering machine is operating properly.* I warned myself not to do that again, if

33

you aren't careful you'll find yourself stumbling into some desperate habit like the middle-aged wretch in the local paper who evidently practiced semiasphyxiation to heighten orgasm and was found hanging by the neck from a tree in the woods with a baggy condom dangling from his lifeless penis. In Speedwell? The desperate soul was trying to feel alive. I considered unplugging the answering machine, except the more disappointed I became about the absence of phone calls and phone messages—worthless shit, the red light accused, miserable last son of a bitch on earth!—the more reluctant I was to throw in the towel. My main concern was Elizabeth. I left the machine on, the constant red light on, in case Elizabeth called from old England needing to talk about something or other, needing me, or just wanting to say hi. Gatsby had his green light, I thought, standing in the kitchen at midnight, and I've got my ridiculous red light. No, the urban dweller was bound to freak out during his first weeks of solitary confinement in Speedwell. That seemed fairly predictable.

For years the ring of the phone meant my daughter calling from San Francisco, where she had been living since college, to let me know what was going on. A doctor's appointment, an emergency hospitalization, the results of blood tests, CAT scans, her flight schedule, a cash crisis. Calls of immense celebration—the MRI was clear!—fluctuated with news of overwhelming sadness, innumerable wrenching messages of life-and-death significance, although we didn't always realize the stakes were ultimate. There were also her everyday calls about friends, the weather, a weekend outing, her love life, calls on birthdays, or on holidays when she hadn't managed to get home. Her voice on the phone! The ring of the phone could still give me pause, thinking her name, and two and a half years later I remained unable to believe or accept that I would never hear her voice again. Hi, Dad, it's me. Those words, never again.

The light on the answering machine in Mary's country house, the unblinking red light, simply meant no messages, but then it got mixed up with my daughter one night during a thunderstorm after too much red wine. I imagined her calling here, listening with amusement or impatience to my voice on the machine, and leaving her message, some response that would be couched in wit, if she was in a good mood, and that would almost certainly make me smile because the thing said would be so her, no one else. Staring at that little unblinking rat's eye on the gray machine, half drunk, but resisting tears, I knew that my daughter would never call and leave a message, that she would never have the pleasure of recording some wonderful observation on the answering machine, if it had been a good day, and I would never experience the joy of listening to her message, whether good news or bad. For the moment the unblinking red light seemed another painfully literal sign of my daughter's absolute, ever-after absence. Thunder tumbled and rolled to the west, followed by lightning that made the dark green outdoors flash against the multipaned window like a looming intruder's vast face. She had loved thunderstorms, a booming storm inspired giddy awe. My father would never turn up on the answering machine either, dead the year before my daughter died. A message from the legendary Ted, whose house this once was, would never make the light blink. He had also died young. It would never be Fitz calling in, for that matter, the scientist with the spiritual side.

Rain drummed on the small house like something willful, I poured another scotch and raised my glass to the weather, my big boisterous companion for the night. Beside me on the antique icebox, the phone rang, causing me to lurch forward, jostling a dollop of booze onto the oak surface. I didn't trust myself to answer it, reluctant to appear the reclusive drunk to whoever this might be, I had that much presence of mind. I waited through four shrill rings, followed by my reserved deadpan voice. *Please leave a message.* There was no response. The person hung up, which left me terribly agitated, a man on a slippery hunk of driftwood still frantically waving—Hey! Help!—as the distant ship passed from view.

There was no response, but the caller had not hung up immediately. Seconds of silence followed my message as though whoever it was had considered speaking before deciding against it. You observe this sort of detail when you're alone in the country, you become a little messed up with this hyperacuity, let's face it. I pressed the Play button on the machine, and listened to those seconds of silence that followed my message, but there was no clue, no discernible background noise at all—like the hubbub of an English pub, the sound of traffic in Trafalgar Square. That phone call had been made in an awfully quiet room. "I've got to settle down, Elizabeth."

Index card #32:
Melville's mother to her brother, following publication of *Pierre*, 1853:
In my opinion, I must again repeat it Herman would be greatly benefitted by a sojourn abroad, he would then be compelled to more intercourse with his fellow creatures. It would very materially renew, and strengthen both his body and his mind.

The constant in-door confinement with little intermission to which Herman's occupation as author compels him, does not agree with him. This constant working of the brain, and excitement of the imagination, is wearing Herman out, and you will my dear Peter be doing him a lasting benefit if by your added exertions you can procure him a foreign consulship.

Out of the blue: a deep blue night scene looking across the shining Seine to Notre Dame.

Dear Dad, staying Hotel de Seine on Left Bank near Latin Quarter. Cafe food is fine. Lots of baguettes. Walk 100 mi/day exploring magical city. Louvre too crowded. Mona Lisa a yawn. d'Orsay better. Trees in Tuileries are butchered. Rip-off artists beaucoup. Almost lost my pack in the Metro. Loved a bare-breasted girl upstairs in Shakespeare & Co. giving herself sponge bath in the sink! Eiffel Tower: too weird. Didn't talk for two days. Paris not really my scene, but digging it to the max. Met some smart students one night. Everybody smokes. Right now on a bench in Place des Vosges. Mom would love it. Miss you.

Love, David.

His handwriting was uncannily similar to his sister's. He was hardly the compulsive letter writer she had been, however, and I'd prepared myself not to hear from him. I read the card three or four times and taped it to the refrigerator. Miss you? When had he last missed me? Paris can be lonely, I thought. Didn't talk for two days! He was traveling alone on his meager life savings (plus a little help from his parents), his first trip to Europe, with two main objectives in mind. He intended to spend two weeks climbing in the French Alps, assuming he'd hook up with other climbers there, and then he'd continue into Italy to retrace the journey his sister had taken through that country when she was his age, twenty-four. David had dropped out of college following his sister's death. Since then he'd worked various jobs in California, Wyoming, and Colorado (housepainter, carpenter, trail-builder, backpacking guide) to support his passion for the mountains and to save for the present adventure, which he hoped, I knew, would somehow bring his future into clearer focus. I'd driven him to the airport only days before I left the city myself. Once we'd checked his large blue backpack at the luggage counter, we had time for a beer. He would join me in Vermont after he returned to the States, shooting for the first week in August, we agreed, provided I was still up there. We finished our beers in silence. David kept his thoughts to himself, you seldom knew what was on his mind, that was his way. When we embraced, his strong arms squeezed tight and he pressed his lips to my cheek. Don't worry about me, he said, I'll be fine. I watched him walk down the concourse wearing his favorite shirt, a bittersweet checked cotton shirt, and faded denims. His solo trip represented a personal mission. Where are you now? I wondered. Here we were in the middle of June and he'd been in Paris weeks ago, so he must have carried the card around for a while before mailing it. The postmark was indecipherable. He was resourceful, sturdy, self-reliant. I'm not worried, I thought, staring at the vivid postcard on the refrigerator. "I'm not worried about you."

A bear appeared outside the kitchen window at about six the following morning while I was filling the kettle at the sink. I gawked, amazed by the glossy pitch-blackness of his shimmering one-hundred-percent-natural fur coat. I guessed male because he was alone and seemed too large to be female, but I couldn't discern any clear evidence of gender. Maybe he was a young bear recently cast into the world by his mother, which would have accounted for his remarkably unguarded manner as he sauntered, pigeon-toed, across the narrow lawn, his tawny snout only inches above the grass. You hot shit, I thought, following him from window to window as he ambled around the perimeter of the house. "Oh, Elizabeth, he's beautiful." In the living room I tapped gently on the glass, but he didn't seem to notice. Outside Fitz's study he stood up, his hind legs planted firmly in the bed of budding daylilies, and seemed to peer into the room. Then I felt he was looking directly at me, through the glass, and I froze until, like a massively bored pet he continued around the garden fence and ambled off into the woods south of the house. I remained staring out the small window in Fitz's study for another minute, as unnerved as a girl who had just been ravished by a stranger's hot gaze. Eye contact with a black bear, Elizabeth, was that for real?

I had an inspired morning, a long-overdo-breakthrough morning, I took a long fern-scented walk in the afternoon, I treated myself to dinner in Brattleboro forty minutes away, the restaurant's laid-back charm spoiled this night by a noisy party of women. When I returned, the red light on the answering machine was blinking.

"Hello . . . remember me? That's an awfully succinct message you've got there. You know, it doesn't really sound like you, but then I've never heard you on tape. What made you break down and get one of these things? I just got here a couple of days ago, during that scary storm, actually. I'll be here for a month as usual. I'm glad I didn't miss the lilacs completely. Hi, Mary, if you're here too. Give me a call."

I liked the voice, clear, direct, relaxed, warm, although I was disappointed, naturally, that the call was not for me. And the message, conveying what the caller clearly didn't know, disturbed me.

The phone rang again two days later while I was in the backyard, and I didn't run to answer it.

"Helen again. I assume you're there, one of you or both of you, or the answering machine wouldn't be on, would it? It's Friday, so I'm looking for a little company. Hate to drink alone, even though I know how. Did you lose my wonderful number? It's 9-6-6-9. Talk to you soon."

I replayed the tape, getting down the number in ink before some unforeseen electronic mishap erased it. My concentration was shot for the rest of the day, rehearsing my succinct speech to this Helen. By the time I'd eaten my supper of beans and greens and sourdough bread, however, I was no longer in the mood to be the black bearer of sad tidings, Friday night or not. Instead I called Mary at her home in Cambridge.

"Some Helen has left messages," I explained. "Obviously she doesn't know about Fitz. Do you want to call her, or what?"

"She comes up from New York each summer, and that's the only time we see her. She'd left last year before it happened. Isn't that bizarre?"

"She sounds pretty familiar with you guys on the Phone Mate."

"That's Helen. Fitz knew her better than I did. She's a Buddhist or something. She meditates. Would you do me an awfully big favor?"

"No, no favors for you."

"You could pretend you don't know me. Just tell her you heard the husband died and that the house came up for rent through a realtor. Maybe she'll have her answering machine on and you won't even have to talk to her. Then she won't bother you again."

"But I phoned you, Mary, because I don't want to call her. It's not my call."

"I just can't go through the whole business with her. She'll have to talk about it. You could play ignorant, and just hang up. I know it's a big favor. Do you think you could do it this once?"

"I can't pretend I don't know you, I'm a miserable liar."

"Thanks, Henry. How is it up there anyway? Is the place working out all right for you?"

"I'm adjusting. I saw a bear the other day."

"How nice for you. I miss it, but I know I shouldn't be there."

"I've planted a garden. . . . Was that the wrong thing to say?"

"He loved that precious garden. His arugula. His broccoli rabe. His Swiss chard was the most beautiful thing he'd ever seen. Have you heard from Elizabeth yet?"

"No, damn it."

"I bet she's having the time of her life. I've got to get off, there goes my call waiting."

I dialed the local number, resolved not to carry the unwanted chore into another day. Chances were good that a woman on her own would have an answering machine fielding phone calls. She picked up on the second ring.

I gave my name. "I'm renting the Underhill house here in town, so I've received your recent . . ."

"Oh? You mean Fitz and Mary aren't there?"

"I'm not sure how well you know the Underhills. . . ."

"I know them very well." An edge of indignation in her tone. "It's a summer thing. This is the third year I've taken this place. I come up from New York for a month. They're practically the only people I see around here, as a matter of fact. You mean they aren't coming to Vermont this year?"

"That's why I called. . . . I thought you should know that Fitz died of a heart attack last summer. You must have left by the time it happened."

A pause. "Who are you? What's your name?"

"Ash, Henry."

"A heart attack? Fitz?"

"Yes. Out in the garden, that's what I heard."

"But . . . that's ridiculous. Fitz? Do you know when?"

"Sometime in August."

"I was here in July. Having drinks in their backyard."

"I'm sure Mary was in a state of shock. She didn't contact everyone Fitz knew. The memorial service was in Wellesley."

"You sound like you know them pretty well."

"I'm Mary's brother-in-law. She didn't think she could handle being here this summer, so she offered the place to me."

"Have I ever seen you around here?"

"I haven't been here in years."

"Fitz?" she said. "Oh my God! Fitz?" and her voice cracked higher. "I can't talk now."

It seemed odd to me, as I thought about it, that Mary hadn't contacted the woman they'd recently been socializing with that summer, one of the last people Fitz had spent time with, presumably. On the other hand, it was plausible that this Helen, whoever she was, had never entered Mary's mind following the death of her husband. Beyond the superficial summer-in-Vermont happenstance, this Helen evidently had no part in their lives.

Saturday: a postcard of the Tower of London addressed c/o Mary Underhill:

> *London seemed oppressive so we hightailed it to Canterbury with its lovely flinty Infirmary in ruins and roses everywhere. Chilham, the first half-timber village, has a little brick castle with hysterical topiaries in a row overlooking Kent countryside, and an alley of ancient lime trees. Beautiful Sissinghurst with its phallic tower and its white garden and hedges made me fall in love with Vita. I missed you to the quick in our frumpy B & B, so came I here alone. Lynn is fun, flirts in pubs with red-faced men, drives like a demon on the left side. Hope Vermont is working.*
>
> *Love, Elizabeth.*

I taped the card to Mary's refrigerator right next to Notre Dame. Two cards in one week! Devil, I thought, teasing me to imagine you raising pints of Courage in a boisterous dark-timbered pub, jerking off in your frumpy B-and-B, turned on by a luxurious tour of gardens in bloom, rubbing it in. Kent countryside!

2 *Loners*

I glanced up from my small gray computer screen in time to see her pass under the maple tree in the front yard, a blue and white blur, basically, walking a bicycle over the grass. By the time I got outside she'd disappeared around the back of Fitz's addition, but when I reached the corner of the building she was not to be seen, apparently circling the house in a hurry, so I was practically jogging as I came around the kitchen side. She'd let the bike drop to the ground and stood looking over the weathered wood fence into the vegetable garden where my kale and collards, my spinach and Swiss chard flourished.

"Can I help?" I called.

Mid to late thirties, not forty, flushed blotchy-pink in the face just now from her bike ride, a pair of sunglasses pushed up on top of short dark wavy hair, a beaded mustache of perspiration above her lip. No makeup particularly, some freckles. Splashy design on her T-shirt. I was careful to hold my eyes on her face so as not to offend the woman.

"Helen," she said by way of introduction. "I had to come over here. I won't stay long."

"I wish there'd been a more tactful way to tell you about Fitz. That must have been a shock, just when you're expecting him to turn up."

"It's like he died the day before yesterday."

I raised my eyebrows. I nodded. "Yes, it must be."

"I want to hang out for a while, that's all. Just be here. Is that a problem for you?"

"I'll leave you to yourself. If I can help," I added, "give a holler." A ludicrous politeness, as if she had come to browse at my tag sale.

"Who planted the garden?"

"I did."

From the kitchen I observed her standing there looking into the garden. At what? What are you looking at? At last she went through the crude wattle gate and proceeded to examine my vegetables row by row. She snatched what must have been spinach and popped it into her mouth. She snipped leaves of arugula, I assumed from my vantage point, and ate them, idly grazing. She stooped again and when she straightened up, throwing her arm out, dirt flew into the air above the garden, falling onto my plants. Suddenly she went down on her knees between the spinach and Swiss chard, down on her bare knees on the dry earth, she brought her hands to her face, and I thought, Give the woman some privacy. Of course, my work-day was over. I couldn't possibly concentrate with this Helen out in the yard. "It's already four o'clock, Elizabeth, what's for supper?"

With the large rosewood-handled chef's knife from the top drawer I chopped English walnuts to a fine uniform consistency. I minced a dozen garlic cloves, working the knife with a practiced rocking motion, until the minced garlic approximated in size the graininess of the chopped walnuts. "You're going to miss this, Elizabeth; you won't find anything like this in old England." Glancing out the east window, I assumed she'd left, but on second look I saw this Helen crouched down, squatting on her hams between my recently germinated beans and the still flimsy onions I'd put in as plants. I needed vegetables from the garden for my dinner; that couldn't be helped.

She didn't look up as I entered, evidently absorbed, altogether taken up with the chore at hand, rather aggressively weeding the row of onions at the moment, leaving a thin trail of uprooted green scraps on the narrow path.

"How's it coming?" I asked, thinking I'd break the ice here. "I've been meaning to jump on those weeds," I added when there was no reply. A half moon of pale skin above her beltless blue shorts and above that a large colorful caterpillar decorated the back of her T-shirt. Unpainted closely trimmed toenails in sturdy Velcro-fastened sandals.

"You don't mind, do you?" she asked. "I used to help him with it. It's still Fitz's garden, isn't it?"

"I thought it was more like my garden," I said, "but I see what you mean, yes," I hastened to agree, alarmed to see her tears. "I suppose it is Fitz's garden. Let's call it my vegetables in Fitz's garden."

She looked up, sniffling, and left a smudge of dirt under her nose when she wiped it with the back of her fingers. "All right, your vegetables in Fitz's garden."

"I came out to get some greens," gesturing with my enameled colander. "Keep working." And there wasn't another word between us while I collected enough arugula, mustard, and spinach for my spicy solo salad. Soon I went on to the field to gather all the dandelion leaves I needed.

Fitz's garden, I thought, busily chopping the dandelion, grating the Parmesan. He'd be proud of his garden this year, wouldn't he?

By the time my dinner was prepared, this Helen had left the Fitz garden and was seated cross-legged beneath the towering maple tree, precisely where the shade of the outermost branches met the lowering sunlight. With the help of binoculars, so I felt I was observing an animal that would flee if I made a sound, I saw her eyes were closed and her hands were resting palms up on her thighs. "Don't tell me that's something she learned from Fitz?" It was a large colorful butterfly in diagonal flight that emblazoned the front of her T-shirt. I ate with my back to the window, but even then it was difficult to concentrate on the meal. I was eating too fast, and for reasons I couldn't fathom my dandelion pesto seemed to have no taste. She was still out there, immobile, by the time I'd cleaned up my dishes. "Should this be getting on my nerves, Elizabeth? Am I overreacting?" I entered Fitz's study, promptly put my hands on his guide to butterflies and moths, and flitted back to the kitchen. After some minutes, by the process of elimination, fluctuating between binoculars and book, I identified the winged creature on the T-shirt—"That's it!" I pounced with a definite pang of satisfaction—to be a black swallowtail, *Papilio americanus*, as distinct from the spice-bush swallowtail or the tiger swallowtail. Whitman had claimed to have a way with butterflies. He decorated his unkillable book with the symbolic image at some point, and once posed for a photograph ostensibly wearing a butterfly on his finger. When I looked out the window again after putting dishes away and wiping the kitchen table the woman was gone, and soon, as dusk overshadowed the yard, the whole episode, the weird coming and going of this Helen, felt something like the sudden arrival and disappearance of the bear a few days before. Unsettling, unpredictable, and by the next day, plowing ahead with my new would-be project, unreal.

Index card #39:

Higginson's observation, meeting E.D. in Amherst, 1870:

I could only sit still and watch, as one does in the woods.

I drove to Amherst, Massachusetts, to visit the Dickinson Homestead where the reclusive poet had lived most of her life. Years before, I had visited Arrowhead near Pittsfield and promised myself never to return. The house Melville lived and wrote in for thirteen years felt sad and abandoned, and weirdly misplaced in the midst of a recent housing development. The dim upstairs bedroom where he'd worked was surely one of the loneliest, dreariest, and most depressing rooms I'd ever set foot in. The distant view of Greylock in the south window didn't remind me of a whale, it seemed the stark embodiment of monumental isolation. The so-called piazza was a flimsy wood porch. The famous hearth was a dark corner. Clearly, you could go crazy in this hilltop house, delicate Elizabeth and children and assorted relations scurrying or shuffling around the rooms, using yourself up on thankless chores half the day, alone by the chimney at night, damned by dollars, thinking about obsessive, desperate characters like Pierre while the wind cried overhead, feelings hurt because Hawthorne didn't want to be your best friend.

Amherst was almost spooky at first glance in its boy-girl college-town cuteness, but the Federal-style brick Homestead, well back from the road behind a long overgrown hemlock hedge and topped with a tall white cupola, was an imposing and handsome residence, at least from the outside. There was a tour every half hour. The only other person going through with me, at three, was a skinny red-haired girl, maybe eighteen, in a green jumper and red ankle-high sneakers, with gnawed fingernails, I couldn't help noticing as she thumbed her brochure. Our guide was a round thistle-haired elderly woman with an Anglophilic accent, who addressed her comments exclusively to the girl, even in answer to my questions. The first floor was empty apart from a few pieces of period furniture, photographs and drawings of the Homestead in various phases of development (an east ell was added one year, a conservatory another, etc.), and pictures of individual family members.

"Now this is a piano just like the one Emily would have played, dear," our guide said, touching the girl's arm.

"Where's the one she played?" the girl asked.

"Well, that's a good question, dear. Now this picture, you see, was taken the year she went to Mount Holyoke. She was only there the one year, of course."

"She must have hated it," the girl said, "I would. Her lips are amazing. What color was her hair anyway?"

The old lady removed a horse chestnut from the pocket of her skirt. "It wasn't red like yours, it was the color of a chestnut," she said, and she held out the nut in the palm of her hand. "And her eyes, she said, were like the sherry the guest leaves in the glass."

The girl glanced at me for the first time and rolled her eyes—surprisingly large and brown—at the ceiling. Looking closely at the famous picture of the poet above a bookcase in the double drawing room, she said, "That's one weird chick. Definitely."

"What's that, dear?"

"A bird came down the walk, he did not know I saw, he bit an angleworm in halves, and ate the fellow raw." Her laugh was a mischievous cackle.

"And then he drank a dew," I said, "from a convenient grass . . ."

"And then hopped sidewise to the wall to let a beetle pass," she cackled. "We rhymed!" She held up her thin hand, fingers spread, and I slapped her five.

"What would Emily have seen out of these windows?" I asked. "What was across the street?"

"Well, not what you see now," the woman said impatiently, frowning. "Not that unpleasant house."

Explosive unmusical sound filled the room. The girl had stepped to the piano and was thumping the creaky untuned keyboard. By the time our guide reached her side, hands raised in alarm, I recognized the opening bars of "The Battle Hymn of the Republic."

"Oh no, dear, you mustn't do that!"

"I wondered what it sounded like," the girl said.

"Come along, we're going upstairs now." In the unfurnished hallway she pointed out "the men in Emily's life." Charles Wadsworth, Samuel Bowles, the editor of the Springfield *Republican*, which had published a few of her poems, her Higginson, and an older man, Judge Otis Lord, whose correspondence with Emily, according to our guide, suggested "a special fondness."

"What a pack of losers," the girl said.

"They were all very distinguished men, dear."

"Not in my book." She pointed. "Never met this fellow attended, or alone without a tighter breathing and zero at the bone." Giddy laughter.

Our guide, who had been at pains to give the poet's life a *normal* spin, so to speak, E. Dickinson as your regular high-spirited young lady who liked baking, gardening, gathering wildflowers, reading, socializing, corresponding, dancing—"What was meant by her POM club, you see, my dear, Poetry of Motion, was dancing!"— now told us the well-rehearsed anecdote, intended to be amusing, of Bowles's futile attempt on one occasion to coax Emily downstairs to join the evening's company. The poet wouldn't be talked down from her room.

"Exactly," the girl said. "The soul selects her own society, then shuts the door. That woman was too busy to bother with some jerk."

"And here's Emily's room," the guide said, plowing ahead with the routine, "and this is the actual bed she slept in. A sleigh bed, they called it."

"Jingle bells, jingle bells, jingle all the way." The girl cackled. "It looks awful short."

There were pictures of the poet's heroes on one wall—Carlyle, Elizabeth Barrett Browning, George Eliot—and Mable Loomis Todd's Indian pipes on another. A headless, handless white dress stood upright in a glass case. Like the piano downstairs, we were told, the chest of drawers here, the small table, the simple side chair, and the cabinet by the bed were very similar to the actual furnishings Emily had lived with. Emily's sister had discovered the hundreds of poems in the bottom drawer of the dresser, the woman explained, pointing, as it were, to the very drawer.

"I thought they were in a trunk or something," the girl said. "I don't think she would have kept them in her dresser."

"No, dear, I'm sure Lavinia found them right in that bottom drawer."

"I doubt it." She turned to the small, maybe twenty-inch-square table. "You mean she wrote her poems at a dinky table like that?"

"Oh, I think it was big enough, wasn't it?"

"She probably wrote them lying on the bed."

"How would you like to wear dresses like that one, dear? Isn't it marvelous?"

"It freaks me out in that glass case. It's like a decapitated mummy or something. What do you think she would have said about that?"

"Who, dear?"

"Emily Dickinson."

"Well, I'm sure I don't know."

"She would have laughed."

We couldn't examine an early first edition of the poems—"Don't touch that, sir! Please!"—which sat on the chest of drawers, but we were permitted to handle a Xerox copy of one of the "volumes" or packets of poems composed of several folded sheets of paper bound with a delicate thread.

"I love her handwriting," the girl said. "It's loose and open and free. It's bold." She looked around the small room. "This is the southwest bedroom, right?"

"Yes, that's correct."

"So how do they know this was her bedroom?"

"Well, it simply *is*. This has always been the Emily Dickinson bedroom."

"But who says? Why are they so sure?"

"I guess her niece, Martha, said so. Martha Dickinson Bianchi, who lived next door, her literary heir. She was very involved, of course, with every aspect of the estate."

"But it's not documented or anything."

"This was—and is—the bedroom of Emily Dickinson. There has never been any question about that."

"Assent, and you are sane; demur—you're straightway dangerous—and handled with a chain." Gleeful cackling punctuated the lines.

"The next tour will be right behind us. Come along, dear. Please don't sit on the bed now, we can't have that."

"This is too weird," the girl said, popping off the bed. "She slept right *there* with all that poetry going through her head?"

Downstairs, our guide invited us to "have a turn" in the garden before we left the premises. The plants were the same plants that Emily would have enjoyed in her day. The grand oak on the east side of the house, she informed us, had surely been there when the poet was alive. "Good-bye," she said firmly, and retreated to the administrative office.

"Let's check out the flowers," I said to the girl. "You can tell me about them."

"A bee his burnished carriage drove boldly to a rose." Wild cackling, big smile. "I've already been to the garden. I've gotta go."

"Some other time," I said.

51

"Say, 'in a long time'—that will be nearer. 'Some time' is no time." Giddy hooting, clapping her hands, delighted with the words she'd spoken. She ran a dozen steps, the red sneakers slapping the pavement, then turned and called, "Bye," waving, and continued half-jogging down the driveway.

I walked through the colorful flower garden, I touched the massive trunk of the extraordinary oak, but I was unable to think about Emily Dickinson or feel her presence or attempt to see what she had seen here. I was absorbed with the red-haired girl. Driving back to Vermont, I couldn't stop thinking about the girl in the green jumper with the red sneaks and the chewed-off fingernails and that laugh. I was intoxicated with this girl, Elizabeth, I adored this girl I met at the Dickinson Homestead, this dazzling gnome.

Maybe I was getting somewhere, it seemed Monday evening as I reread the morning's two and a quarter pages, and also Tuesday evening reading that day's additional page and a half, and again on Wednesday with almost three more pages under my belt. The red light of my Phone Mate remained unblinking and that was all right with me. That was preferable to some off-the-wall call that could cause me to lose an entire day or more, that could take the mysterious inspiring wind out of my sail here, leaving my earnest and willing little boat in paralyzing doldrums again. The little boat, temporarily labelled *Loners*, was beginning to move, driven by some propitious breeze. That's all that ever matters, motion, the bow rising and falling, your homemade colors unfurled, busily engaged even if you don't know where you're headed. That's how I was feeling Thursday as I returned to the house to begin the day's work following a brisk walk to the top of the hill behind the barn through Mary's sparkling deciduous woods. The sight of the bicycle, a marriage between a ten-speed and a mountain bike—it stood propped against the lamppost entwined with blooming indigo-blue clematis—made me want to run for cover. My watch said seven-forty-five. She wasn't in the garden.

"Hello," I called, circling the dwelling, agitated, the day endangered. "Looking for me? Hello."

The red light was blinking in the kitchen like a furtive alarm, but when I hit Play, there was only a woman's exasperated gasp, an expelled breath, saying, "Shit." As I moved toward the living room I spotted her on the landing at the dark top of the staircase.

"I called first, but you weren't here. I can explain," she said, descending the stairs, following me to the kitchen.

"What are you doing in here?"

"When I looked through the screen door, I saw the kitchen was exactly the way it used to be," she said, gesturing to the room. "I expected everything to be gone. But everything's here! I had to come in. Do you understand what I'm saying?"

"No, I don't understand walking into someone's house. Just get on your bike . . ."

"It's like Mary just shut the door behind her. How could she do that? How could she fail to tell me about Fitz? Is the woman *sick*? All year long I assumed he was living his life and would be coming back here again and Mary let me think it, and all the time he was dead."

"You probably would have known about it if you'd been closer to them," I suggested.

"Close? Oh, I was close, all right. You don't understand. The idea was we wouldn't contact one another during the year, we wanted this new beginning each summer. Now. We didn't need to know about our everyday lives. Last year was like meeting here for the first time again, and we wanted to keep it that way."

"Like kids returning to summer camp."

"Yes," she said, deaf to the irony. "I felt like a kid coming back here. That excited."

"That doesn't sound like the Fitz I knew."

"How could Mary do that?" she repeated. "Wasn't that uncon-
scionable of her?"

"You'll have to take that up with her. Do you have her number
in Cambridge?"

"I'll never speak to Mary again. There's something wrong with
that woman. I thought she was a friend. Not even dropping me a
card all year? That's sick."

"Listen, I've got work to do."

"How well did you know Fitz?"

"Come on . . ." I stood on the granite doorstep, holding open the
screen door.

"He was a beautiful man. Did you know that?"

This coolish morning she was wearing faded jeans and a black
cotton sweater with white socks under the synthetic sandals. She
reached to the right of the door and took a large straw hat down
from its nail—Quakerish or Shakerish, with a flat crown and a large
firm brim. "This is his hat," she said, holding it toward me, and
tears surfaced, her mouth crumpling. "Oh, Fitz," she cried, "oh God,
what am I going to do?" rushing through the doorway. Halfway to
the lamppost the woman stumbled, bungling over her sandals, it
looked like, flopping to the damp grass as if she'd been tripped up
on her blind side.

"Are you all right?" But as I bent down to her, extending my
hand, she scrambled to her feet, this Helen, and continued in a
wobbly lurching run to her bicycle. And she was pumping down
the drive before I could remind her she still had the straw hat—
How about the hat?—scrunched up in one hand on the handlebar.
But how could she have been unaware of that?

I pushed the Play button: "Shit."

Upstairs a closet door in the master bedroom had been left open;
a black silk shirt, size X-large, lay with outstretched sleeves on

the bed. "Beautiful man, Elizabeth. Did we know he was a beautiful man?"

An unexpected surprise arrived in the day's mail. The postcard was of Picasso's *Nude Asleep in a Landscape*, 1934, from the Musée Picasso, which made me laugh out loud, coming from my son. A peaceful, voluptuous, happy painting of the painter's midlife muse Marie Thérèse, who Picasso had set up in an apartment for his exclusive pleasure when she was maybe eighteen, soft skin and silken hair, and he was a protean titan pushing fifty.

Dear Dad, Paris was okay, but no moveable feast. Met a Catherine (St. Louis) in a café, but too hyper. Train to Chartres. C'est trop. Skipped Versailles. Hitched southeast, and happier in the wine country. Met a family. Money seems to be holding out okay. Most days on my own just thinking about things. Like tonight feeling far away. Now north of Lyons. Plan to hump it for the mountains, but playing everything by ear. Then Italy. *Comment ça va in Vermont? Take care.*

Love, David.

I read the lines and read and reread between the lines, imagining him in a strange place. Compared to Picasso's serene picture, David's sober text was the other side of the coin. He can take care of himself, I thought, he's stronger and more resourceful than you are. I'm not worried about David. Beloved, that's what the name meant and that's why we chose it.

In the noisy wind that accompanied that night's storm a seventy-five-foot white pine came down partially on top of a lovely white birch right where I'd been reconstructing the wall. I'd worked with a chain saw years before, bucking up cordwood with my first wife's brother during the wood-burning seventies. Fitz's Stihl chain saw along with a gas can, marked *Stihl*, and a gallon of chain oil were together under a plank table in the barn. The saw roared to life with a few pulls. Nuts to have done all that earlier clearing by hand, I saw within minutes of lopping branches from the fallen pine. I made a neat pile on the other side of the wall. The arching birch wasn't broken but when I rolled the pine logs away from it, it didn't swing back up, as in a poem by Frost. Bowed almost parallel to the ground, the tree would never stand straight. I made my cut a couple of feet above the base. When I was little more than halfway through the trunk it exploded upward, sending me backward, the dangerous chain saw still roaring, and projecting the sawed end diagonally into the air with astonishing force, jolting the entire tree behind it. Christ, Elizabeth, if it had struck me in the head, instead of tossing me clear ... Foolkill was the name Vermonters had for accidents of that kind—a mistake so stupid you deserved to die. And how long might I have lain there decomposing before someone turned up Mary's long drive and discovered the putrid body? Turkey vultures, coyotes, and crows would have cleaned my bones. Not so much as a bruise, Elizabeth, and yet I never came so close to being expunged, deleted, blotted out. I paced back and forth before the tree in a daze, talking to the severed trunk, as if my mortality had just dawned on me.

I'm so miserable, my daughter had cried to me on the phone very near the end of her life, prepared to die, she said, so tired of suffering. As I dragged the beautiful birch branches off the field and into the woods, an unusually vivid picture of my daughter piling branches in her uncle's Connecticut woods at age ten or eleven appeared to me—Oshkosh overalls, very pink cheeks, a flannel shirt, and her characteristic frown of concentration as she willingly carried out the task allotted her—not a recollected photograph or a list of recalled details but a rare authentic memory, a reseen moment, which made me stop and hold my breath, conscious of my heartbeat.

I left a message on Sally's answering machine that night, asking her to call, and the next night she did. Throughout the gradual disintegration of our marriage we'd been more civil than angry—we'd married when we were practically children, after all—and sometime later, during the years of our daughter's illness, we found we needed one another as fellow travelers on our shared road of sorrow. Our daughter's suffering, as well as our determination to see her through, our ever-mounting anxiety, and at last, our endless grief overwhelmed whatever lingering tensions remained between us. Neither one of us could have relinquished the parental role to the other. In the last year of our daughter's life we were often together with her, and it was during that impossible time that Sally and Elizabeth got to know each other on some level. Basically, I think, they liked each other. Sally had remained in the West Side apartment; she eventually received tenure at Hunter in the psychology department. While we'd rarely seen each other in the past two years, we talked on the phone every few months, it seemed, mostly to discuss our son's next undertaking, or to work out his holiday schedule between us. Until that night it hadn't seemed necessary to give her my unlisted telephone number in Vermont. But suppose she needed to reach me about something in a hurry? We hadn't spoken to each other since discussing David's European travel plans in March, and when she called she said, "I've been away, I just got in this afternoon. David's all right, isn't he?"

"I'm sure he's fine. I didn't phone you because of David."

"Thank God. You scared the daylights out of me calling like that out of the blue."

"I had a card from him the other day, actually, postmarked Lyons. He was headed for the Alps."

"Isn't he too much? I can't think about him alone on some

damned mountain. It terrifies me. How did you and I end up with an adventurer for a son?"

"I have complete faith in the kid. He could be in Italy by now for that matter."

"Was that your first card?"

"Second. He wrote me his first week in Paris."

"I've only heard from him once, that pisses me off."

"You'll probably get something tomorrow, don't worry. He adores you. How have you been?"

"I'm all right. What kind of a question is that? I've been on a raft in the Snake River for a week. I joined a group, which I was afraid would be awful, but it was great."

"I'm impressed."

"Yeah, I always wanted to do something like that, and it's taken me all these years to manage it. There were a dozen of us, and the whole thing was just wild and wonderful."

"Psychopaths, aren't they a problem with these river trips?"

"Only in the movies, Frog. There was one moron about our age who assumed I was looking for a man, plus these icky newly-weds, who were too absorbed with all their new expensive camping crap to relax."

"You weren't looking for a man?"

"I've got all the men friends I need, thank you. I was looking for adventure and escape, or whatever you call it. But this man . . . the poor fool thought I'd gravitate toward him by the light of the camp-fire like a dusty moth. He had graying hair longer than mine, he swaggered in his purple shorts, an anesthesiologist, I think. He ended up hitting on one of the guides about half his age, who just played him like a pro for a couple of days, then tossed him back. How do these kids get to be so worldly and smart? I would have been afraid of the jerk at her age."

"I don't know."

"Anyway, I feel like I've been away. Like *away*. But it's unbearable around here. Has it been this stifling all week?"

"I'm not there, remember."

"Oh, right. You sound like you're downtown. Where the hell are you?"

"I'm in heaven," I said.

"Fine, I don't need to know. Wait a minute, I want to get a beer."

"I've already got one." As I heard her set down the phone and step away from it, then the muffled slam of the refrigerator, I could imagine her in the quiet kitchen perfectly, although I hadn't set foot in the room for many years. The sounds and sense of her still there in the old place moved me the way an old photograph of a friend can cause a rush of nostalgia.

"Okay, I'm back. Is Elizabeth there?"

"Elizabeth's in England."

"That's right, she loves England, doesn't she? Okay, tell me about heaven. What's it look like?"

"Pretty much what you'd expect—billowy white clouds, patches of pure blue, occasional shafts of light, rolling green fields surrounded by mist-enshrouded hills. Just like the cliche, more or less."

"Sounds like Vermont. David told me that's where you'd be, of course. What are you doing up there, trying to get into a book?"

"I was cleaning up some trees that came down in a storm, with Fitz's chain saw—Mary's husband who dropped dead last year, you know, Elizabeth's sister's husband. I made a stupid mistake cutting a pendulous white birch and it flew up and took my head off."

"You shouldn't use a chain saw out there by yourself. That's dumb, Henry. You could have an accident and no one would even know about it."

"I thought you should know."

"It's not funny, you know. I don't think this is funny. It's offensive. Have you been drinking?"

"Of course not. I've had a few drinks. It's very beautiful here. I guess it sounds like Vermont, but of course it's like nowhere on earth."

"Is this leading somewhere? I hate it when you do this."

"Do what?"

"Annoy me with some nonsense, with something that's supposed to amuse me, and only infuriates me."

"It's not supposed to amuse you."

"*That's* what infuriates me!" There was a pause, and when she spoke again she had changed her tack. "What's-his-name—Fitz? I think you mentioned his death to me. Elizabeth went up there to help her sister in the fall, didn't she?"

"Right."

"Have you run into him by any chance?"

"Fitz?"

"In heaven."

"No, I haven't run into him."

"How about God? Any sign of our Father who art in heaven?"

"Of course not. There's no God, you know that."

In a quiet, more solemn voice Sally asked, "Have you seen *anyone*?"

"No."

"Not one soul? What's the point of heaven if you don't get to see people you want to see? Isn't that the whole point?"

"I don't know."

"All right, Henry, I've had enough, I don't want to play anymore."

"When I was working outside this afternoon I had a very clear memory of her dragging branches on your brother's place at age ten or so. It was fall." I described that day. "Do you remember?"

"Maybe, I'm not sure. So you're up there alone. Are you all right, or what are you?"

"No, I'm fine. Poor Fitz is like a spook around here—his stuff, his house, his garden. I guess that's why our daughter has been so present. I came here thinking I could distance myself and focus on something else, but I keep going back to those years, nothing else seems important. I'm stuck, Sal, I can't seem to move forward. But I've got to, don't I?"

"Drifting down that river I missed her more than ever. I suppose that's why the anesthesiologist looked like such an asshole. It doesn't pass, Henry, it's never going to end."

"But look . . ."

"Look what?"

"I was going to say she's all right now, but that's a ridiculous lie."

"You mean she's no longer suffering."

"She's gone, she's completely gone."

"Not to heaven."

"I'm glad you called back. I shouldn't lay this on you, but . . ."

"You knew I'd call back. I'm going to bed now, I'm exhausted. Good night, Henry. Say hello to Elizabeth."

"Good night, Toad."

Sussex left me feeling all thatched out. Dorset was stoney, with downs, and there in Stinsford lay the heart of Thomas Hardy. Isn't that insane? Today it would probably be his dick. Castle Combe in the Cotswolds was make-believe. Treated ourselves to a fancy meal in the Manor House there. Two lovely boys (maybe thirty) traveling by bicycles bought us drinks, we flirted, shamelessly, but we didn't let them lay a finger on our precious skins. Stratford-upon-Avon was sexy, too. Busloads of people were herded through Anne Hathaway's house. After climbing down the tower at Warwick

Castle my legs went numb and wouldn't support me. Don't let it happen to you! Travel makes me horny; wish you were right here in this special spot, yes I said yes I will yes.

Love, E.

The picture on the postcard was of a knight of Warwick Castle decked out for jousting and mounted on a large black horse draped with a blanket bearing the knight's coat of arms. In the thought-bubble penned in above his head, Elizabeth had written, "I should be writin' a fookin' book right now."

Instead of taping the card onto the refrigerator, I took the Tower of London down. Grateful as I was to hear from the traveler, my wife's messages from old England were for the moment out of sync with my present mood.

~

Lynn drove the small red Ford while Elizabeth read the map, tracing their evolving itinerary—a crash course of quaint unreal towns and famous sights—with the indispensable help of her *Book of British Villages*. The Woolpak Inn in Chilham provided a carving for dinner, glistening shanks of lamb and beef, which made them laugh. Elizabeth loved the view of the countryside from the tower at Sissinghurst, imagining Vita Sackville-West looking out at the very scene. That same day they plowed on to Penshurst with its twelfth-century great room, its pleached apple arbor and carved yew hedge. Before they knew it evening had arrived and they hadn't found a place to stay yet, which caused some bickering over who was to blame. A pub owner phoned a Mrs. Shortwell, who put them in her grown-up daughter's preserved girlhood room. The pink-and-white-canopied bed was crowded with an extravagant collection of stuffed unicorns in pastel colors, which Lynn regarded as some creepy sexual fantasy. "I'm not sleeping with a fucking herd of unicorns." Elizabeth stuffed them under the bed. They hadn't slept together in the same bed before, but their fatigue quickly overcame the awkwardness of getting under the covers. She awoke near dawn to find Lynn, sound asleep, lying against her backside, one arm draped over her shoulder, the way she often woke up with Henry.

They stopped for fruit in Shere and chatted about the notable steeple with an old man trimming a hedge in the churchyard. Milk bottles by doorsteps reminded Lynn of Sylvia Plath, she said, from her days as an English major. The B roads through Surrey were narrow, twisting, canopied tunnels seemingly hacked out of the earth, and, yes, a little scary. Amberley was their first look at thatching, and provoked Lynn to shoot a whole roll of film. Watercress grew in the river at New Alresford. They stayed in the Swan hotel there, luxuriating in a private bath for the first time since London— "I could use a date tonight," Lynn said, "now that my hair is clean"—and ate at a sidewalk café across from blue and cream stucco buildings and felt far from home. They skipped two major cathedrals, Winchester and Salisbury, and flipped a coin over Stonehenge, which came up heads, Elizabeth's call, and meant they weren't going, she didn't want to see that ancient mystery locked up in a cage.

Continuing southwest through Dorset, they came to Corfe Castle where the dwellings of the entire village, in many cases constructed from the remains of the hilltop ruin that stood above the town, were of uniformly gray Purbeck stone, the roofing slates as well as the walls. The pillars of Westminster Abbey's towering nave, she remembered, were of Purbeck marble. It was cool and breezy so near the sea. They climbed the hill to the ancient destroyed castle and Lynn snapped a picture—"love in the ruin," she said—of a mother nursing her infant in the sun. Nan Berwick, an ancient ruin in her own right, ninety-five, she informed them, old as the century, was walleyed and wore bright lipstick on her whiskered face. There was a pitcher of water in the bedroom, hot water from the boiler in the kitchen, and crisp linen sheets on their beds. The twenty-foot-high hedges along the roads used to be beautiful, Nan Berwick said, when they trimmed them by hand. Now they used machines. "Don't you think," she said of Ireland, "they could drag that island out to the ocean and sink it?" She warned them to steer clear of the Midlands. "They had that Industrial Revolution there, you know. Quite beastly."

Each afternoon at about three they stopped wherever they were for cream tea, smearing coddled cream and strawberry jam on scones like there was no tomorrow. At six they'd track down a pub for pints of bitter, which Lynn claimed to be her favorite time of day. Every pub had a cat.

Driving north on the M5, cars flying past on the right as though their little Ford stood still, was scarier than the twisting one-lane roads bounded by hedges. Bath seemed too big and busy to bother with, this trip. Anticipating nothing special, they arrived at Castle Combe, a tiny village in the Cotswolds uniformly constructed of honey-colored stone—oolitic limestone, Elizabeth read. The place seemed more make-believe, more impeccable and unreal, and busier with tourists, than anyplace yet. They checked into a small hotel, then found a pub. The day marked the end of their first week.

Lynn sat back holding her beer with both hands. "I'm pooped," she said. "London seems like last year. Where were we yesterday? When was Penshurst? It all sort of runs together, doesn't it? My head is spinning."

"Maybe we should slow down," Elizabeth said. "This is supposed to be a vacation."

"We're doing pretty well, though, aren't we—as a team?"

"We're doing fine."

When Lynn went back to the hotel for a nap, Elizabeth walked to the so-called Manor House, an imposing brick place set in a spacious park at one end of the town, to make a reservation for dinner. A majestic cedar, heroic in height, dominated the grounds to one side of the building. The town was busy with sightseers, but Elizabeth had this spot, the bench at the base of the tree, to herself. Lynn was right, her head was full of details—a wattle fence, a flowerbox below a windowsill, the dark-timber ceiling of a pub, hedgerows and stone walls and sweeping downs—but the chronology of where and when ran together.

Gustavo was a fool. Impatient, grabby, overconfident, he'd screwed up whatever might have been possible. She'd deliberately left behind the small picture of Henry, cut from a larger photograph, which she had carried in her wallet for years. The point was to get away from him for a while. Now she wanted the picture, she wanted to see his eyes, for example, the width of his mouth, the physical information that made him Henry. How he had pored over pictures of his daughter after her death, trying to see her, and yet the exercise typically proved both futile and wrenching. He would never see her again was the truth the photographs repeatedly brought home to him. Elizabeth tipped her head back, the tree trunk seemed to rise infinitely above her, through distant lateral branches, to odd fragmented shapes of blue. Fear that she might never see Henry again stunned her, the high branches blurred, trembled, and she momentarily closed her eyes. She concentrated on the building across the lawn until her vision cleared, deciding the dizziness had been brought on by bending back her head like that. Not a brain tumor, not this time. A residue of fear remained. Did the sensation qualify as a kind of premonition? Poor Fitz, she thought. She could picture her sister's isolated house in its clearing—the pitch of the roof, the deep shade and patch of lawn—but she could hardly imagine Henry there on his own. Poking around Mary's dim kitchen, reading in the low-ceilinged living room at night surrounded by the spooky pitch dark. If anything happened to him she'd be completely alone, she considered, looking across the undulating groomed lawn of the empty park. More alone than Mary, for example, who still had her children. She could call him—it would be about noon there now—then decided no, she'd been emphatic about not calling. She didn't need to know how his work was progressing. In five minutes he might manage to provoke her. Come on, you're being morbid. Henry is fine.

She showered and dressed in the best clothes she'd brought with her, black on black, which hardly seemed appropriate in pastoral Castle Combe, a place not of this world, but too bad. She found Lynn downstairs having tea and cake.

"I just met the nicest English guy," she said. "He and his friend are on their way to bike around the Lake District. He asked me to dinner. Can you believe that?"

"Yes, you've got your headlights on, for one thing." A clingy rayon dress clearly showed off Lynn's breasts, nipples pricking the fabric, quite a handful. "And you said?"

"I had a date with my traveling companion, but thanks, maybe we'll see you at the restaurant."

"Just what we need."

"Aren't you bored hanging around with me? It might be fun. Vacation, remember?"

"I'm sure I'll collapse as soon as I've stuffed myself."

"What's that by the way?" she asked, reaching. "Those are beautiful. Have I seen them before?"

"Gustavo. I tried to refuse them. I thought this dress needed something tonight and there they were."

Two young men were seated at the opposite side of the dining room when Lynn and Elizabeth arrived and they were waiting in the manor's large living room when the two women, finished with dinner, were on their way out of the place.

"There they are," the red-haired fellow in the moss green jacket said to his pal, loud enough to be heard by them. "Lynn, won't you join us?" He held up a glass of something.

"I'll be back to the room soon," she said to Elizabeth. "Are you sure you don't want a nightcap or something?"

"Oh, I'm sure." At best the men might have been Lynn's age, mid-thirties. They were privileged, attractive, possibly married, and Elizabeth was sure she didn't have the patience to put up with their engaging banter about the States, what everyone did for a living, places they'd been, places to go. She wasn't feeling sociable. "I want to get an early start in the morning," she said. "I'm going to haul you out of bed."

Before she left the building, however, the other man caught up with her, placing himself between Elizabeth and the front door. He was tall with prematurely gray hair, and an insignia of some kind on his blue blazer. "Don't go," he implored. "I'm starved for conversation with a charming stranger from America." Beaming at her like a British twit in an insufferable romantic comedy.

"I'm fresh out of charm," she said. She was starved for sleep.

"You won't reconsider?" he pouted, cocking his head to one side, and his eyes were sad all of a sudden.

"No, afraid not." She turned and retraced her steps to the living room where her friend's laughter was evidently provoking an inspired performance from the guy who'd latched on to her. "Lynn, are you sure you want to hang out with these two?"

Lynn looked up, flattered pink by the jabbering fuss over her. "See you back at the room," she said.

She was awakened by an annoyingly literal, yet absurd dream: a twisting road tunneling through dense vegetation ... furious at Henry for believing he could buy Corfe Castle and rebuild it by hand ... pleading with him to get on the left side of the road ... pleading with Lynn while Lynn laughed as though unable to hear her . . . It was still dark. Her friend wasn't in the other bed and she clearly hadn't been in the bed all night. She considered calling the front desk, but what would she say? Had they gone off in the car? Had there been an accident? Phoning the police seemed premature, yet it was improbable that Lynn would spend the night with the guy. Wasn't it? She grew frightened. Two unknown men in a foreign country. Stranger things had happened. *Prime Suspect*, who was that actress? Helen Mirren? Chief Inspector Tennison. Not spelled like the poet, she thought. If Lynn fucked one of them, she was going to unload on her, goddamn it. Going around with her nipples poking out all over the room. Yeah, you've come a long way, baby. Lynn, won't you join us, the little shit. Lynn, won't you fuck us? Won't you reconsider? I'm starved for charm. If Lynn wasn't back by seven, say, she'd have to contact the police, and if it turned out to be mortifying for everyone, that was tough. I'm surprised you'd leave me hanging like that. Was a phone call too much to ask, worried sick half the night, thinking something horrible had happened to you?

On the other hand, Elizabeth realized, it might have seemed too late to Lynn to call by the time she decided not to return to the room. Or maybe she was too embarrassed to call, or resented feeling an obligation to do so, or simply didn't want to deal with Elizabeth's questions, Elizabeth's disapproving tone, Elizabeth's dismay, having made up her mind to do as she pleased. Oh Lynn, that's stupid, I didn't know you were so stupid. Impressed by a stranger with an Oxbridge accent. I thought you were beyond that sort of nonsense. Six months before, Lynn had given up on a man she'd been with for about two years, a hot shit in the garment industry who'd had a vasectomy following the birth of his second child and wouldn't consider having his potency restored to make a mother out of another woman, period. She refused to buy in to another pre-owned man, she said. When you added the divorced-with-children category to the other out-of-bounds males—married, gay, fat, sick, old, poor, stupid, insane—there wasn't much left.

She examined herself in the full-length mirror attached to the back of the bathroom door, adjusting the door so that she was able to see her body from behind and in three-quarter profile in the horizontal mirror above the sink. Her ass wasn't getting any smaller, her breasts sagged a little, her spine was knobby. Faint stretch marks on her hips, from the unhappy teenage years her weight had fluctuated radically, looked like faded scars. She tried to figure out the last time she and Henry had fucked and couldn't put her finger on it. She remembered a lovely morning that might have been late April or early May, her head dangling off the side of the bed, a swatch of blue sky between the buildings, while he went on and on, eliciting from both of them an unusual commotion. Then weeks of sexual drought, an awful waste, because it was more than a matter of pleasure. If jerking off could make you feel desperate and lonely, fucking made you feel tuned up and hopeful, boosting your fragile joie de vivre. There wasn't a good substitute for genital contact. Every man was another story; she hadn't known that many. No one since her marriage; you good girl. She pressed her fingers between her legs, probing. Nothing doing. Arousal was too far off, too much work. I hope you haven't done something you'll regret, she thought, I hope you protected yourself, you reckless reckless child. That would prompt Lynn's sporting smile.

The sky over Castle Combe was brightening by the time she got out of the shower. She was soon packed up and ready to roll. The sight of Lynn's journal, a black sketch pad, and her white sweat-stained Nikes caused her another moment of fright. Should she have called the police two hours ago? She opened the journal and her friend's unfamiliar handwriting, large and open and loopy, surprised her, too girlish-seeming for a person with Lynn's ambition and aggressiveness. She had been a buyer at Barney's, a young hot-shot, when Elizabeth had worked there years before, and the friendship initiated then had survived their various career changes in retail. Presently Lynn was also between jobs, which was the coincidence in their lives that had made the plan to tour England together possible. Each day of their journey had evidently merited about two pages in Lynn's journal. The travel diary was either the last thing she attended to each day, lying on her bed, propped on an elbow, or the first thing she did over her tea after breakfast. Recalling her friend frowning over her black notebook at Nan Berwick's, hastily getting down all her precious impressions of *that day*, Elizabeth placed the journal back on the bedspread without reading a word of it. She was inclined to regard privacy as sacrosanct, but she also had no desire to know just what observations Piccadilly, for example, the Gore, Harrods, Amberley, or her traveling companion, for that matter, had provoked in Lynn. The woman's private thoughts, if they qualified as such, represented more information than Elizabeth wished to know about her. She would have been reluctant to read the notebook if her friend had put it in her lap.

Elizabeth had never recorded any period of her existence, failing to grasp the point of an exercise so self-absorbed and self-serious. Who in the world would read such a thing, and if it was not meant to be read—and whose little everyday routines deserved that distinction?—why would you write it? Henry claimed that the act of jotting down the ordinary events of the day had become a necessary ritual for him, which represented a confirmation of experience. When he browsed through his journal—the handwriting unreadable to anyone else—there were always small surprises and revelations, he insisted, memories recaptured or clarified, sightings and reseeings, recurrent patterns and themes that persuaded him of the notebook's indispensable importance. To her the habit was more like an obsessive-compulsive disorder, which had the effect of distancing him from experience—you're always *observing*—rather than involving him in it.

"Forget Henry for five minutes," she said impatiently. "Come on, Lynn, give me a break." As if her wish was a command, her friend let herself into the room.

"Give me fifteen minutes," she said, dropping her pocketbook, reaching behind to unfasten her dress as she kicked off her good black shoes. "I need a shower and I'll be fresh as a daisy."

"I'll be downstairs," said Elizabeth. "I hope you haven't done something you'll regret."

"Me too."

"You reckless reckless child."

"Okay, Mother."

Driving through Gloucestershire—they backtracked to Lacock, then proceeded north to Sapperton, Bourton-on-the-Water, Cirencester, the Slaughters—they became bored, they admitted, with the prevailing charm, the orderly, silent villages of stone houses with their stone roofs, as though old England had become too familiar overnight. And today, following a compulsory hour of stubborn silence on the subject, there was something more stimulating to talk about than the scenery, the great downs that swept to the horizon on both sides of the meandering road.

"I had no intention of spending the night with him. I wasn't really drunk. He was telling me stories about his patients."

"You really believe he was a gynecologist?"

"He was ... absolutely ... Stories about cancer, brave women he's known, difficult births. He was smart and sweet and fun, we got to holding hands, and then he was touching my face, my hair, and at some point I thought, Okay, Simon, you're in for it. I felt we connected, incredible as it seems."

"Is that what you call it—connected?"

"He was a wonderfully entertaining storyteller. Once he delivered quintuplets, for instance, a litter of little humans, which was hysterical."

"The Herriot of the lady's infirmary," Elizabeth said. "All vaginas great and small."

"He also seemed a safe bet from the STD angle, an OB-GYN no less. And he was beautiful, didn't you think so?"

"I wonder if he screws someone new every night of his holiday. Where was his sidekick?"

"His friend had gone to bed. He was an investment banker or something. They had separate rooms in the bloody Manor House. You're jealous. Elizabeth is jealous of Lynn for getting laid."

"That doesn't deserve an answer."

"You know what I was thinking?"

"I can't imagine."

"I was thinking I can do it if he can. I decided I was just going to go ahead and see what it's like. I haven't slept with a total stranger since I was twenty-two, I think, on a hike in the Sierra Nevadas. My Rexroth phase. Before retailing."

"I hope he wore a condom. I don't think gynecologists are immune to disease or able to spontaneously prevent fertilization during intercourse."

"I found the thing inside me when I took my shower this morning."

"Well, that's too bad. I'm sorry."

"I'm sure I'm fine."

At midday they stopped at Stow-on-the-Wold and secured a bed for the night at the Queen's Head Inn. They spent an hour browsing antique shops and when Lynn spotted the refectory table of her dreams, ancient walnut waxed to a lustrous finish, she bought it on the spot for about five thousand dollars. "That's how I felt last night," she said. "I've always wanted one. I'm not putting things off anymore. I'm leaping in."

"Wild warrior woman," Elizabeth told her. "Henry would love a table like that."

"When we see another one, go for it. You only live once, right?"

"We don't have thousands of bucks for a chunk of wood. He'd kill me."

They drove on to Broadway, which seemed too tidy, yellow, and infested with bric-a-brac. A balding businessman from Cleveland, struggling with a map as large as a tablecloth, asked, "Are these the Cotswolds?" He reminded Elizabeth of the American in stone-washed jeans stalking her through St. James's Park.

Lynn's escapade kept coming up like an aftertaste in the back of her throat. Over afternoon tea Elizabeth finally asked, "All right, you liked this Simon guy and you have no regrets, but you haven't told me how it was. How it went."

Lynn regarded her friend mischievously. "You're bad, Elizabeth. He had rather compact genitals for a gynecologist, smallish compact balls, and a very average penis, I'd say. I'm no expert. All that was fine, it worked. I suppose I was a little disappointed in the end, of course, but what can you expect?"

"Of course, what can you expect?"

"He was a better storyteller. It was all too quick."

"So the big connection had its limits?"

"Are you happy now?"

"You'd think an OB-GYN would know something about women, wouldn't you? I mean, have some know-how, some appreciation of the woman's point of view. Some heightened sensitivity."

"Not if he's a man." Lynn bit into her scone. "How are we going to live without coddled cream?"

Snowshill, the view down a great steep field where a thin ribbon of road disappeared between overlapping hills, was magical and brought them back to the un-American beauty of their surroundings. Back at Stow-on-the-Wold, however, enjoying their first pints of the day, they agreed they'd had their fill of the Cotswolds.

"How dumb," Lynn said, looking across the square. "How disgusting, wasn't it, screwing that guy?"

"I thought you felt okay about the whole thing."

"Now what? I'll never see Simon what's-his-name again. The feeling you have after an X-rated movie, it's sort of like that. Manipulated, sticky, unsatisfied."

"He probably feels the same way you do. I'm just glad you're all right. You didn't know what you were getting into. You could have been hurt."

"That wasn't a risk. You have to trust your instincts, don't you?"

She hadn't confided Gustavo's overpowering assault to Lynn, or the precipitous fear she'd experienced when he'd momentarily seemed beyond her control. "You can't trust anything as far as I'm concerned."

"I was pretty sure this pretty Englishman wasn't about to cut me up and put me through his wood chipper. What was that movie?" Lynn leaned toward her, gently rubbing the back of her friend's hand. "You're still mad at me, aren't you?"

"I'm really not, Lynn."

"Then what are you down about? You look so gloomy right now."

"I should call Henry. I want to call him, I worry about him, but then when I think about actually picking up the phone, hearing his voice, I lose it, I don't want to talk to him."

"You wanted a vacation from one another, that's the whole point. What's wrong with that?"

"Ever since he left for Vermont, I've felt nothing but relief. All last year we were at each other half the time. Just contrary, impatient, hard of hearing. I don't think I want to go back to that."

"I didn't know it was that grim. I've always liked Henry."

"He can be wonderful. But everything has been overshadowed now. He doesn't know how to have fun anymore. Does that sound stupid? Henry has a marvelous sense of humor, he used to make me laugh—like your Simon character—but that seems lost, as though part of him has been blacked out."

"The laughs?" Lynn asked incredulously.

"I miss him—the original Henry. I miss his unexpected observations, his particular take on things. He used to appreciate everything, he loved walking down the street taking it all in."

Lynn shrugged. "He still seems pretty witty when I'm around."

"That's different. There's a persistent undercurrent of sadness. I can see it in his face. The light is gone. Pick your cliche, there must be a thousand ways of putting it."

"Sorrow befell him. Is that his fault?"

"Of course not."

"It would be a shame if you broke up, that's what I think."

"The idea terrifies me, then I think it might give us both a chance."

"To do what?"

Until Lynn posed the question, Elizabeth assumed she knew the answer. "Our lives are passing by. This is all going to be over," she pleaded, holding out the palms of her hands.

"I see."

~

"Henry Ash calling from the Underhills'," I said to her answering machine. "About the other morning, I know I was a little abrupt. You surprised me just as I was eager to get to work. I think I understand how you must be feeling. . . . Look, feel free to come over again, if that would be helpful or useful to you. Just call ahead so I'll know when to expect you. I hear we're in for another storm," I added, "batten down the hatches," regretting the good-guy message, the idea of my voice on her machine, the moment I hung up.

The threat of thunderstorms lately, the fifty or seventy percent chance of a storm every damn night, Elizabeth, is getting old.

When she called the next morning, I allowed her to deliver her message without interference, rather than pick up the phone: "Helen Trudell returning your call. Yes, the confusion was unfortunate. I can see how you'd be put off, I can't help that. The whole Fitz thing, it all feels so wrong and unfinished. . . . If I could spend some time over there, maybe just have the place to myself for an afternoon . . . I'm confused and angry. I want to feel his presence, feel near him again. I have to accept what has happened and I know it would help if I could be there alone with him. I'm glad you called."

The whole Fitz thing, Elizabeth! You can't be here alone with him because he's not here, not in body or soul, not in his silk shirt or the size twelve Birkenstocks on the closet floor. He was buried almost a year ago in Wellesley, according to his mother's wishes, and that's the end of Fitz, the whole Fitz thing, I thought, the whole thing called Fitz, pacing the kitchen, taking in the pine table, the green painted chairs, the plain unpainted pine cabinets, the dated appliances, the curtainless multipaned windows. Was Fitz's presence discernible in these simple furnishings? Mary was no Vanessa Bell, Fitz no Duncan Grant, making every corner of their dwelling an opportunity for self-expression, transforming everyday walls and doors into decorative art.

An old corner cupboard, painted an antiqued blue-green, contained piles of old *New Yorkers*, some larger serving bowls and platters, candlesticks and cloth napkins. Was Fitz there? A carved Canada goose with a busted beak sat on top of the cupboard. Several baskets of various weave were displayed on top of the cabinets. One contained dried strawflowers and another was filled with wine corks. Clay canisters served as bookends for a number of well-thumbed cookbooks. The Julia Child volume contained various recipes on stained and tattered three-by-five cards and assorted slips of paper, and among these I discovered *Fitz's Blueberry Pie*, *Fitz's Rice Pudding*, *Fitz's Cajun Beans*, *Fitz's Curried Chicken*. The pantry was an intimidating chaos of accumulated household stuff, a long narrow catchall of domestic debris, into which I was reluctant to venture, as anyone would be. There were hats, a giant basket of old sneakers and boots, plastic rain gear, and several extra-large jackets, a jean jacket, a barn coat, an old wool thing, in the mud-room. The low-ceilinged, dirt-floored, fieldstone basement was even smaller than expected because the house had been partially built on a ledge. The small area was dominated by the chimney mass, a fairly recent furnace on a new concrete slab, and a modest oil tank. No wine cellar, Fitz? Headroom was taken up with plumbing and wiring. Some of the timber joists beneath the living room had been replaced. There was only a vacant crawl space under his addition. No, there was nothing of interest in the basement. The bedrooms were minimally furnished and the closets contained nothing but clothes, more his than hers because of course Mary had taken most of her things back to Cambridge with her. A hatchway in my bedroom led to what must have been a shallow attic, and I was certain there could be nothing of importance, possibly nothing at all, in that attic. The woman wasn't going to be climbing into the attic looking for Fitz's presence.

And there was nothing in the simply furnished living room that didn't meet the eye. The books represented Mary's summer reading, stout biographies and nineteenth-century novels by Tolstoy, Flaubert, James, Trollope, and the watercolors on the wall—of irises, a weathered barn, a pasture with cows bounded by pine woods—had been done by Mary, who was no Winslow Homer but far better than most Sunday painters. I was looking for what harm there could be in allowing the woman to spend time alone in the house, because the simplest way to resolve the *whole Fitz thing* was maybe to let her come and get it over with. Let the woman feel Fitz's presence, if she could, accept what had happened, with any luck, and put her unexpected arrival on the scene behind me. An unforeseen last-minute impulse prompted me to designate Fitz's room out-of-bounds—out of deference to his widow's wishes.

"Mary left the room untouched," I explained over the phone. "Until she's dealt with it herself, she doesn't want anyone else in there. That was the only stipulation she made when I decided to take the place for the summer: no trespassing in Fitz's study. Otherwise, sure, come over and hang out for a while."

"I don't need to go into his study," she said. "I rarely went beyond the kitchen when I was over there."

When she pedaled into the yard the following afternoon at two, as arranged, I was on my way out the door—having stashed my notes, my journal, etc., in the out-of-bounds room—determined to avoid an awkward and possibly embarrassing confrontation. We acknowledged one another with a wave, that's all, fellow workers changing shifts. As I drove out of the yard, I observed her walking toward the house in the rearview mirror—like a cautious woman keeping a daring rendezvous.

The highlights of my outing to Augustus Saint-Gaudens's summer home and studio in New Hampshire, now a museum, were his bronze medallion of Robert Louis Stevenson languishing on a couch from TB, smoking a cigarette, and the splendid, pillared, west-facing porch of the modest house. His heroic *Puritan* always gave me a laugh. Today the famous monuments of the standing Lincoln, Robert Shaw and his black Civil War regiment, and the shrouded Mrs. Henry Adams didn't intrigue me as much as the ice house, the evocation of a world when blocks of ice were cut from a pond in winter to last through the summer. The statue of seated Mrs. Adams, who died young, was often called *Grief*, I learned from the young, heavyset guide, but the artist intended just the opposite: "Peace." She smiled. Well, it looked like grief to me. A hundred years ago Saint-Gaudens and his guests made the long journey from New York by train, then toted everything up to the top of the hill by horse-drawn wagons. The renowned sculptor died of colon cancer at fifty-nine, the guide said in answer to my question, but she wouldn't agree that it must have been a high-fat diet that caused the disease.

"Do you know anything about his meeting with Walt Whitman?" I asked.

She was flustered, cheeks rosy, lips pouting, an anxious, overly responsible tour guide, who had been persuaded that she was the custodian, at least temporarily, of Saint-Gaudens's estate and therefore obligated to know everything known about his life. "Walt Whitman?" she asked, blinking. Possibly she was shy, uncomfortable to find herself alone with a male tourist.

"I think they met when Whitman was being photographed and painted and sculpted to death in old age. Saint-Gaudens was thirty years younger, of course." I smiled, thinking of The Good Gray Poet, when I said, "I wonder if he was attracted to the old codger."

"I don't know what you mean," she said. "Attracted?"

"Well, what do you make of his friendship with Stanford White? The notorious men of the day and their New York sex club. What was that note Saint-Gaudens sent to his buddy, I'm your man for drinking and buggery, words to that effect."

The young woman's complexion turned a deeper shade of blush. "Are you being abusive?" she said as though fully prepared to call 911 on her portable phone.

I raised my hands in the air. "Don't you know about those guys—enticing a new batch of aspiring girls into their hedonistic lair every week? The famous Stanford White scandal? He was murdered, remember?"

But she had already started back up the stairs to the front door of the historic house. At the top she turned. Mustering all her indignation, she said, "Please leave."

I stopped at an inn for supper, enormously disappointing sole, and didn't get back to the house until almost dark, hours later than planned. The red light on the answering machine wasn't blinking. Helen had left a bouquet of daisies on the kitchen table with a note: "I really appreciated today. I don't think I'll have to bother you again. God bless." As I went through the rooms, flicking on lights, I could find no further evidence to indicate that she'd spent the afternoon here, which was more a letdown than a relief. What's she been up to, Elizabeth? What did she do with herself all afternoon?

I was in bed slogging through the impossible opening pages of Mary's discolored copy of *The Ambassadors* when the phone went off in the kitchen. I scrambled downstairs to catch it before the answering machine was engaged.

"It's me, Helen, oh my God, something horrible is happening."

"What's wrong?"

"This is horrible."

"What's happening? What's horrible?" and I was practically shouting myself, her alarm spontaneously igniting my own.

"I don't know," she cried, "I was just sitting here ... my heart feels like it's coming through my chest, I can't get my breath, I feel like I'm going to pass out. I tried to call my friend in New York, but ..."

"Should I call Emergency? Does 9-1-1 work around here?"

"Am I having a heart attack? Oh God ..."

"Hang up. I'll call 9-1-1, then I'll call you back."

"Wait! I don't want anyone barging in here. I was just sitting here thinking about things and I burst into tears, then this whole thing came over me." Momentarily, she began to cry. "I'm sorry."

"My first wife went through a difficult period when she experienced panic attacks," I suggested, "racing pulse, breathlessness, fear of fainting, just what you're describing. Maybe you're experiencing a panic attack."

"I feel out of control. My mind is all over the place."

"Helen," I said, conscious of uttering the name for the first time, "try to take some deep breaths. There's nothing physically wrong. You're having an anxiety attack. Try to take some breaths, try to calm yourself."

"I started having these thoughts, I couldn't stop them. It's horrible."

"Try to breathe, okay? Try to take deep, slow breaths."

"Could you possibly come over? I'm sorry, there's no one else to call."

"It's after eleven."

"I don't know what's come over me, I can't stop it."

"Why don't I just stay on the phone until you're feeling better? I'm right here."

"I'm sorry, I know it's asking a lot. I'm ten minutes away, maybe less."

"You sound a little better, do you think so?"

"I'd come over there, but I don't trust myself to drive, I don't want to go out."

"No, you should stay where you are. You're really all right, you know. Concentrate on breathing, try to relax. I'm going to hang up, but I'll be right here, okay? I can come over if necessary, but I think you're going to be fine. My wife went through that. It's frightening, but then it passes. I'm going to say good night. All right?"

"All right."

I poured myself a finger of scotch. "Oh, Sally," I said, observing my long face in the window over the sink. "Sad Toad."

The phone rang minutes later. "I can't stop these thoughts, I'm scared. What's wrong with me?"

"All right, I'm on my way over. Tell me how to get there. Take your time."

However many minutes later, after I'd found the sign for Emerson Hill Road and proceeded less than a mile on that potholed dirt disaster, I turned left at the mailbox marked *Platt*. A narrow corridor through black woods opened to a dark clearing. Anyone would panic living here, I thought. A light on the front porch, which ran the length of the building, revealed that the one-story structure was a sort of crude log cabin. What could I do, Elizabeth? You'd never make a call like that if you weren't in an awfully bad way, would you? This Helen stepped onto the porch in an over-sized T-shirt that reached almost to her knees, waving both arms over her head. "It's all right," she called.

I stepped forward. "What?"

More emphatic waving like a woman stopping traffic, flagging down a train, desperately warning the oncomer to come no closer. "It's all right. I'm okay now."

"All right?"

"Yes. Thanks anyway."

The red light was blinking in time with my pulse as I let myself into Mary's kitchen. I pressed Play: "Have you left? I was going to tell you not to come, after all. Oh no, you're here already!"

Index card #71:
W. W.:
I just did what I did because I did it—that's the whole secret.

I sat before my computer in a state of agitation the next morning—Monday!—scrolling and rescrolling through the haphazard pages I'd written, unable to see what my meditation on the three great loners of American literature was about or where it was going. The door to Fitz's study stood closed directly behind my back. *The Ambassadors* was unreadable. "Unreadable, Elizabeth, no one can possibly endure this stuff that passes for American literature. His doubt was his passion, wasn't it, but doubt didn't inhibit him from sitting down day after day to crank out his turgid impenetrable prose and feel like a bleeding genius in the process. The bag of wind," I cried, flinging the book against Fitz's closed door. "Feathers, Whitman called it. Feathers! He wouldn't have been compelled to write such convoluted, repressed prose if he'd gone out cruising swimming holes and bathhouses with his young pal Sargent, instead of posing for that lofty bombastic portrait of his. Everything he ever wrote was about failing to get it on with another human being. The loneliness of the long-distance writer, Elizabeth, one hand on his pen, one on his dick, doubt for his passion." Venting my frustration against the Master, that's sad, Henry, James's prose isn't the problem here, the sex life of Henry James isn't your problem, the poor man may have been impotent, for that matter, as the virile author of *The Sun Also Rises* suggested. Fitz's door stood closed behind my back, Fitz the aloof, Fitz the unreadable, and at times there was the feeling of Fitz there behind the door. Fitz industriously going about his business in there without a doubt in the world, all his stuff untouched behind the door, Fitz unsorted and unsettled and unresolved behind the door, the brilliant scientist with the spiritual side, the beautiful man. If I could be alone with Fitz, she'd said, but it was Henry who was alone with him, and that was running interference, it was getting in the way, *the whole Fitz thing*, Elizabeth. I picked up the book from the floor and tossed it onto the stuffed love seat against the wall, beneath Mary's wishy-washy irises, and entered the study.

I'd browsed through the bookshelves before, the books didn't interest me, and, at a glance, it was clear that the professional articles from various colleagues could only concern members of a recondite scientific community. "Silk Proteins and the Evolution of Web-spinning Spiders," "Parasitism, Mutualism, and the Evolution of Adaptive Systems," "The Evolutionary Ecology of Virulence," for example, by Albert Fitzgerald Underhill. There was a manila folder of correspondence to Dear Fitz or Dear Professor Underhill, which largely pertained to professional matters, but which I wasn't inclined to read in any case. The only item on the wall was a cheap reproduction of Hieronymus Bosch's *Garden of Earthly Delights*. The room was uncluttered and orderly, the relatively austere setup of someone who basically came here to sit at his computer.

I'd noticed the yellow envelopes of Kodak color prints on top of the bookcase before and automatically turned away from the thought of family snapshots, the Underhills on holiday, the Underhills entertaining guests, celebrating the Fourth of July with Mary's children visiting from the city probably. All snapshots of families on vacation were alike, whether of people, of the yard, of the view, of the occasion, whatever the occasion. And in fact most of the photos were what you'd expect: Mary in front of the house laughing with a couple unrecognizable to me; Mary blowing out a handful of candles on a cake in the kitchen; Fitz in his garden wearing the straw hat; Fitz and the other man and woman posing next to blooming lilacs; three turkeys in the front yard; two distant deer in the mowing west of the house, and so on. There was one picture of the wall of woods bordering the field, which seemed pointless, until I deciphered a blurred blackness beneath a tree, a bear eluding the camera.

Halfway through the second batch of snapshots this Helen appeared framed by the dark of the open barn door and wearing an audacious smile. Here she was with Mary in the kitchen, and again seated with Mary on a massive rock by a narrow stream. In the next change of scene Fitz was dressed in khaki like something out of Africa, standing before a primitive hutlike structure less than his height, composed of green branches, and backed by deciduous woods. There followed a shot of Mary wrapped in a towel at the entrance to this structure, which now had a blue tarp spread over the rustic roof. She waved at the camera as though she was stepping onto a train, off on a trip. An out-of-focus picture captured the backside of a naked person ducking inside the hut, surely a woman, judging from the broadly heart-shaped behind. And then these Vermont snapshots, the last half dozen of them, gave me a laugh—"Whoa!"—for here was Mary and Fitz, or Mary and Helen, or Helen and Fitz lounging outside the hut on a blanket, or posing arm in arm before the structure, or bathing in the glinting stream, casually naked. Sunlight, shadows, forest, smoke, and smiling naked people, Elizabeth, about as provocative as any aboriginal group featured in *National Geographic*. Whoa, I thought, where are the skulls on poles? Mary looked bonier and scrawnier than I would have imagined; Fitz was tan limbs and face with a thin pale torso, his longish uncircumcised penis blind and innocent-looking in the one frontal view of him, standing arm in arm with Helen. This Helen, though discernibly younger than her middle-aged companions, didn't look much different than they did in her skin. The startling thing about the woman, and the notably disturbing detail in the otherwise amusing photographs, was only obvious in the same frontal shot that featured Fitz's penis—her left breast had been removed, leaving a peculiar horizontal scar on that side. Her right breast was half-concealed against Fitz's side. She and Fitz looked warm, with flushed moist faces in the humid green air, and they grinned the candid, unguarded smiles of simple people at peace, let's say, in a simpler world.

It hadn't occurred to me to turn on his computer, Elizabeth, the thought hadn't entered my mind. Fitz and I had always been civil, the one or two times we ran into each other annually, but we had probably never had a conversation that made any difference to either of us. The matter-of-fact candor and forthrightness that existed between possible friends, the implicit understanding, the shared sense of humor, had never existed between your brother-in-law and me. The biologist, I thought, the scientist. We had never expressed the slightest interest in each other's work. I could do nothing to further Fitz's career, he could do nothing to further mine, and although that consideration had rarely influenced my friendships, I gathered it was the sole criterion informing Fitz's relationships. His ambition left no time to make even eye contact with people who weren't professionally useful. In a room of non-scientific types, he was unable to suppress his impatience, his flight instinct. Mary once apologized for her husband's last-minute regrets concerning a little dinner party we were throwing in New York, explaining that he'd been working very hard on an important proj-ect and strangers (our other guests) would only make him tense just when he needed to relax. No one works harder than Fitz, Elizabeth, no one needs to relax from his all-important labors more than your esteemed brother-in-law. Eventually, I wanted nothing more to do with the man, even if that meant risking Mary's friendship in the process. I knew all I needed to know about Fitz—until I stumbled on snapshots of smiling naked people in the Vermont bush, Fitz the native, Fitz the uncircumcised, Fitz the uncorked.

Sitting down before the small personal computer, exactly like mine, seemed more like getting behind the wheel of a familiar car than violating someone's privacy. *Welcome to Macintosh.* Fitz and I also had the same software—WriteNow 3.0—because it was Fitz who had recommended it to me a couple of years earlier when I was shopping for my first computer, always a latecomer to anything that made life easier, Sally would say. I browsed the contents of the hard drive: various drafts of an article entitled "Emerging Viruses"; numerous, usually brief professional correspondences; a folder entitled *Destructive Interactions* contained thirteen items, which turned out to be chapters of a book on the ecological and evolutionary mutation of disease. There was a long list of names and addresses in alphabetical order. A folder labeled *Harvard* contained schedules, syllabi, departmental committee memoranda, lecture notes, reading lists, letters of recommendation for students, etc. The mind of Fitz, I thought, the various compartments of Fitz's orderly, single-minded brain. I randomly opened windows and documents only to click them closed the moment I grasped that they couldn't possibly interest me.

The folder *In Progress* became a window containing one lonely icon with the title bar *Vermont*. I double-clicked the mouse and words spontaneously appeared on the screen in 10-point Geneva type. The cool gray screen made whatever was written there seem distinctly less personal than a manuscript of typed pages, for example, and infinitely less personal than, say, a handwritten notebook. I wouldn't have opened a handwritten journal like the one I obsessively wrote in each day, I couldn't have faced the messy sacrosanct scribbling of a living hand, Elizabeth. No, words on the computer screen were a different matter. I clicked back to the beginning of the document.

3 *Fitz's* Vermont

6/12/94—Sunday.

I'm outside with the *Times*: Helen pedals into the yard! Don't spoil the day reading the paper, Fitz. She's been well. Glad we're here. Her job at Pantheon is frustrating, but she has some autonomy now. She's curious about our recent gruesome murder/suicide, of course. The two girls, roommates, were both biology majors, weren't they? Did I know them? In fact, no, I didn't know them. Now it appears no one knew them. Mary comes out: they hug like long-separated sisters. They're off for a walk: Helen stays for asparagus crepes. Later Mary says, She's so young to have gone through that, meaning breast cancer less than two years ago, a topic that must have come up between them. I'm afraid for her, Fitz.

The journal was a compulsive habit when I was young: haven't kept one for decades: too driven to indulge a useless diversion. Suddenly one June I get the urge. Do you need a reason?

Meditate for half an hour: breathe. Work until noon: crushing soporific boredom. Long walk through woods to the river: strip and settle into the cascading water at the base of the thirty-foot drop. To anyone watching here's an old fool lowering himself naked into the water: narrow-chested skinny-assed old goat with sagging balls. But still alive, still a live fucker. No one comes here. I recline against granite, face and pale shoulders in the sun, the white water coming down: once enough on a good day to be titillating. Not today. Fifty-five. Eternal boy in a dying body. Rock, water, tall trees. I'm the human being here: the sentient creature. The sense of something impending, almost alarm, startles me. The annihilating depression three years ago: didn't want to *do myself in*, but felt I couldn't prevent it from happening. My father's .22 rifle in the closet like an assassin. The psychiatrist: useless words, helpless silences, fatuous questions, ineffectual prescriptions. Mary's anxious intervention was critical: hospitalization. You fear the onset of another such crisis, but that's not what this is about. Slip beneath the white whirlpool of water: gasp in the bright air, coming to the surface. Breath. I want to be honest, I want candor, nakedness, adventure. I no longer want what I have.

Everything can be explained: cause and effect, choices, chance. I understand. I've been fortunate, achieved more than I'd hoped—my place here, an indubitable reputation. Various extras—our home, travel, these summers, the freedom to pursue goals and pleasures—have come through Mary's money and contribute to the appearance of success. Unlike Jonathan, who has achieved more but has less. His four children are not a source of strength or accomplishment or happiness. As adults, with all their grown-up difficulties, they compound his worries, an unending complication. My largely nonparental relationship with Mary's children is undemanding, with few expectations on either side: we enjoy one another more than flesh and blood. Mary, striving to be loving toward them, is alternately disappointed and hopeful, always anxious, and an easy touch for quick cash. Cast down this evening following an unhappy call from Kelly. Illusions concerning the joys of children have evaporated: they are a drain, they rob you of your life.

Helen. The second year of her marriage to a rug expert: diagnosed with breast cancer. Three months following her mastectomy he cannot remain in the marriage: his mother and his aunt have died of breast cancer, his sister lives in fear of breast cancer: he cannot live under the shadow of Helen's breast cancer. He was honest, she says. She's glad to be rid of him, but at the time she felt worthless and utterly alone. Cowardice isn't honesty, Mary says, selfishness isn't honesty. What will he do the next time he must face illness or worse, what will he do when his turn comes, etc.? Breast cancer: how inconvenient for *him*! Vehement supporter! The funny thing, Helen says, he's the one that got me started on meditation: the Buddhist, she laughs, who reserves all his compassion for himself. I hope he comes back as an insect, sure to be squashed.

Her first year here by herself—last year—was an experiment. The place belongs to her father's family, who use it in the winter for skiing. She'd been leaning on her friends too much, burdening her friends, and she decided time alone in a peaceful place was what she needed to get in touch with herself. She was anxious for the first week, stayed up half the night reading and slept away half the morning, afraid she was becoming depressed, then ran into us outside Baker's. I couldn't have gotten through the month without you guys, she says. The uncle's house was available again this year so she took it.

Her clothed body appears normal—medium breasts, smooth sturdy legs, slender arms—she swings a pair of barbells every other day—but it isn't normal. She decided against reconstructive surgery: I want the scar, I accept what happened, I want to be who I am. Accustomed to this appearance of symmetry, that scar is hard to imagine. Mary asks: has the mastectomy interfered with meeting men? Yes, but it's probably me as much as them. I want to feel right about someone before I expose myself, pun intended, and that hasn't happened often. Happened once, to be exact, but when the affair ended, as affairs do, says Helen, you aren't sure what role the missing part played. He'd deny it was a factor at all, there was no dearth of explanations, but if you're me, you never know. Maybe he doesn't either.

We dine just outside the kitchen door. The women across from the man. The younger woman, the older woman. Wood thrush, hermit thrush. Mosquitoes don't discourage us. We go through the magnum of wine. Espresso with our Cherry Garcia. The moon comes up. I say: You both look absolutely beautiful just now. Mary says: Oh brother. Helen places her hand over mine: That's sweet, Fitz. Mary has come to her feet, noisily collecting dishes, and as she reaches for my cup she mimics Helen's words.

Other women have seldom interested me: that's understatement, friend. For years I've been absorbed with my work, haven't allowed the time, or wanted the trouble, or imagined changing my life. Marriage: months will pass without contact, then we will enter a period—two or three days—of sexual involvement: a well-oiled routine both satisfying and disappointing. We are involved in each other's lives, we are considerate, even kind, yet: little physical tenderness. We ignore this, we live quite well without it. The cost is real. The absence of passion and spontaneity: a source of regret, which has made me susceptible to a passing attraction. Preferably anonymous. Seldom women. The dilemma: to invade someone's life on the basis of a mutual deception, to enter what can only lead to unhappiness. You must be young to squander energy in the name of fucking. That's crap, Fitz, life is a flash in the pan. Then the question: how did you live it? Answer: seldom as I wished I had.

Drove to Tom's nouvelle cuisine scene in W., knowing this was a mistake. A hunk of salmon in parchment at the bar along with several drinks. The bartender, another of Tom's imports for the summer—local color—provoked shameless mortifying flirting, so that he and Tom and Bryce must have had a howl in the kitchen when I left, lurching, after midnight. The old closet queen. A beautiful boy with a handsome mouth, bright eyes, and lively small talk. Beautiful hands and even ears. Adrian, no less! Raced home recklessly thinking Adrian, Adrian, Adrian, hopeless, lost, prepared to sacrifice everything. I can never go back there.

Turn to my article: boredom oppresses me. The scientific community is not waiting to hear from A. F. Underhill: what I have to say is predictable from my earlier work. Destructive Interactions. Work done in the interest of a modest self-serving career, not man's life on earth. Jonathan doesn't appear to doubt his task: he seems genuinely engaged in discovery. His mind is more original, more creative, more excitable. He believes in his role, he is motivated by inspired goals, his commitment is persuasive. I do not have an original contribution to make: my work keeps respectable pace with developments in the field.

I can recall the specific moment, hiking with my father in northern California thirty years ago, when I made the decision not to attend medical school. He was a successful surgeon who hoped I would follow in his footsteps, as many sons in those days did: therefore I refused to pursue a career in medicine. The simplicity, the simplemindedness, of the thought is staggering. I was fifty before I faced the truth about my momentous choice. Intuitively I feared for my selfhood, my autonomy. Mary's view: I wished to punish him, this powerful personality, for love withheld: the benign neglect a busy parent's success visits on his children. No: I was given every opportunity to flourish. I didn't want my path laid out for me: I didn't wish to be confined to his world. We made camp beneath an overhanging glacial erratic in a canyon profuse with wildflowers. We built a fire, the starry sky amazing. Dad, I've decided against medical school. All afternoon, hiking, I had prepared an answer to his question—Why?—and even I didn't know my reasons weren't the real reasons. His response was supportive: he wanted what I wanted, sure I'd do well in whatever I chose. He reminded me that my decision then didn't cancel future opportunities: I could always change my mind, I had all the time in the world. If he had been less tolerant—less loving, less respectful of my announced aspirations— perhaps he could have overwhelmed my youthful resolve. *Dad!* In the years since his death the truth has become very clear: my life could have been put to better use. I console myself with the thought that such misgivings and self-recriminations are commonplace. But the alarm that comes over me, a foreboding, is rooted in that recognition. More often my instinct for self-preservation prevails: I accept my life as such, I count my blessings. Here endeth today's self-sermon.

Mary walks across the yard in her blue skirt. I watch her from my room. We're here together, it's that simple.

Friday. Mary, getting dressed upstairs with the tube on, calls us to the bedroom. The aerial picture of a white vehicle, an invisible man inside, moving down a cleared highway, followed by squad cars. First we've heard of this bizarre mess that happened days ago. The cheering crowd's wish: dazzle us: get away with murder. Insatiable

America. We're mesmerized for twenty minutes. Helen asks what team he played for: I don't know the answer. Fitz has lived here all his life, Mary says, but he's a poor excuse for an American. He has no country.

No children, no noteworthy accomplishments, no country. Count your blessings.

Father's Day.
I wouldn't have known. Unpredictably Mary has presents for me: a jar of Vitamin C and a bottle of calvados. Helen, when she comes by this evening, has not been able to reach her father all day—a Chicago lawyer, we learn, who married a woman younger than Helen only months ago. His first wife, Helen's mother, died some years ago. She can't quite forgive her father for failing to *be there* during her health crisis. He couldn't deal with it, she says. The complicated layers of this situation—a death, a new young wife, a daughter stricken with illness—make me woozy. More than I want to know. When she finally reaches him from our place she's cheerfully chatty, betrays none of the bitterness she's expressed to us, and avows her affection in closing. Mary asks, Would it be better for you to confront him with your disappointment? Helen believes he'd only withdraw further, he's terrified for her, not indifferent. She wants to keep the door open. He's the only father I've got. Mary and I walk her to her car, and take turns hugging her good night. *You guys* are great, she says. Half the calvados is gone.

Mary announces: I'm going to have a Fresh Air kid here next year. Maybe two would be better, she adds. Do you know what it could mean to a child to spend some time, etc.? Mary wants to do good, and she's fed up with the garden, reading, her painting. I believe it's a complicated question, I'm not sure what it would mean to a child, etc. That's crap, Fitz. It's a moral issue, she insists. I agree, rather than prolong the discussion. It will never happen. A couple of wild Indians running around here would bring my work to a standstill. Later, Mary stands in the door of the guest bedroom, frowning. She has washed the windows and rearranged the beds. She wants to paint the walls for next year, but she doesn't know what color. They're dingy, she says, they should be bright and cheerful. She can get new bedspreads in Boston. Helen encourages her: she'd love to help out, she loves little kids. You'll have to be chief chef and disciplinarian, Fitz: we'll drag you out to slice watermelon and do the whipping. Offended by this intended joke, Mary remains silent for the rest of the evening. In the bedroom she says, Helen is getting a little tiresome. I think I need a break from Helen.

Is it like missing an arm or leg? Is there a phantom breast phenomenon? No one we know who has been through it has mentioned this.

We don't call: Helen doesn't call. She doesn't come pedaling up the drive. She must be sick and tired of us, too, Mary says. Sex in the small hours: good for us. The man enormous, solid, and Mary's coming accompanied by some wonderful carrying on, mooning oh fuck, etc., all thanks to hormone replacement therapy. What brought that on? Nobody knows. We hardly speak for the rest of the day. At noon I emerge from my study, blinking at the sunlight outside the kitchen windows. Mary lies naked on top of the picnic table—she has dragged it into the sun, near the garden. Soles of her feet facing me so I'm looking up the length of her body. Dips her fingers into the white bowl on the bench of the table: sprinkles water over her torso. Still a remarkably okay body, especially stretched out flat on her back. White towel beneath her. My large straw hat over her face. Daydreaming. Her bush: a dark glinting patch. I put on the kettle, still pondering a sentence about mutant pathogens. Now she's raised her knee. Glad you're feeling relaxed and good enough about yourself today to take a sunbath. Right hand into the white bowl: sprinkle sprinkle. Her hand slides down to her crotch, slipping between her legs to probe: let's see what's going on there. I smile. One good orgasm begs for another. She withdraws her hand, arms at her sides, peaceful sunbather. Come on, Mary, we know what's going on under that hat, behind your closed eyes, the feeling of your body in full sun. My touchstone for the vast norm: she wants what everyone wants. Middle-aged woman lounging on her picnic table at high noon: a thoroughly upright lady, who wants to have Fresh Air children someday. Come on, Mary. As though she has heard a voice whisper in her ear, she reaches between her legs again, testing the water, undecided. Her right hand goes under the hat, to her lips, I know, to carry saliva . . . thither. She has made up her mind, her body has made up her mind. I raise the binoculars, which happen to be handy there on the windowsill. Mary is the more avid birder. Observing her practiced fingers apply themselves to her pleasure I think, How nice. Big word: clitoris. Just do it, like the Nike ad. Suddenly her body jack-knifes to a sitting position, her legs swing sideways as she grabs the towel from underneath. Lower the glasses: Helen is pumping into the yard, and Mary, the hat fallen to the ground, is waving, her towel hastily clutched around her. It's been three days since we've seen Helen. I'm disappointed she has chosen this moment to appear.

Chicken breasts stuffed with chevre and fresh basil on the grill. Perfectly pleasant evening until Mary says, I don't care if I never see your mother again. Fitz's mother is insufferable, she asserts. I should let this go, especially with Helen present, but perhaps for that reason the general denunciation of my aged mother rubs me the wrong way and I come to her defense, how damned decent of her to remember Adam's birthday, etc. Mary insists that Mother has never liked Adam—she called him *too free and easy* on the phone earlier—which makes a gift from her meaningless, a pinstripe shirt, she scoffs, which Adam wouldn't be caught dead in, he's probably already thrown it out. Fitz's mother has always criticized my children, she says, and I've had enough of it. I'm stung by the venom of her attack. Turning to Helen, I explain why the phrase *free and easy* is upsetting: Adam has been out of college for two years and hasn't paid his rent yet, a volunteer cook at a church shelter at the moment, hoping to get an internship with a small film company. Don't start this, Mary says, Adam lost his father at a crucial time, she tells our guest, and it hasn't been easy for him, he's a resourceful creative boy, he's struggling, and he deserves my support. Like flocks of kids hanging out in the city at their parents' expense. Not to mention Kelly, I add, the daughter, a painter slash waitress, she only needs to be bailed out two or three times a year. Kelly is *amazing*, Mary insists to Helen, she works her butt off, sometimes she needs a hand. I'm glad I can back them up, I'm proud of the kind of people they are. What are you saying, Fitz, they're your stepchildren, you sound like you don't like them. You give them too much, I respond: you're afraid to let them be on their own: they're not children anymore. If you'd worked for it, you'd make them work for it. This is below the belt: I've gone too far. You son of a bitch, she begins, her face darkening. Don't tell me what to think or feel! A phrase that has the ring of a battle cry. Let's see you manage without my financial support. Europe twice a year and summers up here and living like a prince in Cambridge! What's wrong for my children is all right for you, isn't it? What's the correlation between your taste in wine and my money? He's the lofty scientist and I'm the lowly spouse who has the privilege of gilding his lily. Well, you don't have to put up with me and my children and my poor judgment and my guilt a minute longer. You can move your *skinny ass* out, Fitz. You can go back to Cambridge and find your own house to live in, unless you want to join your insufferable mother at Heritage Village. All right, I say, we don't need to carry on like this. Don't tell me what I need, she cries, and to emphasize this point she sends her wineglass sailing across the yard showering the dark lawn with invisible droplets, then marches to the house and slams through the kitchen door. Glass unbroken. Helen, who must feel she's just had her first glimpse of the real Mary and Fitz—can such an outburst really come as a surprise to her?—gets to her feet and says she should be going. I apologize: when we feel like hammering each other with our endless everyday issues, we will use anyone, I say, even an innocent Vermont neighbor. If you hadn't been here we would have had no opportunity to indulge ourselves. But Helen, frowning grimly, is sorry, she's just very sorry the evening ended this way. Mary has closeted herself in the bedroom; I clean up the kitchen, finish the wine, sleep in the guest room. We've been here many times before. My part in the evening's charade repels me. I adore Adam and Kelly.

Receive bound galleys of Jonathan's book. Reading this persuades me, page after page, of the mediocrity of my own work. I sit at the computer: fatigue numbs me like a drug. Light rain. Mary, driving off first thing in the morning, returns with her supplies. Soon there is the smell of fresh paint in the house. By the end of the day she has accomplished what she set out to do: the guest room now spanking white. She energetically picks up newspapers she's spread on the floor, she thrusts the balled-up mess of paper into my arms as I stand in the doorway. Take it out to the garbage, she says, the first words between us today. You big stupid prickhole, she adds. The room is white and for the moment Mary is happy.

Chess: Underhill versus the mistake-proof but mindless computer. Beat level four in just under two hours, a breakthrough for me, causing me to hoot—checkmate!—in the silent house at mid-night. Pour a nightcap. I prefer playing the computer, where losing isn't personal. Ten years ago in an occasional game with Jonathan, the stress of watching and waiting for my defeat to unfold was almost unendurable. Ten years later I couldn't possibly submit to the self-examination.

Mary takes our ancient cat to be put down at the vet's (Katz), can't go through with it, and returns home with him. But the poor guy looks beat. Soon, I think.

Mary returns from her outing with Helen, the Clark Museum in Williamstown, animated about some watercolors, loathing Renoir, declining to tell me what they talked about all day, only that they *had fun*, until we're eating. Fitz's goulash! A group of children caught their attention, launching Helen into how her life has changed. In her mid-twenties she'd had an abortion. Later, married to someone she wanted children with, it was breast cancer she got, not pregnant. Now she suspects she would be afraid to have a child, the future has become so uncertain. She wonders: if she hadn't ended the pregnancy, would she have gotten breast cancer? If her body had gone through childbirth and motherhood would everything have turned out differently? Isn't it too much, Mary says, isn't life too much? She's almost tearful: not like Mary. Later, reading in bed, Mary has more to tell me: Helen has confided to her that she was hospitalized for depression following her mother's death and again following her separation from the rug expert. The first hospitalization was initiated by a psychiatrist and the second time she was found by a friend following an overdose of pills. It all seems remote and unreal and not at all her, she told Mary. No one wants to die: the depression, stripping you from yourself, awakens the possibility. All that is behind her now, she's quite sure. Helen asked Mary not to mention these traumas to me. No, Mary says, she didn't tell Helen about my *episode*. I'm puzzled, and momentarily jealous, I guess, that she'd *share* all this with Mary, and yet would I want to be the one confided in? I don't think so.

Unusually warm and humid. I walk ahead on the path through the woods, dazzled by light coming through trees. The women walk side by side behind me, talking incessantly, like girlfriends: clothes in catalogues, a piece in *The New Yorker*, walking versus swimming, how coffee makes you feel, a recipe for chicken, Boston contrasted to New York, Mary's sister, mothers. I leave them to it, walking ahead, as one disinterested, although I miss little of what is said: the enjoyable counterpoint of harmonious female voices. The river comes glinting through the trees, the sound of moving water reaches us: they stop talking so they can pay attention. We descend along a narrow path through beech and oak to mammoth granite outcroppings, where the river cuts through, coursing steeply to the pool. Because this spot is not accessible by car there's rarely anyone here. Don't mind Fitz, Mary says, he's an incurable exhibitionist. Shed of shorts, T-shirt, sneakers, I quickly enter the water. Mary and Helen have bathing suits under their shorts. They paddle and float: happy. Mary stretches out on the granite at the top of the falls, I recline in the frothing pool at the bottom. Helen lowers herself in from above carefully, opposite me. Impossible to make yourself heard here without raising your voice, so she mimes her delight— raised eyebrows, open arms, a smile—and mouths the word won- derful. She has her back to the onrush of water. Close my eyes, holding my face up to the sun like a beauty queen. When I open them, Helen's expression is sober, challenging. She has slipped the straps of the bathing suit off her shoulders, so the cascading water haphazardly reveals and conceals her upper body. She stands then, almost waist deep in water, and holds her arms up like mad Nixon greeting a crowd. Her body doesn't surprise me, it doesn't appear especially unbalanced. I'm drawn to the site of her surgery, the tattoo there, which I'm unable to decipher without my glasses. I stand and wade two steps toward her, stooping to see (Auntie in S. Ray's *Apu* movie): the image of a butterfly in blues and black beginning above the horizontal scar with one wing partially crossing it where areola and nipple would be. Quite spontaneously I touch the tattoo with fingertips, then meet her eyes. Very nice, I pronounce distinctly. The suspense in her face has relaxed into a smile. She offers a brief light hug: Thanks, Fitz, against the side of my face. Mary meanwhile has sat up and is observing us from above, her arms wrapped around her drawn-up legs, her chin on her knees. Later she tells me she'd been shown the tattoo when they were changing into bathing suits. Could Fitz deal with it? Helen had asked, and Mary didn't see why not. I think it was a big deal for her, Mary says. She feels close to us, she tells me. When I ask, Do you feel that close to her, Mary says, Not really. It's a shame, she says, that the tattoo she chose, a butterfly, has become something of a cliche. What comes back to me most powerfully a day later is her voice: Thanks, Fitz.

Butterfly: soul, resurrection, metamorphosis. Now a cliche!

This discussion: whether an ordeal or important adventure changes you, or merely reminds you of your "real" self: reinforces your knowledge of the person you are, compelling you to recognize again this inside self whether you like it or not. I'm aware of the same person, this "me" going back to childhood, persisting through every experience, essentially recognizable despite the strangeness of the circumstances, this "me" surviving tragic loss or unexpected joy intact, rather than being changed by it. This "me" looking down at my father's coffin, for example, unchanged for better or worse by the significant event. Mary tends to be exasperated by this chitchat and doesn't offer an opinion. Helen insists that her experience of breast cancer has changed her. More important: she endeavors to change, she wants to evolve, she couldn't bear to think she's stuck with some essential inescapable self she despises half the time. My point: you can't escape that person, that awareness, even though your life changes, your circumstances, behavior, priorities change. How depressing, Mary says, I'm going to bed, which Helen takes as her cue to leave. In the bedroom Mary says, You make me want to throw up, *you and that bullshit.*

Herman, our nineteen-year-old cat, couldn't get settled yesterday: moving from place to place restlessly. Hasn't eaten for days. I don't know if he's been drinking much. Nothing but fur and bones: moves as though he hurts. This morning it seems more clear than before that he should be put down: the merciful possibility. He seems to clutch the floor in the corner by the bathroom sink. Gently pulling him out of there, Mary calls me, thinking he's died, he's so still. But no. I drive while Mary holds the poor guy on a towel in her lap. The woman doctor examines him and pronounces him severely dehydrated, kidneys no longer functioning, in keeping with the clear pools of liquid we've found near his litter box. Trying to get to the litter box to the bitter end. The vet believes the right thing to do is end the old cat's suffering. Mary nods. Her cat, of course, dating back to her old life with Ted, small children, etc. I have grown fond of him. The vet injects the barbiturate while an assistant holds him and Mary and I stroke him. Death occurs within half a minute. Mary cries large spontaneous tears that drop onto the stainless steel table. She mutters his name. I have a lump in my throat, surprised. We take him home. I dig a hole near the stone wall on the west side of the field, deeper than it needs to be. Mary puts his body in a pillowcase. We bury him. The last cat.

Death occurs.

Meditate. Read: don't work. Kelly, Adam, and his friend Jane blow in for the holiday weekend—a burst of young flesh and blood, pink faces and glossy hair and smooth limbs—and immediately set off for the swimming hole. Adam and friend pitch their dome-shaped tent in the field. Frisbee: attempt to learn a new toss from the expert, throwing it forehand instead of backhand, and fail. Helen is pretty damned good at it "for a girl." Jane is blond and quiet, at least doesn't say a word to me. Kelly says, You're frightening, Fitz, what do you expect? Her new very short haircut provokes Mary to say, How could you? Screw you, Mother, I like it. Helen seems intrigued with Mary's freewheeling grown-up children. Farm-raised salmon on the grill. Jane's navel ring, visible between halter and jeans, leads to the question of body piercing, tattoos, burns and scars, yes, an atavistic ritualism, the primal, marking and decorating the body to express the soul, etc. Jane has three rings in each ear. A recent trip to San Francisco made her want to get into more piercing—that town brings out the best in you, she says—and she came close to a nipple ring. Oh please, Mary says. Lip rings turn me off, Helen volunteers, and she doesn't get the point of tongue rings, which must interfere with basics like eating. There follows a discussion of genital orna- mentation: all about pain and identity, the boy says. But you don't have a ring through your penis, do you? Mary asks. No, Mom. Jane was with a woman recently who had one of those, not through her clitoris, she says, just the hood. The wine and the mood of this family has loosened her tongue. Just the hood? Helen is laughing. Yeah, Jane says, I thought, What am I supposed to do with that? Don't tell me it makes sex better? Mary asks. No, Mother, you aren't missing anything, says Kelly. A mastectomy doesn't figure into this question of voluntary self-mutilation. Surely that thought has occurred to Helen. Does the piercing fad relate to the infatuation with risk and fear—more people than ever jumping out of planes, swimming in shark-infested waters? Why has danger become the vogue? It's about adrenaline, breaking boundaries, feeling alive, these kids explain. I feel alive when I'm aware, alert to the moment, a heightened repose, I suggest, not when my heart is racing and my temples throbbing so that I can't think. Adam, who has sky dived and climbed every vertical face he's laid eyes on, says, You try it, Fitz, then tell me. Kelly adds, Yeah, Fitz, try risking your life for a change. Yeah, Fitz, Helen smiles. Kelly made her first jump last year at about ten thousand feet. I agree to go with her this year in October for her birthday. Shake on it, she says, reaching her slender hand across the table. I swear, Fitz—and she gives me a piercing dead serious look—if you back down on me, I'll never speak to you again. Don't be an asshole, Fitz, Mary scolds. See, Mom won't let you do it. I'll be there, I say, you arrange it for us. Maybe it will change you, Helen says, and winks. Yeah, Adam says, maybe you'll want to do something besides sit in front of that fucking computer. Jane surprises everyone when she says, quite seriously, *Don't pick on Fitzy*. The table explodes with shrieks of the unheard-of name: Fitzy!

Kelly spends a moment at the stone wall where we put the cat to rest. Walking up to me in the garden, she says, I miss Herman, he seemed to be around my whole life, sometimes I thought he was my father reincarnated, like when he would come into my room and get on the bed. Mom must miss him. She explains that while Adam and Jane will sleep together, they aren't lovers, just friends. Kelly wanted to bring her boyfriend, Nick, but he got a chance to go to Canada with a bunch of people and took it. I needed a break from him, she says. Her work is going *really well*, she says, what she's doing now is really her. I'm looking forward to seeing it when we get down to New York in the fall, I tell her. She says, I'm glad you guys have become friends with Helen, she's a *pretty cool chick*. How do you know that? I ask. Kelly says, I know. Flirtatiously, she adds, Just don't go getting any ideas, Fitz, I've seen the way you two hit it off. I'd say she's more your mother's friend, I suggest. By the way, I tell her, I like the haircut, I've always liked short hair on women, you look great. She pushes her hand through her cropped hair and smiles.

Adam and I hike out to Field's Hill at dawn: always extraordinary. He moves with an easy physical grace on the trail, effortlessly ascending the steeper spots, where I become short-winded. He has an enviable broad-backed natural strength from his father, his calves stout and smooth, his ass and thighs powerful. Packed. As I carefully climb over a stone wall, concerned that a loose stone could tumble me, he leaps over it with a spontaneous bound, clearing the top stones with room to spare. I couldn't have done that at any age. He's taut and straight; I'm taller, slighter, stooped from years bent over a desk. His body has a density that makes me feel light and flimsy. He swings off a low irresistible branch across the path: a laid-back ape. No boast in these high jinks, only a sense of well-being, an exuberance in which his strength is taken for granted. We're here to experience the early morning, the woods, not to talk, and there's little conversation. Moving at his usual pace he inevitably puts distance between us. Stop for a moment at the top of Field's Hill: mist in the hills below us. He hopes his recent internship will soon become a real job, he tells me, he thinks it will. Most weekends he goes bouldering or rock climbing with a group of friends, that's how he met Jane. Despite her lightweight appearance she has a wiry strength, excellent balance, and a gutsy streak that make her an *excellent* climber. Her sexual situation is complicated: she's with a woman right now, but she was involved with a man and that's not really over. That whole issue, Adam says, has made them close friends, but that's all. So how's your love life? I ask, and Adam tells me he's lying low lately, since the beloved Jordan has gone to the West Coast. He and Juliet, a friend from college, occasionally sleep together in the city, but that could never be a relationship, just a *sexual thing*. The boy asks: How's Mom, I thought she was a little uptight last night, *like* she didn't seem all that happy to see us, *like* maybe she was pissed because we brought Jane. No, your mother is very happy you're here. I think she's been bored lately, burned out on her work, and doesn't know how to shake it. And then Herman, you know, that was a milestone of sorts. The boy nods soberly. We stop at the river, returning: the day already warm and humid by nine. Adam leaps from the granite on the far side, unimaginable to me, terrifying for almost anyone, clearing the rocks below and hitting the water just right. He has a thick sturdy cock: like the rest of him. He's beautiful, and I experience a rush of pride for the boy. Love, really. I cautiously enter the water, my long thin feet sensitive to the pebbled bottom, like a feeble bare-ass old lady. Would one trade everything for Adam's youth and strength? Oh yes.

Back at the house Kelly and Jane are still sleeping, and Mary is concocting some healthful banana-oat-bran-walnut muffins in her flannel nightgown, her slept-on hair sticking out at the back of her head. Adam grabs her off her feet—Hey, Mom, it's great to see you!—and Mary's surprised smile lights up the kitchen.

Their project for the afternoon is a sweat lodge: Native American body-and-soul-cleansing ritual. Jane gives a little Indian whoop, fluttering her hand against her mouth, mischievous behind that shyness, that sinewy strength visible today in her tank top. I sug-

gest a spot along the stream in the woods that borders the west side
of the property. Adam assures me they won't make enough smoke
to alarm anyone. Late afternoon Helen and Mary and I go to find
our savages and meet them returning. Adam takes us to the impressive impromptu structure: an elliptical lean-to enclosed on all sides,
maybe eight by six feet, the center of the ceiling perhaps five feet
high. The door faces east, Adam informs me. A layer of hemlock
covers an inner layer of birch branches, the rocks in a pit in the center of the cleared floor. They laid a blue plastic tarp over the top
which made the sweat lodge almost completely dark, and held in
the heat. You sprinkle the heated stones with water, etc. Helen is
quite taken with the thing. You've got to try it, Mom, Kelly says, it
really is cleansing, but Mary doesn't like to sweat, she explains, if
she can help it.

The three of them make dinner for us: Kelly's pasta, Jane's salad,
plus a side dish of wild ramps that Adam unearthed in the woods.
The conversation is far-flung: from the trial of the century to the
World Cup to the state of Africa to the Whitney Biennial to an exhibitionist in Adam's building, to performance art, Lucian Freud,
where AIDS came from. Kelly, who has been quiet this evening,
becomes spontaneously tearful at the table, startling everyone. We
lavish concern upon her. I don't know why, I was sitting here feeling happy to be with everyone tonight, just listening, and then I
began to be unbearably sad, I don't know why because I'm not
really, I'm happy. Jane comes behind her and administers a neck
and shoulder massage. Helen says: I often feel so in love with
everything I can't bear it. The table is covered with glasses, wine
bottles, beer bottles. Half a dozen candles burning. Adam is soon
working on Helen's arms, beginning at the shoulder and massaging
to her fingertips. What about me, Mary says, I'm the one that's
strung out, which prompts Jane and Kelly to descend on her with

their healing touch, beginning with the scalp and working down
her spine. I'm going to turn to mush, she says. Fitz is the one who
needs work, Adam states: the rigid professor, the unflexible Fitz.
With his strong hands he kneads into my shoulders, seeking pressure points. Come on, man, relax, close your eyes. Yeah, let's do
Fitz, Kelly says. Her warm fingers caress my temples. Adam lowers
me to the floor beside the kitchen table: Trust me, he says. Jane slips
off my sandals and starts on my miserable feet. They roll me onto
my stomach: three sets of hands all over me: at my head, my back,
my legs. We're going to open you up, man, we're going to peel
away these painful layers of garbage, this self-defensive carapace of
intellectualism you've encased yourself in. Words to that effect.
Helen's laughter: This is great, she says. Mary's square bare feet go
back and forth clearing the table. We're all drunk.

Sunday.
Meditate at dawn. Skip the paper. Spend the morning writing here,
the sounds of the others in the kitchen, gabbing around the table.
Continues warm and humid. The kids do their sweat lodge again
in the afternoon: return hours later in a blissed-out trance. Mary
seems low: feeling disconnected from her children, she says, distant, despite last night. She's feeling disconnected from herself, she
hasn't been working, everything is a potential disappointment,
nothing is enough. This has been going on for some time. Frisbee in
the afternoon for an hour is fun. Shortness of breath must be the
humidity. Our picnic: baked beans, potato salad, first corn on the
cob, grilled brown trout stuffed with sage and rosemary. At dusk we
all walk to the town road and back holding hands in groups of
three: Mary Adam Jane. Kelly Fitz Helen. I like it. The outsiders are
the catalyst that release this adhering warmth. Jane and Helen
don't realize this; they think we're an unusual family, which is also
true. For dessert we have the remarkable cherry pie Adam spent

over two hours preparing bare-chested in the kitchen this morning. He'd brought the cherries with him from the city. Darkness: lightning bugs over the unmowed field and in the black trees bordering it. The glow signals courtship, Helen informs us. The moon there. Helen, Mary, and I are at the picnic table with citronella candles, the kids gone off somewhere. The magical moment occurs: three white illuminated globes, like visiting moons, float onto the dark field among the fireflies. Helen presses my arm: Oh Fitz. Mary leans forward, smiling. The silent globes of light dance over the field. They bought the paper lanterns in Chinatown for this surprise, in lieu of fireworks, I presume. We applaud. There are five lanterns, it turns out, one for each of us, and soon Mary and Helen join the others in the field, five lighted globes gamboling and weaving under the moon. Kelly becomes the choreographer who coordinates them into a coherent dance. I can hear Helen and Mary giggling like girls. Seated at the table alone I'm overcome really: think of Ted, who has missed them growing up, missed it all, dead all these years, a man I loved: I don't deserve this family.

Fourth of July.
Raised voices. I enter the kitchen: Kelly slams out the door. Mary tearful. Mary says: I told her how much I've been looking forward to seeing her this weekend, and I don't feel we've had any time together and I'm sorry, so she attacked me. I told her I feel like she's withdrawing from me or what I do doesn't count, and she says, Mother, don't start, we're about to leave. So now I guess I've ruined the weekend, as usual. I'm always to blame, Mary says, it's always my fault. I catch up with Kelly in the garden, picking greens to bring back with her. What does she want from me? she asks. I urge her not to leave it like this, and an hour later, by the time our guests are packed up to make the journey back to the city, mother and daughter are friends again.

It's been a good visit for me. We're going to open you up, man. Adam confronts me with myself, being himself, being real. I could not do that: cautious, conflicted, without knowing why. Fleeting intermittent sexual encounters left to chance. Constrained with men of my own generation: walking by bars on humid summer nights to look through the open door, listen to the voices, afraid to enter. Flying to Britain and France to meet other men in academic, quasi-monastic settings. Rather than San Francisco or New York. Running from the tall man on the sidewalk who kept pace with me for half a block, imploring. There will be sperm all over the room, I know you want to suck my cock. Fleeing rest rooms where men got hard standing beside me at urinals. In this country it suited me to have visible affairs with women, which always ended in disappointment. The escape into years of hard work and achievement resolved a great deal. I preferred to be perceived as driven by ambition: dogged, disciplined Underhill. In Cambridge only Ted and Mary, and eventually Jonathan were the privileged confidants of my complicated personal drama. Then the eighties, the crushing scourge: it could almost seem that my confusion and ambivalence and avoidance, my tormenting difficulties, had been fortuitous: I was the lucky one, as though the least deserving were to be spared. Grief over Ted's loss threw us together: the unimaginable possibility—marriage—gradually becoming real. I was myself with Mary, this peculiar marriage one of the few places where I could be honest. We would each continue to enjoy the independence we were accustomed to within new reasonable limits—independent travel, for example. I acquired a family: a period of tremendous discovery for me, the bachelor. Mutual sexual accommodation has been an ongoing project, which has actually improved with time. Passion has played no part in it. From the outset there have been long intervals of abstinence. If we had not been already in our forties and under pressure of such unusual circumstances, we couldn't have been so patient and forgiving. Yet this is a source of regret that matures with age. Mary had known the real thing with Ted. Ironically, Adam would seem more like his stepfather than his biological one in sexual orientation. The apparent similarity is superficial. In energy, force, nerve—in character, in sheer balls—he is Ted's son. I love him the way I loved his father: a pure admiration.

Read what I've written: coming clean, even here, comes as a relief.

Catch up on correspondence in the most cursory fashion, I'm afraid. Decide to take a break from my project, the work lately so uninspired. Work has been the only thing that has defined me: even to myself. Hot and humid: badly need rain. Miss the young blood. I'm in the garden when Helen arrives on her bicycle. Eager and positive: jumps in to weed the carrots, squatting on her haunches. She says: Can I ask you something about the other day? You were sweet about it, at the river, but nothing was said. How do you perceive this, you know, a one-breasted woman, were you repelled or what? I guess it's a stupid question, she adds, I shouldn't put you on the spot.

HE: You know I wasn't repelled.
SHE: Does it get in the way? Is it a hang-up?
HE: Do you mean the actual disfigurement, or some abstract fear of illness?
SHE: I mean both.
HE: I don't think I could know until I was faced with it.
SHE: Do you feel faced with it now?
HE: No.

111

SHE: Why not? Here I am, facing you.

HE: The thought hasn't entered my mind, Helen.

SHE: Do you think it would have entered your mind if I hadn't had a mastectomy?

HE: I'm not inclined to plunge my life into crisis, I've got all I can handle at the moment.

SHE: I think there's chemistry going on here, that's what I think.

HE: Chemistry?

SHE: Okay, biology. Your touch excited me. When you reached out and touched the tattoo, I wanted to touch you back. The other night with the paper lanterns and the fireflies, I felt desperate. You think I'm terrible, I shouldn't be saying this.

HE: I don't think you're terrible. I'm surprised, I'm flattered, Helen, but . . .

SHE: You're the person I want to see when I come over here. It began last summer. Am I embarrassing you? I don't meet men that make me feel this way. It seemed important, like I should do something about it, I should tell you about it, I should take the chance, I should risk making a fool of myself. I'm not afraid of risks.

HE: You're not making a fool of yourself. You know it's an impossible situation.

SHE: You and Mary never touch each other for one thing.

HE: We're not kids anymore.

SHE: That's not it. I've learned to trust my instincts. She told me about Ted and how you were all friends and what happened. Ted was it for her.

HE: As marriages go, I think we're doing all right. It wouldn't occur to me to jeopardize that. I'm too old for summer romance.

SHE: I'm leaving in ten days, I wanted to put my cards on the table. She slaps the dirt from her hands. You're a youthful man, Fitz.

She exits the garden. The one-breasted woman. The tone of this conversation is light, smiling, as though we're trading ironic quips, but the undercurrent is swift and powerful. A moment later she and Mary are off for their walk, they glance my way, their raised hands read more like "get lost" than "good-bye."

My sympathy with young men—their bodies, not their minds—represents a kind of nostalgia for energy and vigor, the spontaneity of desire. Picasso's fascinated compulsion to draw hard-ons when he was an octogenarian who no longer experienced them. The apt description remembered from somewhere: a lump of winged lead. That feeling! Mary tells me, No, Fitz, I don't nostalgically identify with girlish wet cunts.

Standing at attention before the mirror in the bedroom—like a prisoner before a firing squad—she says wistfully, I'm losing my appearance. Then your reality will shine through, I quip, intending a compliment. She meets my eyes in the mirror: What a cruel thing to say to me, Fitz.

Frustration indoors: march out to the mowing determined to throw myself into the stone wall project I've promised myself to tackle each summer for years. Body and soul work. I stand there looking at the job: old ruin painstakingly put up by patient rugged forefathers. Not today: return to the house: dejected.

Mary is fed up when she gets off the phone with her sister. Elizabeth is exasperated with her marriage these days. Henry Ash. The poor man hasn't been himself since his grown-up daughter from his first marriage died following a long struggle with cancer. He has devoted himself to a memoir, miring himself in his suffering, Elizabeth complains: wants to suffer, she says, rather than get past it. He pores over photograph albums and journals and the poetry his daughter loved. They have no children of their own, he and Elizabeth. She was fond of the young woman, she played her part during the years of illness, which commenced a couple of years after they were married, but she wants to get on with living now and she feels her life paralyzed by his grief. They seldom go out, he refuses to attend dinner parties, concerts, even movies. They haven't had a vacation for three years. Too many years of their marriage have been dominated by this ordeal. And so on. Mary in turn gets fed up listening to Elizabeth's complaints. Tonight she advises her to think about getting away from him for a while: a temporary separation. That might make him aware of the unhappiness he's causing her. And so on. Frankly, I don't have an opinion about Elizabeth's problems. Helen wants to know about the young woman who died: probes Mary with questions, most of which Mary can't answer. Helen says: Your sister doesn't understand. The man's life will never be the same. She wants to escape the way my husband did because life shouldn't have so much pain in it, because she's entitled to be carefree and happy, because she shouldn't be bound in marriage to a man devastated by the death of his daughter. You encourage her to do something stupid because you want her to be happy too, to stop bothering you with her problems. You're right, Mary says, but Mary hates to be contradicted, she doesn't look at Helen for the rest of the evening. I never met the daughter; I remember her father's face at the memorial service: surprised to be alive!

For the record: Mary drinks vodka tonics or Black Russians, Helen likes kir with extra cassis, Fitz drinks scotch. A sweet time of the day, seated at the picnic table, which we've carried around the house to catch the west light.

7/8/94—Friday.

Just past dawn: a rim of pale light above the trees, Mary sleeping, I stand looking down into the yard from the bedroom window and it takes seconds, two or three seconds, for the sight below me to register, and for the word—bear—to surface. Each time: the same thrill. I always think it's the same bear. His daily route crosses our property is my guess, yet I'm lucky to see him twice in a summer. He plods past the garden, lumbering, seems to pause at the open barn, thinks better of entering, and continues along the north side to the woods. The wall of woods: a magical threshold that confers invisibility as he steps through it. If I raced out for another look he would have already vanished. You don't know what the color black is until you've seen this black, I explain. I want to see him, Helen says. I need to see that bear.

She has been reading an article about female transsexuals in *The New Yorker:* the complicated ordeal of acquiring manlike genitals. In one procedure the labia are gradually stretched until they can be sewn together around synthetic testicles to simulate a scrotum. The clitoris gets to stand in as an itsy-bitsy penis. A more ambitious operation: two incisions are made on the stomach above the crotch, the skin is rolled into a tube and left on the belly until it heals over. Eventually this tube is detached so that it dangles, a lump of flesh that answers the desire for a pricklike appendage, Helen imagines, although what good this item devoid of sexual sensation could be to someone is baffling. Why not just wear a dildo? In a further refinement of the technique, the tube of flesh is connected to the clitoris and rigged up with a nerve removed from the arm so that the would-be dick does tingle with a current of sensation during orgasm. The trouble people go to! Helen says. Submitting to all this pain and trauma because the body you were born with isn't the real you. That real you you were talking about, Fitz. Some surgeons, carried away with sympathy for their patients' wishes, have produced salami-sized make-believe penises apparently, a pound of flesh dangling between the legs. Makes our ordinary desires seem awfully tame and simple, huh? But come on, Mary asks, how can the woman-to-man ever feel like a man if orgasm remains clitoral? No erection, no sperm, nothing really. Helen doesn't know, Fitz doesn't know.

Question: if this female transsexual, now a man, pursues sex with women, is the motivating impulse lesbianism? On the other hand, if the woman-cum-man pursues sex with men, what's that? Is that homosexuality too? Helen knew of a gay man who went through the sex-change ordeal and ended up, as a woman, marrying his former male lover. What's going on there? Are they both still queer? Does the male lover still feel he's in a homosexual relationship now that he's married his former boyfriend even though the guy has decided to be a woman and no longer has a dick? Who's who here and what's what? Who are these people? Whoever they are, Helen says, they make the rest of us look pretty good, don't they? She wonders if bisexuality bears on the issue insofar as there must be a discernible shift in the bisexual's sense of self as he or she alternates between sexes. A pause. Mary says: Beats me, you must have some thoughts on the subject, Fitz, goading me. After Helen has gone Mary says, If she wants to be infatuated with you, she might as well know what she's getting into. All that flirtatious sex chat makes my head spin. She shuts the bedroom door behind her. I sleep in the guest room. This happens in an instant these days: these mood swings, like snapping her fingers. She's anxious, frustrated, volatile, fragile, she doesn't know what she wants. It's not hormonal: it's what life is doing to her. Part of her anger always involves me, so it becomes impossible to comfort her.

A sunny blue day, the woods dazzling. We might as well be heading for the beach, loaded with our blanket, towels, our pail containing the tarp. We want to be cleansed. Leading the way in her tan shoulders and new white sneakers, Mary seems energetic and cheerful. Per Adam's instructions I build the fire east of the hut. Helen in cute blue-and-white headband says, I'm nervous. We bake the stones for as long as the fire lasts, almost an hour. The women have laid the tarp over the top of the structure so that it hangs down on three sides. Mary spreads an old sheet inside for us to sit on. She has hung bunches of sage from the low ceiling. With two pronged beech sticks I transfer the heated stones from the fire to the shallow pit in the center of the hut: a dozen fieldstones of various size and shape, none larger than a cantaloupe. Stooping inside the hut while carrying the hot stones isn't easy for the old man. They glow faintly in the darkness. Mary says: If anyone saw us doing this they'd call 911. Her bathing suit has to go: no damned Iroquois worth his salt wore a bathing suit in the sweat lodge, Mary. In our towels we're a little trio of matched maniacs, almost giddy with the silliness of all this. Careful: don't stumble into those stones. It's too dark inside to see: small glints of light coming through the black wall of branches. Hot already with a bristling dry heat. Oh man, Helen says. She's at the back of the hut with Mary and me on either side. Each of us pours water from the bucket over head and face with the coffee mug. Sprinkle water onto the stones: hiss and steam. The close hot air becomes humid, heavy. Helen stretches out on the ground along the back wall. You don't want a towel on you. My accelerated pulse is almost alarming. The discomfort increases until sweat, like an unburdening, breaks out. Mary declares that she's not sweating, she's intensely uncomfortable: a couple of minutes later she says, I've got to get out of here, I can't breathe. Helen says she's loving it, her head, her voice, perhaps three feet from my hips. She says: I'm sweating from every pore, Fitz, I'm dissolving. Mary cautions us not to overdo it *in there, you two.* I duck out into the bright day after twenty minutes: light-headed, the ordinary air amazing. Helen follows, grinning, toweling her scalp. This trial of heat has made our matter-of-fact nakedness quite irrelevant. Mary, wrapped in her towel, snaps a picture of the happy savages. The three of us stand knee-deep in the stream, scooping water over one another. Mary won't be persuaded to try it again: the heat was giving her a headache. Our second stint in the sweat lodge is less hot, less intense: more relaxing. I've never seen a man who wasn't circumcised, Helen confides quite off-the-cuff. It's nice that you weren't, Fitz. The mood has been emphatically asexual. As though it understands English, my prick nods in the dark. Helen reaches over and grasps my ankle, saying, Do you mind? She reaches to my thigh: God, you have long legs. I'm suddenly hard, to my surprise. She can do as she pleases, my prick has decided now, but cunningly she doesn't go for it, her hand reaches no further. More pasta and salad for supper. Kelly calls as we're cleaning up the dishes: What's this I hear about an orgy? she says. Put Mom on. While Mary's on the phone, Helen says, You make me feel safe, Fitz, you make me feel I'm going to be all right, I don't know why, I know it's important to me.

Mary is in bed by nine. Sit with computer chess—level five!—but don't have the energy tonight to finish a longish game. Close to victory, conceivably two moves away, and I don't want to blow it for lack of concentration.

It's nice that you weren't, Fitz. It has its drawbacks, dear, but of course I agree. Helen has been determined these days to get through manuscripts she has promised to read. The memoir of a woman who cared for her mother through Alzheimer's concludes with the writer's fear that she may be exhibiting the first signs of the disease herself, persuading Helen that she couldn't possibly go through the long publication process with this author. A novel by a young woman about growing up screwing an evil stepfather is *no Lolita* in Helen's considered opinion. The publishing world! She has never heard of Elizabeth's husband, Henry Ash, despite his shelf of books and various grants and fellowships. Those are booby prizes, she says, given for respectable work that fails in the marketplace. The poor wretch!

Five days away from my computer and I'm ready to implode. Whatever its merit, the work is my sole source of worth, and I remove myself from it, even temporarily, at my peril. This little experiment, for example, intended to be a faithful account of the quotidian, becomes difficult to maintain. Honesty is an illusion: one is selective in ways that cannot be understood. What seems noteworthy to me is merely a reflection of the self-serving person I can't escape. Does that describe the way I live as well: my invented life? Mary's voice inside my head—Dry up, Fitz!—keeps me that much more honest, at least.

The feeling: something's got to give. It's what Mary's been feeling as well, I'm sure. We're sick of our life on one level, yet can't imagine it otherwise, remain unwilling to have it otherwise: afraid of the loss, the costs. Ted's death was partially the basis for our marriage, so these years later, with Ted's memory dim, we find ourselves questioning our decision, questioning our lives. We're sitting at the kitchen table following dinner. Mary says, No, Ted's memory has not dimmed, she hasn't been questioning her marriage, as a matter of fact, she hasn't been waiting for something to give, as I put it, but she often thinks about being alone, she'd like to know what that's like, living alone. Because she has never lived just with herself, she says: by herself. Alone. Like Helen over there in that hovel. Alone. Just you, she says, alone with yourself, with your thoughts, without interference. Just you. Doing as you please. Yes, she wonders what that must be like. Yes, she'd like to see what that might tell her about herself. Alone. What depresses her sometimes: the idea that she could live her whole life without ever knowing what it's like to be herself. Alone. She knows everything about being lonely, she says, but nothing about being alone. Yes, if she's sick of anything, she's sick of being lonely, but that has nothing to do with being alone. Calm down, Mary, I had no intention of provoking this tirade, etc. She's out the door. A moment later I hear the car departing. She returns at dusk. I expect her to go directly upstairs without speaking. Instead she bursts into the living room in a state of excitement, bright-eyed, with color. I saw him, Fitz, I just saw him minutes ago as I pulled into the drive, caught in my lights. He was beautiful, she says, he was so beautiful. The bear. Our bear.

Marching up the steep hill behind the barn this morning: the now-familiar constriction girding my chest, accompanied by some shortness of breath. As in the past, I walk through the discomfort and it passes by the time I reach the top of the rise and the path levels out. My heart? I don't think so. My pulse, while accelerated from the uphill exertion, seems normal. The pain passes soon enough without causing me to stop. Stress test with Berkman last year was fine. I suspect a muscular-skeletal problem that radiates from the back, encircling my chest, and is provoked by the climbing motion. As for the degree of breathlessness: normal for someone my age, and clearly aggravated, as it was this morning, by heat and humidity. With cooler, drier air the breathing improves considerably. This is not denial, I'm saying—to whom it may concern!—but a reasonable assessment. Mary dismisses the heart question with a snort of derision: I'm too thin, too pink, too diet-conscious, too vain and crotchety. Call Berkman's office, nevertheless, and schedule another stress test for early September. The contrast between Robert, who received bypass surgery before an incident damaged his heart, and Peter, who waited until a heart attack almost killed him, is very clear. Do the test, Fitz! Schedule a checkup with Swanson down the hall for the same day—the old prostate. Two stones with one bird. Bird seems grand lately, as Mary points out one morning, shaking her head, amused. Horn o' plenty. Other blessings: the mind isn't mush, the knees haven't gone, the bowels are willing, piss is a clear stream, whites of the eyes still white, aches and pains just typical wear and tear.

Helen has cropped her chestnut hair almost as closely as Kelly's: wishing to return to the city obviously transformed, she says, by her month in the country. People only believe what they see, Fitz, especially in New York. Mary claims to like the haircut, although she didn't like it on her daughter. The three of us pitch in to concoct supper out of the garden. Helen talked earlier with her father's young wife, she says, who is determined to cover the house in Ralph Lauren shit, so now she'll never set foot in the place again. She has pedaled her bike over here this evening so I insist on giving her a lift home after dark. In her driveway she reaches over and snaps off the ignition: I want to make myself clear, in case I haven't already, Fitz. This doesn't happen to me, she says, I haven't felt this way about anyone for a long time, I want to do something about it. And so on. She reaches beneath her cotton dress, raising her hips in the same motion, and slips off her underpants. Here, she says, stuffing them into my lap, feel them, Fitz, how do they feel, tell me what you feel. I protest, basically, amused: Mary will send the Coast Guard looking for me if I'm not back soon. Are you coming in or not? she asks impatiently. I can't, really: love to on the one hand, but . . . She deftly grabs the belt buckle on my trousers with both hands: has it half undone by the time my hands cover hers. Life is too short, Fitz, haven't you heard that before? She snatches the keys from the ignition. I'm kidnapping you, she says, you and that uncircumcised prick of yours. So we're both laughing, getting silly. In fact, the feel of the moistened underpants excites me. Okay, she says, she wants me to know just how crazy this has become: she's been fantasizing about having a child: I mean, your child, Fitz. I realize that must terrify you and saying it does not further my cause, but I can't get it out of my mind. There I am being pregnant and then having it with you in your face mask in the hospital, and nursing the little guy with my one beautiful breast, honestly, Fitz, I've been imagining it all week, and we've never even fucked, that's getting out of hand, isn't it? The upshot of all this: we sit there too long, we embrace, she opens my pants while I enter her with my hand, and so on, finally saying a warm good night like old friends, and when I return Mary is at the kitchen table in her flannel nightgown, arms embracing her drawn-up legs, chin on knees, feet peeking out. I don't like being humiliated like this, she says. Do you think it's humiliating for me to sit there while you smile at her and touch her arm and smile some more and ignore me? I thought she was my friend too, you know, she says. I don't like sitting here alone in this pitch black wondering what you two are up to. The answer, of course, is nothing, as you know perfectly well, Mary, and so on, but she's frazzled, she's hurt, she felt both of us ignoring her tonight. At last she retreats to the bedroom again, shutting the door firmly behind her. I'm in the room getting the evening down here. The thought that this Helen would actually do it, that she would have a child—Underhill's only child—is slightly intoxicating. It's as though this is an island where we have both washed up, finally realizing we're the sole inhabitants, free to do as we please.

Mary: not talking this morning. Pointless. Drives off before noon without letting me know. Spend some hours scraping and painting windowsills white, a project I've been putting off all month. Am I doing it to please her, I wonder: this isn't a simple question. Marriage shouldn't inhibit either of us from going out into the new: pursuing our vital selves. The everyday wretchedness is nuts, while each of us is still capable of much more. Dry up, Fitz! I'm surprised to find she isn't back when I return from my hike. Helen calls: she's been working her ass off all day, and is ready to kick back, how about it. I explain that Mary went off in a huff: can't begin the cocktail hour without her. About last night, Helen says, I haven't changed my mind, I still mean it. By seven I'm pissed off: where are you? By dusk I've become anxious: this isn't like her: to let me worry. By dark, I call Kelly and get no answer. Call Adam: no answer, of course not. Call Helen. It's only ten o'clock, she says, Mary wants you to fret. Call Elizabeth finally, thinking she may have heard from her sister today, but her husband answers— Henry!—and I hang up without speaking. Soon after eleven the phone startles me: Helen wondering if she's back. Well, I'm exhausted, she says, I'm turning in. I'm here, Fitz, she says, if I can help. Put things away, my little surprise dinner, saving the salad greens and pitching the overcooked clam sauce. A good night for fasting. The thought that something dreadful has happened, an accident in some remote location, begins to work on me. I plead with her, come on now, to return home safely, and to make it quick. I'm frightened. Adam's recent photograph of her (arrived yesterday) taped to the refrigerator—Mary in baggy blue T-shirt laughing with her eyes closed, goofy—upsets me. Coyotes howl west of the house: I step outside to listen, the sky wonderful. I'm in a state, seated at attention at the kitchen table, when the headlights come bouncing into the yard. She enters looking rather fresh, given the hour. She asks: Still up? When I'm through scolding—Where have you been? How could you do this to me?—she says, Look, I called this afternoon, but you were out, and when I tried tonight the line was busy, so you can stop being an asshole. She'd taken herself to Burlington, she reports: a gorgeous drive, visited that Shelburne Farm, had a lovely solo meal: she needed a day to herself, and intends to do it more often. Being locked up here all day with you, Fitz, is enough to drive anyone crazy.

7/15/95—Friday.

Light rain is welcome. Return to my project for several hours today, browsing through the pages, and decide it's better than I thought. The three of us have a long hike in drizzle: the women in matching yellow plastic ponchos like schoolgirls. Clears enough for me to cook scallops skewered with roasted peppers on the grill. Corn on the cob. Helen's hands on the corn, for example. Elizabeth calls before dark. Helen and I take to the dusk-filled yard. This has been an important month, she says. I feel stronger, Fitz, I feel less afraid. She'd been withdrawing in the city, accumulating anxieties, preoccupied with illness, with dying. Now she's prepared to return, although I wish I could have another month here, she says. She wants our Cambridge address and phone number. Should we plan anything, she asks, maybe a weekend in October, or dinner in New York, etc. Time speeds up back in the real world, I remind her, with work, family, holidays, innumerable obligations and commitments. Chances of getting together are actually slim, as absurd as that may be. More interesting: let's skip the effort to stay in touch, let's just have this here, this extralife encounter each summer, as though returning to an island, world unto itself, and so on. Getting together elsewhere wouldn't be the same. We would call it a *fiendship*, she proposes. You aren't ready yet, Fitz, it'll be better to have the kid next year. And the woman jabs me in the gut. We shake on our little pact—I'll be here!—and Helen grabs me around the waist with both arms. It's been good for me, she says. Mary comes out carrying her glass of wine. Her sister remains unhappy in New York, bogged down in misery with Henry. Elizabeth never liked me either, I remind Mary: maybe it's men in general. Helen describes our plan— same place same time next year—and Mary likes the idea. Later in the bedroom she says, If she turns up here next year, I'll leave: you can sweat it out alone, Fitz.

7/16/94.

Helen stops, as planned, her Honda packed full, the bike on its rack on the trunk. Okay, you guys, I guess this is it for a while, almost tearful. We exchange firm hugs. Helen has mementos: some fancy scented avocado body lotion for Mary, and for me a large cream-colored ceramic bowl, suitable for serving pasta. You shouldn't have, Mary says, we have nothing for you. She doesn't want to linger. She toots the horn once, and down the drive she goes. An oddly touching moment, so that Mary says, Now I'm going to miss her.

Work: no new pages. Walk out into the yard at evening. The impact of her absence is unexpected and disturbing: the yard feels empty. I walk around the house, billowy clouds reflecting a rose-gold sunset. The feeling that of course we won't see Helen again, despite our rather fanciful promise: the year will intrude with old and new faces, change, and she will have something better to do next summer. The thought:

You blew it, Fitz.

8/1/94—Mon.

Astonishing letter (forwarded from Harvard) from Andrew's son in CA, in his twenties now, informing me that his father died a month ago at his home in Tuscany. Over twenty-five years ago we were young men hiking in the Apennines. I couldn't accept his capitulation to marriage: an Austrian girl he'd met in Rome. Ridiculous, Andrew! An American girl would have been out of the question: she had to be foreign, remote, incapable of knowing him at some level. The truth: I wanted him to myself. And then his decision to remain in Europe. Ridiculous, Andrew! He was older: I couldn't influence him. For years I went out of my way to see him whenever I was in Europe: the last time years ago. He only returned to the States occasionally for brief trips: we exchanged annual holiday greetings. Now clear why I haven't heard from him for the past two years. Dead of prostate cancer at sixty-two. Only sixty-two! The boy believed I would want to know. I have no basis, I realize, for grasping this death: I recall my friend as a young man on a mountain trail in hiking shorts and sturdy boots. I knew his son's name, of course, I have always known it, and yet the signature at the bottom of the page startles me to tears: Fitz.

Mary and I will talk about separation rather casually, yet go on as usual, including, as this morning, occasional sexual encounters in the small hours when the old man's testosterone peaks. Mary's strong hands, coarse and callused from yard work, might be the hands of a man. She's had no patience for my moping over Andrew these past couple of weeks: withdrawn, beyond reach. Part of this was anger toward her—as though she's responsible for the life I've led—for my failure to pursue other possible lives. Marriage: a theater of blame. Scared, though, that I could tumble into another black hole. This death, especially, makes me examine my life. Talking to Adam and Kelly on the phone we remain the cheerful folks in Vermont. Our typical strife would exasperate them: isn't it a joke to be questioning everything at your age? Haven't you got it figured out yet?

Drive by Tom's restaurant late afternoon. Crazy. A half hour later I return to the place, sit in the car for five minutes before mustering the nerve to walk in. A waiter is folding napkins at a table. Does he suspect why I'm here? The person behind the bar is a woman I've never seen before. Polishing silver. Order a beer, but leave before finishing it. Just luck that I haven't had the opportunity to humiliate myself.

I leaf through a catalogue from The Nature Company in the kitchen, waiting for the water to boil. The age of catalogues: nothing in these pages I want. Mary enters from outside, hands dirty from the garden, carrying her Carpe Diem coffee mug. How about this crystal carving of a baby seal? I say. How about some wind chimes to hang under the eaves? Enjoy the enchanted song of the wind, it says. Mary drops a Longlife teabag into her cup, fills it with the water I've just heated, and heads back outside into morning sun. Fuck chimes, she says.

Already the middle of August, and we intend to return to the real world before Labor Day this year: much to do. Eager to visit Adam and Kelly in the city. He's temping to earn some money—good man!—and Kelly has an appointment with her gallery person for a studio visit. Her studio in the tiny five-story walk-up is also her bedroom and her living room. Her devotion to her work! She might make it if there was any justice. There is none. I haven't completed what I set out to accomplish this summer. Including stone wall. Helen played a part in that. She is on my mind a month later: our little pact of silence that much sillier. It would be an interesting kick to see her in the city, while Mary was meeting her sister for an hour or two, for example. Yes, I think so: I want to see her. This evening: my blueberry pie! Mary smiling her blue smile.

8/20/94—Sat.

Fasted yesterday: superior to food. Mary declined. Up at five this morning: manic birds. Meditate for an hour, and manage a feeling of deep calm. Clearing the garden: our second crop of beans almost ready to be picked, and in the nick of time. The walk, the river. I slip on a slick rock at the top of the falls and pitch forward on granite, landing on my side: shaken, but unhurt. Mary scolds me when I relate the incident later. Naked middle-aged man found with cracked skull in Bear River. We whip up our pasta, salad, bread, wine. It seems clear: Mary and I here as though meant to be. Yet the opportunity with Helen: an extraordinary windfall. Vanity! As I fell, I glimpsed myself tumbling over the edge. My life, I thought—as if I saw it whole, a fleeting random inexplicable interval, a moment so brief that no hope should be denied. Step outside this evening: wood thrush. A male bluebird silently revisits the nesting box by the west field. The evening light! Around midnight, Mary asleep, I walk down the drive for there's a full moon. The moist air absolutely still. There's low fog and the fog-filtered moonlight illuminates the land, the trees. An ecstatic night. The house there and the wall of woods: a ghostly black in this remarkable glow. Mary, Jonathan, Ted, Adam, Kelly, Andrew, my father, Mother, and yes, Helen too: my irreplaceable dead and living. The feeling of joy, sudden joy: almost unbearably piercing.

Today at dinner following the evening news: I take my Buck pocketknife out and open the three-inch blade and hold it up between us. I could cut your throat with this, I say. Mary nods, smiling. I ask: Are you frightened? She shakes her head, smiling as she chews. Why not? I ask. Why aren't you? This strikes her funny: she laughs beautifully. I have never touched her in anger; she's the violent one: the knife thrower, the door slammer, the raging upturner of furniture. Tonight she's happy. Later, I observe her from the window as she strides toward the compost at the edge of the woods with our bowl of discarded scraps: square-shouldered, chin up, bouncy.

We're here together, it's that simple.

4 *Fire of Bones*

A flood of 0s—000000000000—rapidly appeared following the word "simple," causing me to jerk my hand away from the keyboard, my thumb, to be precise, which had accidentally come to rest on the large 0 key as I sat staring in anxious disappointment at the screen. Deleting those 0s, I clumsily expunged the period following the word "simple" as well, so that I then had to type a new period onto the screen. Whoa, watch it, you're manipulating the original document here. I hit the Save command, and pushed away from the table, holding up my hands as though the plastic keyboard was too hot to handle, a dangerous remote-control device intended to detonate distant unknown targets. My inadvertent zeros reminded me of the malleable and volatile nature of text on the screen. It was practically impossible for me to sit before my computer, after all, without altering the arrangement of words that appeared there, without constantly revising ad nauseum.

I read the document *Vermont* in one sitting, almost without looking up, and I wanted to read it again immediately, at least selected passages, to scroll through it again for details of particular interest. Everything written there represented news to me, every scrap of information was news about Fitz or Mary or this Helen, and I wanted more, I realized, I wanted to keep reading. *He was a beautiful man, did you know that?* You poor bastard. *We're here together, it's that simple.* Poor pompous bag of wind. *The feeling of joy . . . sudden joy.* I understand, Fitz. What was that you said about children, they drain you, and yet the idea of an Underhill child, Fitz's child, that seemed extraordinary, didn't it? Quite extraordinary. Decisively, in the next moment, suddenly emotional, I clicked Close, and shut down Fitz's computer, promising myself not to turn it on again. Absolutely not, Elizabeth.

It is now safe to switch off your Macintosh.

You want more, yes, you want to continue reading, you want the new information to keep coming, that's what everyone wants, always, but there is no more, no new information. It is ended, finished, over and done with. This life stopped here, and everything that might have been can never be, and must remain forever unknown, unread, just as all that continues to be, our lives, cannot be known to the person who is gone. Unbearable! These thoughts were unbearable, and I became choked up again as I studied my daughter's picture in the living room. I had brought framed photographs of Elizabeth and both my children to Vermont with me because I foresaw that I would need them here. I suspected I would want to have pictures to keep me company in my verdant isolation, and I had been right. However much I disliked and mistrusted other people's photographs, I treasured my photographs, *our* photographs.

I ventured into the deciduous woods, following abandoned logging roads and the narrow paths used by snowmobiles in winter, green undulating paths bordered by hay-scented ferns, which forked several times, leading to more paths, taking me further than I'd been before, but I didn't come upon the remains of a sweat lodge, for one thing, and, more disconcerting, I failed to discover the trail to the river with its Norman Rockwell swimming hole. You'd think Mary would have volunteered such a summertime detail, wouldn't you, Elizabeth? By the time I felt lost I saw sky up ahead, indicating an opening in the woods, and soon walked into the mowing west of the house, realizing my hike had taken me in a wobbly irregular circle.

Darkness had arrived by the time I finished my dinner—meatless chili—and a song on the radio as I cleaned up the dishes—*My love is like a sea, baby!*—provoked me to finish the bottle of inexpensive red wine, and then I was shuffling the pictures of Mary and Fitz and this Helen again—the butterfly tattoo suddenly visible to me, didn't know how I missed it the first time—seeing them a little more vividly now. I guess we didn't know Fitz all that well, Elizabeth, did we? Scientist with the spiritual side. I flicked the switch at the back of his computer—*Welcome to Macintosh*—and promptly switched it off again. The important thing was to put it out of my mind—the *whole Fitz thing*—and get on with my own work barely in progress, the document in my own Classic II entitled *Loners.* Tomorrow was Tuesday, the twenty-seventh of June, and what did I have to show for my six weeks of solitary confinement in Vermont? Using the rectangular magnifying glass that came with Fitz's one-volume OED, I studied the photographs more carefully. The tattoo was brave of her, such a radical contrast to the pinkish nipple of her other breast, heartbreaking, this impossible curse of illness. Her bush was an impenetrably dark thicket. The dangle of Fitz's dick told that his arousal factor was zip, although his smile was impressive, all right, a handsome man, beautiful might not have been an exaggeration once. We never knew you, and now you're unknowable, unknown. You were right here this time last year in the thick of your personal experiment, worried about the real you, how to be, your accomplishments, Fitz, your uppity prick, and now there's no you, there's no being one way or another. Mary's brave smile in one of the photographs reminded me of Elizabeth when she was trying to put an acceptable face on feeling left out and pissed off—like those unexpected visceral occasions when Sal and I poured out our grief to each other. Sad Toad. Life changed forever. Period.

I dialed this Helen's number—"You have reached . . ."—and hastily hung up. What did I intend to say to her? I've been examining pictures of you naked under a magnifying glass, wondering where that sweat lodge is anyway, and how about the swimming hole Fitz talks about here on his computer?

"Christ, Henry, what time is it? Nothing frightens me more than the phone going off after I'm in bed."

"You're in bed already? It's only ten, Mary. Sorry about that."

"I'm in bed by nine every night, Henry, ever since Fitz died. It's no fun being alone at night."

"That's one of the reasons I'm calling, actually. I know he died in August, late August, but I couldn't remember the date. I want to say the twenty-first for some reason."

"Is that what you're calling about at ten o'clock on a Tuesday night? Why on earth do you care what day Fitz died? Honestly, Henry, what's happening to you up there?"

"Here I am in your house, Fitz's house, and . . . I don't know, it was bothering me."

"You've called me more in the past few weeks than you have in the last five years. Elizabeth can't be away for any length of time, can she?"

"Am I right? The twenty-first?"

"It was the twenty-third, a Tuesday in fact. It was a beautiful day following a gray raining week, an early fall day, a perfect day. Tonight we're going to have Fitz's beans, Mary, Fitz's Special Green Mountain Beans. We were planning to leave in a week. I can see him going out the door with the colander. Jesus Christ, now you're going to have me upset."

"Being here is strange, Mary. I'm sorry I never got to know Fitz very well."

"Oh rubbish, Henry, you two were hardly civil to one another. Is there anything else? You've upset me, damn it."

"What do you hear from Elizabeth?"

"I've had one card from her. From the Cotswolds. She wants to live there now, she belongs in England, she says, like a bleeding hedgehog, she feels like she's finally home."

"I thought she'd outgrown that nonsense."

"Whatever happened to our neighbor up there? Has she stopped bugging you? She called here, you know?"

"Did she? It's Helen, isn't it?"

"Thank God I was out. Her message said she was shocked to learn about Fitz, she was sorry, would I call her. Well, I have no intention of calling her, I have all I can handle without adding Helen to the list. So far, she hasn't called back."

"She wanted to stop by one afternoon, so I let her come and get it over with."

"Spare me the details. Be careful, that's my advice concerning Helen. I'm getting off now. Please don't startle me like this again, Henry, I thought you were one of my kids calling with a horrible emergency. I don't have the emotional stamina for another crisis. Have you heard from either of them?" she added. "Kelly or Adam?"

"Why would I hear from Kelly or Adam?"

"Kelly was talking about getting away, but they must have decided on Maine or Block Island. Forget I mentioned it. How am I going to get to sleep now?"

"I won't bother you again, Mary. That's a promise. No more calls to Mary Underhill."

"Don't be so melodramatic, Henry, just don't call me after nine." She replaced the receiver with an abrupt click.

Chatsworth in Derbyshire had a maze we were forbidden to enter. The library was a gilded fantasy. Miles and miles of Cumbrian stone walls. We took off our shorts and waded into the water at Thirlmere—Thrillmore to us. We arrived at white, rose-covered Dove cottage too late to get inside. Decided to go for Scotland, after all, reaching Inveraray late afternoon. Two small glasses each of single malt made us walk along the water (Loch Fyne) holding hands like girlscouts, before skipping back to our stately white hotel. Lynn has acquired a cute Scottish accent. We met black-faced sheep as we hiked up breathtaking Ben Nevis, the high point so far. Awesome Glencoe was lonely. We're off to ancient Edinburgh on Firth of Forth. I don't want to come back.

Love, E.

Oh, remember when I used to look like this.

The picture on the postcard was a black-and-white portrait of Virginia Woolf as a young woman: soulful, beautiful, demure. I taped it to the refrigerator, next to the picture of laughing Mary, which had been there all along, of course, presumably from the preceding summer. I kissed my index finger and touched it to my son's *Nude Asleep in a Landscape.*

Dusk, another day gone, another week gone. I hadn't foreseen the impact of being here, becoming embroiled in the *whole Fitz thing*, this Helen turning up full of happy anticipation only to be knocked down and hammered by tragic news. I'm sure it was a mistake to turn on his computer, to open the document entitled *Vermont*, to read it from beginning to end in one sitting. I now knew *more* than I wished to know about Fitz, about Mary, about this Helen with one breast, and even you, Elizabeth. Especially you, I thought, shaking my wooden spoon at the postcard. You *complained* to your sister about your pathetic, grief-stricken husband? Henry

Ash the downer, dragging you into the airless cellar of his hopeless sorrow? I figured you for a soul mate, aggrieved in your own way, faithfully standing by me through thick and thin! "And you thought it was time I snapped out of it. Holy shit," I murmured, standing over the stove, stirring fresh minced parsley into my tomato sauce. Surprised to be alive. You're right, I couldn't bear sitting through another Merchant-Ivory production, I couldn't stomach Nancy Zweig feeling entitled to snort her politically correct opinions all evening just because she'd given us a meal. Movies and dinner parties! Intercourse with fellow creatures! The soul selects her own society and shuts the door. We all wish life could be a lark again. I understand, Elizabeth. "But life can't be a lark again," I said, dumping the linguine into salted boiling water. There's no going back to life as a lark. "I thought you understood that."

The journey *intensified*, was Elizabeth's word, as they drove north. The steep hillocks of the Peak District seemed diminished by the sweeping fells of the wilder Lake District where the intermittent sight of water was a welcome change. A sporting vacation of camping, hiking, or cycling—That's not them, Elizabeth announced each time people on bicycles were seen—was evidently the way to discover the beauty of the region, but they weren't at leisure to spend a week there so they settled, essentially, for driving through, staying one night at a farm not far from Grasmere. The faraway south of England, that older, richer, denser world, seemed to accumulate historical and cultural weight as they progressed northward. The endless stone walls and stone buildings finally seemed a bewildering achievement, as though men had done little more here for hundreds of years than pile up miles upon miles of perfect everlasting stone to enclose brilliant green fields and pastures like the stitching of a vast quilt. But if the Lake District had been stirring it hadn't prepared them for the dramatic landscape they entered north of gray sprawling Glasgow. Steep immense fern-covered hills rose from the shores of Loch Lomond and went on heaped up to the horizon. "Stop," Elizabeth said, and they had to keep stopping along the way, thrilled with green hills, sheep everywhere, vistas, these lochs. "Look at Scotland!" There was wind and sun and blue sky and the air was bracingly cooler. The Lake District seemed a miniature version hardly worth pausing to observe, if you were bound for Scotland. Late afternoon, the westering sun illuminating the hills a bright deep green, they rounded the north end of Loch Fyne and the row of spanking white buildings that composed the small remote village of Inveraray came into view across the water. As they passed over a narrow stone bridge, Lynn said, "There's no going back. Isn't that how you feel?" There was a room with private bath at the Argyll Arms Hotel. The four malt whiskies the two of them tried were Dalmore, then Dalwhinnie, followed by a Glenkinchie, and one called Cragganmore. The sky was still light at eleven o'clock. They walked to the water just slightly tipsy, holding hands. Gulls whirled over the shore. "Oh, this is perfect," Lynn cried, and clasping Elizabeth in a sudden hug, she pressed her lips to the side of her face. "I love it." Sweetly, the sound of an accordian faintly reached them from the hotel across the road where a sleepy Great Dane and a vigilant little terrier lay inside the open door of the lobby.

They both bought heavy wool sweaters at a tiny shop packed floor to ceiling with Scottish goods and run by a woman whose big beautiful blue-eyed infant gurgled and chortled contentedly, surveying the store from its infant seat high on a stack of tartan blankets. The eighteenth-century castle with twin conical towers, home to the Duke of Argyll, looked like something from Legoland. Of the bicyclists who passed through the village, the most noteworthy was an old pistol with woolly eyebrows, an enormous horn on the handlebars of his bike, and a stout black trunk strapped to the back.

They stayed two nights, returning to the sweater store once to steal another look at that cherubic bairn. Lynn invented a story about star-crossed lovers that made the child the duke's true heir.

The route north took them through even more remarkable country—converging mountains, a castle ruin, Loch Awe, and larger Loch Linnhe—and quite by chance, because their map hardly called attention to it, they found themselves at midday pulling into a small park—sheep, pasture, a farmhouse—where a foot trail to snow-capped Ben Nevis began.

"Can we do this?"

"Sure we can," Lynn said.

Elizabeth changed into her Patagonia shorts. They both wore sturdy sneakers and tied their new sweaters around their waists. An English couple in Inveraray, decorators who specialized in pub furniture, had told Elizabeth they'd been coming to Scotland for years but they'd never seen the mountains, usually lost in rain and mist and clouds, so clearly. Today was another cool shiny day with amazing visibility in all directions. A sign cautioned hikers that eight people on average died on Ben Nevis each year. The narrow footpath began as a gradual uphill slope, but soon grew steep and stony, wending through grassland and ferns. Lynn walked ahead, ascending at a faster clip, her tied-back hair bouncy, her bunchy calf muscles reminding Elizabeth that the younger woman worked out religiously three times a week in a downtown gym. Elizabeth had never hiked up a mountain before, she was thinking, she'd never seen anything like this. Green undulating hills overlapped one another as far as the eye could see in every direction. As suddenly as a cloud blocking the sun, it seemed to her, the slope the path was cut into became dangerously steep, the drop to her right almost vertical. She kept her eyes on the path, one foot before the other, don't look down, that's all. Her breathing grew rapid. When her right foot slipped in loose gravel, she froze. Far below, the thin straight line, like a hairline crack dissecting the valley, was the road that led back to Fort William, whose clustered rooftops were just barely discernible. She was unable to move. If she slipped off the path she'd tumble unstoppably to disaster, and if she attempted to move at all she'd certainly step off the path. She couldn't take a normal breath. Oh God, Elizabeth, get a grip. Lynn had moved out of sight up ahead. There were other hikers, of course, but few and far between—it was the middle of the week—and she was alone with the mountain, that was the feeling. Just now there wasn't another person in sight. She abruptly sat down with her back to the inside of the path and scuttled on her bottom, pushing with hands and feet, to the safe grass behind her.

"Elizabeth," Lynn called from above. She was almost skipping as she plunged down the trail. "What happened? Are you all right?"

"I don't know if I can keep going. This path . . . I'm all shook up," she said, clutching grass in her fists.

"It gets easier up ahead." She stooped and took her by the arm. "Come on, I'll give you a hand."

"Don't help me. I really have the jitters."

"This is safe, it really is. It would be hard to fall."

"Go on ahead. I just need a minute to calm down, then I'll catch up."

"You sure?"

"I'm sure."

She thought, You go ahead and have a nice dinner, dear. I'm not going anywhere. Her mother had added, I don't know what I'd do without you, Elizabeth, you're such a wonderful girl. You're a joy. Goddamn it, she thought, and she pounded the hard ground with her fists, afraid to move. Her mother had been alone to face her last moments alive. Oh, don't be so sentimental, that probably didn't make a damned bit of difference, probably not. If she were to fall to her death then and there it wouldn't make a damn bit of difference if someone was holding her hand, would it? Of course she wasn't falling, there was nothing wrong with her, she was fine. Her mother had lived in Scotland the first ten years of her life, but she had probably never laid eyes on Ben Nevis. This place had nothing to do with her mother.

An elderly white-haired man wearing a turquoise shirt, stabbing the ground with a walking stick, came marching down the trail and Elizabeth got to her feet. "I'm awestruck," he said, red-faced, breathing heavily. "I'll never be the same after that." He was British. "Never."

When she continued uphill her fear, like a trapped bird that had discovered the open window, was gone. Perched on a boulder around the next bend, Lynn snapped her picture as she came into view. "See, I knew you could do it."

After two hours of climbing, they reached a grassy mounded plateau. A shallow oblong basin of clear water there, a miniature loch, was cold to the touch, although the day was sunny. A half dozen long-haired black-faced sheep went on grazing with no apparent curiosity about their visitors.

Elizabeth asked, "Are they dangerous?"

"Yeah, they're really wolves in disguise."

From here, Loch Linnhe was visible beyond mountains that looked mossy in the distance, a blade-shaped swath of shining water, and beyond that more hills and peaks swept to the horizon in gradations from green to gray-blue.

"Now I can die," Lynn said.

"Don't talk like that."

"You're a regular trooper all of a sudden. What happened?"

"I don't know. I was petrified, then it passed."

She didn't need to hike to the next high point, though, the present plateau was more than enough, so Lynn went on alone, "to see what I can see," she said. There was a steady cool breeze and Elizabeth pulled on her charcoal cable-knit sweater. She walked past the pool of water to the far edge of the hilltop near an outcropping of granite and looked down. Who could run and leap out into that instant nothingness? Never. The seemingly uninhabited vista, three hundred and sixty degrees around, made her feel displaced, quite pointless. Utterly indifferent to her presence, a large shaggy ewe went on grazing about five yards away. Daring herself, Elizabeth moved toward it cautiously, crouching, one hand extended, there, can I touch you, you creature . . . but as she reached out, the animal darted skittishly away. That baby at the wool shop—its round pink face and big round eyes—what a picture. Local people were probably in and out of the place all day just to get their baby fix, to chortle and grin. She'd become slightly gaga about babies lately whenever she spotted one in a grocery cart, for example, snug in its infant seat, or strapped to its father's back going down Prince Street.

The critter had turned and was now facing her. Elizabeth tore a fistful of tall grass from the ground and tentatively stepped forward. "Nice girl," she said. "Look what I have for you." The black-faced sheep stared, and its large dark eyes gleamed, Elizabeth thought, with a sensitive intelligence. "You have everything up here, don't you? You're on top of the world. You're also very pretty," she said. "Do you take it all for granted? Are you the happiest ewe in the world?" She stretched out her arm and the animal leaped away again, hammering the earth with its hoofs.

She'd waited until she was forty-five to hike up the side of a mountain in Scotland. Never be the same after that. Henry should have been here, that would have done them good, making the

climb together. Then maybe lovemaking in some funny inn following a lamb carving, parsnips, potatoes, beans, frothy pints of Scottish ale, a lovely warming nightcap of Cragganmore neat. Yeah,
Henry, she thought, looking out over the desolate landscape, when
will you climb Ben Nevis now? Never. You missed it.

She dropped the handful of coarse grass. Squinting into the
wind, a pain like cramping pressed on her lower abdomen, making
her catch her breath, and her eyes filled, causing her vision to
momentarily blur. Four years before, without consulting Henry or
anyone, she'd decided to end a month-long pregnancy. Given the
turmoil in Henry's life at the time, her decision seemed unavoid-
able and she'd never questioned it. Now, as if this revelation was
what she had hiked up Ben Nevis to discover, and maybe the whole
point of her present journey, her confident choice suddenly looked
like the mistake of a lifetime. She marched across the grassy plateau
squeezing her skull. Two of the sheep scattered, startled by her
sudden movement. The child—her child—would have been three
years old now, a demanding gigantic human in their midst, transforming every aspect of their lives, she thought, hers and Henry's,
so that everything about their life together would have been colos-
sally different. A dark stain on her shorts puzzled her until she saw
that her finger was bleeding; she'd cut herself on a blade of grass.
Right after they were married she had halfheartedly tried and failed
to become pregnant. Several years later, while no longer intent on a
child, she had become casual about birth control. Then, faced with
the eventuality under unfavorable circumstances, she'd hastily
sought an abortion as though correcting a clumsy error, removing
an awkward confusion, before anyone was aware of it. She had
been forty-one. The mountainous horizon seemed to fly away from
her on all sides, limitless and unreachable. All they had lost. She
wanted to scream. Rushing to do the right thing, she'd gotten it
completely wrong. The staggering blindness of it. How stupid

can you be! They were miserable, she and Henry; a child, making life so much more than just the two of them, might have changed everything.

"Oh God," Lynn called, striding toward her, "you should see it up there, it gets better and better." She was grinning. "What's wrong?" she asked then. "There's blood on your face." Lynn touched her temple.

"It's nothing, a little cut."

"You're pale."

"This place is freaking me out. I've got to get back down to terra firma."

During dinner at the Ballachulish Hotel she described what had come over her on the mountain. Lynn, clearly wishing to comfort her, supported the decision she'd made four years before. "It was selfless of you, Elizabeth. You were thinking of other people."

"There's no such thing as selfless. It was new life. I quashed it."

"I would have done the same thing."

"Lately I've become obsessed with babies, naturally, now that it's pointless. I was never like that. One afternoon I followed a father with an infant on his back for three blocks just to watch the little face oogling and ogling. That was the only time I've ever been pregnant, that was my chance."

"I don't follow that part. Why is it too late?"

"I'm forty-five years old, for God's sake."

"And ten years from now maybe you'll look it."

"I'd probably hit menopause before I got pregnant."

"The world is crawling with kids who need homes."

"Well, I'm not picking one up this trip, am I?"

The soup was called cock-a-leekie. Their bed at the Ballachulish Hotel was layered with three wool blankets, a quilt, and a bedspread. Breakfast was creamy porridge.

It was an uncomfortably cold morning, a dense steel-gray sky low overhead. While they'd been told the wildness and thrill of Scotland was still ahead of them to the north, they decided they'd gone far enough this trip, they wouldn't top yesterday, and so headed toward Edinburgh. The stretch through Glencoe was austere snowy peaks and denuded ridges with jutting rock face, precipitous waterfalls, perilous ravines. A historian had named the glen "the very valley of the Shadow of Death," Elizabeth read, owing to the slaughter of Macdonalds in the late seventeenth century, but the place deserved the name apart from historical events. Proceeding southeast the bleakness made Lynn speed and she had to swerve dangerously at one point to avoid sheep walking down the center of the road. Elizabeth couldn't get the phrase out of her mind—the valley of the shadow of death—and wished she hadn't read it. Call Henry today, she told herself. You've got to call him. The landscape gradually grew friendlier, and when the sun popped out, they stopped by a loch in the Trossachs for an hour.

"Ben Nevis was it," Lynn said, holding her face up to the sun, eyes closed, hands folded in her lap. "I feel like we're near the end of our trip."

Elizabeth had donned her straw hat and sunglasses. "Well, we're only halfway, dear thing." The waitress's name for Lynn at the Ballachulish Hotel: dear thing.

"Please leave a message? That hardly sounds inviting. Let's see, it's Friday night at . . . oh, let's call it eleven-fifty, according to my Swiss Army wristwatch with its little red cross. I'm a pretty accurate lady. This is Helen, in case you haven't recognized my recording voice. Helen Trudell is what's on my driver's license. No driving tonight, or I might whiz right over there to visit. I've been drinking Black Russians. That was Mary's drink, you know. If you can't fuck them you have to drink them, that was one of Fitz's little jokes. The cocktail hour began at five sharp, which is when it always begins here in old Vermont. Wonderful word: cocktail. Yes? Fitz said Vermont meant True Cunt. Not Green Mountain. You may not know that he could be very naughty. Clever, gentlemanly, and perverse, that was Fitz. The cocktail hour began at five sharp this splendid thirtieth of June, and it is now eleven-something following a carafe of Black Russians. Or cossacks. Mary's drink. Oh, she's something, that one. I tried to like Mary, but she's a tough cookie. I don't like to drink alone, but sometimes you have to. Please leave a message. I'm trying. I don't remember your name. I wasn't paying attention and I don't think I ever heard it. I asked at the P.O. but Rita wasn't there and the other little part-time twat didn't have a clue. It all comes care of Underhill, she says. Fine. I want to say Hugo, but it can't be Hugo. Could it be Otto? As in ottoerotic? Two of my favorite names. It's Friday night, almost midnight, the cocktail hour began at five, and yes I'm a tad drunk in old Vermont in my terry cloth cassock. I felt tense buying a fifth of Kahlua and a fifth of Absolut just for me, like I was renting an X-rated movie to take home and watch alone. I'm usually a good girl, I never drink, really, which may be why I'm so drunk now following a fistful of Black Russians. You're a Fitzful, I used to tell him. If you're there listening to this, fine, go ahead.

"I've been here for a little more than two weeks and it feels like ages. I used to be so excited when I dialed this number. So I wanted to dial it again. Please leave a message. Didn't Fitz leave one for me? That's something I want to know. Isn't there a message from Fitz for me? How could this have happened? A few weeks after I left! Oh, Mary, that's too much. We always had marvelous conversations after midnight with the big quiet Vermont dark enfolding us. I should be a poet. Please leave a message. I can't believe you're dead, and I can't bear it. Do you hear me? Now that you're dead I can tell you the whole truth and nothing but the truth: as a lover and a friend you were the crème de la crème. I know it sounds corny. Please leave a message. I'm a tad drunk, but I know exactly what I'm doing. Talking into your machine is better than talking to myself. Do you understand? Am I getting through? Friday night alone in Vermont with everything else just as it was—the starlight, the air, the black trees. The house sitting there just as it was, everything just as it was except that nothing is the same. Oh boy, here I go. I didn't feel near tears a minute ago, I didn't call to leave a message of tears, no, I beg your pardon, I do not cry in front of strangers like some fucking actress. I'm no actress. I just miss him acutely, being here. Please leave a message. You've been very helpful, I'm glad you were there to be talked into. We can both forget about this tomorrow. Good night, neighbor."

I listened to the message a second time, looking into the shadowed dark of the yard from the darkness of the kitchen, aware of the evening chill on my bare skin—I'd leaped from bed and stumbled downstairs at the ring of the phone—then pressed Save on the Phone Mate, quite certain there would be no other incoming calls tonight to erase the recording, and yet also pretty sure I'd want to check out this Helen's midnight riff over my bowl of oatmeal as daylight invaded the yard.

"It's about noon on Saturday. The name isn't Hugo or Otto, it's Ash. Henry Ash. I received your message this morning. Always a pleasure to hear a human voice in the solitary confinement of Vermont. It feels like we've both washed up on an island in the wake of the Underhills' disaster. I've seen your distinctive footprints in the sand, and you've seen mine. The cocktail hour gets going over here at five, too, so bring your Black Russian, if you feel like it, or you'll have to settle for scotch. I'll expect you unless I hear otherwise, how's that?"

I mowed the lawn, I went out and bought some hummus and corn chips, carrots and celery, a half pound of jumbo shrimp, and a waxen chunk of local cheddar. I showered and shaved and put on my black T-shirt with clean jeans like I was the horny hot date of a personal ad in the *New York Review of Books*. I straightened out the kitchen, keyed up with an almost sexual anticipatory edge, to tell the truth, as the cocktail hour approached. By five-thirty expectation turned to exasperation, and by six I said, "All right, fuck it, Elizabeth," and poured myself a drink, fed up with the way people were, annoyed that I'd set myself up to be let down by this Helen.

"This is Helen, I just got your message and, let's see, I guess it's too late now, almost ten. I spent the day in Woodstock with a friend from New York, otherwise I would have been over. So . . . let's do it another time soon. Get this, I bought a kilt at Scotland-by-the-Yard!"

But thanks to my earlier disappointment, I had regained perspective and come to my senses. Well-meaning, distracting companionship with a troubled stranger in the sticks was not what I needed to spark the inspiration and concentration necessary to wring something of merit from my precious time here. Solitude was the state most conducive to work worth doing.

I was surprised, when I awoke, to find the room dimly visible and the backdrop of pale luminous first light defining the close dark leaves in the window, for I never slept through the night without waking at least once. As I lay listening to the ecstatic birds, I was perplexed by a vaguely recollected dream, uncomfortably real, of my tall thin daughter, with hair short enough to reveal her perfectly symmetrical head, looking in on me from the doorway of the present room as I slept. When I noticed her and began to lift my head, she raised her hand and said, quietly but distinctly, "Don't get up, don't mind me, we're fine." When I looked again, she was gone, and I then evidently descended into a dreamless sleep, as if succumbing to the power of her words. Unlike Sally, I almost never dreamed of our daughter. To my regret I had only rarely been visited by an authentic recollected image of her, a genuine memory that hadn't been prompted, for example, by photographs, which so often seemed to inhibit real memories by tyrannically taking their place. Don't get up, don't mind me, we're fine. Staring at the brightening sky in the window, I imagined her awakening to another day, knowing she would die, my vision blurred with tears, and I sobbed out loud, calling her name.

Move, look alive, just two, three pages a day, adding up to thirty thousand words by the time you return to the city—that's all!— a hundred pages and you're back in the saddle, working again, two hundred pages by New Year's, a new book a year later. Signed, sealed, delivered. Just sit down and stay put until two, three pages are done each day without fail. Headstrong Victorians wrote thirty or forty pages a day by hand—slam, bam, thank you, ma'am!— never changed a word.

I knew perfectly well that the door to the master bedroom had been wide open when I went to bed. The interior doors were always open, except for the door to Fitz's room, yet the fact that the door to the master bedroom stood shut this morning didn't register until I was downstairs in the kitchen and heard a sound come from that room directly overhead. There was a distinct sound of movement, then silence. I noisily opened and closed the back door, but that didn't provoke a response from above. I stepped outside to glance up at the window of the master bedroom, but no shadowed figure—no rural terrorist!—appeared to be looking down. I considered driving to Baker's, which opened at six, but that would only give the intruder an opportunity to flee, and how embarrassing my story would sound in any case. Grabbing the wrought-iron fire tool from behind the stove, I marched up the stairs, decisively thrust open the master bedroom door, and sternly demanded, "Hello?"

The room smelled of warm bodies, of warm breath and humid skin. There were two persons under the sheet. Neither moved. I firmly shook the bedstead. "Hello?"

Mary's son, Adam, raised his blond head from the pillow, squinting, moistening his full lips. "What time is it?" he managed, a harsh whisper. "What's up?"

"It's six," I said. "You startled me."

He raised himself to an elbow, supporting his head with his hand. "We got in about three. We didn't want to bother you. We've got a key."

The girl pulled the sheet off her shoulders without opening her eyes. "'Swarm," she muttered. "Adam, not now, okay? I want to sleep." She rolled onto her other side, facing the edge of the bed, her blue T-shirt bunched around her waist, revealing black bikini underpants, and resumed sleeping.

"I wasn't expecting company," I said.

"Yeah, it was pretty spontaneous. Someone said let's go to Vermont, you know. Mom said you've been up here for a while."

"How long are you planning to be around?"

"Couple of days. For the holiday, you know." The boy dropped back onto his pillow. "Catch you a little later, okay?" He added, "Good to see you, Henry."

A tall woman with short dark hair, dressed in a red plaid flannel shirt that reached to her thighs, stood helping herself to a glass of water at the kitchen sink as I entered the room from the staircase. Kelly.

"I hardly recognized you," I said. "You people scared the hell out of me."

She drank. "Boy, that's good water. I thought I heard voices. We didn't want to wake you earlier. I was in there on the couch. I need a couple of more hours."

I suggested she move to the guest room upstairs, the unused bed.

"Good idea, that couch is messing up my back. Hi," she said, lightly pressing a discreet kiss to my cheek as she passed in her bare feet. "See you in a little bit."

Panic came over me, a nauseating wave of alarm accentuated by an accelerated pulse and constriction of the chest, as I approached Fitz's library table where the blank unilluminated screen of my little Mac sullenly stared across the living room like a child to whom a promise had been broken.

I fled to the Clark Museum in Williamstown, a mausoleum erected in a pasture, looked like, thinking an outing was the best way to cope with the sudden invasion of Mary's children. "Back by dark," my note read. Their temporary presence would prove less disruptive, I decided, if I kept my distance. I loved Remington's painting of the blanketed Indian scout on horseback, isolated in the foreground of a snow-covered night landscape, dazzling and vast, beneath a starry ice-blue sky, looking down on a far-off settlement atwinkle with yellow lights. Frozen in that solitary moment for all time, but the painting wasn't about loneliness or longing. Our Indian friend wanted no part of that cozy nestled world below. Do you? I thought, squinting into the painting. In the same room, *The Women of Amphissa* by Sir Lawrence Alma-Tadema portrayed a dishevelled group of classically gorgeous women with wild red, blond, black hair, languorously lying around in diaphanous white garments or leopard skins, bare arms and bare feet, following an exhausting night of Dionysian revels. It could have been a picture of my daughter and her college girlfriends as far as I was concerned. They were surrounded by a gathering of kindly, curious workaday women, who regarded them with sympathy, bewilderment, and envy. Adolphe-William Bouguereau's *Nymphs and Satyr* on the adjacent wall inspired a similar rush of emotions in me. Four voluptuous, luminous-fleshed rollicking young women were dragging the reluctant mighty man-beast to the water's edge with devilish glee and irresistible determination. With her firm feminine fist, one of the nymphs grasped the single upright horn on the sylvan deity's curly head in a manner so unmistakably erotic as to be momentarily arousing to someone who'd been secluded in Speedwell for weeks. In the room of Impressionist paintings I spotted a woman whose smart haircut and folded arms, along with the intense pout with which she viewed paintings, and the sudden briskness of her stride when she decided to move, reminded me so strongly of Elizabeth that I smiled at her as we passed each other near a Degas ballerina on a pedestal. Like Elizabeth, the woman, if she noticed my nod, refused to glance in my direction. Exactly like you. I killed an hour browsing through a deserted bookstore in town—"I'm afraid we don't have anything under that name," said the bookseller, peering at the blue screen of her computer. "Did you say Ash or Rash?"—grabbed a Reuben sandwich for supper at the thriving deli next door, and Sunday was over, I thought, for all intents and purposes.

Brilliant light intermittently flickered through dark deciduous woods as I approached the house, and coming into the open, I saw flames at the back of Mary's place, a sight that made me suck air through my teeth, "Oh my God, Elizabeth." As I turned the corner at the large maple and pulled up before the barn, I saw that it was a bonfire in the mowing west of the house, the burning smell heavy and sweet, the intensity of combustion audible in the still air, an irresistible summons, basically, rather than disaster. Walking into the field I could hear voices softly singing—blush!—and I spotted the small choir on the far side of the blaze, a swaying silhouette facing the man-sized flames from a tolerable distance, arms encircling waists, and the song, Oh Jesus, Sally, that "Bridge Over Troubled Water," Sally, circa 1970. There was a pause, someone's arm raised to strike the new note—four people present, I realized, not three!—and they launched, fervently, into the next movement of the song. Sail on by, I thought, just sail right on back to the house, it's been a long day. But who's the fourth person here, I wondered, so I stood to one side, staring into the fire, too, while they strove on with this anthem, Toad, two kids from the suburbs, but they struck a cord, they had our number . . . we're with you, you're going to be okay . . . and my daughter's shining, hopeful face appeared at the center of the flames, smiling and singing . . . everything will work out in the end, trust me. Easy, I thought, hold on now. They climaxed their concluding crescendo with a ripple of self-approving applause, and the four of them collapsed into a clumsy embrace. I turned toward the house, thinking I hadn't been noticed, but before I reached the lilacs bordering the yard the boy called out to me—"Henry!"—bounding over with his impassioned face, smelling of wood smoke, beer, sweat, and marijuana.

They'd held up supper as long as possible, he explained, "This great Indian dish, Fitz's Curried Chicken, with kale and collards, Fitz's Corn Salad. There's plenty of leftovers. But now that you're back, how about joining us?" His face was blackened and smeared from tending the blaze, and in the moonlight his sincere bloodshot eyes and his big off-white smile had a manic brightness.

"The fire shook me up. Do you think this is all right with your mother?"

"We called her today and asked her to meet us here, but she couldn't get it together. Last night at about midnight the three of us felt we needed to do something, so here we are. And this afternoon Helen, who you've met, right, comes pedaling into the yard, which makes it even better." He gestured to the fire behind him.

"Needed to do something?"

"To mark the anniversary. Fitz, right? This was the last time we were with him, Fourth of July last year, so we thought it was the right time to get together, and we wanted to do it here. Definitely here."

"I see."

"Celebrating Fitz, that's the idea. That song, like that was one of his songs."

"Simon and Garfunkel?"

"You missed the Beatles medley." Adam laughed. "The Fitz tapes, he kept a box of them in the car. We managed almost all of *Abbey Road.*"

"How about that," I said, nodding.

"There's beer in the cooler over there."

"It's been a long day."

"Suit yourself. We'll probably be out here all night."

Helen, this Helen, caught up with me in the yard, in her bare feet, her jeans rolled to midcalf, a collarless short-sleeved white shirt. "We've been playing phone tag or something. I decided to come over this afternoon and these guys were here, which was just incredible. The best thing that could have happened." Her smile was convincing. "We've been laughing and crying all night."

"Sounds like fun."

"No, fun isn't the word. It's important. We were all here together last year. Are you going to join us?"

"I'm bushed, I'm going to turn in."

"Right," she said. "It's not your loss."

Fire of bones. Adam had gone to some effort to create the event, for the original architecture of the burning structure, composed of pine and hemlock and birch from various decaying piles around the field, had been discernible in the aggressive blaze. I could see the play of firelight from the kitchen, but not the players in the *whole Fitz thing* ritual. I took a scotch to the living room and sat down before my Mac, but only a fool would turn on the computer at this hour, while a bonfire celebrating Fitz raged outdoors.

The photograph of my daughter on the tea table had been taken during the last summer of her life while she appeared to be quite well. She was standing in the herb garden at the Cloisters wearing a straw hat, quince trees branching behind her. I'd taken one picture of her standing there smiling wonderfully, unguardedly, but then she'd caught herself and said, No, wait, do it again, and the second time around the smile was gone and the face she presented made a direct, unflinching statement: This is the last summer of my life, I'm dying and I know it. That was the snapshot I'd brought to Vermont with me. The photograph of my son portrayed him sitting on the summit of a mountain, one of his mountains, with snow-covered peaks receding behind him. He'd taken the picture himself, using the timer, for it had been a solo climb. His open straight-on expression was remarkably similar to his sister's. In appearance they were remarkably alike, in fact, and perhaps in temperament too. The snapshots I'd brought to Vermont were not the most flattering pictures of my children, but for me they told the truth about each of them. Their faces shared a bold seriousness, I thought, a defiant independence. They were never joiners, they never fit into groups comfortably, they never enjoyed group sports or group outings. From an early age it was clear that they would never enter the world of various professions or organizations. They were never going to be lawyers or business people, for example. They would never seek their fortunes in Hollywood or Washington, D.C. From an early age it was clear that they wouldn't lead lives devoted to the acquisition of worldly power and/or money. They were going to go their own way, making their lives far more difficult than necessary. Why? I asked myself. Why did we make ourselves practically unsuited for anything but stubborn solitary lives spent working at self-imposed tasks that only allowed you to scrape by. Why were we the way we were? Why did we feel it wasn't our world—our business world or religious world or political world or sports world, for that matter? I didn't want my children to suffer—God forbid! I wanted them to be happy!—yet I knew they couldn't escape the costs of being who they were. How did it happen? How did you become the person you couldn't help being?

Elizabeth, in the version of her displayed on Mary's oval Queen Anne tea table, was sitting on the massive dock at Port Clyde in her khaki shorts and navy blue sweater, waiting for the boat to Monhegan. She looked happy with her sunglasses shoved up on her head and her recently colored hair attractively tousled by the wind. She looked even more attractive in this marvelous picture, taken a half hour before the bout of seasickness that spoiled her ride to the island, than she actually was. Just last summer, I thought, last August. Moved by the beauty of the outer cliffs, she commented that Mary had never been here because she was always in Vermont for the summer, but maybe it would be fun if she and Fitz joined us next year, they'd probably love it. And then we returned to New York to find the red light blinking on the answering machine, Mary's recorded voice saying Fitz had died of a heart attack only days before and where were we, how could we go off without telling people where we would be?

I poured myself another scotch, observing that the bonfire hadn't diminished. The flames, if anything, leaped higher. "Fire of bones, Elizabeth." Good fire was what I thought the word meant when I was a boy. My daughter's body was cremated, I thought, and I repeated the sentence aloud, "My daughter's body was cremated." No one suggested that we accompany the body to the crematorium, not the undertaker, or the minister of the Unitarian church, or anyone we knew. I don't think I realized people could be present at the

155

cremation, in fact. That seemed a necessary procedure, rather than a sacred ceremony. The body was taken away and a few days later the family was presented with a box of white and gray bone fragments, which was all that remained of this person, this remarkable human being. It never occurred to Sally or me or anyone we knew to be present for that event, and no one suggested the possibility to us. What were we thinking, Elizabeth? Where were our heads? Sally and I, her mother and father, had left her alone in the funeral parlor and alone at the crematorium. Horrible! And because I had yet to witness a cremation or even set foot in a crematorium I didn't know what my daughter's body had been subjected to, or what had taken place. I had no images of the event whatever, so I was left to imagine her lying in the pine box being consumed in flames, her body clothed in her favorite dress and wrapped in a quilt made by her grandmother, this mature young body reduced by fire to a box of black-flecked white and gray bone fragments. That box was still with Sally; she couldn't let it go. Neither of us could decide what we wanted to do with our daughter's cremains. Cruel word. It was a mistake not to have been with her at every moment. "Yes, you would have expected that," I muttered, staring out the window. Why hadn't anyone told us, why hadn't Pease, the undertaker, during our meeting to discuss final arrangements, suggested the option of being present at the cremation? Why hadn't I known better? Stupid son of a bitch, bringing the empty whiskey glass down on the counter with a crack. That was over, the mistakes and missed opportunities had already happened, and there was nothing to be done except to press my hot face into my hands.

How could people bear to bury their dead? I thought, observing the bonfire from the bedroom window where it burned in the center of the field beyond the lilacs, framed by nearer trees and the backdrop of dark woods. I could think of any number of buried people without feeling anything one way or the other, but

156

I couldn't think about my daughter's body decaying in a coffin underground, without a kind of horror. The idea of *her skeleton* surviving in a fancy box underground—leg and arm bones, hands and feet, pelvis, ribcage, skull, teeth—horrified me. I had failed to be at the crematorium, but I had no doubt whatever that cremation was the most appropriate way to deal with the dead. Transformation by fire seemed absolute, clean, the most direct unmitigated passage to extinction. "Wonderful person," I whispered, staring through the west window at the brilliant play of light in the center of the mowing.

From the bedroom I was able to make out dark figures standing near the blaze in a close group, so I imagined they were singing again or had simply *come together* arm in arm to share the moment. "You missed the Beatles medley," I muttered. Fitz's mother had insisted that her son be interred, according to Mary. The old woman wanted her son *planted* in the Underhill plot in Wellesley, Mary said, and there was to be a ceremony to install an impressive granite marker on his grave sometime soon, perhaps later this summer. Hundreds of people had stood by Fitz's grave while the minister recited his final blessings, and many of them had placed a single rose, provided by the funeral parlor, on the coffin, which had not yet been lowered into the ground, before returning to their cars. The thought of Fitz's body in that massive metallic box—his long bony body and his large handsome head lying in the tufted wine-red plush interior of the costly coffin—wasn't comforting. It's horrifying, I said to Elizabeth. Don't bury me, I told her. I want to go up in flames. This Helen hadn't been there. She hadn't even been told he had died. Oh, Mary, that's bad, that's too much. Yet here she was bonding with Kelly and Adam at Fitz's bonfire, while the widow was back in Cambridge sound asleep by now.

I returned to the kitchen, agitated, looking out the window at the brilliant shape-shifting flames, as wide awake as I would have been if I'd been contending with some emergency that was bound to have me keyed up for hours. Sleep was out of the question. Unexpectedly and unstoppably the thought of my daughter's body in the maroon body bag, being transported to the funeral parlor in the back of the undertaker's vehicle by the tall man who had come for her, arose before me. I had helped him place my daughter's body in the maroon bag. We asked him not to close the bag over her head, not to zip the bag all the way up over her face, and so he didn't. As he wheeled the gurney out of the apartment, she appeared wrapped in a large bunting, Sally said, with her beautiful sleeping face protruding. Yet I'm sure he zipped the bag over her head the moment he was away from the door and headed for the elevator. He couldn't take her through the building and out into the street without concealing her completely. Then the tall man, who was alone, maneuvered my daughter's body into the back of the vehicle, and got behind the wheel and drove off. I'd never thought about this before. The man behind the wheel, and my daughter's body in the maroon bag lying behind him. I should have been there, I should have been with her every moment. How did he handle her body as he moved it from the car or van to the funeral parlor? What a gruesome name for the place! It astonished me to think that I had never thought about any of this before—the body alone in Pease's in a pine coffin, transported to the crematorium, unloaded . . . "I should have been with you," I said, catching my reflection in the window, "I never should have let you go through all that alone."

If anything the bonfire seemed bigger and brighter than before. Fitz's bonfire. "Forgive me," I muttered, "we didn't know what we were doing, we didn't know any better." None of us did. We're a fucking stupid bunch, aren't we, Elizabeth? Why don't we ever know anything? Why didn't the tall man from Pease's ask me if I'd like to come along with him? Because most people wanted nothing to do with it, I answered. Because it was customary for most people to behave just as we had behaved. We had washed her body and clothed her in her favorite dress and wrapped her in the quilt before the man from the funeral home had arrived. We gave instructions that everything was to remain just as we had arranged it. We had wanted to do everything for her ourselves, so how had we overlooked the possibility of remaining with her at all times and accompanying her pine coffin through the cremation process? Why had we behaved so stupidly? "Forgive me," I muttered, "it's a stupid life, it's one stupidity after another."

Fire of bones. Adam and Kelly and this Helen and whoever else was out there, they've got the funeral pyre, yes, but there's no body. Fitz is pickled in his state-of-the-art Cadillac coffin in the Underhill plot. The bonfire made perfect sense, the only honest way to honor the body of a loved one. Transformed by fire, set free in flames, transfigured. To think this happened to you, my daughter, just as you were coming into your own! After all you'd put into being alive! "Get over it, is that what you'd say?" I muttered. "Cheer up? Put it behind you? Everybody dies? Oh, Elizabeth."

I dialed Sally's number, but had the decency to hang up on the third ring, before I awakened her, although she probably wasn't there anyway, off to the Vineyard or somewhere for the holiday like everyone else in New York. The truth was I seldom called Sally when I was in the city. It was only since I'd been in Vermont that I'd discovered this impulse to phone her, a desire to hear her voice, to tell her what was on my mind. Don't be so indulgent, you have no right to enlist Sally in your sleepless nights.

"You and your England, Elizabeth," I said, squinting at the photograph of Virginia Woolf taped to the refrigerator. "You and your castles and Cotswolds and coldhearted friends." Lynn the traveling companion, Lynn the vixen, Lynn the loyal Elizabeth listener. Is that what Lynn advised: It's your life, don't let him drag you down, tell him just get over it?

The slap of the screen door made me jump, while the sight of my dark figure standing by the window in the unlighted kitchen was surely what caused the person barging into the house to gasp with fright.

"Jesus," she said, pressing a hand to her chest, taking a deep breath, "that was intense. Can I turn on a light?"

"I'll get it, I was just on my way upstairs," I said. "There we are."

"Adam told me I could find some Bag Balm around here, that ointment farmers put on cow teats." A red-peaked cap partially concealed her eyes. "Over the stove, he said," and she was already reaching into the cupboard, a swath of bright skin bared between a snug black halter and beltless cut-off jeans. "Got it! There should be gauze and adhesive tape somewhere too," she said, pulling open the silverware drawer.

"What happened?"

Rapidly, she opened and shut one drawer after another. "Adam burned himself. He can get carried away, you know."

"That's quite a blaze."

"Yeah, another wild night in Vermont," she said.

"Here it is, sterile gauze and medical tape. Is he all right?"

"He'll be fine, he just said, Get me the Bag Balm. I'm Jane, by the way. Bye." The screen door whacked shut behind her as she hurried back to the bonfire.

"Jane," I said, nodding. "You've got the whole gang here, Fitz."

A mature person would simply go about his business without a thought for these young people and their celebration. A mature adult would sleep soundly, husbanding strength for the day ahead, undisturbed by matters that didn't concern him. They were practically children, with the exception of this Helen. A mature man wouldn't be pacing through the house from window to window, thinking about young women in halters and cut-off jeans singing around a bonfire. You're as excitable and uncertain and eager as a damned teenager when it comes to strangers gathered around a fire at night. Three young people show up for the Fourth of July and you're beside yourself, you're like a chained dog.

You can't get this Helen off your mind. You think your *experience* has made you the sort of mature person who isn't intimidated by pain and suffering, who can understand the fears, the private anguish, of the likes of this Helen, and therefore might be of use. Brilliant! I'd always resisted the impulse to collar people like a reformed drunk and tell them I understood what they were going through. Always distrusted healers and counselors and therapists and preachers—all Sally's soulful knowing colleagues in the healing racket!—and yet you think you know some things about the loneliness of the cancer patient, the loneliness of having a breast removed, you know something about loss.

Look at you, and I stared at my reflection in the window where the distant fire burned brightly, you call that a mature human being? You see a young girl in denim cutoffs and a black halter and you're prepared to make an absolute fool of yourself. You've been in Vermont too long, you haven't laid eyes on fellow creatures for too long, all kinds of fellow creatures. "Calm down," I said, and walked outside, looking straight up, and inhaled several deep dizzying breaths of the fragrant night air.

They were gathered in a close huddle to the left of the pungent fire, now a collapsing teepee of stout logs burning on a crimson heap of breathing coals. As I approached the site, their muffled humming resolved itself into the hymnlike intonations of "Kum Ba

Ya." Oh Lord, Elizabeth, listen to this! I stood prodding the blaze with a long stick, while this clutch of humans rhythmically swayed to their murmurous chant nearby. Like a sorrowful animal, I thought, looking directly into the heart of the fire. Remember our campfires, Toad, our young family on a canyon slope under the vast sky like the last people on earth, the faces of our entranced children lit by firelight. Everything already promised to them. The sound of the fire filled the pause in the singing, provoking me to poke a smoldering log.

It was Kelly, I guessed, who burst out with "The Christmas Song," featuring roasting chestnuts, Jack Frost, tiny tots, which was spontaneously taken up by the others, pitching their voices to high heavens. This a Fitz favorite too? Muttering the familiar lyrics despite myself, I struck the stubborn log and it erupted into flame. Oh boy, Sal. Come on, man, you can't break down out here. Christmas and Nat King Cole! Even in July this stuff could tear you apart.

In a moment the heat on my face made me step back. I decided to return to the house unnoticed, but then the song was over, the moaning huddle broke up, and Helen—*this Helen*—walked up to me. "So, you couldn't stay away," and stepping closer as I continued toward the house, she asked, "Are you all right?"

"Just the smoke," I explained, "the heat," rubbing my eyes, blinking.

"Something happened," she confided. "I can't explain, you had to be here."

The other three began circling the fire hand in hand like children in ring-around-a-rosy, in manic contrast to the mood of the song. They were actually skipping through the foot-high grass, so they appeared to be leaping. The second time around, Adam, taking up the rear in bare feet, snatched Helen's hand—"Come on, you guys!"—tugging her along. How you'd hate this, Elizabeth, this antic gallivanting, this hoopla. Turning away from the irresistible inferno, I headed back to the house, satisfied that I shouldn't have come out here in the first place.

Before I reached the edge of the field, I heard them racing behind me, and in the next moment they were skipping around me in a large circle, holding ... *sparklers*, I thought, recovering the word, your favorite childhood firework, which emitted an unmistakable whisper as they threw off white glittering light. I stared, smitten by the effect, hadn't seen sparklers for fifteen years probably, and the Fitz gang closed in on me, momentarily raising the brilliant sputtering wands together above my head.

"Winner of the Sparkler Crown for Hanging in There," Kelly called out, laughing, beautiful, and inspiring a burst of hoorays and bravos.

"Henry Hang-in Ash!" Adam announced. The large white bandage on his left forearm flashed below the upraised glittery light.

Too startled to summon a reply, I glanced from one grinning face to the next for a clue to what was going on. They turned back toward the bonfire, and each sparkler fizzled like a species of giant lightning bug blinking out.

"Hang out with us for a while," Helen said, surprising me again, for I didn't realize she'd remained behind. "Come on," taking my arm, "you look like you could use it." When I declined, she pouted disapprovingly.

Back at the house, I caught sight of myself in the small oval mirror in the mudroom. "You look like hell, man. You look dangerous." This Jane turns up dancing with herself in front of the fire on smooth tan legs, swinging with Nat King Cole in her cut-off blue jeans on a balmy July night, and you turn into a horny adolescent. No, you no longer observe the unfurled colors of young women. You get used to them striding around lower Manhattan like plucky princes. You outgrow them. A bona fide grown-up becomes bored with the merely young. A mature man knows what inappropriate means, he knows what offensive is, he knows the difference. "I must be drunk, Elizabeth, I've had more whiskey than I realized."

Sparkler Crown!

I don't think I can pull it off, to tell the truth. Here I'm trying to *hang in* as though everything hasn't changed! Whatever I was before, I'm no longer that person. The attempt to persist with business as usual, aspirations as usual—what a hopeless fraud. Stealing up to Vermont for the summer to get into something new—that's a joke, Elizabeth. That's not going to happen.

"You know what you could use," I said, taking Elizabeth's part with a quasi-British accent. "You could use a bit of the stiff upper lip, buster. A strong cup of Twining's Earl Grey tea and a dose of the stiff upper lip. Count your blessings, and get the bloody hell on with it. Because the night is coming, you can be sure. Living is one loss after another, and there's nothing for it but to bear one loss after another right up to your last breath, and that's the end of it."

I hear you.

"What's going on here is one death after another in no particular order and in every conceivable way until everyone is dead."

Why don't human beings get used to it? People the world over have grown numb to countless deaths of all kinds occurring daily, even in their own backyards, but no one has become numb to the death of a loved one, death in the garden, death in the master bedroom. You suffer your own, Elizabeth, every human suffers his or her own in the same way everywhere. Life without the beloved person is unbearable, and perhaps your insistent tears help you to feel a pain you crave. You are loath to *adapt* to this loss, you refuse to *get used to it*, afraid you'll lose this redeeming sorrow, which is all that's left of the beloved person. Your pain is all that's left.

"Henry?"

"Don't sneak up on people like that," I said, turning from the window. The top of her head was hardly a foot from the top of the narrow antique doorway.

"I'm all partied out, I can't sleep out there."

Moonlight informed the small guest room so that I left the table lamp between the two beds, the only light here, turned off. I suggested she use her mother's room.

"Their room, you mean. I'm not comfortable with that. Mind if I sleep in here?"

"Suit yourself, I'll take the couch tonight."

"No one has to sleep on the miserable couch. I've shared this room with all kinds of people, summer and winter. It's called bunking it. Don't worry, I don't snore. That fire," she added, "I feel as smoked as a hunk of salmon."

"You smell smoked."

She made pleasurable humming sounds as she showered in the bathroom next door. When she returned to the bedroom, she was dressed in a long pale T-shirt. She stood by the window that looked out to the mowing and the still-visible fire. The fresh scent she'd brought into the room, I realized, was Mary's avocado body lotion. Her short dampened hair was combed back behind her ears. Kelly had already graduated from college by the time I married her aunt, so she must have been pushing thirty now, I thought, observing her from the twin bed. A grown-up woman, for heaven's sake, although she almost always went around like a kid in her blue jeans and T-shirts, her snug tops and nifty little black skirts. Neither married nor a mother, not a svelte business type on the make or a straight-arrow young professional striding down a career track. She was an artist who waited tables. Elizabeth and I had been impressed by a winter exhibit of her paintings almost two years before in a small downtown gallery, a series of medium-sized oils that focused on a small community flower garden surrounded by a chain-link fence at Third Avenue and Houston. Entitled *Garden in the City.* There were individual portraits of the racially mixed bag of city gardeners, vignettes of plants and insects, scenes of the garden in various seasons, some set in the larger congested squalor of the surrounding neighborhood. The meticulous drawing and impeccably labored surfaces of the paintings reminded me of the careful early work of Lucian Freud. I remembered the location of the actual garden because I had walked over to check it out one day after the opening, and several afternoons that following spring I had gone by to see what was doing. Kelly's garden in the city had seized my imagination, I recalled now, observing her at the window. I'd never thought of Mary's daughter as a committed, accomplished, and possibly brilliant young painter, and yet that's what she was. While I'd continued to think of her as a recent graduate of Cooper Union who *hung out* in Soho and earned her keep by waitressing, almost ten years had passed and she had gone on to become quite the painter. She knew what work was, she knew what loneliness and frustration and disappointment were all about because that's what you got for your efforts to make original art in this *civilization* of ours. The sports civilization, the entertainment civilization, the business civilization, the money civilization. You had to be a weirdly inspired oddball to get up each morning in your tiny hovel in New York City and muster the wherewithal to feel like an artist. It was all but impossible to maintain your own little flame of creativity in the face of such human and inhuman wealth and misery. To return from the towering, thronged, devastating streets to your tiny, stifling hovel and roll up your sleeves and get busy making your all-important contribution to the world: remarkable! You're an exemplary young woman, your mother should be proud of you.

She folded her arms across her chest, causing the T-shirt to rise slightly, exposing a pale puffed-out wedge of underpants. She pressed the palm of her right hand to the windowpane, as though reaching to something beyond the glass. In the next moment she silently buried her face in her hands, hunching her shoulders. I repressed an impulse to cross the room and ask what was wrong, and when she turned from the window, I feigned sleep. She slipped into her bed as quietly as possible.

"Are you still awake?" she whispered. When I didn't answer, she resettled herself in the bed, and the gentle movement of air as she rearranged her sheet wafted a scent of avocado lotion my way. Helen's gift.

I shifted my weight.

"Henry?" she whispered. "Are you awake?"

"I must have dozed off while you were in the shower," I said, smacking my pillow a couple of muffled whacks.

"Can I bother you for a minute? I'm worried about Adam. He's always up to some reckless stunt like he doesn't care what happens to him. He's wild."

"He knows what he's doing, though, doesn't he? He looks like he can take care of himself."

"He loved Fitz. He was a lot more devoted to him than I was, let's put it that way. Maybe because he's younger. I was already a senior in high school by the time they got married."

"Too old for a new father." I was propped on an elbow now, watching her. Kelly lay on her back, the sheet pulled up to her armpits.

"He burned himself tonight, for instance. It was horrible."

"That's what Jane said. He's all right, isn't he?"

"You don't understand. Here we are having our first Fourth of July Fitz celebration. We took turns telling about times we remembered with Fitz. Fine. Adam kept lugging logs to the fire, his bonfire couldn't be big enough. He started talking about how we were here but Fitz was gone. Everything went on as ever, everything was just the same, and he didn't understand how that could be. Fitz had died and Adam couldn't feel it somehow. Fitz was gone and he was just sitting there watching the fire and he could get emotional and talk about how he missed him, but he couldn't feel it."

"Did you understand what he was saying?"

"He wanted to feel something. All we could do was sit around singing songs . . . he kept going on about this. He was tending the fire with a wrought-iron bar from the barn. Helen was saying she understood what he meant, trying to placate him. He had deliberately heated the iron bar in the bed of coals, which looked like lava or shimmering metallic red velvet. He took the iron from the fire and held his left arm out and pressed the burning tip of it into the underside of his arm." She raised her arm and rubbed the smooth underside with her thumb, grimacing. "Right here. I smelled his flesh burn. This took forever. Then he flung the poker down. Helen and I were in tears at that point."

"Jane came to the house for the ointment."

"She helped him dress the wound. She was awfully cool about it. Maybe she understands self-mutilation. Maybe branding is nothing new for her. How could he?"

"I don't know."

"I don't think he's ever done anything so . . . excessive. What next?"

"That wound could get infected," I said. "He should have a doctor look at it."

"Can you imagine David doing something like that?" she asked.

"No. But David can also be a daredevil. He takes risks."

"I've heard. How is he anyway?" she asked, deciding to digress. "Isn't David in Europe or somewhere?"

How David was seemed far too complicated a subject to be broached just then with someone who hardly knew him. "Last I heard he was headed for the Alps. He's probably on a mountain right this minute. I assume he's fine. I insist upon it," I added.

A moment later she said, "Mom says Adam is a lot like our father was. I remember him, but not that well—mostly from pictures. I feel much closer to Fitz, although Fitz was never like a father to me."

"What was he like?"

"He was my big pal. He didn't interfere. He didn't tell me what to do, he didn't get disappointed in me and make me feel like shit half the time. That's Mother's job. Fitz didn't have that obsessive, worried parental thing going. I didn't need to make him happy."

"Sounds like you've thought about it."

"I have. My mother loves me a hell of a lot more than Fitz did, there's no doubt about that, but she drives me crazy. Love is the problem, people who love you."

"Of course."

"They want something in return, they want you to love them back, which usually means being the way they want you to be."

I fluffed up my pillow again, discouraged by these observations of hers. My daughter's struggle for so-called independence had taken place under impossible circumstances, with the clock running. Yes, love was the problem. "It's complicated, isn't it? Wait until you're a parent." I told her.

"I know how a parent feels. I wish I could control my mother, I wish she'd stop disappointing me, I wish she'd be the way I want her to be."

"What's Mary been up to?"

"She's becoming a recluse. She and Fitz had quite a social life in Cambridge, but now she seldom goes out. I've warned her, after a while people will stop inviting her. I don't want to worry about my mother. I haven't seen her since her birthday in April. That's awful of me, I suppose, but whenever I make an effort we end up arguing. She never has food in the house, she goes around in the same damn clothes, her Cambridge spouse uniform. She reads two books a day—from the nineteenth century. Come on, Mother, you've got to go out, you've got to see people, and so on. I think she's developing that fear of leaving the house."

"Agoraphobia."

"She says Fitz's death has knocked the wind out of her. All she did was complain about him, he was always at his office, off on a trip, meditating in a French monastery."

"The scientist with the spiritual side."

"But last winter took the cake, her Saks fiasco in Boston." She turned her head toward me, gnawing the side of her thumb for a second.

"Her Saks fiasco?"

"Elizabeth didn't tell you about it? They're very close, those two, they're a lot alike. Two weeks before Christmas Mother was picked up in Saks for stealing. She went through the store stuffing anything at hand into a satchel, and was stopped on her way out. Someone had been observing her."

"Mary did this?"

"Exactly. My mother, who's worth at least a few million. She had a bunch of gold credit cards in her pocketbook. She should have been arrested, but the store looked up her Saks account, which was dandy, you know, and decided to fine her five hundred bucks instead. If she'd been an ordinary poor person, who needed to steal, they would have thrown her in jail. Can you imagine risking that kind of humiliation?"

"Sounds crazy."

"My therapist, Lydia, says she wanted to get caught. It wasn't stealing, it was a cry for help. Lydia thought she should go on medication immediately. Of course Mother doesn't believe in therapy. How convenient of her. I was so angry I couldn't look at her. My sympathy reached a new low. I could have used that five hundred bucks."

"Are you sure Elizabeth knew? I would have heard about it."

"Elizabeth tried to cheer me up over the whole thing—it was almost funny, she said, a symptom of holiday stress—but I wasn't buying. It's like Adam, I don't know what she's going to do next. Why am I worried about them, instead of the other way around?" She paused. "Sorry, I'm chewing your ear off. Adam got me all wound up. Fitz's bonfire brought all this crap boiling to the surface."

"Don't apologize. I understand."

"I was always worried as a kid. By the time I was thirty I thought I'd know what was what, you know, I'd calm down, I wouldn't have to be anxious all the time. Did you feel that way?"

"I don't think so."

"Well, guess what, girl, everything just builds. Instead of worrying my mother, I get to be worried about her. Do you know what I mean?"

"I do, yes."

A pause. "What are you doing up here, writing a book?"

"That was the plan. I've been dragging my feet, I'm afraid."

"And Elizabeth is in England. I remember when she was having her big affair with you. I was still in school. We'd meet downtown for coffee and she'd look fabulous because she was going to meet her mystery man in the Gramercy Park Hotel at three. We had this little routine, we got to know each other. I think she was always nervous, so she wanted to meet me first and kill time and distract herself. She'd have coffee and brioche, then she'd down a glass of white wine just before she left."

"For Gramercy Park?"

"She usually walked over—to get her heartbeat under control, she said. I loved it."

"What were you, a junior? Your aunt was corrupting you."

"I was a dazed senior, actually, and Elizabeth was this exciting woman in her thirties. It was our little secret. Mother didn't even know about it. Then that summer the whole thing was out in the open and there you were, Elizabeth's mystery man. She used to tell me she wasn't into marriage, she didn't know why people had to be married. I guess you changed her mind." She tossed back the sheet. "Beer goes right through me," she said.

Relax, I thought, as I listened to the woman urinate, an urgent hiss in the hallway, for I realized I was clutching the pillow in a fist, my shoulders tight, my left foot cramped up. I reached for the instep and vigorously massaged. Yes, Kelly had been a senior in art school the year I became involved with Elizabeth, I remembered clearly, because that spring we had agreed that I wouldn't attend the talented niece's graduation in the city and Elizabeth would forgo my daughter's graduation from college in New England as well. We had been seeing each other with increasing frequency since the preceding fall, but neither of us had been ready to get involved with the other's family yet. "Yes, Elizabeth, I remember that year quite well."

Kelly quietly crossed the room in her bare feet and slipped back into bed. "Good night, Henry, I'm pooped out all of a sudden."

"Listen, I don't want to leave you with the wrong impression. The Gramercy Park detail couldn't have been Elizabeth. She used to come over to my apartment on Tenth Street. You might have met her for coffee beforehand, but the Gramercy Park part had to be someone else's clandestine rendezvous."

She raised her head from the pillow. "Oh, it was Gramercy Park all right, and it was Fridays. Because of the weekend discount."

"My first marriage was over, there was nothing to conceal. We stayed at my place more often than hers because we preferred the Village to Eighty-first Street. But it wasn't a secret."

Her smile was visible in the moonlit room. "I don't know what to tell you, Henry. Looks bad, doesn't it?"

"You mean Elizabeth was shacking up in the Gramercy Park Hotel Friday afternoons while she was *head-over-heels* in love with her future husband?" I said, emphasizing the hackneyed phrase. "Does that sound like your aunt to you?"

Kelly laughed. "Those window designers can be pretty wild, man. Being with her on those Fridays was heady stuff for me, that's all I can say."

"Maybe it was all an invention intended to titillate her niece, a romantic embellishment."

"If that works for you, Henry, go with it. I can't keep my eyes open." She said good night again.

Elizabeth's niece didn't snore, but her slow regular breathing only feet away—how enviably she fell asleep!—might as well have been snoring, as I listened and couldn't stop listening. Friday afternoons at Gramercy Park! This *mystery* didn't bear thinking about. You didn't own her, I told myself. I quietly moved from bed to window and could still make out the fire in the field. Adam's self-inflicted wound made me cringe, his Fitz-brand, I thought. What sort of person was capable of holding a red hot iron to his arm like something out of Bergman. Beyond Bergman for that matter. Get the Bag Balm, Jane! What did such an act express: self-love or self-hate, self-sacrifice or self-abuse? Was such an act self-assured or self-despairing, self-glorifying or self-forgetful, self-dramatizing or self-effacing, self-fulfilling or self-destroying? Keep it up, I thought, watching the fire from the window in boxer shorts, play your word game while someone else takes the iron rod from the fire and presses it without hesitation into his flesh. Did he hesitate? Something happened, Helen said, you had to be here. Self-reliant or self-immolating, selfish or selfless, self-knowing or self-satisfied, self-seeking or self-surrendering. Keep it up, Henry.

My bunk mate had not moved from where she lay stretched out

on her back. I attempted to breathe in sync with her unconscious breathing and maybe lull myself to sleep. She's actually a beautiful young woman, I saw, observing her profile, the *flawless* skin—exemplary!—framed by short dark hair. She must have gotten her father's nose because her straight prominent beak didn't resemble Mary's rather petite number in the least. Her dead father's nose. Her brow was unlined, two silver rings in her pretty left ear, a half smile on her slightly parted lips. Her left hand lay on top of the sheet by her side, silver rings on her middle and index fingers. Her chest moved just discernibly with each breath she took. Toes sticking up, a long narrow valley between her slightly parted legs. A wonder really. A living wonder. An artist who waited for her moment to arrive. I threw back my covers and scrambled from the bed. A light sleeper might have awakened; Kelly didn't budge.

The fire had been reduced to a mound of burning coals maybe seven feet in diameter. No way to treat a hay field, Graves would say. Some distance from the site, Adam and Jane, I assumed, lay together under a dark puffy comforter, possibly an opened sleeping bag. I moved quietly, determined not to wake them. The wrought-iron bar was stuck upright into the ground by the fire, a blackened lance pitted yet smooth to the touch. I thrust it into the shimmering coals, and sat down on the plank bench that usually stood against the south wall of the barn. I held my hands out to the heat. The iron bar, where it was embedded in molten coals, now glowed as brightly as the coals themselves. I took it from the fire and held the incandescent tip close to the underside of my left arm. Remarkable! Adam's wound would eventually become a large raised badge of scar tissue, which he would bear for the rest of his life, whereas the undersides of my arms were unmarked, smooth and unsullied as the undersides of your blue-veined breasts, Elizabeth. You should be here, we could use you up here in Vermont. Forget England,

Elizabeth, you've got plenty going on right here in your sister's backyard. We've got bloody Shakespeare right here in old Vermont. I brought the iron tip as close as possible to the pale skin of my arm, its concentrated heat forbidding. The distance between my teasing gesture and the act of actually pressing the red hot bar into my flesh was great, and for the moment, I realized, insurmountable. Adam was someone who would inflict such a wound upon himself, and I was a person who would not. I was sorry he had branded himself with an iron bar, yes, I could hardly condone such an act, and yet I regretted more that I hadn't done it first. Viscerally! Spontaneously, I thought, driving the crimson end of the bar into the ground at my feet.

Gradually, almost imperceptibly, it seemed, the sky brightened and euphoric birds began their maddening morning songs. The bulky purple surface of Adam's sleeping bag moved and this Jane got up from it, reaching for the sky in her red plaid flannel shirt— Kelly's shirt?—her blond head tipped back. She wobbled on tip-toes into the wet field for ten yards or so where she squatted, holding her shirttails around her waist. She wiggled her behind hula hoop–wise before standing up again. With her back to me she remained very still, as though listening. Ephemeral patches of mist hung suspended over the mowing like limpid islands of light. A faint plume of smoke ascended from the remains of the bonfire. The red shirt dropped behind her to the ground, and this Jane broke into a light-footed jog for the far corner of the field. "Hark, Elizabeth!" And the air ringing with birdsong, Adam's gleaming bunk mate rounded the corner of the field with arms outspread, her body atilt, exactly like my daughter's girlhood imitation of a jet plane banking in for a landing—zoom!—and then she came through a cloud of ground fog, running toward me, her firm breasts bounc-ing, her hair fly-away, her pubic bush a small earthy smudge. When Jane spotted me she gave me a little wave, rapidly wagging her hand, grinning, before veering off in another direction like an ecstatic 737. Sail on silver girl, I thought, blinking back emotion, for heaven's sake, get a grip, man, and turned away from the field, shining now with the first glints of sunlight.

You can be heartbroken and, in the same breath, bowled over by a radiant girl cavorting over a field at first light. Outrageous, I suppose you'd have to say, Elizabeth, and I'd agree with you. We become outrageous as we stubbornly drag the persistent longings and hankerings of youth into midlife, and beyond. The *aging process* is not a pretty picture. We cling to our dwindling selves until the bitter end. That's all we know. *Living is all we know.*

From the screen of lilacs I glanced back to the brilliant green mowing. Sprinting flat out in fire-engine-red jockey shorts, his chin up and arms pumping like *Chariots of Fire*, Adam caught up with this Jane as she circled Fitz's spent, smoldering bonfire, swung her off her feet and over his shoulder in one powerful swoop, on the run, and dashed off for the far side of the field, the beautiful kidnapped girl shrieking laughter.

At Adam's age, I wasn't sweeping naked girls off their feet at first light. I was already married to Sally, and we'd already had a baby, whose beautiful and brilliant fits and starts represented all the excitement we could have hoped for.

They appeared to be back under the sleeping bag when I returned from Baker's with large brown locally fresh eggs, Pekarski's smoked bacon, English muffins, a lemon, a pound of Sumatran French roast. Even Baker's store now stocked gourmet coffee beans and a machine that produced an almost powdery espresso grind. Remember our youthful experiments with *oeufs pochés*, Toad? This morning I wasted a handful of eggs before I recovered the knack.

Helen came, tapping, to the screen door. "It's me," she said, stepping into the room. "Are they still sleeping? That was quite a bash." She smiled. "I like your apron, Henry. What's up?"

I'd donned the slightly soiled white apron that hung inside the pantry door, the better to master my quasi-hollandaise sauce. *Fitz* was written across the left-hand corner of the bib, in the red cursive appliqué once seen on the shirts of gas station attendants. That couldn't be helped. "I was bored," I said, adjusting the heat under the frying pan. "I didn't hear you drive up."

"I rode my bike. Are those poached eggs? Why, you doll." This morning she wore a simple pale blue cotton jumper over a white short-sleeved shirt opened at the throat. Bare feet in her sandals.

"Eggs Benedict is the plan."

"How ambitious. I've already had my Cheerios and banana, darn it." She added, "I learned some things about you last night."

"You can't believe what you hear," I said, prodding strips of bacon.

"Only good things, actually. What can I do here?"

"Nothing at the moment."

Like a man wearing good trousers she abruptly jerked back the front of her skirt as she sat down in the black Windsor by the kitchen table, raising the hem of it midway to her thigh. "It's humid already. Is there coffee?" She sat facing the room, her sturdy freckled legs stretched out before her. A dark smudge on her right ankle was grease from her bicycle, I decided. Rather than a melanoma.

"Wonderful coffee from Indonesia. Let me get you a cup."

"I didn't realize we were in the same business. Books, I mean."

"We're not," I said. "That's not my business."

"I've been reading the worst stuff in manuscript. All by writers highly touted by their avid agents. Doesn't anyone know the difference anymore?"

"Evidently not. On the other hand, there's a writer under every rock, isn't there? There are probably forty or fifty of them right here in Sleepless Hollow alone. It gives you the willies."

Laughing, she said, "That's true too."

"How do you take your coffee?" I placed the steaming cup on the table before her.

"Black's fine. What do you call it, Sleepless Hollow?"

"The peace and quiet keeps me awake."

"Who picked the flowers?" Pointing with one finger to the wilting bouquet of daisies and buttercups and red clover and ferns that I'd picked a couple of days before.

"They're company, they listen to me."

She blew over the top of her coffee, she sipped, then carefully lowered the cup to its saucer. "Yum." She waited until she caught my eye to say, "They told me about your daughter. I'm sorry."

"How brave of you. Most people wouldn't mention my daughter."

"I'm not most people." She slipped her hand into the open collar of her shirt. "I lost my left breast thanks to what the mammogram detected." She reached across her chest. "There's nothing there."

I didn't appear surprised. "You seem well."

"I am well. I'm great."

The possibility of candor, of outrageousness, carried a charge. "Do you get used to it, or is it always there, missing?"

She gave an amused grunt, impatiently shaking her head. "Yeah, you get used to it and it's always there, missing."

"I thought they were becoming more conservative about radical surgery. You know . . ." I faltered. "It's none of my business, is it?"

"Wasn't lumpectomy an option? Of course it was an option. I wanted to avoid radiation and chemo. We made what we thought was the best decision. My doctors and me. No one else had an opinion."

"You can help me set the table," I suggested, "if you want."

The hollandaise sauce had cooled, growing a bit stiff, and when I attempted—easy now—to rewarm it, I went too far, so the gala brunch came down to slightly overdone poached eggs with bacon and English muffins. Neither Kelly nor Jane could face eggs, they said, and they never ate bacon. Adam, wearing only his soiled shorts, the filthy bandage on his arm, his square bare feet battered, ate three or four eggs doused with ketchup, wiping his plate clean with his muffin. An hour later, unexpectedly, they were packed up and on their way back to the city with the girls up front, Kelly driving, and Adam in the backseat. He had an unmissable Fourth of July party to attend on Fire Island, Kelly had to work that night, and Jane said she wished she could stick around, but she had no choice in the matter. There were hugs good-bye and then Helen and I stood waving in the driveway like a somewhat forlorn married couple who had just hosted a successful weekend and were now relieved, yet sorry, to see their guests depart.

"I have some reading to do," she said. "What are you doing for the holiday? Wednesday."

"I'm working," I said, although the night on fire, as I already thought of it a little melodramatically, had been slightly shattering, if not transfiguring, and for the moment I wasn't entirely sure what "working" meant.

She straddled her bike like a schoolgirl in the pale blue jumper. "That's the spirit."

"Careful," pointing, "you'll get grease on the hem of your dress."

"I'm not going to be here that much longer," she said. "Don't be a stranger, Henry. Let's talk soon."

"Maybe we can get dinner one night," I suggested. "I'll give you a call."

She stood on the upraised pedal to shove off, her slender forearms tensed as she pulled up on the chrome handlebars, and the front wheel twisted in the loose gravel. Passing the gray barn, seated squarely on the crotch-friendly seat, erect as an eager plebe, she raised her right arm above her head, fingers splayed, as though stretching for an overhanging branch just out of touch, without looking back. How do you know I'm watching you? I thought. The round bell, mounted on the handlebar within thumb's reach of her right hand, tingled distantly as she coasted into the woods, amplifying the silence around me. Back indoors the red light of the answering machine, my mute accusing companion, glared from its corner of the kitchen.

5 *The Stone Wall*

A necessary and substantial stone wall had formerly bordered the north side of the mowing. The fieldstones were there, as they had been on the west side, but again all tumbled down and covered over with decaying leaves and branches, ferns, grapevine, and honeysuckle. I was out there by eight each morning and stayed out until four or five in the afternoon with a gallon of water, a handful of Fig Newtons, an apple. I discovered new techniques of lever and balance to maneuver seemingly unmovable stones into place. Holes were soon worn through the fingers of my leather gloves. The wall was beautiful to me, as it progressed along the edge of the woods, defining the cultivated green field. I cleared unwanted brush and overcrowded small trees, mostly birch and poplar, as I went. I kept Fitz's binoculars near at hand to identify the insistent racket of the ovenbird one morning, and the monotonously repetitive serenade of the red-eyed vireo the next. As always the sight of soaring red-tails gave me pause, and contentious crows flying over the field made me smile. The solitude felt right. When you talked to stones, they listened. "It makes a lot more sense than banging your skull against the gray screen of a computer, Elizabeth, doesn't it?" You go to bed tired and wake up rested, you need a new hole in your belt, pulling it tighter, your chest as firm as your arms, your hands coarse and strong for a change. We have Fitz to thank for leaving us the work, but you have to ask yourself, why didn't he savor it himself, "the stout pleasure of juggling stone, Elizabeth, the weighty gratification of a personal monument. Apparently he was never that desperate," I said, and stumbled forward, falling, as I shoved a massive stone sideways into place.

"Are you all right?"

I hadn't noticed her come across the field, wheeling the bike by her side. I stood up, brushing the front of my pants. There were superficial scratches on my arms and across my stomach, barely breaking the skin, like a woman had taken her nails to me. "Lost my balance," I allowed. "That monster was heavy."

"Who were you talking to?" she smiled. "I could hear you from over there."

"The stones need to be coaxed, they like to be flattered and cajoled."

"You're going to split a gut if you aren't careful."

Sweat running down my spine, still panting, my blood seemed to block my ears. I waved at hovering gnatlike insects with my honey-colored bee hat. "What brings you over?"

"It's Friday again." She lifted a paper bag from the basket attached to the front of the bike. "I brought a single malt and some bread and Stilton. I called a couple of times; your machine wasn't on."

"I've been out here all day." Indicating the completed length of wall. "I've done that much since I last saw you. Improving the property."

Setting the bike on the ground, she climbed onto the wall and walked along the top of it for ten feet or so, sneakers so white they had to be new, hands on hips. Her jumper was linen—Elizabeth had bought something similar for her trip—her shirt lavender, cuffs folded back. I knew her wristwatch was Swiss Army somehow, although I hadn't noticed it before. "Feels pretty solid, Henry." She confidently jumped to the ground. "I bet it's more fun than sitting at your desk."

"What time is it?"

"A little after five. Cocktail hour, remember?" She reached out and pressed her fingertips to the bony top of my shoulder. "You're burned, my friend."

"Tired of being pale. I want to feel like a he-man again."

"Your shoulders look like raw meat. Is that what you mean by he-man?" A fleck of lipstick on her teeth when she smiled. Her dark hair, glinting various colors in the late afternoon light, gave a clean fragrant scent in the warm air. "So here I am. Remember your invitation last week? How about it?"

"I'm a mess. I need a shower."

"How long can that take? Why was your machine off anyway?"

"I got sick of that little red light," I told her. "It was ruling my life."

"I'll wait outside," she said as we reached the house.

But when I returned to the yard, showered, shaved, and so on, like you've got a blind date, I thought, she wasn't to be found. The air was remarkably still, the evening light gave the surrounding dense green foliage a burnished glow. The dark behind the trees, leading into the woods, was black. The song of a hermit thrush, which I'd learned to distinguish from its cousin, the wood thrush, arose from inside those woods, ethereal, mysterious, yes, bodiless and unearthly, Elizabeth, that's the word for it, so that the stillness that followed was even more profound, as if, as I listened, I was aware of the woods and sky around me listening, the silence listening, and in that instant my daughter's face appeared, seemed to appear—no, not really her face, but an intimation of her presence—in the red-gold clouds on the western horizon, tinged by the evening sun, and I heard her say, It's okay, which were among the very last words she spoke to us, her mother and me, and those words were followed now by the pure flutelike sound of the thrush again, causing me to cry out hoarsely, staring at the sky, unable to understand any of it, a young woman dead and me alive to know these moments of such inextricable beauty and pain, in which the longing to live cannot be separated from the longing to die.

My eyes were deftly covered from behind, fingers pressed them closed, causing me to freeze.

"Boo," she said.

We sat on either side of the picnic table, the French bread and Stilton cheese and our glasses between us. We sipped scotch and flirted with the food while she talked about the manuscript she was working on, the serenades of coyotes lately, movies last seen, etc., until dusk, when she unrolled her shirtsleeves and began reaching below the table to smack her ankles. Being eaten alive, she said, and she went to some trouble, as she attempted to stand, extricating her long legs from under the table. "I think I'm drunk, I'm not used to that devil whiskey," hissing the word.

"I better give you a lift home. It's too dark to ride your bike."

"It's too dark to go home," she said. "I'm sick of that place. Aren't you starving?"

New Hampshire public radio was playing Mozart violin concertos, which was enormously helpful as I sautéed spinach and garlic and walnuts, the large pot of salted water set to boil on the back burner. I couldn't call you, could I, and yet you had no way of knowing what might be going on with me, so why not check in after two or three weeks? Postcards are a decidedly one-sided mode of communication, aren't they? Maybe I'd amputated my leg with a chain saw or hanged myself in Fitz's barn. People hang themselves in Vermont. Maybe I wanted to talk to you about something important, Elizabeth.

"How's that," she said, "enough?" Holding up the teakwood bowl of salad greens—mustard, arugula, red leaf, spinach—which she'd rinsed and spun dry and torn into bite-sized pieces.

"Loads," I said. "The oil and vinegar are in the right-hand cabinet." You were always a passionate salad-lover, weren't you? Well, we've had the best salads here in old Vermont this month. You discouraged me from planting the garden, Fitz's garden, but you should see it, baby, it's wild, it's quite wonderful. You mean you never had a hankering to hear my voice? Each time I left the house, I anticipated your voice on the answering machine when I returned. No such luck.

"God, this is beautiful," said this Helen, rapidly becoming ever more familiar right there in the kitchen as she mixed up our salad dressing in a water glass, referring to the Mozart, which happened to be the Third Concerto. "What was he, twenty or something when he wrote this?" Her fingers were long and very pink beneath the unpainted bluntly trimmed fingernails. A violinist's hands.

"Even younger. Seventeen or eighteen, I think."

"How old was he when he died? My age?"

We listened to the piercing adagio. Helen quietly tossed the salad. I sampled the boiling linguine. The kitchen was comfortably warm and warmly lighted. Should have been there, Elizabeth, I think that's what it comes down to, I thought, addressing her in some future confrontation. I shouldn't have been holed up alone in Vermont all summer and you shouldn't have been traveling through England with Lynn. Elizabeth the unreachable.

I resisted the potentially cruel temptation to use the large cream-colored bowl from the cabinet next to the stove for my pasta, anxious that the sight of her farewell gift to Fitz might spoil the taste of everything for her.

Seated at the pine table, worn and scrubbed to a bleached smooth finish, we raised our glasses of cheap, palatable Montepulciano. Helen was smiling with compressed lips, a canny, provocative expression.

"This is hilarious," she said. "Sitting at this table with someone called Henry Ash. You're not supposed to be here."

"That's what I've been thinking," I said. "It seemed like a great idea back in New York during February."

"Did you know Fitz very well," she asked, "or what?"

"No." We saw each other maybe once a year during family gatherings, I explained. The sisters maintained a telephone relationship, which seemed to suit them fine. I was sure she knew far more about Fitz than I did, I told her.

"My Fitz experience was limited to a few weeks in the summer," she said, "but it was an intensive course. I sort of desperately latched onto him, he was so tall and twinkly and calm. We might have gone on to have nothing to do with each other, if we'd had the chance. Now Fitz has been stopped in time and I'm left where we were. I know it's nothing like what you've been through."

"How do you know what I've been through?"

"Of course I don't know."

"Thank you."

A long narrow face with dark prominent arching eyebrows. The inside of her right eyebrow intersected a vertical crease when she frowned. Imaginary vertical lines drawn from the pupils of her eyes would intersect the corners of her full mouth, I observed, as she bent over her plate. There were small silver rings in her ears. When she raised her eyes, I was surprised they were blue. Oh, a dark fleck on your oval chin.

"This is pretty damn good," she said.

I touched the skin below the corner of my mouth. "A bit of parsley or something there."

186

"Oh no." Brushing at it. "Gone?" Smiling, her mouth was framed by a double parenthesis of attractive lines.

"Gone." I hadn't had a meal alone with another woman since we were married, not counting Sally of course, not counting Margaret from the department, and it was quite extraordinary, Elizabeth. It seemed like a terrible mistake to forgo the pleasure of a stranger's company. There's so much information right under your nose, so much to observe and take in. I needed to do this more often, I thought, observing now that she was wearing contact lenses, which perhaps contributed to this blue, yes, and there were patches of roughened redness coming through the thin gloss of makeup just below her cheekbones, the onset of acne rosacea possibly, which had begun to afflict Sally in her thirties too. What had first seemed the bloom of health eventually made Toad look as ruddy as a drunken sailor, especially during times of stress. I liked the something vulnerable about such inflamed imperfections.

"Let me get the Fitz situation straight. He was the charming friend and neighbor in old Vermont or there was more to it than that? I don't think I understand just what was going on."

"We had our moments; I don't know where it was going. Probably nowhere."

"What about Mary?" I asked. "She was around, wasn't she?"

"One day Mary would seem like a friend and the next day she wouldn't talk to me. I wasn't into Mary. Anyway . . ." She seemed to reconsider her intended remark, then said, "Let's talk about something else."

"There's no dessert," I said, standing to clear the dishes.

With our coffee we sipped the whiskey neat, Knockandu, half the bottle gone by now, some bombastically heroic symphony on the radio. Moths at the window. We appeared to be all talked out.

"I'll run you home," I suggested, carrying our cups to the sink.

"I can't go back there tonight. It's too dark and creepy."

"You don't mean that. You've been there for weeks."

"Do you mind if I stay here? This once. If I go back there tonight I'll probably sit up until dawn. I can't face that, I feel jittery, like anything can happen."

"Tell me what could happen."

"I could start having thoughts I don't want to have. I don't know what comes over me. Suddenly I'll think how simple it would be to get into my car and drive it into a bridge abutment at a hundred miles an hour. How easy it would be to hang myself with the clothesline in that shitty backyard. These thoughts come into my mind as if I'm really going to do it, I must go through with it, I can't help myself. Even though I desperately don't want it to happen."

"Like the night you called in a panic?"

"Yes. It's terrifying. Do you understand what I'm talking about?"

"No, I can't say I do."

"I don't want to be alone, that's all. I can sleep down here on the couch."

"I'll get you a blanket and a pillow. What about your eyes?" I asked.

"My eyes?"

"Don't you have to take out your contacts and put them in a sterile solution or something?" Elizabeth, for example, couldn't be caught overnight anywhere without the paraphernalia for her contact lenses.

Puzzled, Helen said, "I don't wear contacts. My eyes are one of my strong points. What gave you that idea?"

"I don't know."

I left my door open, as usual, and remained alert for any sound of movement from downstairs. When I got up to take a leak, I couldn't resist quietly descending the staircase partway—nut descending the staircase!—to see if there was light coming from the living room, the cold light of a computer screen, for example. Fortunately, it was dark. I'll just sleep in my jumper, she'd said, it can't get much more wrinkled than it is. *No problem, Henry.*

Maybe we've been miserable long enough, Elizabeth. Here's Fitz the tall and twinkly and calm, fretting about how to be, up to his neck in regrets and misgivings and missed opportunities, hoping for some change to visit him from left field and set him straight. Then he walks into the garden and drops dead. Given the prevailing senselessness of life, we might as well do as we please. Have I said that before? These hard years haven't been fair to you, and our present unhappiness isn't fair to either of us. You should have your life, and I should have mine, whatever that may be. We're stuck and we have to get unstuck. Here endeth the first lesson of Vermont.

"Henry?"

Curiously, I hadn't heard her come up the stairs. She stood in the doorway holding the pillow and the blanket against her body with both arms. Bare feet, I thought as she walked across the room.

"It's too weird down there by myself. I'll just flop here, okay?" When I didn't answer her, she quietly laid herself down on the other twin bed. "Oh, that's better, I can stretch out my legs."

You're dangerous, I thought, you're out of control.

"Good night," she said, exhaling an emphatic sigh.

"Good night."

A long lonesome cry, brilliant and resonant, pierced the dark outdoors, riveting me as I lay there, and soon followed by an eerie high-pitched yodeling like a fit of howling hysteria.

"Listen!"

"Shh."

The cacophony rose and subsided, a swarm of maniacal creatures, finally reaching a crescendo before it abruptly stopped, as though a switch had been thrown. Silence surrounded us again.

"I love that," Helen said, "the wildness."

"I haven't heard them so close. They sounded like they were right there in the woods."

"I wish they'd been around the other night. Adam and Jane were dying to hear them."

"You forget they're out there," I said.

"I saw one going across Graves's pasture when I first got here. I was on my bike. It was tall and its fur was thick, a sort of brindle, beautiful. Walking fast in a straight line. I felt like Little Red Riding Hood. But in a good way," she added. "People used to shoot them on sight. They comfort me."

"Do they?"

"They remind me of everything that has nothing to do with us. We're not the only thing here, my life isn't that important."

"You need coyotes to tell you that?" I said. "Trees and toads and sunsets must have the same effect."

"Oh they do. How about flying geese? I *love* them."

"I saw the bear when I first got here. Sauntering around the house."

"*The* bear? There's just one?"

"You're right, the sight of him was comforting."

"Fitz loved them too. Coyotes. One night he stood out in the field howling, hoping for a response. No answer. Which is worse," she said, shifting her weight on the bed, "consciously slowly dying, aware of leaving, or being snuffed out without warning like Fitz was? Or which is better, let's put it that way." She was facing me, propped up on her arm.

My pulse accelerated.

"He didn't suffer," she continued, "I suppose that's to the good. Wham, like a bolt of lightning. But I think Fitz would have wanted to know, to go through it."

"To die," I offered, "rather than be killed."

"Yes. Doesn't it seem more unfair to get snatched away like that, without time to prepare? Everyone lives as though death is far off, but if we knew . . ."

"Of course we know." A forced laugh.

"People live as though they'll all get to be ancient and die in their sleep after they're worn out. It's this dumb society. They're sold gruesome murder and juicy bone-crunching violence all day long, for entertainment, but plain old inevitable, everyday death, never heard of it."

"They?" I asked.

"I don't think I'm going to live to be old," she said, "I don't live as though I have all the time in the world to do nothing. I try to pay attention."

Helen's words paraphrased statements my daughter had made to me when I was still hopeful that she would be completely well, cured of her illness. Until then I had no intention of allowing her plight to enter the conversation.

"My daughter was conscious of her dying until her last breath. She baffled and astonished me. Right until the very end, though, she was living, she went on being herself, living each day as it came—not dying—until she ceased to be." I gave up. "What am I trying to say? I'm not making myself clear."

"That's what I mean about Fitz. He was robbed. I want to know, I don't want to be snuffed out by a car crash or a heart attack."

And the *thoughts* she'd talked about: what did they represent?

"They scare me, but that's not me." After a pause she said, "Are you afraid of dying?"

"I don't know."

"You don't?"

"I'm not dying."

"Exactly. And you can't imagine it."

"I've thought my daughter has changed me in that respect. She's shown me how to die. I can die if I have to. But I suspect if I was diagnosed with something dreadful tomorrow, I'd be very frightened. We can't help ourselves. We want to be alive."

"Everyone is afraid to die?" She added, "Like me?"

"Everyone wants to live until living becomes impossible. Then you concede. I saw my daughter come to that. She couldn't change it. She sat there with us, completely herself, talking, making decisions, even joking, waiting to die. From Saturday to Wednesday. We said good-bye and she died. It remains unbelievable to me. It happened."

"It sounds like you did okay, Henry."

"I believed I was doing all I could. Now I regret I hadn't been with her more, said more, done more, understood more. The longing can be unbearable."

"You'd always feel that. You can never do enough, can you?"

"She wasn't a child, she only wanted so much from me."

"You wouldn't want her to be suffering if it had been you that died. You'd want her to enjoy life, you'd want her to be happy."

"Of course."

"Well, that's what she'd want for you."

"I know that. I'm working at it."

"My father," she said, and she laughed, "he's never had a conversation with me about my mastectomy. Here's a smart, well-educated, successful man with a new young wife, and we've never talked about what's happened to me."

"That's nuts."

"I've run the gamut of emotions about him. He can't help it, he can't face this. You know what, I forgive him. It's easier for me to let him off the hook. My anger was only hurting me. He wasn't even aware of it."

"That's smart."

"I expect nothing from him, which gets lonely, but I think it's lonelier waiting for something that's never going to happen."

"I understand," I said.

"You make a pretty good roommate slash girlfriend, Henry. I feel like it's three in the morning our first night in the dorm."

"The Fresh Air kids from New York," I muttered.

"The what?"

"Nothing, a bad joke."

"When this happened to me, I was a wreck. My breast! I was afraid all the time. The cancer would come back, I was going to die. I was jealous of anyone who seemed normal and happy. There were two essential friends in New York. Without them . . . I can't imagine . . ."

"You seem to be doing well. Have I said that to you before?"

"I can go along just fine for months, then the fear moves in on me again. The news about Fitz floored me. I almost left, but that felt like running away. Adam and Kelly saved the day. Our bonfire. But here I am in this funny little bedroom with someone I hardly know. That can't be a good sign, can it? You must think I'm demented."

"I'm in here with you," I said, "what's that make me?"

"You're a brick, Henry, despite your severe demeanor. I was pretty sure about you."

"How so?"

"You have kind eyes."

"That sounds a little phrenological of you."

"I trust the eyes." A moment later she said, "You want to hear something crazy? I thought if I had a kid I'd be safe. If I had this little person to be completely responsible for, who was completely dependent on me, I'd *have* to be all right. Love would triumph. Or maybe the miraculous biochemical event of pregnancy and child-birth would destroy any incipient cancer cells. I couldn't be preg-

nant and get sick at the same time, that would be too awful. If I had
a baby, I couldn't die. How's that for logic?"

"It makes absolutely no sense. On the other hand it sounds as
plausible as any other plan."

"I was positively serious, frantic. But then there was no one volunteering to be stud of the month," she said, "so end of story. I
couldn't go the sperm bank route."

When I awoke Saturday morning, surprised I had slept, she was
gone, although it was not yet six. Her note on the kitchen table,
scrawled on a piece of paper taken from my desk, only said, "Talk to
you soon. H."

*Yorkshire had stone barns and undulating downs and the men in
pubs wore caps. Thirsk was the setting for all things great & small.
We shambled through crowded York. Another cathedral! Gigantic
roses. Sore feet! Today we split for the North Sea, dying for a change
of horizon, and found the most spectacular Dover-like limestone
cliffs packed with gulls and lovable puffins. Lynn burst into tears.
This is our holiday's holiday. Our B & B has bowling in the
backyard and birdwatchers in the bar. Tea and scones with coddled
cream and jam every day at 3:00, but I'm skinny from hoofing it.
Hope your monkish devotion in Vermont is fathering a masterpiece.*

Love, E.

It was a postcard of Edinburgh Castle darkly towering above
Princes Street Gardens. This discrepancy between the purchase of
the card and the writing of it disappointed me. Why? I thought.

As if Scotland had been a turning point, their southward journey
was characterized by a certain impatience. They couldn't be bothered
tracking down points of interest in dour, blackened Edinburgh and

only spent one night there. The beauties of Yorkshire, its dales and stone barns and cobblestoned town squares, would have thrilled them more, they realized, if they had seen this part of the country before Dorset or the Cotswolds, the Peak District or the lakes. They began to voice their differences. Lynn drank too much; she'd rather piss in the sink in the middle of the night than leave the room to use the toilet; she would tell her life story to anyone who asked; she couldn't pass a gift shop without examining the junk inside; she had to stretch or meditate or whatever she did for twenty minutes every morning in her underpants. Whereas Elizabeth's need to control the itinerary and schedule the day's events, Lynn told her, her picky attitude toward food, her complaints about the lack of privacy, her plain unfriendliness toward strangers trying to be helpful could drive Lynn "up the fucking wall sometimes." They were sick of the English breakfast each morning and the bloody carving of lamb or beef with boiled vegetables at night. They were sick of their clothes, the same two or three getups one day after the next, the sight of one another from morning to night, the tiny interior of the little red car, almost every aspect now of life on the road. One rainy day in Richmond Elizabeth spent the afternoon reading in the room of their B-and-B (*Pride and Prejudice*), which felt wickedly indulgent, while Lynn went out shopping for shoes and returned in a new summer dress with all her hair cut off. "Do you love it?" she asked. "I love it," Elizabeth told her. The new Lynn was a relief. They'd anticipated a few days in York, the medieval walled city, but found it too crammed with tourists, too hot and smelly and commercial. They fled the next morning for the coast, seeking sea air, and came by chance—Elizabeth's arbitrary hunch—to Flamborough, where spectacular chalk cliffs faced the North Sea.

The tall massive cliffs went on indefinitely in a sinuous line sculpted with undulating uniformity—ribbon candy, Lynn said— and craggy with carved-out caves and recesses and arches. Lush brilliant grass grew to the very edge of them. And woven through the grass along the edge there were dense cushions of something grasslike with pinkish-lilac flowers in clusters. "Armeria, dear," an older woman told her, "or sea pink. Isn't it perfect?" Enormous and boisterous colonies of birds, gannets, an Englishman informed Elizabeth, as well as puffins, and various gulls, including kittiwakes, he pointed out, inhabited these cliffs, making Flamborough Head a birders' paradise. Like something otherworldly, thousands of birds floated and sailed in and out of mist and fog below them. "It's the real wild thing, isn't it?" the Englishman asked, clasping Elizabeth's arm. He had binoculars, a 35mm camera, and a video camera, as well as a raincoat, an umbrella, and a three-legged collapsible stool with a triangular leather seat. "I'm touched, I'm disturbed, I'm astonished," he said, and there were tears running down his wind-burned face. "Yes," Elizabeth agreed, "astonishing." But she didn't need birds to be bowled over by the beauty of the place. They found a room at the Flameburg Hotel, a small place run by an emphatically cheerful middle-aged couple, and decided to stay the weekend.

The fog shrouded Flamborough Head each morning, but the day brightened by midafternoon, when she could discard her sweater. She spent hours walking above the agitated sea, watching the birds drift on still wings in and out of view. Happiness was non-sense, but on their second day she felt happy here. The wet salty breeze in her face, the racket of these seabirds, the deep churning of the water below—yes, happy.

She followed a gull, maybe a kittiwake, as it glided directly into the fog fifty feet below her and disappeared. You wanted to believe in an afterlife, the everafter of the soul, but you couldn't believe it. What did people mean when they talked such stuff? What was the point? They didn't mean you didn't die; they meant some special part of you, that soul of yours, lived on somehow or other. In the hereafter. What did people mean when they talked about knowing their dead mother was looking down on them: I know she's listening, I know she's watching, I know she knows everything that happens. What a horrifying idea. Your mother, who didn't know anything about you while she was alive, began to get the whole picture now that she was dead. Your daughter is in a better place, your daughter has gone to a better place, your daughter's better off. Henry wanted to wring their necks for such sentiments. I know we'll meet again. What was the point of such folderol? How was that a comfort? It didn't change your wretched life on earth one whit, did it? Gustavo believed in God, to take one example of a believer. Oh, that was rich, tirelessly finagling his connections to puff up his career as the man who could make art out of other people's tragedy. Our Father who art in heaven's got everything under control. Let the rivers of blood come down, we've got it covered. How could people talk about God's will, for heaven's sake? As though all the pain and suffering was good for us. First of all I want to thank God for helping me win this Grammy Award. My thanks goes to God for this Super Bowl trophy, which really belongs in His trophy room in the sky. Thank God, God decided to save me while He was wiping out everyone else in that plane crash, that hurricane, that typhoon, that genocide, that cancer ward. I don't know why I'm alive, but I thank the Good Lord, He must have had His eye on me while everyone else was going down the tubes. God's will works in mysterious ways, all right.

No, she didn't want to believe in a hereafter after all. This was plenty, thank you, the here and now, this was mystery enough, unfathomable enough, miracle enough. I'm with Henry on that score. This place even looked like heaven in this light, although the life-and-death battle went on minute by minute, the birdshit was flying, and they squawked about it, all right; these winged creatures raised a bloody ruckus as they glided and flapped between nesting site and sea, their paths of flight crisscrossing bewilderingly. Insatiable angels in paradise. Twice she had spotted dead birds floating on the water. Life was too beautiful and too ugly, too much and too little, too long and too short. There were no healing answers to what went wrong and no good reasons for what went right. As she looked out over the cliffs abounding with birds, half-obscured in blowing mists, her personal predicament appeared quite clear and uncomplicated to her. If you were alive, you had to live somewhere. She was with Henry. Her life was with Henry. The decision was more than half the struggle, and the relief that went with it offered a kind of peace.

Her hand went to her chest, touching the necklace she had told Gustavo she didn't want. By casually wearing it, she'd thought she could divest it of sentimental value, reduce the ornament to its mere thingness, whereas refusing to wear it endowed the object with too much importance. In fact, she had left the small blue box on the table at the Gore, she'd been so incensed with him, but the girl at the desk had retrieved it, and then Elizabeth couldn't bring herself to simply discard the necklace. Why was that? Because it was simple and beautiful and looked good on her, because it was worth three hundred bucks, because Gustavo had chosen it for her and wanted her to have it, because she loved the name lapis lazuli. She unfastened the gold clasp at the back of her neck and held the necklace balled up in the palm of her hand. So blue. It was imperative to reach the water rather than let it fall to the rocks below, so she needed to get quite near the edge of the cliff. Oh how foolish, how melodramatic. Well, I'm sorry. She hesitated. Kelly would love a lapis necklace, for instance. You didn't throw money away. She reached back with her left hand and aimed high, spinning the necklace out into the air. Unfortunately, she couldn't lean out far enough to see where it landed.

"Elizabeth!" Lynn came toward her at an awkward arm-swinging jog, handsome in her white fisherman's sweater from Inveraray. "Look where you are!" Her friend took her arm with two hands. "You're too close. Get back."

"I feel happy today. I feel revived."

"Did I see you throw something?"

"Oh, nothing."

"Look where you are. Come away from here."

"Where have you been all afternoon?" she asked, allowing herself to be led back from the cliff.

Lynn had driven to Bridlington, exploring, and ended up at a vast sandy beach, complete with donkey rides, where she'd taken herself for a long walk. It was warmer there. One distant length of the beach, distinguished by large rock formations, turned out to be a nudist scene—a dozen or so middle-aged men, nonthreatening gentle souls, strutting their stuff in the breezy buff. "They looked so odd naked—amorphous, creaturely, with this fuzzy blur of fur in the middle."

"Were they all together?"

"Everyone seemed to be alone." One man was doing yoga, another meditating, a third seemed to be conducting an invisible orchestra, while the others strolled along the water at respectful intervals from one another, striking poses. "It was a movie. I loved it," Lynn said. "They were great."

"Did they mind you being there?"

A couple of them waltzed by to check her out, and she realized her hair had them confused from a distance, so she pulled off her T-shirt and went topless. "I instantly ceased to exist." She grinned. "So let's hear what you're so happy about."

"I miss Henry."

"Since when?"

"Since today."

"How did you figure that out—that you missed him?"

"It just came to me. I don't know how. I can't imagine the here and now without him."

"What a cute idea," Lynn said. "I'm glad."

Phyllis—*Phyll* to the regulars—had to be eighty-something, and tended the bar at the Flameburg Hotel with authority, impatiently twisting her whole body as she coaxed the amber bitter into the glass. Lynn was *Lovey* and Elizabeth was *Pet*. They hadn't intended to let themselves in for another city before returning to London, but Phyllis insisted that Cambridge was not to be missed, and she enlisted other customers, each more overbearingly chipper than the next, to support her view.

"You'll be a smash there, Lovey, and Pet will positively bring the house down. Oh, won't that be marvelous for the pair of you."

"You know we aren't exactly a vaudeville act on tour, Phyllis."

"Oh, but you are, Pet," said Phyllis. "Everyone's bonkers about you, aren't they?"

The new note Elizabeth detected in Phyllis's tone—the vain old lady didn't like her one bit—took her completely by surprise.

Sunday morning I returned from Baker's with the *Times* to find the light on the answering machine winking at me from its corner in the kitchen.

"Wow, Henry, that message is about as warm and welcoming as a wet blanket. You sound like the last man on earth. Are you there? We just got back late last night, more like two in the morning, or I would have called immediately. The apartment seems to have survived fine without us. Just stuffy. I have a little case of postpartum blues, I guess, but it also feels good to be back. Can't wait to talk to you. Bye-bye."

The sound of her voice, at once familiar and different, moved me more than I'd anticipated.

There was another message awaiting me in the afternoon when I returned to the house after several hours of humping the stone wall. "Where are you?" she said in a singsong voice. "It's me. Back in unbelievably hot and sticky New York. Grocery shopping practically did me in. I assumed you'd be slaving away up there. Are you taking the day off? Call me A.S.A.P. because I'm getting a little worried about you."

Later, just as I was replaying her saved messages for whatever veiled meanings I may have missed initially, the distinctly Vermont ring of the phone made me jump. All right, pick it up.

"I thought I better give you a break after the other night," Helen said. She had a chicken roasting in the oven. "Free range, Henry. Come over. It's my last Sunday up here."

"What time?"

"Now."

"I have a phone call to make, then I'll be over." I paced the kitchen, returning repeatedly to the postcards arranged in the order I'd received them on the refrigerator: the Tower of London, a mounted knight in heraldic armor, Virginia Woolf, Edinburgh Castle. I'm not ready, I wish I felt differently, Elizabeth, but there it is.

I contributed Swiss chard—we sautéed it in oil with garlic—and a bottle of Spanish wine to accompany the free-range chicken, plus carrots cooked in orange juice, quinoa with French lentils and parsley, and a tomato-onion-basil salad. The screened porch, already in dusk at the back of the house, was just large enough for the narrow table, covered tonight with a blue-and-white gingham curtain Helen had borrowed from a bedroom window, and two chairs from the kitchen. The tall bouquet of ferns, white mallow, and gold yarrow stood at the end of the table like a circumspect chaperon. Soon the woods outside our candlelit porch were pitch black. An intermittent breeze sounded like gentle rain and caused a nodding branch to brush the screen as though the big dark night wanted our attention. Solid puddles of off-white wax gathered at the feet of Helen's new candlesticks, tin hog scrapers she'd found in a Bennington antique shop. Her short sleeveless black dress seemed to cause her to cross her legs reflexively when she sat down.

"I've been happy and positive all day," she said. "I had a good talk with my friend Ellen, who is definitely leaving this dud she married six months ago. He looked great on paper, but turned out to be obsessive about his possessions. Too boring. Then I read something wild by a young unpublished writer named Kate Kenney. A girl is climbing a tree, drunk and pregnant. She falls, cutting her leg badly. The scene changes and she's accidentally drowning her infant in the kitchen sink. Then it flashes back to *her* mother giving her a bath when she's pregnant with the child she'll eventually drown. When her mother can't get her daughter's blood off some stones outdoors she buries the stones. That's just the beginning. I want to publish this kid. To celebrate I biked all the way to the mountain, I felt strong and tireless. And here I am dining with a new friend." She reached across the table with her glass and clinked the one I was holding. "How's that for a day in Vermont?"

"Perfect."

"What excitement did you have?"

"There was a message on the answering machine from my wife, back from her month in England. That was probably the highlight of the day."

"Is she coming up?"

"Vermont isn't her scene, but I don't know, maybe she'll want to get out of the reeking city after a few hot days."

"How was England?"

"Thatched, cobblestoned, half-timbered, stiff-upper-lipped, charming, ironic, bloody wonderful . . ."

"You're a dyed-in-the-wool Anglophile."

"I haven't spoken to her yet, I'm pissed off at her."

"Should I ask why?" she asked.

"She's been in England and I've been here, I guess that's it."

"Isn't that what you agreed upon?"

"Of course, that was the plan."

Laughing, she put her head back, then placed her longish hand just below her jaw, partially encircling her neck, and drew it down her throat, finally pressing the hollow below her Adam's apple—largest cartilage of the larynx—with three fingers.

"It's warmer tonight," she said. "I like it."

"Why is it called an Adam's apple?" I asked pointlessly, touching my prominent example of the thing.

"Because Eve stuffed it down his throat," she said soberly.

"Very plausible. Why are you frowning?"

"Nothing. It's silly."

"It's something. Tell me."

"Fitz asked me the same silly question once, that's all. Why is it called an Adam's apple? And that's what I said to him." She smiled.

"You must have done that," I said, tipping my head back. "The same gesture." I put my hand on my throat, pressing the hollow spot there. "Watching you, he had the same thought I did." The branch brushed against the outside of the screen, causing the candles to flicker. "A gesture revisited."

"It's a clever idea."

I want to see your scar. How could you say that to her? It would take an unusual woman to want a tattoo, wouldn't it? A butterfly where your breast was. What butterfly Fitz didn't say. Would you settle for a generic image when you could just as easily choose a black swallowtail?

We picked up the dishes and extinguished the candles. In the kitchen I said, "Let me help you clean this up."

203

"No, it will only take a minute. I want to do it."

A chaste hug, our upper bodies barely touching as we said good night at the door. "You better call your wife, she's probably concerned about you."

"She'll assume I've gone off for the day."

"Where would you go?" She folded her arms across her chest, suddenly curious.

"Italy. My son's going to be there. Maybe he's there already, in fact."

"A day trip to Siena?"

"Wouldn't that be nice?"

"I'll go if you will." She placed her hands on top of my shoulders to offer a maidenly kiss on the cheek.

Elizabeth picked up immediately. "I was worried, Henry." Her voice sleepy. "Didn't you know I'd be back today, the ninth?"

"I had it written down somewhere, but I couldn't find it. So how are you? How was the big trip?"

"Well, I'll probably never go anywhere with Lynn again."

"Oh?"

"She didn't want to get up and get going in the morning, she wanted to have big leisurely breakfasts and chat with strangers. Drove me crazy. She drank too much white wine every night, that was half the problem. And I couldn't drag her out of the shops. I'd want to go to the Tate and she'd need to spend the day antiquing."

"You'll have to find another best friend, I guess."

"Don't get your hopes up, Henry. Of course we're still friends."

"Even though she ruined the trip?"

"Listen to you. I just got back and you're being ornery."

"I'm joking. I know you had a great time."

"I had a complicated time."

"The limestone cliffs sounded pretty neat."

"The birds! Any creature that gathers in great numbers is creepy. A million puffins in one place aren't cute."

"Your postcards were ecstatic."

"That's what postcards are, Henry. Cheerful, reassuring. Do you expect me to tell the grisly truth on a postcard?" A pause. "How are you doing? What have you been up to?"

"Grunt work for the last few days."

"What's that mean?"

"Reconstructing stone walls. I'm getting the hang of it, I'm into it."

"What stone walls?" she asked, striking a familiar note of annoyed skepticism.

"Around the hay field. You know."

"No, I don't know."

"They wouldn't have been visible to you before."

"Oh good."

"Some sections of wall are intact. Most of it has partially crumbled and been overgrown with brush over the years, but the stones are still there. I like the toil, I'm becoming a he-man."

"Just what we need. You realize no one is ever going to notice. I don't think I've ever set foot in that field."

"I notice. You've been in the land of stone walls, Elizabeth. Kent stone, Dorset stone, Cotswold stone, Yorkshire stone. You can't imagine England without its bloody stone walls, can you? It wouldn't be England."

"Don't tell me you've got Mary's backyard looking like England."

"Not quite."

"How much is she paying you an hour, or are you busting your balls for nothing? I didn't think you were that fond of my sister."

"I'm crazy about Mary, but that's probably not why I'm doing it. Oh, I also have quite a garden going. We've had great salads."

"So," sigh, "you've been engaged in futility the whole time?"

"That's pretty strong language, Elizabeth."

"How about the reason you went up there? Are you making progress on that front?"

"Speaking of futility, you mean?"

"You said it, I didn't."

"I was getting into something, then I got thrown off. It's been difficult."

"Naturally. Who's we? You said, We've had great salads."

"I've taken to referring to myself in first person plural. The isolation has that effect."

"Don't you ever see anyone up there? How about those chamber music concerts in that church?"

"Kelly and Adam dropped in for the Fourth. With some Jane. Just here for a couple of nights."

"That must have been exciting for you. How were they?"

"Intrusive, agitating."

"Poor you. I'm sure Mary was given a full report of the visit. I haven't spoken to her yet."

"That reminds me, what's this about kleptomania?"

"What are you talking about?"

"Kelly said her mother was picked up in Saks for stealing last year."

"Oh, that was nothing. Mary was mortified, naturally. She made me promise not to tell anyone. I'm surprised Kelly mentioned it to you. That wasn't very loyal of her."

"I was surprised you hadn't mentioned it to me. What other secrets do you two have?"

"I told you, Mary was humiliated and I promised. What's wrong with you tonight? Why are you so pugnacious?"

"Tell me about the trip. Three highlights."

"Not now, Henry. I'm still exhausted."

"I haven't spoken to you in over a month."

"And you don't sound thrilled to hear from me, frankly. It's late. Let's talk tomorrow."

"All right, go back to sleep."

"I was getting worried, I mean it. Did you tell me where you were all day?"

"Just in and out. I forgot to check the machine for messages earlier."

"What do you hear from David? Anything?"

"I've had two cards so far. How about that? He's fine, he's on his journey. You know David."

"I've missed you. I wish you were right here in bed. He-man!" she added. "Sleep tight, Henry."

We said good night.

A dazzling picture of Mont Blanc from the French side was a marvelous find in the mailbox Monday morning—How about that, Elizabeth!—although it made me a little concerned because all this mail—three cards in two months—wasn't like the kid.

Dear Dad, Chamonix sort of sad, but the mountains magnifique. A relief to get here. Rode telepherique de l'Aiguille du Midi just for fun. Some great hikes. Bunking it in dorms or refuges (cheap). Annecy was Disneyland. Now at Val-d'Isère: the best. Good rock climbing. Want to do a peak, if I find a partner. Most everybody is with somebody. Lost my watch and broke little finger on left hand: no big deal. Might change plans and keep moving.

Your son, David.

You broke your little finger? He'd never broken anything before. And it was unlike him to lose his watch. That must have been a bad moment. Maybe he was lucky he hadn't broken his arm. Maybe he was lucky he hadn't fallen to his death. Don't even think that. Put that thought out of your mind. The emphatic phrase *your son* was not at all like David either. He's not himself, I thought, he's out of his element, he's been on his own in a strange land for too long. Most everybody is with somebody. The postcard wasn't dated, the stamp again indecipherable, so I didn't have any idea where he was at that moment. The mountains or Italy. Must remind him to always date his correspondence. Twenty-four years old and he was still writing a postcard without putting the date on it. He could have gone off on a solo climb, attempting a peak, after all, and . . . Put that out of your mind. He's fine, David's fine. A busted pinkie was what he said it was: no big deal.

I had begun at the east end of the north wall, which abutted a massive red oak at the edge of the private road. My goal now, I realized Monday, resolutely fitting one stone to another as they came to my hands, was to bring the north wall, progressing about ten feet a day, to meet the west wall, which had been in better shape from the start, with less brush to clear, and where the work had gone quicker. What seemed unattainable at the outset had gradually revealed itself to be the whole point, the Sleepless Hollow master plan. Couldn't see it before, that's all. You had to follow the stones, working away until you discovered where you were going. Same old story.

The red light was blinking when I returned to the house in the afternoon. Insistently, urgently. "It's me. This is my third call today," she said, "so this time I'll leave a message. I thought you were going to call me this morning. Wasn't that what we said last night? I hope you aren't trapped under some boulder you shouldn't have been trying to lift, unconscious. The heat and stench of the city are more obnoxious than I remember. Maybe I'll drive up for a few days after all. Should I rent a car, or do you think the red wreck is trustworthy? I'm going to sit here and wait to hear from you. I'm sitting here waiting, okay?"

But she wasn't in, at least she didn't answer the phone, when I called following a shower and a wonderful scotch, which I enjoyed seated on top of the picnic table overlooking the garden, feet planted firmly on the bench, rehearsing what I wanted to say to her, the evening serene and windless, hermit thrush, wood thrush, and veery all singing their hearts out, mosquitoes tolerable. I called again, following my soup and salad supper. On my third attempt to reach her, I couldn't repress delivering the lines I'd practiced for several hours at this point and had made up my mind to speak that night. "Me again for the third time. I thought you were waiting to hear from me? I've been thinking, let's go with the original plan after all, even though I'm torn and would love to say come up. I've worked myself into this altered state, via the miracle of solitude, I feel full, poised, and your arrival, while more than welcome, is bound to throw me off balance. You'd be climbing the walls around here within days, you'd have to return to the city, hating the solo drive all the way, and I'd have to begin all over again to get back to where I was, et cetera, and another month half gone. Of course, I want you to do what's best for you, so . . . here I am waiting for your call, Godot." Wishing I could retract that meaningless concluding cuteness the instant I uttered the last word.

The phone went off at six-thirty the next morning as I was putting the kettle on. She'd gone out to dinner and a movie with Lynn last night, she explained hastily, returning too late to call. "What's going on, Henry?" she asked. "When I went to get the red wreck I remembered the muffler was shot, so I spent half the day getting the damn thing fixed. Finally I'm ready to roll and I get this downer message. I thought you were dying for me to go up there. You make it sound like I'd be intruding."

"I'm just thinking in two days you'll burn out and . . ."

"If that's how you feel, I'm not sure I do want to drive all the way up there to feed the bloody insects and sit in the dark while you . . ."

"Listen to yourself." I laughed. "That's my point."

"No, I was eager, Henry, I couldn't wait, I even packed some stuff, but now you've completely squelched that."

"You know you couldn't bear the thought of being stuck up here, especially if I'm trying to work. Don't turn it around and make me the heartless villain."

"You astonish me, you really do. I thought you'd be happy I was coming."

"All right," I said, "it's not even seven yet. If you leave within the hour you'll be here by midafternoon. It promises to be a beautiful day. Once past Springfield the drive is a tonic. I'll pick up some filets, we'll have a cookout. We've got vegetables from the garden, we've got coyotes, bears, wood thrush. You'll love the sky at night. A ruby-throated hummingbird comes around twice a day. Okay, I've got a lot to do before you get here. See you soon."

"I can't feel good about going up there now. I'm hurt, Henry, you hurt me."

"Just hop in the car, you'll be here before you know it. Come on, I want you to come up. You must have pictures to show me."

"No, you've put a complete damper on my little surprise. I feel deflated."

"I have to go in four different directions for the meat, bread, wine, so I've got to get a move on. I'll see you this afternoon, I want to show you what I've been up to."

"I'm not coming, Henry. And don't ever make it seem like this was my fault. You always blame me, but this time it wasn't my doing." She snapped the receiver onto the wall. Beside our Sierra Club calendar, I thought, picturing her in our small kitchen at that moment, her startled eyes agleam with anger, her pale mouth spitting the words, "you bastard," as she paced before the sink in bare feet, I imagined, dressed in the terry cloth bathrobe, "You did it, you bastard."

"Good," I shouted, storming through the screen door, "perfect, Elizabeth," into the absolutely peaceful green fragrant yard. "Great," I shouted, causing a doe near the cluster of lilacs to bound across the field in hopping leaps, her snow-white flag of distress enormous as it flared straight up off the end of her.

Inexplicably, stones for the north wall petered out about twenty feet shy of the west wall, putting one hell of a damper on my big project. What should have been a splendid defining northwest corner was a baffling gap wrecking the whole works. Easy now, there's no obligation to finish something you never should have begun in the first place. The stone wall was nothing but a little diversion, a little recreational *hobbyhorse*, in lieu of the damned push-ups and sit-ups and pull-ups, all the various conditioning *ups* intended to keep your ass in one piece a little longer. You'd have to be desperate to spend hours and days and weeks toiling senselessly at a wayward project for nothing—for zero compensation—and yet the minute this ill-conceived project is thwarted, the moment you can no longer pursue the desperate *stone wall project*, you're beside yourself, the wasted hours and days and weeks are *ruined*. To have come this far only to be stopped cold. That's what you get for squandering your precious time and energy over the virtually invisible, the sublimely stupid, I thought, kicking through the ashes of the bonfire as I marched across the mowing.

Perhaps forty feet into the woods at the south end of the field— "C'est la vie, Elizabeth!"—I discovered a remarkably intact, isolated stretch of stone wall, which must formerly have been the southern boundary of the field. While I was reluctant to disturb a remnant of labors past, what could be the harm in putting these idle stones to work in my wall of the moment? I had only to cart them along the west wall in Fitz's efficient plywood garden cart, which could handle at least a half dozen substantial stones at a time depending on their size, and I'd have my northwest corner.

Madness, I was thinking an hour later as I trudged my third or fourth load of stone the length of the field, stripped to the waist and sweating my buns off. There would be numerous such trips, I foresaw, an endless journey of such trips. The slight, even trivial upgrade toward the middle of the field had become a Sisyphean obstacle by my fourth push. I paused to get my footing at that point, to shift the burden from arms to legs, and Fitz's garden cart began to roll backward—Do you see this, Elizabeth?—"No, you miserable . . . ," pitting myself against the weighted cart, "wayward, desperate, senseless . . . ," panting by the time I'd shoved over the hump there and was rolling for the unconstructed corner of the wall.

On the next round, Helen came striding across the field, waving, as I staggered behind the leaden cart.

"Hey, Spartacus!" she laughed. "What ya doin'?"

As I met the resistance of the upgrade, brought to a momentary standstill, she fell in next to me, throwing her weight behind the aluminum handle, grasping it with both hands, and the cart jumped forward. "One two three, go," she cheered as we dumped the load onto the accumulating pile.

"Be careful," I said when she seemed to lurch toward the cart under the weight of a too-large stone, "I don't want you to hurt yourself."

Shoving the sleeve of her white T-shirt up to her shoulder, she made a muscle with her right arm, her hand a fist. "I'm strong," she said. "Feel it."

"You're hardly dressed for manual labor." Pleated khaki shorts and bare feet in the Velcro-fastened sandals.

"Feel it," she repeated.

With thumb and two fingers, I squeezed Helen's firm bicep as though sampling a peach or an avocado for ripeness. "Pretty impressive."

"I guess so," the woman said.

The senseless chore went far more quickly now, with what felt like half the effort, Helen's sturdy, much smaller hands on the aluminum handle next to mine. Nice veins stood out along the tops of her wrists extending along her smooth tan forearms. Her face was soon flushed and damp and the thin T-shirt clung to the dampened skin of her back. Each time we approached the slight upward tilt of the field we broke into a brief jog, raising our heels to prance like a pair of ponies in their traces, our breathing audible. One two three, heave! We shared my gallon of water. By midafternoon we had carted all the stones I would need to complete the wall.

"Let's quit, Helen." I extended my hand. "Way to go."

She slapped my open palm, nodding. "I needed that. Look at me," she said, brushing the front of her soiled khaki shorts. "Is my face as dirty as yours?"

"Filthy."

"Why do men sweat more than women? I'm boiling. The river would feel great. Do you ever go over there?"

"I thought there was a river nearby," I told her, "but I haven't found it."

She hadn't been there herself yet this month, she explained, because the spot was just isolated enough to feel a little creepy to a woman alone. Her bathing suit was in the trunk of her car.

"See, I haven't had this on once this summer," she smiled, emerging from the house. Between the tan line left by various shorts and the snug bottom edge of her black suit there was a wide band of distinctly paler skin.

"I'll be right out," I said. I resorted to a pair of pinkish-splattered khakis, which I'd cut off above the knee while repainting our bedroom shell-beige during last summer's heat wave in the city. Remember our quarrels over colors, Elizabeth?

We followed the trail that led through the woods south of the house, Helen leading the way. But where I had always stuck to that trail, gradually turning west and circling back to the house, we now continued south down a steep unmarked bank until we met another narrower path I hadn't walked before. The woods here were beech, birch, and straight towering oak. Within twenty minutes there was the sound of moving water and soon our path ran parallel to a shallow rocky stream, never more than fifteen or twenty feet across, bordered by ferns, moss-covered rock, and outcroppings of granite ledge.

Helen looked back at me. "Beautiful," she asked, "or what?"

Around the next bend the sky opened up and the Bear River—as it was called, Helen informed me—cascaded over a steep step of expansive ledge, tumbling to a deep pool that spilled into two smaller streams around an upstanding boulder at its nether end. Helen walked in up to her knees and slipped under the clear moving water, popping up downstream, blinking and smiling, and I thought, Why are we so unhappy? When she lowered herself into the basin of whirling whitewater at the foot of the precipitous drop, leaning back and closing her eyes, I decided to leave her alone. I was floating on my back, observing a married-looking pair of unmoving cumulus clouds, when the top of my head gently bumped her shoulder, causing both of us—"Oops!"—to splash, startled. This struck a funny chord, tapping us in to the silliness of the whole situation—two grown-ups rather solemnly paddling around here as though this wasn't child's play—so we were suddenly splashing and spluttering and repeating "Oops!" and laughing in that way that provokes or permits the unguarded silly person *who still exists in you*, I marveled, to surface for a minute here. I couldn't remember the last time such *merriment* befell me, Elizabeth. With dark hair wetly plastered around her clean face, altogether unmasked by her uncontrollable yaps and grins, this Helen suddenly looked like a kid without a care in the world.

The skeletal remains of last year's so-called sweat lodge were nowhere in sight, and when I clumsily attempted to introduce the subject—"Kelly mentioned practicing savage rituals by the river, a sauna or something," I said—Helen steered clear, only volunteering that Adam was evidently the family expert on Indian rituals, and so I dropped it.

Back at the house she said, "I'm pooped, I'm going to go home and collapse, but I'll be here in the morning. I want to help you finish that wall."

No messages awaited me on the answering machine. You see the fun we could be having, Elizabeth, oh, you'd love to haul rock for an afternoon before hiking down to the uproarious river for a dip with the crawdads and deerflies and the little nibbling fishies. Feel it, I thought, lying in bed wide-awake in the dark, the moon in the window for a while, rethinking narrow fists on the aluminum bar of the garden cart like a nymph's hand on a satyr's single horn, smooth slender arm firm as an avocado, a sprinkle of freckles on her chest visible in the black swimsuit, all perfectly normal-seeming, sturdy calf muscles flexing along the path. I'm strong, feel it. Just feel it, oops, *so* funny, this slow getting-to-know-you song and dance, getting to see who still exists in you. Let's face it, you never wanted to be here, Elizabeth the unreachable, Elizabeth with two breasts and no scars or butterflies. What's going on, Henry, you hurt me. Honestly, aren't you afraid of dying? I don't think I'm going to live very long, but . . . how odd of us, two strangers bunking it the other night, that couldn't happen now after all we've been through today, one two three, oops, rethinking arms and legs, revisiting gestures and expressions. What next? I didn't know what I'd find in Vermont, you can't foresee what happens, like Fitz dropping dead picking string beans, snap, just like that, end of story. What's the fuss, Elizabeth, why all the sound and fury, you've got to ask yourself, alone in your bed on Tenth Street, Helen alone down the road, Kelly alone in her hovel, Sally alone uptown, me alone in a haunted house, everyone jerking themselves off to sleep probably, oops, oops, oops. Everyone knows it's now or never, and yet everyone is alone—everyone is *dead or alone*, Elizabeth—and nobody knows what's going to happen next, no one can plan it. Just remember I told you to come up here, those were my last words, leave now you'll be here in no time, we can cook filets and fuck ourselves silly, and you said no, that's what you said.

Helen arrived at nine with a thermos of coffee and those delicious little junk-food crumb cakes, wearing blue jeans today, a long-sleeved jersey, and a pair of large canvas gloves she'd picked up at Baker's, along with our snack, on her way over. Rather than merely interfering, as I feared she might, she was a willing apprentice, eager to be directed by ye old wall builder, and the big project progressed more rapidly and smoothly than ever before. At noon we went to the house and rounded up onion, arugula, cucumber sandwiches. By late afternoon we put the final, carefully selected capstones in place, fussing and rearranging a bit to get the crowning northwest corner right. We walked into the middle of the field to check out our achievement from a distance—our futile senseless invisible accomplishment, Elizabeth—and this Helen, taking my arm with both hands and turning toward me so that her forehead pressed against my shoulder said, "I'm sorry, but I could cry."

"Don't do that," I replied. "It's not that bad."

"It's so beautiful," she said, "it was such a beautiful thing to do, I mean it."

"Well . . . there it is."

"Let's give it a name," she said, tugging my arm, nudging me. "What do you want to call it?"

What shall we call it, Elizabeth? "How about The Wayward Wall?" I suggested.

"You're joking, but I'm serious."

"I didn't imagine calling it anything."

"I think we should call it Fitz's Wall," she said, "or the Fitz Wall." When I didn't reply she asked, "Well? What about it?"

I was nodding, pouting probably, thinking this over, squinting to bring the wall, which now—remarkably!—bordered the field on two sides, into clearer focus.

"Henry?" Tugging the arm.

"All right, Fitz's Wall."

With hands folded under her chin and elbows on the kitchen table, Helen leaned toward me over her empty plate—our supper had consisted of spaghetti with Pekarski's extra hot sausage, a bountiful mixed green salad, and most of a magnum of okay cabernet—her face, her sunburned nose especially, shining in kind candlelight.

"Thanks for today, Henry, for letting me help out."

"It's not every day you get to work on the chain gang."

"I feel bushed, and a little woozy." She smiled. "I better go soon."

"Will you be all right driving?"

She said, "I'm leaving Friday. I can't believe my month is up already. On the other hand I feel like I've been here for ages." She sat back in her chair. "Thank goodness you were here. I don't know what I would have done."

Alarm made me sit up straighter in my black Windsor chair. "Friday? We should have dinner tomorrow. A little farewell occasion. I'll make something."

217

"When's your wife coming up? Elizabeth," she said.

"We aren't sure yet. That's up in the air." Thanks to the wine, I said, "Listen, you can crash here if you want. If you'd rather not go back to your place." Jabbering to make myself clear. "Everybody's alone in their lonely little hovels, you know."

She smiled skeptically. "Crash?" she asked, raised eyebrows. "That sounds like it would hurt." She added, "I really appreciate the thought. A woman likes to be asked."

"You've already *slept over*, after all."

"Oh I better not. You don't seem like a girlfriend anymore."

"That's not what I meant, it really isn't."

"Well, it's what I mean. I think I'd like to stay, frankly, but that wouldn't be smart. I don't need to do something stupid to kick myself about all the way back to New York."

"Of course not."

"Us single girls have to use our heads or we just end up beating our brains out." She tipped back in her chair, reaching for the ceiling, a big stretch. "Of course, maybe we can make one little exception now that we've bonded over the stone wall." She sat forward again, bringing her hands down onto the table. "Don't look so frightened, I'm kidding. I'm not just another girl, am I? There are special considerations here."

As though downshifting into an abrupt change of direction I said, "Let's plan on tomorrow night. I'll do something special." I stood up from the table. "How about five?"

Turning to me when we reached her car, she said, "Give me a hug, I think it's safe out here."

She deliberately placed her body against me, the whole of her warm substantial body, as though to say, *I'm strong, feel it*, and the imprint of that forthright hug, the close piquant scent of whatever fragrance she was wearing, was still with me by the time I cleaned up the dimly lighted kitchen and stretched out on my narrow twin bed in the guest room for another restless night in Speedwell.

I reached into the barn-red mailbox at the entrance to Fitz's private road expecting nothing from Elizabeth, of course, now that she was back, and withdrew a black-and-white postcard of Lucas Cranach's 1526 version of Adam and Eve. Wonderful fruit-laden tree with entwined snake, peaceable animals, leaf-covered genitals. A thin, bearded Adam seemed to be scratching his head, perplexed or anxious about Eve's tangible offering, while she wore a knowing, daredevil, almost smirking expression, her left arm fully extended overhead, the hand grasping a branch, and her exposed armpit contributing a convincing dash of eroticism to the highly stylized scene.

> *This skinny guy reminded me of you, honest. Cambridge feels like Paradise Lost. Velvety green courtyards, huge amazing hollyhocks, the Cam with straw-hatted boatmen punting along, Market Hill festive with tables of fruit under striped awnings. This is where you* should *have gone to college! Marlowe and Milton were here! Lynn and I went to Evensong at St. John's College Chapel and fell in love with all those sweet singing boys. Think I'll have to zoom up to Vermont, after all, once I get back. I've got something to give you, it's ripe and it won't keep.*
>
> *Love, E.*

No, it won't keep, Elizabeth.

In Cambridge Lynn began shopping for souvenirs—enormous college scarfs for her nieces, a sweater for her sister, a cravat for her father. The city was full of attractive young men and women on bicycles, who frequently rang their bells as they whizzed by, tall on the seats, earnest, hair blown back, sitting pretty. An Englishman about sixty asked Elizabeth to dinner as she stood on Clare Bridge and watched the green water of the Cam flow beneath her feet. "Do I look that hungry?" she asked, and he explained, "No, you look perfectly forlorn." Not far from that city, James Rothschild's mammoth, vulgar and, to them, laughable Waddesdon, created to house a fanatic's collections of glittering, gilded French stuff, made her feel she was in a giant coffin. Like Vermont's town of the same name, Woodstock existed for tourists. Blenheim Palace, within walking distance of their B-and-B, bored them to pieces. They left Oxford within an hour of their arrival, unable to take another tour of anything. That evening, back in London at last, they dropped off the little red car at Horseferry Road and booked into a tiny hotel at Cadogan Gardens in Chelsea, a short walk from Sloane Square. The place had been recommended by Phyllis and it was fine.

Okay Italian food at a small place called Paradiso was a tremendous relief. They sat near the railing on the small balcony above the main room of the restaurant.

"We did it," Lynn said, raising her glass of wine. "I'm ready to go home."

"It was almost too long, wasn't it? I've had enough."

"Summer in New York. I'm sure that will get old in about two days. I've got to start beating the bushes for a job."

"I've made up my mind, I'm heading north as soon as possible."

Lynn would go into her engaging weekend guest mode, she said, wangling sudden visits to the Berkshires, the Catskills, Block Island, if possible. She intended to spend the morning at Fortnum & Mason stocking up on exotic relishes and preserves in fancy packages to dispense to unsuspecting hosts in their summer hideaways.

Elizabeth said, "You're welcome to visit us in Vermont at some point. Maybe August. If Henry's working, I'll be climbing the walls for company."

"You never called him, did you?"

"It was better this way—incommunicado. I've been very good about postcards."

"Why don't you call him right now. That would be a surprise."

"We'll be in New York tomorrow night." She sipped her Chianti. "I can wait."

"Maybe he won't want his solitude interrupted? Then what?"

"That's unlikely. It gets lonely in Vermont." She added, "I should bring him a little something, shouldn't I? I'd decided to skip presents, but now . . . I should have *something*."

Directly below them the four or five tables against the wall were pulled together end to end and places busily set to accommodate a large party.

"I'm glad we came early, it's going to get noisy in here."

"I like noise," Lynn said.

A busload of children flooded the restaurant, that was the impact, circling the long table, clambering onto chairs. Silverware clattered to the floor, and controlled adult voices called out instructions. When the dust cleared, it took a minute for Elizabeth to sort out the situation. There were three couples in their forties more or less, all of them white and evidently British, and there were six children, two per couple, she deduced, and the children, all between the ages of three and six years old, were Asian. Most of them were Chinese, and the others might have been Korean, she guessed, and Vietnamese or Cambodian. For all the hullabaloo, the six parents in the crowd remained calm, ostensibly delighted with the unwieldy occasion, and patient with the kids, who burst into sudden fits of seat-changing and blurted out, "Spaghetti and meatballs!" or

"Pepsi," or "Garlic bread," as though they were quite familiar with the dining routine here. The children were happy—at least there was no whining or crying—and each one of them, she thought— round smiling face, black straight hair, black bright eyes—beautiful.

"Here's what we were talking about," Lynn said. "Remember?"

"What decent people they must be," Elizabeth said. "Courageous really."

"They're your age, that's what I was saying."

"The children are amazing, aren't they?"

"They grow up into real people, that's the catch."

"Don't be smart."

By the time they were leaving, the food had arrived at the long table below them. Two of the children were in tears, one marched around the table, stomping, another spooned spaghetti into his water glass, while the smallest child had dumped his plate into his lap. Chatting among themselves while addressing the minute-by-minute demands of their children, the adults were imperturbable.

"I'd probably make a mess of it. Look how relaxed these people are."

"You'd be fine, Elizabeth."

"I'd destroy the poor kid."

"Why do you say something like that? You'd love it to death."

"Exactly," she said.

That night, lo and behold, she dreamed she was on the ocean at night with a boatload of Asian children. She recognized the boat, a white dory that had come with the cottage her parents had rented for years on the Maine coast. She was rowing the boat through dark clamorous seas, maybe Frenchman Bay, furious with Henry for not being there to help. Waves continually crashed over the bow, and with each wave another child was washed into the ocean, leaving a wake of helpless children in the water. Lynn shook her awake.

"You're dreaming," she said. "You were almost shouting."

She remembered the dream in the morning—how trite and awful!—which made it worse. "What was I saying?" she asked Lynn.

"I think you were saying 'Henry.' Calling his name. You weren't exactly coherent."

She walked down Sloane to Harrods, arriving practically when the doors opened, and immediately became defeated, traipsing through the men's department. She wasn't going to buy clothes, for heaven's sake, she wasn't going to buy a tweed jacket or good shoes, or a Liberty tie, she wasn't going to get him a wallet or a watch or a bloody chess set. As she fled the store, the window displays made her feel weak. How many more years could she endure . . . oh stop, forget that! Without a clear destination, walking was easier than the Tube or a cab. She marched up Knightsbridge to Piccadilly, then turned onto Bond Street. The day was overcast but humid, muggy. No, she wasn't going to buy him an antique table or a clock, a suit of armor or a chunk of garden statuary. The wounded toe, which hadn't flared up for two weeks, began to throb as she continued toward Regent Street. A gift from England! How about riding clothes, how about a whip? Honestly, Henry, what do you want? She wasn't about to buy him a damned book, that was certain, or a bowler hat. He didn't want *things*, was the truth of the matter, which made him impossible at Christmas or his birthday. Henry went around in the same clothes year in and year out. His dresser drawers were full of unused ties and shirts and socks from holidays past. One year she'd given him a handsome leather jacket and he'd never worn the thing. He had sweaters that were still like new. What could you do with a man like that? He wasn't interested in gadgetry, electronic notebooks, or cellular phones. He didn't golf, for example. He wasn't a collector of anything special. He sat in front of that damned computer until it was time to take a walk each day. Okay, Elizabeth, don't get angry, just get the gift.

Piccadilly Circus was loud and congested and hopeless. She

checked her watch: after eleven. She had to be back at the hotel by one in order to get to Heathrow on time. A slight panic seized her as she foresaw herself returning to the hotel empty-handed. Anything, Elizabeth, it's the thought, remember. Yeah, what thought? Lynn was at Fortnum & Mason. Wouldn't you love some royal marmalade, honey? She wasn't going to lug home a fifth of scotch when he could buy the same bottle at a discount on Broadway. That would be desperate. A sweater from Inveraray would have been perfect, she realized. The authentic, handmade article purchased in that real, wild place. Where was your head, Elizabeth? You always wait until the last minute when it's too late. Why had this whole gift issue just dawned on her with such urgency? Henry didn't care one way or the other. God knows, there was British knitwear all over the city, if that's what you wanted. All the way from Scotland, though, that would have been the point of it.

She sat at the edge of the pool in Trafalgar Square. Children waded in the water on the far side. Great numbers of pigeons in one place were repellent. You've got an hour, calm down and think. She fished her London pocket guide out of her leather bag and turned to the shopping section. Just back on Regent there was something called The Scotch House. There, Elizabeth, you see? She flew on sore feet. She became hot and bothered over the right sweater, and finally chose one almost identical to the bulky fisherman's sweater Lynn had bought herself, the sort of classic item anyone could use. She caught the Tube back to Knightsbridge, then raced down Sloane, scolding herself the whole way, racing, always racing. Lynn was already out front with their luggage, waving her arms, when Elizabeth reached the hotel, and almost simultaneously their cab arrived to take them to Heathrow.

"I could wring your neck, Pet."

"Sorry, I've had a frantic morning."

"I hope Henry appreciates it."

Their driver had been to the States three times, he volunteered, and he was eager to return once more. "I love Las Vegas," he said. "God bless America just like the fellow says."

"What fellow?" Lynn asked.

"Your Clinton. Isn't he the one?" He added, "Shame, though, isn't it?"

"Excuse me?" Lynn said. "Shame?"

"Can't keep it under wraps, can he, the poor devil?"

"What's he talking about?" Lynn asked her friend.

"Just get us to Heathrow, please," Elizabeth put in. "We're in a hurry."

At the Our Garden produce market I chose snap peas for a change of pace, some brilliant red peppers for roasting, and searched in vain for avocados that were ready to become guacamole. I drove fifteen miles in the opposite direction for fresh salmon, and another ten miles out of my way for a bread with character, the radio turned up on an old happy Fleetwood Mac tune at one point—"You make lovin' fun," I sang along—various of Helen's words and gestures from the night before replaying repeatedly, just something appealing about the woman, as Fitz knew, despite himself.

"I don't want to play games, Henry. Please call me today, okay?"

The second message was from my would-be dinner guest: "Hi, it's me, let's see, at about one o'clock. I've been packing and whatnot. I've decided not to come over tonight, after all, I'm a little blue, thinking about Fitz and this weird month here. I'm pretty sure I'll never be back and I think I just want to have a quiet time by myself this last night. It's been quite an adventure, these summers in Vermont. I know you'll understand. Last night was a fine farewell dinner anyway. I'm leaving first thing in the morning, hoping to get to the city by midafternoon so, let's see . . . I guess that's it, but . . . oh . . . I'll call later to say good-bye."

Only a bullying fool would pester the woman after she'd made herself perfectly clear. I refused to make an embarrassing spectacle of myself Helen's last night in Speedwell. Yet if I was a person who simply did as he pleased in such situations, I would have picked up the phone and cajoled her to come over after all, I told myself, looking closely at my son's postcard from Paris on the refrigerator door, *Nude Asleep in a Landscape*.

Picasso gave the impression of a man who almost always did exactly as he pleased. The various women in his life existed as flesh-and-blood muses, inspiring conspirators, or slavish selfless devotees. When his everyday living arrangements no longer promoted and inspired his necessary artistic output he changed them, period, plowing on from one woman to the next the moment the person he was with no longer suited his purposes. Picasso was a monster. Yet there were few artists as productive as Pablo Picasso. A large Picasso exhibit like the one a few years back at MOMA gave the museum-goer the impression that the indefatigable artist never had a bad day. Nothing interfered with his art-making—no depression, no disappointment, no frustration, no longing. The moment a relationship with a woman began to interfere it was promptly resolved. Picasso was a happy man; that's the impression one got walking through a colossal exhibit of his work, happy because he was always making art at a feverish self-renewing, self-inventing, self-sustaining pitch, which was possible because he always mastermined the circumstances that made it possible. Short bullish Picasso insisted on being in control of his life as well as his art, which was why he was so productive and happy, if he was happy, and ultimately why he lived so long. People in control of their lives are happier and live longer. Unless they come down with a dreadful illness. Unless they are unlucky. Why aren't we more like monstrous Picasso, Elizabeth? No one's like Picasso. There's only one Picasso and there's no one like him. Are all the hundred-year-olds jogging around the golf courses in Florida people who were always happy and in control of their lives? They're people who have mysteriously escaped countless fatal accidents and numerous mortal illnesses; they've been lucky, if living to be a hundred is lucky. Picasso seemed happy and productive right until the end of his life, but the last self-portrait wasn't happy. The artist in his last self-portrait looked monstrously surprised, as if he was astonished to find himself losing control of his life after all, astonished to be dying after being alive for only ninety-plus years, while there was still so much to do.

Why not plow under the feelings of others and just do what you want at all times? Because we grasp the other point of view, we respect other people's wishes, we don't believe our wants necessarily come first. We refuse to treat people like garbage, we try to be reasonable and considerate and kind, that's the problem, Elizabeth, we want to be kind and good, although that doesn't work either.

Waiting for Helen's phone call, I found it difficult to do anything else, even read the first sentence of the second chapter of Book First in *The Ambassadors*. "He had none the less to confess to this friend that evening that he knew almost nothing about her, and it was a deficiency that Waymarsh, even with his memory refreshed by contact, by her own prompt and lucid allusions and enquiries, by their having publicly partaken of dinner in her company, and by another stroll, to which she was not a stranger, out into the town to look at the cathedral by moonlight—it was a blank that the resident of Milrose, though admitting acquaintance with the Munsters, professed himself unable to fill," I read for the fifth or sixth time that night, unable to hold the sentence in mind or move beyond it. Who wrote such sentences, Elizabeth, and who read them? You can't read sentences by Henry James if you have something else on your mind. Chances are, your mind will never be free and clear enough to accommodate sentences by the Master, especially those sentences painstakingly composed for *The Ambassadors*. In order to read *The Ambassadors* you must enter an altered state, an *Ambassadors* trance, in which you are susceptible to zero distractions, especially the ring of a phone. In a fast-paced age of mindless distractions, James's novel will have few readers, Elizabeth, let's face it. Did you visit his memorial in London? I wondered, reminding me that just as I was anxiously waiting for the phone to ring in the Speedwell house, Elizabeth was waiting for the phone to ring back on Tenth Street in New York City. Just as Helen was getting on my nerves as I paced between the kitchen and the living room in Vermont, I was undoubtedly alarming Elizabeth as she sat in the bedroom watching television, I imagined, in our air-conditioned apartment. You're being a real shit, man, don't do that to her.

By eleven I knew Helen was not going to call to say good-bye as she said she would. What has happened in the past few hours? Are we not to hear from you again? "He had none the less to confess to this friend that evening that he knew almost nothing about her ..." I began for possibly the tenth time that night. I slammed the book shut—"All right, Elizabeth!"—I walked across the kitchen and just as I was reaching for the receiver to place my call the miserable phone—There you are!—at last went off, startling me, now that I was no longer expecting it to ring, as viscerally as a harmless garter snake underfoot alarms a person strolling through a sunny garden.

"For heaven's sake, Henry, I was getting really concerned and having horrible thoughts. I was ready to contact the Vermont State Police and send them over there to see if you were all right. Why haven't you called?"

"I was just about to," I said. "I was reaching for the phone this very minute."

"I don't hear from you Tuesday or all day Wednesday, so I call today and leave a message and you still don't call me. What's wrong?"

"I urged you to come up, remember, and you cracked the phone down, that's what happened."

"I was hurt, you know that. I was dying to see you when I got back, and you were cool."

"While you've been gallivanting around England with Lynn, I've been underground in Speedwell, Vermont, so a little misunderstanding is understandable, don't you think? You returned in a chipper mood of expectation, but I was buried in my own garbage, so you were bound to be disappointed. Do you want me to apologize?"

"I'm glad it's so crystal clear to you," she said impatiently. "You make it sound like you've been in the trenches, for crying out loud. What garbage? You've had the whole month to yourself in a beautiful place to do as you pleased. I missed you, I couldn't wait to see you, and you were a cold fish. I might as well be some tiresome distant relation you can't be bothered with."

"You're exaggerating. The upshot was I told you to come up, I'd have dinner ready. You hung up the phone."

"God, I hate that reasonable, holier-than-thou tone. You sound like a goddamn book, you know it. I'm sick of it."

"Are you?"

"I'm sick of being put on hold while you bury yourself in your *garbage*. It was a revelation being away from here for a change. There are normal people out there, Henry, laughing and talking and enjoying themselves. Millions of perfectly decent workaday people out doing things and going places and just living and being,

Henry, while you sit in your damned tower buried in *garbage*. You *asshole!*" she concluded, furious. "Yes, sick of it. You were a *zombie* while you slaved on that last thing of yours."

"Don't work yourself into a state, Elizabeth. Calm down."

"If you live with a zombie, you become a zombie, that's what I've realized. Going around England surrounded by normal men and women I felt like a member of the human race again. Look at all the people, Elizabeth. How amazing! We must stop living like zombies, that's what I promised myself. I'm not going to live like a zombie."

"I thought you couldn't wait to see me."

A pause.

"I couldn't, Henry," she said somberly, with possibly a dash of tears. "It's true, I couldn't wait to see you. I'm tired and sad," she added. "I'm hanging up now."

"Wait . . . ," I began, but our connection had been broken.

And what disturbed me more than that unhappy conversation with you was the fact that Helen hadn't called, as promised, and I was left to wonder, recalling the last few days we'd spent together, what must have transpired her last night in Vermont, what thoughts and feelings, that had made her change her mind.

I was up at dawn, but I waited until seven-thirty to dial her number. There was no answer—and no answering machine to take a message—there was only the obnoxious incessant ringing in my ear, which could go on indefinitely, I thought, stubbornly refusing to hang up the phone until the shrill ringing in the small sunless ski house, the lonesome Vermont semishack on its dirt road, became a kind of shriek.

The hazy overcast morning promised to be a warm humid day. The stone wall was finished, no more stone wall project to escape into, no more futile stone wall project to pit myself against and expend myself upon. I couldn't face remaining indoors and all that that implied. I wasn't prepared to get in the saddle again, to bridle my little Mac, and spur my hobbyhorse named *Loners* into unknown territory, Elizabeth. Not today. But I couldn't face the garden either, the futile and pointless chore of weeding and hoeing, thinning and trimming. A hemlock stood dead in the woods along the private road, a fifty-foot-tall eyesore that I glared at each time I came and went, but I was in no frame of mind to fool with the chain saw, the rip and roar of Fitz's saw. You can't face being either indoors or outdoors. Where does that leave you?

People hang themselves in Vermont, Elizabeth, the precious solitude of the sylvan setting provides an excellent dark-green backdrop for hanging yourself, whether you pull off an instantaneous orgasm in the bargain or not. A mature man who hangs himself to heighten his sexual response is right next door to committing suicide, you'd have to say. The big death is surely implicit in the longed-for little death. Ejaculating into a condom with a rope around your neck has got to be closely related to coming to grief willingly. Still, the preferred method of doing yourself in is probably the gun in the closet—the father's twenty-two in the closet, I thought, snapping my thumbs.

"Do you think it's here? Aren't you curious?"

I climbed the narrow staircase two steps at a time and went to the deep closet in the corner of the master bedroom, pushing past musty clothes on hangers, feeling blindly into the dark corners, and emerged a moment later holding an elegant little single-shot twenty-two rifle that I knew had once belonged to Fitz's father. Fitz must have contemplated shooting himself in old Vermont, you see, and Mary had come to the rescue. In my first investigation of the house the very day I arrived I'd spotted a small box of bullets in the cabinet above the refrigerator, which was evidently Fitz's combo liquor-medicine cabinet and still contained half-empty bottles of sherry, rum, crème de cassis (but no scotch, no calvados, no great bottle of wine) along with aspirin, Mylanta, various vitamin supplements, herbal bug repellent, cold tablets, tubes of Retin-A, Preparation H, expired suntan lotion . . .

There were probably more self-inflicted gunshot fatalities in Vermont than self-inflicted hangings. When Fitz considered shooting himself in Vermont with his father's twenty-two he was contemplating the typical way out. That must have happened before my time, Elizabeth, although it's surprising you've never mentioned a Fitz crisis to me, unless it was so long ago as to seem inconsequential—slipped your mind. Kicking through the kitchen door, I slipped a small bullet into the dainty rifle's firing chamber, if that was the name for it, and snapped the gun shut. Vermont meant True Cunt, according to Fitz, but Mary wasn't a True Cunt, in Helen's estimation. You and your sister are a lot alike, Elizabeth, you're awfully damn tight in your AT&T relationship, I thought, pulling back the hammer on the twenty-two. The gun had to be a freaking antique if it belonged to Fitz's father, who'd probably had it when he was a boy out nailing squirrels and chipmunks and starlings for a lark. E. Hemingway and V. van Gogh shot themselves to take two famous examples. I raised the gun and sighted along the barrel. Melville's son and Frost's son took their lives, the male offspring of monstrous American originals. There was a dull pop when I fired, plus the trivial sound of a single bullet tearing through foliage, and the thing I'd aimed at, a huge inedible zucchini plunked on top of the fence post days before, unscathed.

"Shit."

I loaded again, stalked closer to the humongous useless and tasteless vegetable and drilled a bullet through it. Reloaded and let the miserable zucchini have it again. Fitz's gun works, all right. Guns are frightening, Elizabeth. No one in his right mind wanted to have a gun around the house, and certainly no one in his wrong mind. Fitz couldn't have contemplated shooting himself if he hadn't had his father's quaint old twenty-two rifle in the closet. Fitz had too damn much in the closet, Fitz's closet was too full, wasn't it? I slipped another bullet into the gun and blasted—pop!—into the air. I reloaded with my back turned to the garden, then swung around, cocking the gun as I drew down on my target, and nailed the abnormally large green vegetable again, this time causing it to fall off the post. Frightening, Elizabeth. With the same haste that I'd sought and found the rifle I returned it to the back of the closet, and I flung the remaining handful of bullets into the woods behind the barn—"Disgusting!"—as though casting them out of the world.

With other people around, you have to watch yourself, to paraphrase a line from a Franz Kafka diary, but when there's no one around you have to watch yourself more carefully. I'd been anxious about my impromptu visitors, my sacrosanct solitude invaded, but now that all visitors had gone the Vermont getaway felt spookier than ever. Dutifully, I pushed the small reel-type hand mower over the tawdry lawn of red fescue, plantain, dandelion, violets, oxalis, emergent crabgrass. The lawn wasn't one of your hang-ups, was it, Fitz? You didn't have the obsessive-compulsive lawn disorder of the average homeowner, which is fed and nurtured by the poisonous chemo lawn services patrolling the suburbs, broadcasting brain damage and birth defects in their spanking-white trucks. Fitz the scientist wasn't fooled. The beautiful man. Helen had the nerve to lay her cards on the table, to make a grab for her private-sperm-bank-bridge-over-troubled-water, and you were saving it for some dreamed-up hard-on, although you couldn't resist at least one occasion of touch and go in the front seat of the car like a pair of fumbling adolescents, her nymph's firm hand fisting your old horn. What did she call you, a Fitzful?

It wasn't like her not to call as promised, I thought, swatting still prevalent, maddeningly persistent deerflies as I marched down the narrow forest path. The sun had burned through the haze and this aimless day had become all the more oppressive as the temperature rose higher than it had since my arrival. Two months ago, the summer now more than half over. Your own personal Vermont Yaddo: dreamer! What I'd always considered *Mary's place* had become *Fitz's place.* How could I have anticipated such a development, including the appearance of Helen, recalling her on the trail ahead of me, leading the way in Velcro sandals, on her sturdy freckled legs, the khaki shorts a bit baggy in the seat, her lively hair glinting in dappled woodland light. Beautiful here, huh? Overheated and eager by the time I reached ye old swimming hole, I hastily stripped and dunked myself.

"All right, let's give it a try, Fitz."

Climbing cautiously over wet slippery granite I eased myself into the turbulent basin of tumbling whitewater at the bottom of the resounding falls. A cry—"Boy oh boy!"—involuntarily escaped me. Bracing myself with my legs, I sat back on an invisible shelf of submerged rock so that the plummeting water pleasantly coursed over me. Oh that's nice. I closed my eyes—Boo!—recalling Helen lowering herself into this mind-blowing whirlpool a few days before, and then, comfortably adjusted to Fitz's former seat, I was visited by a fairly clear imagining of Helen directly opposite me in the water taking down the top of her black swimsuit, except in my shamelessly erotic version of the moment she wasn't exposing the reality and result of the radical medical procedure she'd suffered, she was simply and provocatively baring her breasts, a matched wholesome twosome in my fleeting fantastic glimpse, and as she pulled the suit down further, as it were, uncovering sparkling spit-curled pubic hair, I felt the pulsating flow of water suddenly become irresistibly—oops!—stimulating. I opened my eyes, startled and possibly ashamed of the pathetic, even cruel fantasy I'd succumbed to. Oh Helen, I thought for the first time—her name, that is, in just that way. Oh Helen.

With other people around you have to watch yourself, but when there's no one around you have to watch yourself more carefully.

A mist had become visible now as it blew off the top of the falls in the late afternoon light, a mist composed of thousands of tiny sparkling beads of light, and I was reminded—spontaneously—of the sight my daughter had reported to me very near the end of her life. A vision of dancing droplets of light had appeared at her window one night, which she accepted, or wished to accept, as a comforting visitation of angels. "It was amazing, Dad!" I spoke aloud, hearing her voice. Slipping under the water's tempestuous surface I allowed the familiar upswell of my longing and loneliness for her to pour forth as the now dark and numbing torrent of the Bear River cascaded over me.

Breathe, I thought in the next moment, holding myself beneath the surface, just breathe the water into your lungs, isn't that possible? Just stay down until you must take a breath and then breathe the water. But of course voluntarily inhaling water wasn't possible. I held my breath, I couldn't stop holding my breath, Elizabeth, and when it became difficult and slightly dizzying and then actually impossible to hold it an instant longer, I simply stuck my head above the surface, coughing and gasping, seeing stars for a second in the blinding sunlight, and deeply inhaled the sweet Vermont air, thinking then of how valiantly and brilliantly—without a thought of ever giving up—my daughter had struggled to live, prepared to live under any and all circumstances, to accept whatever limitations necessary to go on with life, and how well, how keenly and engagingly, she had lived until her last breath, until breathing had become absolutely impossible. That's the only way to be, I thought. The only way to honor the memory and the love of life of those who were *lost* was to go on living as fully as possible. The only way to honor life was to go on living. The only way to live was to go on living.

I dressed and quickly laced on the hiking boots and scrambled over the massive granite ledge to the path. The woods were illuminated now a spangling green-gold in the westering light, and the shining beauty of the place only fueled my urgency so that I soon fell into a loping jog. Come on, hurry. As I'd come to the surface of the water moments before, it had dawned on me why Helen hadn't called as promised. I'm feeling a little blue, Henry, I just want to be alone. People hang themselves in Vermont, Elizabeth. Every month of the year someone is found hanging from a tree in Vermont for one reason or another. Look at the trees, I thought, speed walking through the sun-spangled deciduous forest. Every tree in the woods was a hanging tree, every damned oak, maple, ash, birch was a perfect opportunity for self-destruction. It's a wonder there aren't men and women hanging from every one of them; it's remarkable there are any people left in the state. The only way to live, Helen, is to go on living. I slammed through the screen door for my car keys.

My daughter had come to grasp the *beauty and wonder* in the midst of all the everyday garbage, that's no exaggeration, Elizabeth. Beauty and wonder were words she was not afraid to use, and they could often apply to what others regarded as ugly or trivial. She wanted to live, she never questioned that desire, and yet she couldn't go on living. While everyone who gets to live, everyone *sentenced to life*, mopes from morning to night with hows and whys and what's the uses. The gravely ill person can often be the most hopeful and positive and alive person in our midst, while anyone in good health thinks he's Hamlet. That's fucked, Helen! No, the only way to honor those who have died is to go for the beauty and the wonder. That's something you've learned, I told myself, that's something that pain and sorrow has taught you. But you wouldn't know it, would you? You're still a *zombie*, you still don't have beauty and wonder under your belt, you're still afraid to live, I thought, speeding toward Helen's summer hovel fearing the worst.

For what I was bound to find when I pulled into the dismal sunless yard a mile down Emerson Hill Road had become very clear, it seemed. The Honda would be parked by the side door as usual, the small thrown-together ski house would be dark and unwelcoming, with no signs of life. I would be compelled to make the short impossible walk around the side of the dreary isolated dwelling to the backyard where the screened porch stood beneath the widespread limb of a venerable sugar maple. Oh God, Helen. I have these thoughts I don't want to have, like I'm going to drive my car into a bridge or hang myself from a tree in the backyard. That's not me, but I can't help these thoughts, which seem more like commands, like inevitable occurrences. Coming around the side of the house I would see the woman's body in the stylish sleeveless black dress vertically suspended from the mighty outflung limb. She'd been hospitalized following her mother's death, and again following an overdose of pills in the wake of her marital breakup, which had come on the heels of disfiguring treatment for the most devastating illness. "And now Fitz," I said, "her Fitzful," steering onto Emerson Hill Road, perhaps the most lightless and airless and altogether depressing stretch of potholed dirt road for miles.

"What hill, Elizabeth? Emerson Hill Road is no damned hill."

I accelerated anxiously as I turned left at the mailbox labeled *Platt* and I had to hit the brakes as I pulled into the small deserted clearing. The Honda was gone! I left the car running as I circled the house, glancing into the spare curtainless linoleum-floored kitchen, the vacant screened porch, the tacky wallpapered bedroom. The double bed had been stripped and the naked mattress and box spring made the room seem the unfortunate setting of impoverished acts. Okay, Henry, are you satisfied? She didn't hang herself after all. What was that about? I asked myself, taking deep slow breaths of relief. You panicked, pal, you became hysterical there for a minute! And yet I was still agitated, possibly more agitated, as I drove away from the place, knowing that Helen had indeed left and would not be back.

I pulled up to the Underhill mailbox at the entrance to the private road expecting nothing, of course, and I didn't immediately recognize Fitz's wide-brimmed straw hat—a detail quite forgotten—as I removed it from the mailbox and unfolded it. An envelope bearing my name in block letters—HENRY—dropped into my lap. The card it contained was a reproduction of Adolphe-William Bouguereau's sumptuous wacky *Nymphs and Satyr*, 1873. So she'd made the same daytrip to Williamstown this summer that I did. Her handwriting was of the almost indecipherably small variety that I associated with highly intelligent, fastidious copy editors. Was that how you began your career in publishing?

Dear Henry, I'm afraid the evening got slightly emotional and out of control. I intended to call but couldn't find the right time to do it. Then it was too late. Now it's three A.M.—who said it was always three o'clock in the morning when you can't sleep?—I know I'm up for the day, so I'm out of here. I just wanted to say thanks again— for that funny "sleep-over," the stone wall, some good food—and so long. I hope the rest of the summer is good to you. Isn't this painting pure Vermont? Would you rather be the satyr or one of these nymphs? (Fitz said: "Both.") I would have been happy as a nymph—

naturally!—but my Vermont days are over. At the last minute I decided the hat should stay here.

Take care. Helen

Walking toward the silent house with its blank staring windows and black screen door, I realized it was Friday. Another Friday, I thought, turning in a circle to take in the garden, the barn, the field, these utterly silent ten acres surrounded by their tall dense perimeter of woods. An unusually downcast Crusoe glanced at his reliable quartz Timex, Elizabeth, and saw that it was the cocktail hour, right on the dot.

6 *The Writing*

I sat at Fitz's stout old-world library table, which I had yet to regard as *my desk*, to scroll and rescroll through *Loners*, reading and rereading the summer's work so far, unsure where my meditation on nineteenth-century American originals was going or how to get there. I pondered Helen's card, which sat on the table to the right of the computer, unable to decide just what she meant by giving me this picture of four naked women tugging a reluctant man-beast into ye old swimming hole. Four luminously fleshy merry-maiden-types playing with a shy shaggy sylvan deity who appeared to be afraid of the water. Helen intruded, that is—Would you rather be satyr or nymph?—as I tangled and untangled various thoughts and themes concerning Melville and Whitman and Emily Dickinson, the loners club, I thought, the American genius club, until, almost midnight on Saturday, I pushed back my chair and strode across the room, my glass and the almost empty bottle of wine in one hand, and entered Fitz's musty workroom, which I'd sworn I wouldn't do.

Welcome to Macintosh. I clicked open the document entitled

Vermont and reread the entire forty-plus pages of the thing, with special attention to those sections pertaining to Helen, as though Fitz's summer journal was something for the beach, an irresistible page-turner. You're hungry to read about Helen, you're developing a Helen obsession, you're becoming a Helen nut. Be careful. Fitz's *Vermont* was even more engaging and intriguing the second time around, my left thumb on the command button and my right thumb on the down arrow. I'd forgotten very little, in fact, but my new insight, my new sympathy with this Helen gave new life, all the more poignant for being tinged with eroticism, to the Bear River episode and the sweat lodge episode and the moment in Fitz's car, for example, when the forthright lionhearted heroine slipped off her moist under-pants and thrust them into the man's lap. I leafed through the few photographs of these wannabe-aboriginals again, which also struck me tonight as both sad and amusing. Sad, Elizabeth.

"Poor Fitz!" I muttered, looking around the carefully constructed room he had built for himself to last his lifetime. The floor was wide oak; the real plaster walls had chair rails embedded in them, which must have made the plastering easier to master. The paneled pine door and the tall mullioned windows with their deep sills and beaded surrounds, as well as the beaded baseboards, had been handmade by Fitz. The facing on the bookcase was in keeping with the finish work on the windows. The ceiling was taller than expected, I realized for the first time, to heighten the feeling of space. It was a beautiful room. Good job, man. He'd left the wood-work natural, while painting the walls pure white, so the room had a soothing air of Shaker-like simplicity. A certain kind of gay man was drawn to the clean austere style of that celibate religious sect.

Fitz's secret life was no more pathetic or absurd than any-one else's secret life, your little inescapable inside self, your little inescapable thoughts and feelings, all the ever-present hopes and fears and pains and desires known exclusively to you. Everyone lived secret lives, I thought, seated before the cold light of another man's computer at midnight, which was what one meant by admitting that one could never really *know* another person, Elizabeth. A cliche that offered comfort to the profoundly disappointed. What are we afraid of, I ask you.

I clicked Close on *Vermont*, disappearing the document into the *In Progress* folder where I'd discovered it in the first place. I scooted the arrow across the gray field of the desktop, intending to hit Shut Down in the Special menu and noticed something I hadn't seen before. The Trash icon in the lower right-hand corner—below folders labeled *Letters, Harvard, Destructive Interactions*—was bulging in its cartoonish telltale way, as ostensibly full as a trash barrel on Broadway. Funny we hadn't observed that before, Elizabeth, Fitz's miniature garbage can.

It contained one item entitled *Untitled*, which only meant that while the writer had initially decided to save the document when faced with the choice, he hadn't bothered to give the thing a name. I hastily clicked the icon and got the inevitable message box: *The WriteNow 3.0 document 'Untitled' cannot be opened, because it is in the Trash. To use this item, first drag it out of the Trash.* Why hadn't Fitz gone into the Special menu and hit Empty Trash? Mere oversight, or had he been ambivalent about obliterating what he'd written? Maybe it was the hour or the wine, but I found I was ambivalent about moving *Untitled* into the open. "... First drag it out of the Trash" sounded like asking for trouble, salvaging something scheduled for oblivion. For all my infringements on Fitz's privacy here, ransacking his Trash felt like trespassing.

"Oh bullshit," I muttered in the next breath. Tipping back my glass of red wine, I shoved *Untitled* onto the desktop—effortlessly!— and of course opening the document—click-click—was about as difficult as flicking on a light switch.

Shangri-la, VT

August 21, '94

Dear Helen,

Now that you're gone . . . Sunday: languid, lacking. It's ten P.M.: Mary has gone to bed with her old friend George Eliot, a man of a woman, presumably. My *Destructive Interactions* has reached a crisis: will have to wait until I return to real life. Rest assured: the work is all there, I simply can't face the writing at present. I walk, meditate, fast, fuss in the garden: more like a monk than a man of the world. I'm mostly okay with this routine, and then I'll experience an inner revolt, heart lurching, anxious that I'm in a free fall from which I'll never recover, never be productive again: have I inadvertently committed some irremediable mistake that can never be clear to me? It's not like depression. I've thought I'm waiting for an event that will jump-start me and return me to myself: like an agnostic waiting for God to appear so he can go ahead and become a believer. No one I know will catch a whiff of this distress: the uncomfortable suspicion that I haven't followed the right path, realized my would-be best self: lived as I ought to have lived. I've rarely been at home in my own skin: how do you fix that? Life pissed away on personal ambition in a rarefied cloistered setting. My self-absorbed bachelorhood, redeemed by dogged achievement, wasn't pretty, but then escape into marriage was a matter of accommodation, convenience, safety. Of course I can love and care for Mary—in my way!—but the arrangement has always excluded whole mountains and valleys in each of us. Already in our forties we both accepted this lesser landscape. I never gave a thought to the *issue* of offspring: until now. An inadvertent irremediable mistake? Offspring: the word has wings! I've never mentioned Andrew to you: my traveling

243

companion when we were young men. Our lives diverged, the years passed. Can I tell *you* the truth? I think he was the love of my life. The other day I received a letter from his son informing me that Andrew died in June. I felt—I feel—frantic. . . . The urgent point of this letter: I want to see you when I'm in New York in September, I want to tell you what I haven't told you, I wonder what is possible, the wonder quickens my blood. . . .

Careful, buddy, leave things just as you found them. I returned *Untitled* to Trash, causing the barrel in the lower right-hand corner to throw its chest out, and closed that window. But then, as if reverting to an automatic reflex provoked by the bulge of the little garbage can in the corner, I darted to the Special menu and clicked—uh oh!—Empty Trash. Whew, I thought, as the message box containing a giant cautionary exclamation point appeared: *The Trash contains one item. . . . Are you sure you want to permanently remove it?* Anxious I might still unintentionally screw up, I managed to click cancel and hastily shut down the machine. "You're jealous?" I asked myself in dismay. "You'd begrudge a deceased man his last letter?"

"It's me, Henry, You've got to change that greeting on your machine, it sounds like I've reached an asylum in Finland, for God's sake. Aren't they supposed to be the most depressed people in the world, obsessed with the polka? Pick up if you're there, will you? Please?" A pause. "So where *are* you? It's two o'clock Sunday afternoon. Aren't you supposed to be strapped into your high chair in front of the computer drooling onto your bib? That's meant to be funny, not mean. When did we have that last dreary conversation, Thursday? You see, I've been a good girl and left you alone for two whole days. I thought that was a good idea. Actually, Lynn and I were visiting her broker brother—just the opposite of broke—and his frazzled wife and three kids on Block Island. We couldn't remain in this stifling city. I spent half my time taking ticks off Susie, Lynn's decrepit golden, with rusty tweezers. I notice you haven't tried to call me. Or did you try and decide not to talk to my machine? Anyway, the ocean helped clear my head. You were right about the misunderstanding. I don't know exactly what that was about, except it was getting pretty silly. I guess I overreacted, but I don't want to get into it again. Let's not, okay? Anyway, if you still want me to come I'll zoom right up there. I mean I want to. So . . . I'm here. Talk to you soon."

I dialed our New York number anticipating the machine, frankly, but the real you answered the phone.

"Aren't you screening these days?"

"I'm just sitting here waiting like a good girl. So . . . what's cookin'? The red wreck is right outside," she hastened to add, amping her tone to upbeat. "I bought myself a pair of indestructible hiking boots. Gore-Tex–lined. The soles look like a Mack truck. They make me feel like Catherine the Great. I almost fell off Ben Nevis, you know."

"There's no point in beating around the bush. It's pointless for you to drive up here. I wouldn't be much company. I'll be home in another month anyway, six weeks max. I need the time, Elizabeth."

"Goddamn it, Henry, you just don't want me around, do you?"

"It's not about you."

"That's what people say when they're fucking somebody else. I think we better beat around the bush because I don't understand what's going on."

"I'm not fucking anyone else, Elizabeth, believe me."

"How am I supposed to know what to believe? Kelly said there was some neighbor up there. I know Mary has mentioned her to me. From New York."

"When did you see Kelly?"

"We went out for lunch today."

"Checking up on me?"

"I haven't seen her for ages. She said you weren't very friendly when she was there. You were distant. Aloof was her word, I think."

"Like I said, I wasn't expecting company. Helen left, she went back to New York."

"Yes—Helen. Kelly said she's quite a character. *Intense,* no less."

"I don't know what she means by that."

"I thought you were alone up there. Now I hear there were all these people."

"I told you Mary's kids turned up. Don't be alarmed, Elizabeth, I haven't been enjoying myself."

"Oh Christ."

"I haven't been having the time of my life."

"I'm sure you haven't, Henry. No, I'm not *alarmed* about that."

"You shouldn't be."

The ensuing seconds of silence were surely more telling than what we'd said.

"To tell you the truth I don't feel like driving up there alone and then driving back alone."

"I know that, so why are you giving me this runaround?"

"You don't sound right, that's why. I want to know what's been going on up there. You worry me."

"I'm fine, I think I'm finally getting somewhere. Don't worry."

"Kelly said something about a Fitz remembrance night or something. You didn't say anything about that."

"That's why they were here, apparently. I wasn't involved."

"He hardly had anything to do with those kids. I can't imagine why they're so devoted to him."

"Maybe that's why. They aren't kids anymore."

"He wasn't an easy man to live with, I know that much," she

said, seizing upon unfortunate Fitz, I thought, to curtail the tension between us. "Don't get Mary started on Fitz."

"Is anyone easy to live with? You always claimed they had a pretty good marriage."

"When he wasn't infatuated with some queer in a French monastery, or having a crisis."

"Fitz?"

"Henry, everyone knew Fitz was gay or half-gay. Is that a word?"

"I didn't."

"I'm exaggerating. Actually, almost no one knew. Mary married him with her eyes open, but they kept the bisexual twist under wraps. The children weren't to know. I'm not sure what they know about it today. It's ironic, of course, that Adam turns out to be the real McCoy."

"His crisis? Was that another taboo subject?"

"That was years ago, a full-blown crack-up, apparently. I've never known the details; Mary and I weren't close then. She would allude to it when she was down on his case. Why are we talking about this stuff now? Fitz is gone."

"You brought it up. And Fitz is hard to avoid around here. He's remarkably present. Should I be surprised that you've never mentioned these home truths to me?"

"It was long before us, Henry. It never occurred to me to mention it. We almost never saw them. Maybe Mary swore me to secrecy. I don't remember."

"Well, that doesn't surprise me."

"What doesn't surprise you, Henry?"

"That your first loyalty would be to your big sister."

"This conversation is going downhill fast." Full stop. "I better go before you manage to piss me off. I'll call again later in the week. Or how about you call me for a change?"

"You call whenever you feel like it and I'll call whenever I feel like it. Why don't we leave it at that?"

"That sounds fair," she said. "I can live with that."

I stood before the narrow five-foot mirror that was screwed to the back of the bathroom door. "Gorgeous. Perfect." Precancerous keratoses defaced the freckled forearms along with minor scratches and scrapes; thin skin peeled from sunburned shoulders leaving irregular pink patches; a bluish-yellow bruise the size of an avocado mottled the left thigh, a temporary souvenir from recent labors, Elizabeth. But the dark, slightly raised mark on the skin below the ribs wasn't a melanoma. Neither was the black freckle on the back of the thigh just above the crook of the knee. Everybody sported an average of thirty or so moles or molelike imperfections, said acne-scarred Goldstein, the skin expert. Sun damage to the edge of the lower lip would have to be treated eventually. Don't wait until you need a wedgie, he'd advised. The so-called crow's-feet were like something done with a knife. A cloud of furriness afloat on the aging chest, uninspired dick in its nest of kinky hair, hair loss above the ankles, long bony feet. Hardly your average satyr, pal. A damned haircut might help the whole picture. I stepped closer to scrutinize my image more carefully, drawing my fingers down the summer-in-Vermont-weathered face, tracing the outline of nose and lips, and I was unable to discern there the influence of my tall father's large features, for example, or my mother's smaller fairer ones. I was unable to see anything of my daughter's clear blue eyes in the deep-set, red-veined eyes in the mirror or her *Women of Amphissa* nose or her long thin arms and fingers or her beautiful hair, which had gone through radical transformations with each course of cancer treatment. I caught no glimpse of my son's smooth handsome brow or his strong white grin or his firm muscled torso and lower body. Nor was there a trace of Sally written anywhere on my body, despite the many years we'd given ourselves to each other. And not a sign of you, Elizabeth, either. No one but yourself, you're no one but yourself. Surprised to be alive. Yeah, you got that right. I'm losing my appearance, that was one of Mary's lines. Yeah, I hear you. We're here together, I thought, peering into the mirror in Fitz's bathroom, that's all there is to it.

I had been determined to remain at the library table until the kindling of informed intuitions and thoughts and instincts concerning Dickinson and Whitman and Melville caught fire. It was all there, the raw material for an illuminating meditation on the American soul as gleaned in the hidden lives and astonishing works of three original American misfits. The insatiable hunger and coveted reclusiveness, the monstrous confidence and uncertainty, the isolated longing and hopeless repression that gave birth to such prodigious and creative energy made for an extraordinary story of American self-discovery and self-definition. Whatever the frustrations of composition I no longer exactly questioned the value of my project— until I sat down Monday morning, following my disturbing phone call with you, and read the first twenty-five or thirty pages of what I'd written in brief intermittent bursts over the past two months, inchoate speculations on three strange and elusive people substantiated by various bits and pieces of evidence from their works and lives. Oh boy! My penetrating observations about the psychosexual rage of the author of *Moby Dick* and *Pierre* and *Billy Budd*! Henry Ash's thoughts on Emily Dickinson's love life or Walt Whitman's relationship with his father! You hardly knew the first thing about Fitz, for heaven's sake, who was married to your wife's sister and would sit down with you *in the flesh* once or twice a year for a good meal. Suddenly, scrolling and rescrolling through my painstaking sentences, I became so repelled, Elizabeth, repelled and mortified, that it was not enough to shut down my machine and walk away

249

for the morning. You must clear the decks, you've got to rid your-self of this self-serving, self-saving, self-deluded project, this would-be meditation. You've got to discard the document *Loners* right this digital instant. No going back, I thought, deftly moving the labeled icon to the miniature Trash barrel—bulge!—in the corner of my screen. Melville was Melville, Dickinson was Dickinson, Whitman Whitman. You're you, that's all there is to it. They lived and did their work and died, difficult cases of invisible greatness, secret greatness. They're dead and gone, and what remains is the work they left behind. They all lived secret lives, and the lives they lived in secret, even in the midst of so-called loved ones, certainly remained secret from us. Things worked out for them *after death*, so to speak, which was just sheer luck, but lucky for us, not them. Surely they knew what they were doing, to some extent, yet in the end they couldn't know what they'd done. Neither Melville nor Dickinson and not even Whitman, despite his optimistic egomania, could have known, or even had reason to believe, that their work would eventually be heralded as permanent American Literature. Such a thing cannot be known. We all live secret lives, and we never know what we're doing. Enough, Elizabeth. I clicked Empty Trash in the Special menu and before I could change my mind or even read the big question in the message box—*Are you sure you want to permanently remove it?*—I speared OK with my tiny black arrow, the little garbage can spontaneously deflated, and my over sixty pages of something called *Loners*, the summer's work so far, the new beginning, was obliterated, causing me to sit back and stare anxiously at the mute blank face of the machine for quite a while, thinking, Easy, just take a deep breath, you're okay, kiddo, it's not the end of the world, it's not over.

The red light was blinking when I came in from my daily inspection of the stone wall, where I raised a toast each evening now, to my daughter or my son, to my father or Fitz, to my Herman Melville or Helen, or to you, Elizabeth, to whoever happened to be on my mind at the moment. I pressed Play and it took a second for me to identify the stressed, breathless commotion as a woman's uncontrollable sobbing. The person had been in tears as she dialed the number, evidently, and just went on crying inarticulately, as she waited for Henry Ash, presumably, to pick up the phone. Seconds later, with a wet sniffly groan of exasperation, she hung up. What a terrifying sound, I thought, glaring at the Phone Mate, a little shaken. I hit Play and listened again, but there was no clue to who the caller could be. Terrifying.

When the phone rang later that night, it was Sally, the last person I would have expected to hear from just then in Vermont.

"Did you call earlier and get the answering machine?" I asked.

"I'm sick of those things. You can never talk to anyone anymore."

"There was someone sobbing on the machine. I can't imagine . . ."

"I assumed you were still up there. How's it going?"

"It's Vermont. It's a scream."

"Well, I just . . ." she caught her breath, and her clear strong voice was shaky when she continued. "I called because . . . I'm sorry, Henry, this isn't fair."

"Have you heard from David lately?" I said matter-of-factly.

"I got a card a few days ago. From Verona. He sounds wonderful. The Alps were awesome, but now he's on his pilgrimage. I'm so proud of him."

"I can't wait to see the kid. We planned on him coming up here after he gets back, you know. Maybe a couple of weeks from now, right?"

"He mentioned that before he left."

"So what's unfair? You called because . . ."

"I was looking at pictures and letters and stuff and I completely lost it. I can't believe she's absolutely gone and I'll never see her again. I haven't felt so overcome for months. I guess it was David's card that got me started. David in Italy. I was listening to her music and looking at pictures . . . and her wonderful letters, her scrunched-up handwriting . . ."

"I know, Toad."

"I miss her so much."

"I know."

"All day long. Constantly. I know you know. It's unbearable, and so unbearably lonely." She sniffled. "I don't think I can stand it any-more. Maybe I'm a good-for-nothing wimp, I must be. I know she'd never want me to mope around like this."

"You're no wimp, Sally. It is unbearable and you bear it. But you're right, she'd never want you to go around despairing. Most of the time you don't. Do you?"

"I was leafing through one of her books and I found a poem she'd copied out on a postcard. It was addressed to David, but she never mailed it."

"Really?"

"She messed up a word toward the end and tried to correct it and then must have decided not to send it after all. Anyway, finding it was like hearing from her again, like getting another card from San Francisco. Her brother's name and address in her handwriting. It just floored me."

"What's the card?"

"It's a black-and-white photograph: two people in wide-brimmed hats standing on a precipice with their arms around each other and their free arms stretched out, embracing the wonderful view before them. A canyon, I guess."

"That's her all right."

"Can I read you the poem? That's why I called—to tell you, and read the poem."

"I'm eager to hear it."

"It's Wendell Berry, 'To the Unseeable Animal.' " She read the poem and when she was finished she said nothing, allowing the language of the last lines to resonate in the silence between us. "Henry?"

I swallowed, too disturbed for the moment to talk. "Yes."

"It's so her. I wanted you to hear it too."

"It *is* like hearing from her again."

"It's wonderful, isn't it?"

"Yes."

"Who could I call? I had to call you."

"I'm glad you did." A question occurred to me. "Where did you find it? What book?"

"It was in a book about dying. *Who Dies?*"

"Amazing," I muttered.

"What would I do if you weren't there?"

"Don't worry about that. I'm not going anywhere."

"Well . . . Are you managing any breakthroughs up there in the woods? Are you making progress?"

"I think so. I'm feeling inspired actually."

"Good for you. Okay, I'm going to say good night now."

"Good night, Toad."

I unearthed a woman's three-speed bicycle, a green Raleigh dating back to before the first ten-speeds, in a corner of the barn among some clay pots, a rusted scythe, a cracked mirror. I'd noticed the bike before without imagining it was ridable. The tires were fine once I filled them with air, the brakes worked okay, the gear shift stiffly shifted. I hosed it down and squirted some all-purpose oil on the chain. I had to adjust the wide seat, which had been set a tad higher than was comfortable for me. So it must have been Fitz, not Mary, who rode the bike, I figured, or had been the last to ride it.

Tall in the saddle. Hadn't pumped a bike since our weekend at the Vineyard the year we were married, Elizabeth. Pushing off made me grin, and flying into town down the steep mile-long hill was a giddy thrill. I made it all the way to the top on the return—pull, baby!—standing on the pedals, hauling on the handlebars, my groceries (one can of garbanzos, two bulbs of garlic, a pound of pasta) in a good-sized basket fastened to the handlebars with leather straps. The next day I'd take an exhilarating two-hour ride, I promised myself, and soon enough I'd be up to a full day's outing, sailing under towering trees, alongside babbling streams, through the green green hills and undulating farmlands of old Vermont. The forest-green Raleigh seems to have appeared just when we needed it, Elizabeth.

The message awaiting me—blink blink blink—was startling and disheartening and exciting all at the same time:

"Hi, Dad. It's me, calling not far from Siena. I've hooked up with some great people, a family actually, who rent an ancient place out in the country here and they've asked me to stay with them for a while. Paul and Jessica, they're with their mother, Maggie. I feel like they sort of saved me, you know. You'd like them. Anyway, we want to do some hiking in the mountains and just be here. So I'm probably not going to make it back in time to get up to Vermont as planned, after all. No big deal, right? I had to call Mom because she was going to meet me at the airport, and she said I should talk to you too. So . . . I'm having a good time, everything's fine, and I'll see you in New York. So . . . I guess that's it. Sorry I missed you. Love you, Dad. Bye-bye."

My exasperation—no, my pain—at having missed his call gradually gave way as I replayed the message, pressing Save in order to replay it later, to the pleasure, the thrill, of his voice reaching me from Italy. And it was wonderful that he'd *hooked up* with *great people.* Wonderful that everything was fine and he could extend his big trip. I only regretted David's change of plans for the briefest selfish moment. Who would choose a week in Vermont with the old man over extra weeks in Italy with someone named Jessica? He had the rest of his life to visit his father. No, the phone call was a tremendous relief. Knowing where he was that very day—near Siena—was tremendous, and the surprise of his voice, the sound of that absolutely distinctive, unmistakable, one and only voice, that was a rush.

It hadn't occurred to me before now, not once, to amuse myself with Fitz's game of computer chess, a compact plastic box just about the size of my copy of *Moby Dick*. It was Thursday night, I was bored, and tired of reading about women's health issues (Mary's paperback copy of *The New Our Bodies, Ourselves*). When I removed the black plastic cover, a game appeared to be in progress, White and Black already thoroughly engaged. I switched on the machine and two little red lights winked to life, one of them indicating that it was White's move. A nice feature of this computerized game allowed me to verify the present position of each of the chess pieces. Their remarkable placement was indeed the result of pressured play, the game implicitly under way, waiting on White. While I recalled references to solitary chess in Fitz's journal, I didn't remember just what he'd written, and so I had to turn on his Mac one more time and scroll through his tragicomic *Vermont*. An early passage boasted of besting the machine. Much later that fateful summer, Mary snug in her bed, he noted: *Sit with computer chess—level five!—but don't have the energy tonight to finish a longish game. Close to victory, conceivably two moves away, and I don't want to blow it for lack of concentration.* Back at the library table I pressed the tiny button labeled *Level* on the chess set and five little red lights blinked on.

Thank goodness I had the presence of mind not to jump in and make a move, irrevocably changing everything as it then stood. As I unraveled the lay of the small chess board and began to appreciate the complicated web of contending forces at play, gradually grasping the difficulties this particular game presented, *gradually glimpsing Fitz's mind at work,* Elizabeth, other questions, other issues began to dawn on me—weird scruples ganging up as I sat alone in the pitch dark of a Vermont night. Was it okay to toy with Fitz's unfinished game of chess? Faced with a Fitz sculpture still half-concealed in a block of stone, would you get out your hammer and chisel and finish the job? Come on, the computerized game in progress was no work of art. And there was no obligation to preserve what death had prevented a man from completing. Was there? On the other hand, there was certainly no obligation to play out the game. Fitz believed he was *close to victory*: what if you lose? Another alternative was simply to erase the game Fitz had left unfinished, to press New Game and have your own damned high noon with the electronic opponent. "You're making way too much out of no big deal. It's *just a game*," I protested at last. "Every aspect of Fitz's life was *left unfinished* in a manner of speaking."

Yet I remained unwilling to take up White's queen, say, and press her firmly to another square, thereby engaging the computer's circuitry and irreparably altering all that Fitz had achieved so far. What were my chances of making the move Fitz would have made? What were my chances of beating level five? "I'll feel like shit if I lose, Elizabeth, that's for sure." A dry run seemed smart. Safer to puzzle out White's triumph before engaging the unforgiving machine. I turned the thing off.

I sketched a diagram of the board: White: king on a7 (first file, seventh rank), queen on b6, rooks on f4, h5, bishops on e4, h8, knights on d8, e6, pawns on b7, g3. Black: king on e5, rook on g7, bishop on h6, knights on e2, g5, pawns on c3, c6, d7. Fitz imagined he was a couple of moves from checkmate, so I reduced the game to just such a problem: White to mate in two moves. While White clearly had the advantage, bound to win eventually barring brainless missteps, the Fitz challenge upped the ante.

It would be foolish to describe the next few hours of false moves and head-scratching and beer-guzzling. If I missed the heat of play, where each and every move was met by a response, it was no less stressful to think through numerous tries before testing my solution on the board. You enter a trance, you become a monomaniac, to exaggerate slightly, your head throbs and spins, you become nauseated and damp with concentration and anxiety. A question squeezes your skull with constant pressure: What am I missing? What am I failing to see? The various chessmen began to dance before my eyes incoherently. At one point, standing back from the library table in a kind of horror at the effort I'd invested in this fucking chess ordeal, I felt I really was losing my mind. I cracked open another beer and sat down to the task again. The whole time I was aware of Fitz looking over my shoulder, Fitz breathing down my neck, Fitz the chess champ, Fitz the aloof, Fitz the scientist with the spiritual side, Fitz the beautiful man, Fitz the deceased. Fitz was present, and ultimately the feeling arose that this was less a contest with the computer or myself than it was a contest with Fitz—in which my win would be his win as well.

The moment of truth arrived at two in the morning. I restored the players to their original verifiable positions and turned on the game. I was confident I'd discovered the so-called key and yet it was still heady, Elizabeth, it was still a big moment in Speedwell when I made my bid, when I took my man and moved him diagonally only two squares, and sat back to wait for Black's answer. The simple computer was slow, and despite the seeming inevitability of the outcome Black took long minutes thoroughly trying every possibility its circuitry could see. I had correctly anticipated my invisible opponent's doomsday response. Then it was time for my calm stately queen to step forward, just one step, and as I pressed her firmly to the small black square the little red checkmate light spontaneously flashed on, blinking hysterically—checkmate, checkmate, checkmate—and I suppose the outcome should have seemed anticlimactic to me at that point, but it didn't. "Checkmate!" I cried, leaping to my feet in the silent living room. "Checkmate, goddamn it!" Clapping, throwing my arms overhead, exhausted and half-drunk. "We did it, Fitz," and I picked up your photograph in its frame, Elizabeth, and my daughter's photograph, and David's photograph. "We did it," I repeated. Yeah, sure, we did it. And suddenly there was a lot of stuff surfacing, I guess, thoughts and feelings and memories building, rapidly becoming infinitely more knotty and confounding than any chess game, until at last I stumbled outside into the moonless night, shaking my fists to star-studded high heavens, tears streaming down my hot face.

You wouldn't point to my solo chess victory as a turning point—that would be nonsense, Elizabeth—but as I stood in Fitz's yard at two in the morning following that exhausting uncalled-for trial, I seemed to see myself as an unseen animal might have observed me from within the black woods: a man making a peculiar fuss out here all by himself, releasing puny cries and sobs to be swallowed by the silent dark—a ludicrous and baffling creature—and a calm came over me, my mind cleared, and as the huge silence, heightened by the song of tree frogs and unidentified insects, settled around me, I realized that a period of my life had ended—would have to end—and a new period was to begin. What I felt at that moment in my bones, so to speak, seemed the culmination of the whole haunting summer-in-Vermont experience. I came here to be alone and work, to urge myself into a new project in order to go on with life *as is*—and I tried, I did try, Elizabeth—but I discovered that wasn't the way.

Friday morning, wide-awake and pumped despite little sleep, I sat down at Fitz's beautiful antique oak table from England with its almost black patina and began to get down in language as spontaneous and natural as possible, as artless as possible, everything of importance that had occurred here since I'd pulled into the long private drive two months before, all based on my daily notebook, which had been a fastidious and compulsive practice for twenty-five years. I often wondered what compelled me to scribble down what was thought and said and done by myself and others every blessed damned day of the week when one day of my life was so much like another and my record often seemed a litany of everyday habits, recurrent themes and pet peeves, repeated observations and conversations from one season to the next, one year to the next. The journal-keeping was a kind of scriptomania, I often thought, more like an obsessive-compulsive disorder, as Elizabeth said, than a valuable means of self-expression. And yet I couldn't stop myself from scribbling the familiar mundane events of my day in the large ledgerlike notebook. If a day passed without being accounted for in the notebook, I experienced a mounting panic—almost as though my failure to write down the essence of what had transpired that day meant that *nothing* had occurred. Early Friday morning I began rethinking and reseeing everything that had gone down in Vermont, typing everything into my computer as rapidly and expeditiously as possible, terribly anxious to get the bare bones of the narrative, which closed out a whole period of my life, on paper. I didn't question my urgency, I never considered what would become of the document, if it would or should be read by a living soul, even you. I was only certain I had to get the Vermont interlude down on paper, period, and I had to do it at once. I was on fire, Elizabeth, Tyger! Tyger! burning bright.

Late in the afternoon I would jump up following eight or nine productive hours at Fitz's noble table and pedal my ass off for an hour or so on Fitz's forest-green girl's bike, zipping over smooth blacktop under tall trees, gulping deep breaths of fragrant summer-in-Vermont air. I alternated an easy hour-long loop that took me along the Green River with a tougher longer loop that took me in the opposite direction over four exhilarating hills, grinning like a manic daredevil on the death-defying downslopes. The final uphill pull each day became easier with each outing, legs and lungs stronger and braver, Elizabeth, so that I began to feel reborn; that's hardly an exaggeration. One day a long, staggered file of twenty or so young cyclists, teenage boys and girls of various races, wearing white helmets and Day-Glo orange bandoliers, were walking their bikes up the hill I was headed down. "Where's your helmet?" they cried, pointing. "Hey, asshole!" "Nice bike, old lady!" I took my hands off the handlebars, that's how I was feeling, and stretched out my arms like a flying crucifixion and their laughing whoops and catcalls and good-natured applause resounded in my ears as I sped past them. Another day on a steeper hill a black bear—*the* bear, I thought, realizing the creature plodding onto the road was too big to be a dog—lumbered directly into my path from the dense woods and didn't seem to notice me as I swerved perilously to avoid him. I'd been longing to see another bear before my Vermont days were over and that sighting added to the sense of completion that seemed to be in the offing. I ate from the garden for the most part—there was still kale and Swiss chard, basil and arugula, there were now green beans and cucumbers and squash, with tomatoes on the way—supplemented with pasta and canned beans, a hunk of fish or chicken. At night I'd go over the pages I'd written that day, I'd jot in my notebook, and hit the sack by eleven, determined to be fresh when I arose at six. So you had the writing by day and the bike in the afternoon, you had the garden, you had the evening scotch as you made your evening round, and there was the sky at night before you turned in. That's what we had, Elizabeth. We were on a roll.

I came to that point in my narrative when, only weeks before, I'd discovered Fitz's journal in his computer. Without a qualm, I copied his *Vermont* onto a floppy disk and pasted it into my document entitled *Fitz*. Fitz's journal was an integral part of my Vermont story, that's all there was to it, along with the telephone conversations and phone messages that I'd transcribed into my notebook, along with your postcards, Elizabeth, and David's gripping cards— all crucial elements of the unfolding drama. Clearly, as you'd say, I didn't consider my right to appropriate these materials or anyone else's rights in the matter, I didn't consider what might become of my document called *Fitz*, I was voracious, I was prepared to do whatever was necessary to tell the story. Everything had to go in, each twist and turn of the whole Vermont experience that had brought me to the clear, present moment.

It was Saturday, yes, that I stood at the end of the drive and roared with laughter at my son's latest postcard, a picture of Michelangelo's *David*. Oh that's wonderful, I thought. Priceless. But his rather succinct note—*I'm doing better today, headed for Orvieto, but yesterday almost hit bottom in Florence. Following my sister's footsteps through land of art and beauty, you know, I'm pretty overwhelmed, more torn up than healed. It's hard. Okay, though, glad I'm doing it. Feel like I'm ready for Vermont now. See you soon. Love, D.*—just about broke me up, until I realized, rapidly walking back to the house, that this card had been written prior to his recent phone message. Yes. His sudden happiness in Tuscany was the last word, not his understated pain. So that's what you meant by "saved." And then I adored this

Jessica, whoever she was, for her split-second, as I saw it, last-minute rescue. That can happen: the mysterious right person turning up out of nowhere just when you least expect and most need him/her to appear. That sometimes happens, I thought, like a hand reaching out at the precise last instant to prevent you from stepping off a cliff or into oncoming traffic. It happens. Bravely retracing your sister's footsteps, following your sorrow, can lead to a Jessica. It can.

The phone rang twice while I was plowing ahead at my table the next Tuesday, but the caller chose not to leave a message either time. When it went off again, as I was cleaning up my few dishes that evening, I answered it.

The silence on the other end made me repeat, "Hello." Then, "Hello? Is someone there? Can you hear me?"

Just as clear as a bell Elizabeth said, "What the fuck, Henry?"

"Oh, it's you. Hi."

"It's been over a week since we talked. I thought you'd call. I was afraid to *disturb* you. You tell me, what am I supposed to do?"

"Has it been that long?"

"Yeah, it has."

"I've been absorbed, working. Like a trance, you know? I'm hot."

"No, I don't know. Is it still Emily Dickinson and that crowd?"

"Something new."

"What does that mean? Is it going to be a book?"

"I doubt it. I'm not thinking that far ahead."

"Well, I don't know what you're talking about. You've gotten awfully damned mysterious."

"Maybe you'll read it sometime. No mystery."

"You're writing something I'd read? That is new." She took a breath, enough small talk. "Is something happening up there? Are you seeing someone?"

"Let me look around. I don't see a soul."

"I'm serious, Henry."

"Haven't we had this conversation? I haven't laid a glove on another woman since we've been married. You know that."

"There's a first time for everything. What are you so happy about? You sound almost jolly tonight. It's not like you."

"Are you disappointed?"

"Do you have to have a wisecrack for every word I say?"

"I guess I'm feeling jolly tonight. What can I tell you?"

"I had a drink with your pal Robert the other day," she said, switching to the conversational mode, backing off, I thought. "He called to discuss some scheduling problem, thinking you'd be back by now. I gave him your number up there. Anyway, he said let's get a beer, so I met him at Beardsley's and we ended up having a light supper in the bar. His rap was Cynthia this and Cynthia that. I guess the divorce crap is finally getting done. She's taking him to the cleaners, she won't get a job, she's living with someone in Chicago, she's blown her relationship with their daughter, and on and on. I guess that's why he asked me out for a drink: he had to unload."

"Fun."

"It was fun. That man is *hilarious*. He should write a book called *Cynthia*. He says he's unbearably lonely. After twenty-five years with her he can't adapt to her not being there. He screws someone new every two weeks apparently—he's never been so *cunt crazy*, he says—but he misses the everyday thing, Cynthia in the morning, Cynthia at night. Of course, I know exactly how he feels at this point."

"Does he want to screw you?"

"Robert won't touch you unless you're under thirty-five. He talks to me like a buddy. So anyway, I want to know when you're coming back."

"You seem to forget that you encouraged me to do this, you thought it was just the ticket, remember."

"I didn't realize it would seem so long."

"It's not even August. I need another couple of weeks, I think. I'm not sure."

"I had my checkup with Bello. Mammogram, Pap smear, the whole works."

"And?"

"They won't have the results for a week. I'm sure I'm fine."

"What makes you so sure?" It was a real question.

"That's a nice fucking attitude. You think something should be wrong with me?"

"Of course not. I'm sure you're fine too. I'm glad you feel that way."

"Jesus Christ, Henry. I hope so."

"Did Robert say he was going to call me?"

"I think he can wait until you're back. You've got a pile of stuff here from school. I didn't think you wanted to bother with it. I've paid the bills of course. What a nightmare. I'm going to make some calls and start the job search. I'm ready."

"Good for you."

"As long as you're up there, I intend to do some things I've been wanting to do around here."

"Like what?"

"I want to paint the kitchen for one thing. It's dingy. And I'd love to paint the floor in our bedroom—some exotic design."

"I don't think you should get into all that."

"Why shouldn't I?"

"What color are you talking about in the kitchen? I like the kitchen the way it is."

"I haven't decided. Don't worry, you'll like it."

"I don't want the bedroom floor painted, damn it, it's a good oak floor."

"It's a bore. I want to give this joint a lift, I'm tired of the way everything looks, I'm sick of it."

"Shouldn't I have some say in the matter? It's my apartment, isn't it?"

"That's bullshit, Henry, I've done everything to improve our happy hovel. What do you mean, your apartment? Since when?"

"I don't think you should go to the trouble, that's all."

"It's not trouble, it's fun. When I walked into this place three weeks ago, I hated it. I'm a visual person, Henry, I need to alter my surroundings every so often. I feel like a prisoner in here. I need a change. Of course you could live cooped up like a monk in the same dreary four walls . . ."

"Your voice, Elizabeth, you're shouting. Paint what you want to paint. Paint to your heart's content."

"I will. And you'll love it, wait and see."

"Okay, I'll wait and see. I've got work to do, I've got to go."

"Call me in a couple of days, all right? Don't make me worry about you. I miss you."

"Don't fall off the ladder, okay? The last thing we need is a broken leg," I said, very aware of tossing in the pronoun as a little token of affection. "Good night."

A pause.

"Henry?"

"I'm still here."

"You're a prick."

"But what?"

"But I wish you were here to fuck me."

"That's a cunning tease."

"I'm horny."

"Married people don't have phone sex, Elizabeth. Snap out of it."

"You're never tender, you bastard. What happened to your tenderness?" she asked. "All right, good night. Now remember, call me."

So complicated, I thought moments later, looking closely at the snapshot of her on the dock at Port Clyde, waiting to board the boat for Monhegan. You look so happy. My wife! Of course, the part of me that loved you recoiled at the thought of painful impending troubles, and a long-distance phone call was not the occasion to bring the trouble down on us, Elizabeth. Nor would a letter have been appropriate. I had to be there, I saw clearly, we had to sit down face-to-face and look at what our lives together had become. But first I had to follow my inspiration and finish what I'd started. The night of Elizabeth's phone call was the fifth day of *the writing*, as I thought of my spontaneous and artless outpouring, and I had well over one hundred pages of something called *Fitz*, which included Fitz's journal, *Vermont*.

Three days later I reached that point in the narrative when—less than two weeks before!—I'd discovered Fitz's letter to Helen in Trash. Stubborn qualms caused tightness in the large muscles across my shoulders. Pilfering a dead man's Trash, how could you do that? I paced the room before the illuminated screen of my humming computer. I ended work early and went further than usual on the bike, pumping the question before me over half a dozen Vermont hills. In the end, back at the house, I strode into Fitz's workroom without hesitation and quickly went through the several steps necessary to copy his unsigned letter to Helen onto the floppy disk that already contained his journal, and all in the same motion, as it were, I pasted it into my document-in-progress. Every word of Fitz's letter in Trash, like everything else included in *Fitz*, was essential to the story. It couldn't be left out. As his italicized words burst onto the screen of my Mac I felt only relief.

Then, out of the blue, Elizabeth, as I read and reread the Fitz love letter now safe in my document, and recalled my excitement upon first finding it, I was struck with a possibility that hadn't occurred to me until that moment. *Please leave a message. Didn't Fitz leave one for me?* Helen had asked in the long riff she'd left on my Phone Mate, very recently transcribed from my notebook. The qualms arose again, to be sure. A letter in the trash could hardly be constructed as a message for anyone, and yet the trash had not been emptied, which was more along the lines of a letter that remained undelivered. Yes? And maybe the divine intervention–like discovery of the almost lost detail endowed the finder with unforeseen prerogatives. Think what it would mean to the woman. Think what Sally's discovery of an unmailed postcard from our daughter had meant to both of us. Send the letter! By the time I'd printed it out and called Pantheon for the address—"Yes, Ms. Trudell is in today. Shall I connect you?" "No, no, that's not necessary"—and sealed the letter in a white business envelope, I was convinced that Helen deserved a copy of this last word from Fitz.

My handwritten note simply said:

Dear Helen, I came across this unsigned letter in Fitz's workroom and while he evidently hadn't sent it to you—that is, I assume he didn't send a copy—I thought, at the risk of being meddlesome and worse, you should have it. Hope this sits all right with you.

Best Wishes, Henry Ash.

P.S. I'll call you when I return to the city. Maybe lunch or a drink, if that works for you. I'll look forward to that.

Simply!

New reservations dogged my steps as I walked to the mailbox at the entrance to the private road. It was Friday. Helen had left this corner of Vermont just two weeks before, not to return. Surely she wanted to put the *whole Fitz thing* behind her. Why cause the woman more sleepless nights? Of course, it wasn't Fitz's love letter as much as my own oh so spontaneous postscript—I'd spent an hour composing it—that made me balk. Why, I asked myself, what are you afraid of? Take the leap. With quickened blood, Fitz, I put my envelope with its erotic Georgia O'Keeffe stamp into the red barn-shaped mailbox and shut the door. The matter was now in the hands of the U.S. Postal Service—numerous hands—which gave fate, to wax a touch melodramatic, a last chance to have its say. As I retraced my steps to the house, that modest act—my leap!—seemed the very gesture to bring the whole summer-in-Vermont interlude to a close.

And three days after that, the eleventh day of *the writing*—just yesterday, Elizabeth! Monday, July 31—I reached the point where I began, the Friday, that is, when I opened a new document entitled *Fitz* and began getting down my Vermont narrative at full tilt, as inspired as Ishmael bobbing on Queequeg's coffin. I labored until evening on the all but final pages, at pains to get our last conversation letter-perfect, then I scrolled through the document from the beginning just to get the feel of the whole thing. *It is now safe to switch off your Macintosh.* I was smiling as I stared at the silent empty screen.

Outside, a beautiful evening, with its shadows and gilt-edged, green-gold light, was in full swing. I circled the garden, popping a cherry tomato into my mouth—sweet—and proceeded past the lilac bushes and across the mowing, skirting the site of Fitz's bonfire, a bed of ashes that would heal with next spring. That's a wonderful stone wall, Helen. I stepped onto the top of it and walked along the solid, carefully placed capstones, avoiding the lichened patches, to the northwest corner. My permanent contribution. Can you dig it? Beyond the bright green field, the white cape, with its classically pitched gray wood roof and stout chimney, sat firmly nestled among gleaming trees and shrubs, backed by tall shining woods—in its impeccable seclusion, Elizabeth, its exacting solitude. That's it, time to pack it in. I couldn't say I'd learned all the place had to teach me—hardly!—but I was sure there was nothing more for me to do here. I would hang out for another week or so, I figured, a little holiday—clean the house, clear out the garden, leave the place better than I'd found it. I raised my glass of Lagavulin (a present I'd bought myself the night before in anticipation of completing my document) and drank to my season in Vermont. I'm alive, I thought, as I stood on Fitz's wall, I can live, I intend to live, that's my promise, I declared, addressing my daughter, that's all I can do, all anyone can do, and I raised the glass again, Elizabeth, getting a touch emotional, and shouted, "O take my hand, Walt Whitman."

As I started back across the field—*splendor of ended day floating and filling me*—I imagined walking down my tree-lined city street again, turning onto Broadway to be engulfed in the noise and traffic and heat and stink of it, swept up in the rush of bodies and faces, each and every face extraordinary and different, hundreds and thousands of faces constantly approaching and passing you as you strode along in the opposite direction. Halfway across Fitz's field I was seized with a hunger for that excitement again—Mannahatta!—a longing for the crowds of beautiful and not-so-beautiful men and women, and in the middle of all the strangeness and difference and danger, the sudden miracle of a face that you know, a smile you know, coming toward you.

7 *Bear River*

Mary awoke before dawn. Her pointless dream, an incoherent jumble involving vaguely familiar but inconsequential faces, frustrated her. She had to pee but she didn't want to get out of bed. In Cambridge she now slept in the center of the bed she'd shared with Fitz, but here, though the bed was smaller, she was more comfortable on the right side. Two pillows placed under the covers end to end occupied the other side, a little stratagem she'd devised the first night. If it helped her sleep, she thought, so what? She rolled onto her back against the pillows, stretching her legs and feet until one of her ankles cracked. Sex, if it happened at all in those last years, had almost always occurred in the hour or so before dawn when quite by accident, it seemed, they found each other in the mood. More often in Vermont than Cambridge. Blind semiconscious groping. She reached under her flannel nightgown. Dry as a toad, Fitz would say. Fifty-three. That's young today, Mother, her daughter scolded. It didn't feel young. When she had been indisputably young, her young husband's death had permanently limited her capacity for happiness. Fitz's sudden death was an event that had occurred within the realm of the possible, by comparison, and yet it marked an equally radical change in her life. She couldn't imagine the anxious trouble of someone new and unknown, the risk and exposure. Men her age wanted younger women—naturally!—and she didn't want an older man. Living with Fitz had often meant being alone; that didn't frighten her. Her life with men—there had been two—was over and done with, she'd told Elizabeth, and for now that decision was a relief. Elizabeth didn't feel the same way about herself, and she shouldn't have, of course. She was eight years younger, after all. On a good day Mary's slender energetic sister could pass for a woman in her thirties.

The sky lightened behind the dark branches in the screened window, the smell of the air wonderful. She moistened her fingers, curious, arousing herself just enough to experience the pulse of blood in her ears, that pleasant rush. The maddening pull of the sensation baffled you, she thought, reaching farther, better now, there, much. She'd had no patience for this only moments before, Jesus, Mary, honestly. Fifty-three. That's young today. Could have fooled me, she thought, but suddenly you're . . . oh all right, good Lord. Does anyone understand this? Fitz entering her only as she was beginning to come, the fullness suddenly amazing, causing deep shuddering waves of release. That bumper sticker they saw on the way up: Orgasm Donor. A kid with a ponytail in an old green pickup. Come inside me. Now. Boy oh boy. Do you understand this? How can it be so important? She squeezed her hand between her legs, trembling, calming her breathing, and lay still. I can't believe you're gone, she thought. When she opened her eyes to the brightened sky—Fitz—tears blurred her vision, she impatiently threw back her covers, pale blue sheet beneath a white quilt, and sat up. Ridiculous, she thought, honestly, Mary, ridiculous. It was Friday, get a move on.

When she heard Elizabeth directly below her in the kitchen, Mary realized she hadn't heard her go downstairs, and had to wonder if her sister had noticed inadvertent sounds coming from the master bedroom as she stepped out of the guest room. Well, I'm sorry.

The Vermont outing had been at Elizabeth's insistence. Mary had resisted, unwilling to let herself in for all that, less than two years since Fitz's death. Once she'd gotten past the shock of arrival, however, the old place was familiar rather than forbidding, more comforting than she'd anticipated, and she found herself remembering Fitz in a good way, without the anger. There had been many summers, Vermont held some of the happiest memories of their convoluted marriage, and now she was glad she'd faced coming here. It felt like an accomplishment, as if she'd regained an important possession that had seemed lost to her. Even the surge of sadness, arriving briefly each morning and each evening as though the light on the horizon was a message from Fitz, was not unwelcome. She knew it was worse for Elizabeth—every aspect of the place was news, piercing and staggering, a revelation. But that was partly why Elizabeth had come. She wanted to get her nose right down in the pain, as if inhaling this Vermont air might be healing, Mary thought, or at least clear her senses. And there was the thing she'd come to do. God yes, get it over with.

Elizabeth had been after her since spring—she couldn't go alone—and Mary finally agreed to the week of the Fourth. She'd driven to New York on Sunday and managed to take in two big exhibits with Kelly. *Picasso and Portraiture* at MOMA—he painted with his prick, she told her daughter—and, far more important and powerful to Mary, *Winslow Homer* at the Met. His incandescent watercolors. She'd missed Adam, who had already left to spend July leading groups of teenagers through the Sierra Nevadas, a windfall opportunity that had come his way through one of Fitz's former students, oddly enough, whom Adam had coincidentally met in a winter yoga class in the city. She and her sister had driven to Vermont on Tuesday, a day ahead of the holiday traffic, stopping in Bennington for supper and reaching the house at dusk. Entering the place, Elizabeth said, "I feel like I'm visiting the scene of a crime." Wednesday was rain all day. They'd cleaned the house, rearranging furniture, converting Fitz's study to another guest room—for they were expecting guests—dragging out an iron bed with box spring and mattress that had been wrapped in a plastic tarp upstairs in the barn. They'd laundered bedding at a Laundromat in the neighboring town, and bought groceries and beer and wine to last most of the week. Elizabeth kept to herself and Mary let her be. Thursday, the Fourth, was sunny and they'd spent most of the day outdoors. They mowed and raked the lawn; Mary pruned the mock orange and deadheaded the lilacs. The enclosed vegetable garden was a sorry sight, a tangle of weeds, sage, malva, Johnny-jump-ups, dill, surprisingly, all mixed up with the remains, the rotted and dried leaves and stalks, of last year's garden, but there was no point in bothering with it for the short time they intended to be here.

The constant rainfall all spring right through June had prevented Graves from haying the field yet. The grass stood as tall as Mary's shoulder, and seemed wild and beautiful to her. Late Thursday afternoon she'd walked through the field scouting for fawns bedded down in the tall fragrant grass. They were hard to spot in a heavy crop even when you were on the lookout for them, and one year Graves had shredded one with the mower. The animal's instinct was to stay put and the approach of the tractor could not make it move. The restored stone wall at the north edge of the field, invisible with the tall hay until you were next to it, surprised her, becoming all the more remarkable as she walked the length of it. A stout impressive wall now bordered the west edge of the field as well, she saw, yes, remarkable, something of a feat. Last summer, during the tense time following her return from England, Elizabeth had referred to Henry's stone wall project disparagingly—Has he gone completely off his rocker? she asked—and Mary had never imagined anything so . . . substantial. Fitz had talked about restoring those stone walls for years. When Mary returned to the house she kept her discovery to herself, rather than risk a scene with her sister.

It was after seven by the time she had dressed and made the bed. She smelled coffee as she entered the kitchen, but Elizabeth wasn't in the room. She was standing inside the tangled defunct garden, holding her coffee mug with both hands, dressed this morning in pleated khaki pants and a white shirt. Elizabeth tipped her head back then, staring at the sky, and in the next moment she stumbled forward dizzily, as though losing her balance. The cup dropped from her hands.

"Are you all right out there?" Mary called, and let the screen door slap shut behind her.

"Hi. What a morning," she said, raising her arms to encompass the idea.

"I just saw you drop your coffee."

"I know, damn it, it slipped out of my hands." She stooped to pick up the mug.

"What are you doing anyway?"

"I'm just standing here."

"I'm going to have a boiled egg. Do you want one?"

"I can't eat eggs first thing in the morning."

"You better eat something, you're too skinny."

She'd taken *The Ambassadors* to bed with her, having come across her old copy of the book on the table in the other room, and now over breakfast she continued reading where she left off, altogether absorbed with the fastidious precision of James's leisurely ruminating prose, Strether's luminous consciousness. "Beyond, behind them was the pale figure of his real youth, which held against its breast the two presences paler than itself—the young wife he had early lost and the young son he had stupidly sacrificed," she read, smiling. When Elizabeth entered the kitchen she didn't look up.

"It's so gorgeous out, it's almost too much. What are you reading?"

Mary held up the book. "I haven't read it in twenty years. I feel like Alice. I've opened a door and dropped right out of the world."

"How was your egg?"

"Perfect." Her sister's eyes were red, she saw, and that exasperated her. She didn't want to talk about tears. She asked, "Did you sleep last night?"

"I woke up around three and I couldn't get back. Did you hear the owl?"

"I didn't hear a thing."

"There was an owl for quite a while. It was wonderful." She rinsed her mug at the sink. "What time do you think Kelly will get here?"

"She said noon. I hope they make it in time for supper." Kelly and Jane, the friend her daughter had acquired through Adam, hadn't been part of the original plan for the week, but when Kelly learned her mother and her aunt were going to be in Vermont for the Fourth, she assumed the weekend would include her. She wanted to be there. Henry's son, David, who was central to Elizabeth's plan—he was due to arrive tomorrow, flying from San Francisco to New York especially for the occasion—would surely appreciate the presence of the younger women. God knows, Mary didn't want to be responsible for keeping him entertained, if that was the word for it under the circumstances. And now Elizabeth could ride back to New York Monday morning with Kelly, which would save Mary the trouble of that trip. The whole situation actually worked out much better this way.

"What are you doing this morning?" Elizabeth asked.

"I'm going to sit here and drink coffee and read for an hour, then I'm going to wash my hair and I'll make the kiwi torte for dessert. Why, was there something you wanted to do?"

"No. I'm just restless. I think I'll go for a good long walk." She tore a paper towel from the roll by the window and blew her nose. "It's still safe to walk in the woods around here, isn't it?"

"It's hardly eight o'clock."

"It's so beautiful out there right now. The woods are sparkling."

"Do you want me to come? Or do you want to be alone?"

"No, I think I'd rather be by myself."

Mary went to the stove and turned on the heat under the kettle. "Why don't you walk over to Field's Hill, that's pretty up there."

"That's what I was thinking."

As Mary reached to the cabinet where the coffee filters were kept, Elizabeth stepped toward her, her eyes pleading, Mary thought, and they embraced, which was hardly typical of them. They rarely touched each other. Mary awkwardly patted her taller sister's back. "You smell good," she said, letting go. "What are you wearing?"

"Something of yours. It was in the bathroom. Avocado maybe?" She walked to the door.

"It might be buggy, you better wear one of those straw hats."

Elizabeth took a hat down from its nail near the door and pulled it on. "Okay, I'm out of here."

"Are you all right?" Mary asked, stooping to a tone, an automatic utilitarian shorthand, she loathed—that awful quasi-psychotherapeutic caring bullshit—but which had become so much a part of the vernacular as to be irresistible.

"Yeah, I'm all right." Rather than let it slam shut, she quietly closed the door behind her.

"Let's see, '... stupidly sacrificed,'" she read.

He had again and again made out for himself that he might have kept his little boy, his little dull boy who had died at school of rapid diphtheria, if he had not in those years so insanely given himself to merely missing the mother. It was the soreness of his remorse that the child had in all likelihood not really been dull—had been dull, as he had been banished and neglected, mainly because the father had been unwittingly selfish. This was doubtless but the secret habit of sorrow, which had slowly given way to time; yet there remained an ache sharp enough to make the spirit, at the sight now and again of some fair young man just growing up, wince with the thought of an opportunity lost.

Marvelous, Mary thought, nodding. Everything here was new to her, sentence for sentence, as though she had never read Strether's story before.

"For heaven's sake," she muttered, approaching her daughter and Jane as they stood next to their white rented car, stretching. It was just past four. She reached out and firmly brushed the top of her daughter's head with her hand. "Oh Kell," she said. Her daughter's dark hair might have been cut with a butcher's knife. Her face looked drained, Mary thought, even puffy, and her clothes, an oversized gray T-shirt, paint-splattered jeans that hung off her hips, were sloppy. She was too old to go around like that. She would lose her prettiness if she didn't ... and Mary reached her hand toward her daughter's face, thinking maybe it was her period that made her so pale.

Dodging her mother's touch, Kelly stepped closer to offer a perfunctory hug. "We made it," she said. "This is Jane, remember? She visited Cambridge last winter."

"How could I forget Jane?" In men's overalls over a snug white T-shirt, the blond girl glowed; that was not an exaggeration.

"It's great to be here again," she smiled. "I love your house."

"Is David here yet?" Kelly asked.

"Tomorrow." She added, "I don't know if I'm ready for that."

"Where's Elizabeth?"

"She wanted a nap before you showed up. Your hair looked so lovely last week. I remember you standing in front of that Picasso sleeping nude and I thought . . ."

"Mother, don't start. I just got here." She added, "What's for supper? We haven't had anything but a bag of peanuts all day."

"Honestly, Kell, how . . ."

"It's *my* hair," she stated firmly.

⌒

Honestly, Kell, you looked so lovely, how could you . . . enough to drive you fucking nuts, that worried frown, like I'm ruining my life with a haircut. Well this morning I had to walk over an unconscious body at the bottom of the stairs, then hopscotch through the shit on the sidewalk, human shit, Mother, not dog shit, and human shit is worse, believe me. God forbid I say anything about the way you go around, like you've joined the ranks of sexless middle-aged women with short gray hair in that goddamn skirt when you could look great if you tried, buy whatever you want, tooling around in a fifty-thousand-dollar Land Rover as if driving to the grocery store is a freaking safari. Winslow Homer has more to say to her than Picasso, right, Mom, perfect, exactly, and what I do is too difficult, too prickly, too off-putting, as you put it, too weird, you mean, too ugly, even a garden in the city turns out to be disturbing and edgy, well, right, the garden happened to have a chain-link fence with barbed wire around it and a bloody syringe under the daffodils. I'd like to take those irises that have been hanging on the wall for ten years and eat them and shit them onto the sidewalk on Second Avenue, is that vulgar and ugly enough for you? I don't want to be pretty, Mother, it's not pretty to have losers leering and yanking their dicks every time you walk by, feeling exhausted and beat up to start with. Cockroaches everywhere you look when you turn on a light aren't pretty, the smell of piss and garbage isn't pretty. The black guy at the end of the street yesterday smashing his bicycle with a pipe, he was beautiful—I couldn't take my eyes off him—but I thought he was going to hit me. What are you looking at, lady? Nick falling all over that little twat from Connecticut at Jonathan's party wasn't pretty, it was humiliating to me. Three months ago he was begging me to have a kid for crying out loud. You don't even know about that, Mother. Maybe that's why I got my hair cut. There are all kinds of whores everywhere you look who aren't pretty. I've been working late every night, knocking myself out to finish the biggest thing I've done, so I was really looking forward to getting here until we got here. You're so predictable, Mother.

Elizabeth entered the kitchen smiling. "Hey you," she said, grabbing her niece into a firm hug—they had seen more of each other in the city over the past year, now that Elizabeth was on her own—and Kelly decided to lighten up. "This is adorable," her aunt said, touching the back of Kelly's head.

"Do you think so?"

"Positively."

"Well, Mother here just pissed me off to no end about it."

"Do I have to like it?" her mother asked.

"Yes, you have to like it."

"All right, you guys, no squabbling, that's not why we're here."

"Amen," Jane said, neatly uncapping a beer with her Swiss Army knife. They'd picked up two six-packs of Harpoon in Massachusetts. She tipped up the bottle, then held it at arm's length. "Don't you love this guy on the label?"

"Fitz's favorite beer," Kelly said, "that's why I bought it."

Her mother was setting out smoked trout and blue cheese. "I don't know about that," she said, adding, "it might have been one of them."

"Mother, trust me, it was Harpoon."

"Okay, Kell. If you say so."

"I say so."

"Knock it off, you two. Enough."

"To Queequeg," Jane said, "the best harpooner of them all. Was he queer or not?"

"Who?" Elizabeth asked.

"Queequeg," Kelly said, "remember him cuddling up with Ishmael at the inn."

"The Spouter Inn!" Jane laughed. "I just finished reading it."

"Ishmael was the queer," Mary said, "not Queequeg."

Kelly observed her mother smear a lump of blue cheese over a cracker with her strong veined hands, soiled and stained from the work she'd been doing around here. She added a wedge of trout on top, the whole item down the hatch, followed by a large swallow of red wine. Her eyes were bright, her lips moist. She'll live to be a hundred, her daughter thought. Propelled by an irresistible emotion she moved to the woman and fell upon her shoulders, burrowing her face against her mother's neck. "You're too much, Mother, you're too fucking much."

"What, Kell, what is it?"

"You're too much," Kelly said, "you're an animal. You know I love you."

"Oh, my big beautiful girl," Mary said, laughing then, holding her. "My artist."

As the meal progressed—raviolis with sun-dried tomato pesto, salmon, spinach salad with a walnut-Gorgonzola dressing—the four of them warmed to their evening together. Jane's stories about her three cats in the city—how she'd rescued them (from an ex-boyfriend allergic to cat fur, from a French restaurant where she'd worked as prep chef, from a scary weekend on Fire Island) and how she'd nearly lost each of them (on the subway, down the fire escape, to a neighbor's dog in the hallway)—were funny and winning. Mary and Elizabeth got into summer vacations they remembered from childhood, which made it seem—hilariously to them—as if they'd been raised by different parents in entirely different places. Mary's exotic dessert was a hit. They listened to an Ella Fitzgerald tape on Jane's Sony cassette player, goofily singing along here and there—"Bewitched, bothered, and bewildered"— while they did the dishes. The older women washed, Kelly and Jane dried. They walked down the long drive arm in arm, Kelly contentedly between her mother and Elizabeth, so beautiful out here under moon and stars, fireflies in the trees and over the tall hay field, that no one said a word the whole way back.

Kelly was in bed with her book—*Shackleton's Boat Journey*— when Elizabeth returned from the bathroom in silky-looking flesh-colored long underwear. She paused to look out the window. "That sky blows me away," she said. She brushed off the soles of her thin bony feet before she slipped between sheets. "How about the peace and quiet around here?" She smiled. With no makeup, her face was smooth and polished, with pink lips and becoming crow's-feet. "We get to be roommates. Isn't this fun?"

"How do you get to look like that at your age?" Kelly asked. "What's the secret? Mom's a wild animal and you're Audrey Hepburn."

"Don't embarrass me," she said, and propped the pillow up

behind her back, drawing up her knees so that her legs beneath the covers formed a steep peak. "Now for my half hour dose of fierce prose. It's almost my favorite time of day. Have you tried this?" She held up a large white book with a black spine entitled *Extinction*.

"I tried something of his, but I didn't have the patience. I need paragraphs, I didn't know when to stop reading."

"Once you start you can't stop. I just picked it up one night. There are all these books around the house I've never read."

"My hero of the moment is this guy." She held up her paperback. "He saved his entire arctic expedition from *extinction*," she said, emphasizing the word. "Not one man was lost."

"They could have used him on Everest this spring. Can you imagine?" In May eight people had died attempting the summit, owing to poor judgment, it seemed, bad weather, and bad luck.

"Did you hear the telephone conversation between the man at the summit, freezing to death, and his pregnant wife in New Zealand? They *patched* her in. The technology makes my head spin. Don't worry about me, he said. So heartbreaking."

Elizabeth was frowning, somber suddenly. "At least they had a chance to say good-bye."

For Kelly the ensuing pause was awkward. "How do you feel about being here?" she asked. "You weren't sure about it last winter."

"I keep trying to see him here, but it's peculiar. I just don't associate this place with Henry. It's not like your mother with her years of memories, Fitz informing every detail."

"Mom seems to be good, doesn't she?"

"She does, she said she's glad she came after all."

Kelly decided to pursue this new vein, deflecting them for the moment from the more difficult issue. "God, she pissed me off when we got here. I've been working my ass off, and she's worried about what I look like."

"She's your mother, what do you expect?"

She decided to go further, as if a shared confidence might be compensation for her aunt's quickly altered mood. "I haven't told her this, and I don't want her to know."

"Now what?" Elizabeth said, smiling skeptically. "Something good I hope."

"I had an abortion three months ago."

"I'm sorry."

"I wanted to tell you, but the time was never right, and then we haven't seen each other for a while."

Elizabeth had been under the impression that Kelly's Nick, gainfully employed as a jacket designer at . . . Houghton Mifflin? . . . had been ready to marry her. "What's he afraid of?" she asked.

"Oh, he wanted it, he was thrilled. I have my work to do, I couldn't be strapped with an infant now. I think I've pretty much had it with Nick."

"You're kidding?"

"I realized he doesn't really know what I'm about. He didn't understand my decision."

"It's always sad, though, isn't it?"

"I did what I had to do, and I don't regret it. I'm not going to mope about it."

"I understand, believe me. But it's always unhappy, that's all I meant. I'm sorry you had to go through that."

Hearing what she'd missed the first time, Kelly asked, "Have you ever gone through it?"

"Yes," Elizabeth said, enunciating the sibilant word to convey that she intended to say nothing more about that aspect of her life, not tonight. "Let's read for a while and go to sleep." But it was Elizabeth who broke the silence moments later. "What are you thinking, Kelly?"

"Do I look like I'm thinking?"

"You're frowning. I'm sorry if I said the wrong thing. My empathy is a little rusty. I wish you'd told me when it happened. I know how lonely it can be."

"I was thinking about this time last year actually. I was right here in this room with Henry, and now I'm here with you. You know?"

Elizabeth nodded. "Of course I know."

"I don't remember what he said, I just remember him listening. I'm sure I did the talking and all I talked about was me. Fitz's bonfire. That seems ages ago."

"Who else was here? I know you've told me, but tell me again."

"Adam, of course, and Jane, and Helen, who used to rent a place out here somewhere."

"That's right—Helen. I couldn't remember."

"Is she here this summer?"

"I have no idea. How would I know that?"

"I ran into her months ago. Did I tell you?"

"I don't think so."

"Maybe January because it was snowing. I was hurrying somewhere and she called my name. I didn't recognize her all bundled up in her hat and coat. Oh it was on Broadway. She was coming out of Kate's Paperie and she wanted to drag me into Dean and DeLuca's for lunch. I couldn't deal with it."

"With what?"

"Her . . . enthusiasm. She was all over me like what a wonder it was bumping into each other. How was Mary? How was Adam? I'm always confused when I run into a familiar face in the city—someone from elsewhere—as though it's an anomaly. I guess I'd rather remain anonymous, invisible."

"You sound like your mother."

"I have a confession to make. I mean, I just thought of it."

"I love confessions."

"She also asked about Henry. How was Henry?"

"Who?"

"Helen. I don't even know her last name. Do you know what I'm going to say?"

"Of course not."

"I told her I hadn't seen him since summer. I felt terrible about it afterwards, I was ashamed, like I'd betrayed Henry and even you. I just didn't want to go into all that standing on the street. Do you know what I mean?"

"Kelly, why would I care what you said to some stranger I've never met?"

"I felt like I'd committed a sin or something. I felt awful."

"You didn't want to stop and talk in the first place, and you weren't prepared to get into Henry. I understand, I can imagine doing the same thing myself."

"Do you forgive me?"

"Now you're being ludicrous."

"Say you forgive me."

"All right, I forgive you. I'm turning out the light now. Okay?"

In the darkened room, looking across the low ceiling to the window brightened by moonlight, Kelly's recollection of the last time she'd slept here, Henry occupying the bed where his wife now lay, became all the more vivid. He'd turned onto his side with his back to her, just as Elizabeth was now. They'd talked about Fitz, Adam's impulsive act that night, her worries about her mother, her youthful infatuation with her attractive aunt. Henry had looked very well, fit and robust, and he also seemed strung tight, smoldering, anxious to keep his distance from them, shy about sharing the room with her, his intense unease visible in his eyes as he listened to her talk. She couldn't remember him smiling, for example. She had wanted to say something about his daughter's death, even two years later, for she had never expressed a word to him about that calamity in the few times they'd met since it had occurred. The omission made Kelly feel stupid. They'd been about the same age, she and Henry's daughter, and although they had never met, Kelly had followed her story through Elizabeth and her mother. She believed she knew the sort of person this had been, she identified with the way the young woman had purportedly coped with illness and faced the end of her life. She regretted not having known her. But she had failed to say any of this to Henry the night they shared the same bedroom, she didn't know how to bring it up, or whether she should. At the time she'd thought his detachment had more to do with his work, the project he'd come here to pursue, and the perceived threat to that fragile process which their temporary invasion represented. Henry, she thought, he was right there, I could have reached out and touched him. She was frightened, staring at Elizabeth's back in the dim room, at least they had a chance to say good-bye, she thought, how horrible, how ludicrous, forgive me.

She moved to the other bed and lay down next to Elizabeth, wrapping her arm around the woman and pressing her face against her shoulder.

"Kelly, what is it?"

"I just want to be here for a minute."

Her aunt turned, extricating her arms, and returned Kelly's hug, squeezing back.

"Elizabeth, I'm so sorry. It's so fucked up. How do you bear it?"

"I only wish we'd had more time. After those grueling years I thought we were ready to have our life, I thought it was going to be good now."

They both became tearful for a minute and when that passed they lay there quietly holding hands.

"Then I think of David," Elizabeth said, "half his family is gone."

"When did you last see him? He's living in San Francisco, isn't he?"

"He was in New York at Christmas visiting his mother. We had lunch downtown. We still talk on the phone every so often. He sends me a postcard occasionally. I think he's a great kid. He's painting houses right now, but once he meets the residency requirement, he wants to go to Berkeley and finish his degree. Philosophy, I think."

Kelly heard the smile in her voice. "What's he plan to do with that?" she asked.

"You'll have to ask him. Philosophize, I guess."

"Are you nervous about him coming?"

"Of course. He's never been here. I'm sure it's a pilgrimage for David."

"I remember him at the memorial service. It was only the third or fourth time I'd ever seen him probably. He didn't look like anyone else, did he? It was as though he had an aura or something. In his black turtleneck."

"Suffering is what you call it. He was dazed, stunned. He'd just gotten back from Italy. We had to locate him there first. His mother almost went berserk."

"He read that poem as if . . . what? As if it was a sacred text. That was extraordinary. I was holding my breath. Do you remember it? The poem, I mean."

"Oh, what was it?" Elizabeth said. "How could I forget something like that? I have a copy of it at home."

"About hoping there's an animal somewhere than can never be seen or . . ."

"Yes, the unseen animal. Or maybe unseeable." She squeezed Kelly's hand. "Thank you."

"For what?"

"Remembering the poem."

Kelly idly rubbed the palm of her aunt's hand with her thumb. "I guess I've never really thought about it before, but what was Henry working on anyway? Wasn't that the reason he was up here?"

Elizabeth nodded. "That was the reason," she said, as if that fact of the matter was particularly disheartening to her. "I haven't touched his computer. He was on to one of his projects. At the time I just couldn't face . . . whatever. I was never Henry's ideal reader, that's no secret. I'm giving the computer to David, who was thrilled with the idea. I've brought it with me. He can read what his father was writing if he wants to. It's his now."

"I was only wondering. I realized I had no idea what he'd been working on."

"The notebooks are practically indecipherable. I'm not ready for that yet either. In fact, I'm ambivalent about ever opening them. It seems like trespassing. Shouldn't everyone be entitled to their privacy? I'm sure I'll read them eventually, but it's too soon, it's too sad. I'm not explaining myself very well, am I?"

"You don't have to explain anything."

"If I thought there was something I should know, I'd feel differently. But that's not the issue. It's not as though there would be any surprising insights or revelations in those pages. I honestly believe we understood each other as well as two people can. Goddamn it," she added, closing her eyes, refusing more tears.

"Your name came up the night Henry and I shared this room together. Naturally," Kelly added. "I must have told you this already."

"I don't know. He was probably pissed off at me for being in England with Lynn."

"I don't remember his exact words, but I remember feeling he was awfully hung up on you."

"Hung up?" she smiled.

"Yeah, he was missing you big time."

Her aunt's cool hands were suddenly on either side of her face, and then Elizabeth pressed her lips against Kelly's forehead. "I should have driven up here as soon as I got back to New York. I was trying to go along with what he wanted. I stayed home to paint the stupid kitchen."

"There's no point in thinking that way. Things happen."

"Well, it was nice of you to tell me he was missing me big time." After a pause she asked, "Is it the truth?"

"I think so," Kelly said.

~

David arrived shortly after noon, driving a little black something-or-other that belonged to his mother, I think, Jane wrote in her intermittent notebook for 7/6/96/Sat. Beautiful Elizabeth was on edge like a girl waiting for a date with Mr. Unknown. She'd made a loaf of banana bread that was damp in the middle and burned around the edges. Mary, red-faced, in a sweat, had begun tearing the weeds and leftover debris out of the garden, turning the soil with her long-handled shovel. She said she woke up this morning knowing she wanted a fall garden of beans, beets, and rutabagas, and she'd gone to Baker's for the seeds. What she didn't use or give away would be for the critters. Kelly had set up her portable easel at the edge of the hay field and was making a *plein air* painting of the apple tree on copper in her nineteenth-century straw hat. I watched him taking things in as he walked through the yard, finally seeing this place for the first time, this was why he'd come. When Elizabeth introduced me, he shook my hand, staring, like I was going to interview him for some key position. He was wearing a ponytail, a faded blue Bob Marley T-shirt, shorts frayed around the edges, and hiking boots. He was average height, handsome, with strong arms and legs, and warm large eyes. Maybe I could see the family resemblance to his father. Right away I liked him.

I decided to give Mary a hand in the garden while Elizabeth went off with him in the Land Rover. He wanted a tour of the countryside and to see where the accident had occurred, Mary explained. They had things to talk about. I wanted to be sure I had the story straight so I quizzed her about it. Henry had been flying down a long steep hill on a bicycle just when a truck going in the opposite direction had pulled out to pass a straggly column of cyclists likewise headed up. I had seen the files of twenty or more goofy-looking teenagers on the roads around here in orange vests and white helmets from the Young People's International Cycling Camp, a sign said, a few miles away. I seemed to remember it was a UPS truck for some reason, but Mary said she was pretty sure it was Federal Express. In any case the impatient moron shouldn't have been trying to go around them on that corner and so on, although that's what an accident was, everything conspiring to go wrong in an instant. Mary didn't know what David expected to discover driving down the road where it had happened; Elizabeth would be better off if she didn't dwell on every miserable detail. There was some hopeless legal action pending. Of course Mary had known Henry, she said, ripping up rotten stalks of last year's plants with her bare hands, but it wasn't as though they were close friends. Fitz and Henry were very different, she explained, or they all might have seen more of one another. She didn't know David at all, she was here for Elizabeth, she said, and she'd be awfully glad when this day was over. It was a perfect day, a serene sunny Vermont day, all sky blue and deep green, the sparkling air amazing. I trundled the packed garden cart to the compost heap at the edge of the woods. We turned the soil and raked it smooth and planted the different seeds in rows. I'd have to come back in the fall to see these beans and beets and rutabagas, I told her, and she said it would be wonderful if we all came back here for a weekend in October.

The path was only two-people wide so David and Elizabeth walked ahead with Mary in the middle and Kelly and me taking up the rear. He toted the knapsack slung over one shoulder. Everyone seemed to be chattering normally at first, but talked less as we went deeper into the woods—gleaming woods—as though we might see something if we kept quiet, and by the time we came parallel to the Bear River no one was saying a word. Elizabeth put her arm around David's waist at one point. His back was straight and he was looking straight down the path. Just as I realized I was feeling nervous, the sound of the river suddenly audible, Kelly reached over and took my hand. We went single file down the steeper path to the granite ledge where the river cascaded precipitously over the crashing foaming falls, which threw off a dancing mist in bright slanting sunlight. It was almost five o'clock. The waterfall was far more impressive than I remembered and rather than dropping to a defined basin, it poured itself into a wide expanse of turbulent ongoing riverflow. The swimming hole had been obliterated for the time being. David set the pack on the rock and climbed down along the falls, disappearing around the bend below. Kelly held up her arms and mouthed the word *wow*, I think, because you couldn't hear anything but the sound of the river. David returned, moving quickly and confidently as he climbed back up to us. He nodded to Elizabeth, pointing to the falls, and I realized he was saying, Yes, this is the place, this will do. Elizabeth ushered us back from the deafening rush of river and we huddled in a close circle. Four women and a man. David held the square blue box taken from the knapsack and read something handwritten on a piece of paper about the seasons and the earth and remembering. Then Elizabeth read a poem about "the hour of lead" and "letting go" from an old paperback edition of Emily Dickinson, which she had in the back pocket of her jeans. One of Henry's favorites, she said. It was a little awkward as we arranged ourselves near David, who stood on the granite promontory directly over the falls, dangerously close. He opened the box and took a fistful of his father's remains, like bony gravel, held them straight out over the white rushing water, opened his hand and let them go. Elizabeth reached into the box and did the same thing. The mist, illuminated by the late afternoon sun, drifted back on us, wetting our faces. David tipped the blue box and let the rest of the ashes slowly pour into the river. There were hugs and so forth. Mary gestured to Kelly and me and when we drew back from the river she said, Let's leave them alone.

Our dinner was roasted cornish hens with Mary's amazing fresh pesto and Kelly's huge salad. We ate outside on the picnic table, which made the occasion more open and relaxed, I think. Kelly took some snapshots. We paused to remember Fitz and Henry, then a toast to Adam off in his Sierras, and we raised our glasses to Mary's fall garden, Elizabeth's new job at Lord & Taylor, Kelly's painting of the apple tree, David's upcoming sea kayaking adventure, and my first-to-be-published story—Yay!—in BOMB. We went on toasting Mary's house, the Bear River, Vermont, the hay field, bluebirds, and other stuff, which got kinda silly and funny with everyone putting down the wine. We were feeling no pain by the time we'd cleaned everything up, singing along with Ella again. David was pretty quiet the whole time, maybe we were too much for him. It was dusk and melancholy when we walked down the long drive, Elizabeth and Mary arm in arm quietly talking. David wanted to sleep outside when he knew I'd brought my new tent so I helped him set it up between the lilacs and the hay field. He came in to say good night to everyone. Elizabeth walked him outside and when she returned she thanked us for being there today and said she was exhausted, she was going to bed. By ten o'clock Mary and Kelly had gone upstairs with their books as well.

My room had been Fitz's workroom and there was still a bookcase of his books, a computer, a printer, etc., shoved into one corner with some cardboard boxes of stuff, which Mary was planning to bring back to Cambridge with her. I stretched out on top of the iron bed with Hemingway's *The Garden of Eden* where at the moment the Catherine character was into some bisexual or transsexual trip where she wanted her husband to become her or she wanted to become him, but I was kidding myself. I walked through the dark living room to the slightly darker kitchen, pretended to get myself a glass of water, and pressed my face to the window. I wasn't worried about Kelly or Mary, frankly, but I knew Elizabeth would disapprove. I returned to the bedroom. I was thinking about how he looked when he arrived—surprised—the walk through the woods, the whole incredible business at the river, his brave solemn face, and now he was alone in this place in Vermont in somebody's tent. I knew he was leaving in the morning and I knew I wasn't going to talk myself out of it. I wanted an adventure. I took a Harpoon from the refrigerator. Beautiful outside, starry and still and everything dimly visible. Are you awake in there, I said, everyone went to bed and I'm still up. He must have been lying inside fully dressed because he came out of the tent immediately and he still had his boots on. We sat on top of the picnic table and drank the beer. I told him about this time last year, the huge bonfire we'd kept going all night. He just listened. The mosquitoes finally became too much. I went for another beer—the light in the upstairs window had gone out—and we moved into the tent because we didn't want to be in the house. We talked about places—Italy, San Francisco, New York—not people. I did most of the talking. Finally I said, I'd like to stay out here tonight. Is that all right? I went into the house for my pillow and the blanket. We slept with our clothes on. When I awoke a little later, my back was to him, his arm was around me, and his hand was covering my breast. I placed my hand over his and went back to sleep. At dawn, maybe five-thirty, we were both awake, and I just wanted to observe him, his face, while he lay on his back staring at the brightening ceiling of the tent. What are you thinking, David? He talked a little about his sister and his father. One thing he couldn't stand was his sister not knowing what had happened to their father, the way everything went on happening that she couldn't know, and now his father not knowing either, like the only people who needed to know what was happening couldn't know, etc. Did I understand what he was talking about? I said, Yes, I think I do understand. Long silence. I touched his face and said, You're beautiful. I traced a finger down the center of his forehead and his nose and over his lips like this was a movie, and he didn't move. I made up my mind and asked him if he wanted to make love, using those words, rather than have sex or fuck. Then he looked at me, his eyes widening, and said, No, not really, he had no protection, besides this was fine the way it was, he liked just lying there with me. Don't get me wrong, I told him, I wasn't a loose woman or something. It was Vermont, I said, the whole thing happening here. We lay for quite a while watching the day brighten through the tent, not saying anything, holding hands between us, and I think we both felt pretty good about being there like that. I definitely did, just as happy we skipped fucking.

We were the first ones up, which seemed like a little luck. He left about ten, the four of us like a mixed bag of cheerleaders waving and hooting good-bye as he drove out. Mary didn't envy him the long drive alone. What's he thinking? she asked. I think he's going to be fine, Elizabeth said, adding, God knows why. I thought so too. It was another *splendid* day, as Mary would say. She spent it cleaning all the multipaned windows on the first floor inside and out. When Kelly asked, Why, Mother? You aren't even going to be here, Mary said they needed it, nothing made a house as bright and

294

cheerful as clean windows. Elizabeth volunteered to shop for supper, then took herself for a walk in the afternoon. Kelly finished her
plein air painting and presented it as a gift to her mother. I took
down the tent, read for a while, went off exploring the woods,
and ended up sunning myself by the river. Now—almost six Sunday evening—I'm writing here at the picnic table, I hear Mary and
Elizabeth talking in the kitchen as they *whip up* our supper, and
right this second, as I pen these very words—how's this for up-to-
the-minute realism, *plein air* writing?—Kelly comes through the
screen door with two glasses of white wine. She sits down opposite
me and places one glass directly in front of my notebook and says,
What are you writing about, Hemingway?

Each morning, as she awoke, his forever-after absence, his new
nonbeing, was a fresh astonishment to her. Death was a wonder.
The person with whom she wanted to share her amazement was
Henry, of course. Nothing seemed more important, tremendous,
and yet living—continuing to live—meant that almost everything
went on more importantly than the absent person. The extinguished person. The illuminated face on her small alarm clock said
three-thirty. The room was dark, stars in the window. Who was her
sorrow for? From the time of his daughter's death until his own,
Henry had hardly escaped his grief for a single day. Now his
anguish seemed pointless. He couldn't help himself. Anymore than
I can help myself, she thought. Yes, maybe she understood more
now, and she understood less. If she imagined her own life coming
to an end within a year or five years or ten, nothing seemed more
pathetic and futile than stubbornly bearing heartache and regret to
her solitary grave. You had to go on living, you couldn't help that,
there was nothing to be guilty about. Dying was what defined

being alive—that simple truth had never been so glaring—and suffering was mostly a question of random timing.

You wouldn't say that to David, though, would you, as if the way to get through the rest of life without his sister or his father was just to lighten up about it. He had his work cut out for him, she thought. He'd gotten out of the car at the site of the accident and walked uphill for half a mile along the side of the road as though searching for something lost. Several cars slowed to pass him. He picked up a handful of sand and gravel and looked at it before dusting off his hands. He walked up onto the bank and sat on his heels among the tall ferns with his head bowed. He didn't know what to do with himself. There was nothing to do. When he returned to the car, she asked him what he made of it, the site of the accident, but he didn't respond. Later at the river, he was rigid; he had made up his mind to be stoic. They would have preferred holding their Bear River ceremony on the anniversary of Henry's death, but July had been more convenient for them than August. The date didn't matter.

Her father had also died when she was in her early twenties, but she'd hardly known the man, or suffered the loss, more engrossed at the time by a new boyfriend almost twice her age. Her first passionate affair taught her the lesson life taught repeatedly: you don't get what you want. Alan's cruelty had revealed itself within weeks but she went on living with him, sometimes fearfully, for the next several months, finally escaping to her mother's house only when it seemed she might really get hurt if she stuck around. What a sad little controlling twerp Mr. Brilliant Charming turned out to be with his silent rages and jealous ultimatums. How naïve she had been then, imagining herself lucky, wanting to be happy, expecting to be happy at some point. Most of the time you didn't know what you wanted, but if that exalted goal ever seemed within grasp, you immediately began to learn the innumerable reasons why it wasn't going to happen. Each possible happiness became a lesson in its unattainability.

She observed Kelly's sleeping face in the bed beside her. Everything ahead of her, you wanted to say, but that was already hard to believe. The young woman submitted to social and economic deprivation in order to pursue her personal, inimitable art. How did anyone hope to get ahead in that heartless, fickle scene? Kelly had spent a year making twelve paintings for her next show. Once the gallery took its cut, she came out working way below minimum wage, even while selling her paintings for as much as the New York market could bear. Now she was looking down the barrel of another year of arduous labor, while making ends meet with a half-assed job. You couldn't be an artist was the lesson her life was teaching her. If she ever lucked out of her financial straits, there would be no lack of even more withering obstacles lined up to oppress her. You couldn't be on your own in your little lightweight body, you had to commit yourself to some towering voracious entity of glass and steel. How much easier to have a lousy job with cozy benefits, returning home just to veg out rather than roll up your sleeves and get on with your *real work*, sure to be lost on the big insatiable world out there. The final crushing indignity was that no one cared, not a whit. Why should they? No, Kelly wasn't going to get what she wanted, and yet she couldn't help being who she was any more than Henry could, for that matter. Her guts and talent and tenacity were a curse. She'd been lucky, Elizabeth thought of herself, not to have possessed enough of such qualities to make the art life a serious temptation. As it turned out, she made a decent living. The tawdry, market-driven fruits of her labor had a measurable impact on a huge audience, which translated into a reliable paycheck.

Nobody got what they wanted. Everybody got what they didn't

want. Lovely Ted snuffed out, only in his thirties. Fitz struck down
in the garden at—what?—fifty-five. He had seemed to possess a
certain equanimity, an insouciant air, although that was surely not
the truth about anyone with Fitz's ambition, who played his cards
so close to the chest. David was already filled to the brim with what
he didn't want, and it was bound to weigh him down for years to
come. The likes of Gustavo, she considered, seemed to cruise along,
as though above the fray, but that was nonsense too.

He had called her that September, maybe October, soon after
he'd returned from Europe, as he'd promised he would. Her grief
had made her open, tender, forgiving, and she actually welcomed
the sound of his voice. He was in New York, he wanted to see her
as soon as possible, he'd thought about her constantly since their
meeting in London. When she told him about Henry, there was
utter silence on his end, which might have gone on indefinitely, it
seemed, so she attempted to rescue them by retelling details of the
accident's aftermath—the harrowing trip to Vermont, the memorial
service in New York, her recent months of numbing dismay. Gustavo
was shocked, of course, at a loss for words, and concluded by saying he regretted intruding at such a difficult time. She wanted to
protest—seeing him might do her good—but before she managed
to speak, he was hastily terminating the phone call. If there's
anything I can do, Elizabeth, please let me know. Anything, he
repeated. He gave her a number. He would check on her in a
month, he said. Perhaps she'd feel like getting supper or something
then. And without waiting for her to reply, he hung up. He hadn't
called since, not in the last nine months, not once. No, cruising
along wasn't the name for it. Gustavo had promptly bailed out. His
conduct, insofar as she took it to be conclusive evidence of the
man's character, gratified her—the way a guilty verdict might
assuage the vengefulness of a murder victim's family. Gustavo had
grasped the wisdom of putting his personal interests and desires

before any other considerations. He was successful, all right, ambitious, winning, and useless to anyone. Utterly useless.

A noise, a muffled crashing, startled her. She thought she'd heard something earlier, a kind of rummaging, but dismissed the thought when there were no further sounds. Now she heard another thump, which caused her to sit up. Kelly, rolling onto her other side, remained asleep. Elizabeth stepped into the narrow hall and saw that Mary's bedroom door was open. The sounds of activity came from the kitchen. She pulled on her jeans and a hooded sweatshirt and went downstairs.

The kitchen was strewn with piles of various belongings as if the place was being packed up, the people moving out. There were assorted canned goods, plus bottles and jars ranging from empty to almost full. An old waffle iron, for example, an electric coffeemaker, an old metal fan, miscellaneous vases, platters, ceramic bowls, tin cookie boxes. An array of cleaning and polishing agents, assorted aerosol cans, sandpaper and steel wool. There were several closed cartons marked fragile. An open box of empty mason jars. One pile had evidently been designated for old boxes of cereal and crackers: Quaker oats, for example, Cheerios. A pyramid of gallons and quarts of paint stood on the kitchen table next to a bunch of paintbrushes. Near the screen door articles of clothing—jackets, shirts, pants, shoes—had been tossed into a heap three feet high.

She could hear her sister muttering to herself as she struggled with something back in the pantry, a deep roomy closet to the right of the refrigerator, which extended into the mudroom, creating an inside wall there.

"Mary?"

She emerged from the pantry carrying a wooden-legged ironing board, which had a yellow sheet pinned to its padded covering. She was in her bare feet, her unruly hair unkempt and her flushed face smudged with dirt. Her khaki Bermudas and the oversized Grateful

Dead T-shirt, probably Adam's, were filthy even in the dull incandescent light of the kitchen. Mary's cheeks and knees as well as her hands and feet looked coarse and reddened from her exertions.

"What are you doing up?" she asked Elizabeth.

"How could I sleep with this racket going on? What are you doing down here? It's hardly four in the morning."

"I couldn't sleep. Can you believe all this stuff was crammed into that pantry? There's still more in there."

One grouping consisted of badminton rackets, a football, a Wiffle ball and bat, an odd little hatchet, a coil of rope, a canoe paddle, a pair of cross-country ski poles, an old leather satchel. There was a small pile of screwdrivers and pliers, a pair of pruning shears, and a jar of mixed nuts, bolts, and screws.

"So what are you doing?"

"Half the stuff needs to get thrown out. Maybe Kelly can use some of the kitchen paraphernalia. Some things stay here."

"You picked a good time to delve into it, Mary. Aren't you returning to Boston when the rest of us leave?"

"I'll see what I get done. I'm cleaning out that *fucking* pantry, Mary, if it's the last thing I do. Fitz's proclamations." She smiled. "That pantry *haunts* me, he said. This is the year, Mary, this is the year of the pantry. He couldn't bring himself to face it."

There was a small pile of old bricks, a fiberglass fishing pole, a shoe box of chessmen, and a large net, which Elizabeth guessed was a butterfly net.

"Well, you've unearthed quite a mess, that's for sure. How long have you been up?"

"A couple of hours. I'm cleaning the whole thing out, then I'm going to paint the walls and shelves with whatever paint I've got there."

"Isn't that a little excessive?"

"Then I'm taking everything that's going, to the dump."

Elizabeth moved to the pile of clothing by the door. "These clothes weren't in the pantry, were they?"

"That's what got me started—cleaning out his closet upstairs. That's all going to Goodwill."

"Really?" She held up a plaid flannel shirt. "This is like new." She picked a black silk shirt from the heap along with a perfectly good leather belt. "There are some nice things here."

"Well, I don't know anyone Fitz's size, do you?"

"It seems a shame. What a nifty jacket," she said, lifting the arm of a tweed sport coat. "How about these shoes—from England—and this sweater? Made in Ireland, it says."

"Elizabeth, I've looked at everything. Take whatever you want. Otherwise, it's out of here. I'm sure some poor souls will make good use of it."

"I'm surprised." She stopped before she put her foot in her mouth.

"I don't need to be sentimental about Fitz's clothes, for God's sake. What am I going to do with them? They're going to Goodwill first thing this morning."

"I'm sure you're right, I just couldn't do it. Henry's personal things seem like part of him. I know that's ridiculous. I just can't pitch the stuff out."

"You will when you're ready."

"What's left? I'll give you a hand."

"I want to do it myself, I really do. Why don't you go back to bed?"

"I couldn't sleep now."

Mary disappeared into the pantry again, and Elizabeth casually, as it were, began sorting through Fitz's clothing, holding up a cotton shirt, a pair of pants, a sweater, as though she might come across an item worth salvaging after all. She found a single brass key in the watch pocket of a pair of Levi's, a number of restaurant receipts in the side pockets of two sport coats, along with two ballpoint pens, a tube of Chap Stick, a brittle cigar, a program from a local concert of chamber music, and a crumbling and yellowed white rose. The front pocket of a weathered canvas barn jacket, which had hung in the mudroom, contained a handful of sealed envelopes with stamps on them. Two were official business: New England Telephone and Northeast Utilities. Two bore handwritten local addresses: Robert Graves, the neighboring farmer, and Ben's Service Station respectively. And the last envelope was addressed to a Helen Trudell in New York City.

Mary staggered out of the pantry with a bulky contraption grasped in her arms.

"I'd forgotten about this. The year we were married we went to Italy, remember, and this was our present to ourselves. Our Baby Gaggia. We designated it our Vermont espresso/cappuccino machine. It worked fine for the first few years, then it began to leak. It was never the same after that."

"Couldn't it be fixed?"

"Fitz tried. The thing kept busting. Good-bye, Gaggia."

"Really?"

"Do you think you can fix it, Elizabeth? Baby Gaggia is going to the dump," Mary said, stooping to place the bulky chrome-plated machine on the floor.

"I found this key. Do you recognize it?"

Mary turned the brass key in her hand. "Ace," she read. "Where was it?"

"In a pair of blue jeans. In that little watch pocket they have."

"Honestly, Elizabeth, ransacking his clothes?"

"I felt it the minute I picked them up, that's all. Do you know what it goes to?"

"I can't imagine. One more lost key." She tossed it into a box of dump-bound debris. "I'm not saving it for anything."

"And these," Elizabeth said, holding the envelopes. "Didn't you notice them? Bills that didn't get mailed, I guess."

Mary shuffled through them quickly, and pitched them into the same box. "Now that's funny. No, I hadn't noticed. I'm sure the bills caught up with me the next month."

"That must be your friend Helen, right? Don't you want to open it? Just out of curiosity," she added.

"Yes, our friend Helen. Fitz was always dropping people notes. No, I'm not the least bit curious."

Elizabeth retrieved the Helen envelope from where it had slipped down along the side of the box. "Well, I am. Mind if I open it?"

Mary deftly snatched the item from her hand and stuffed it, crumpled, into the box again. "Yes, I do mind. You wouldn't open it if he was alive."

"Relax, Mary, I didn't mean to upset you."

"Just leave it."

Jane entered the room wearing a vast turquoise T-shirt, squinting, rubbing her eyes. "Is there a problem? I heard your voices." She took in the room. "Holy shit, what happened in here?"

"Sorry," Mary said, "there isn't a problem. We're just bickering. I'm cleaning out the pantry."

"It's kinda early, isn't it? Not even light yet." Jane helped herself to a glass of water at the sink before shuffling out of the room. "Okay, see you in the morning."

In a moment Elizabeth said, "Maybe you should hold off on some of these things. You might regret it later. What's the rush, you know?"

"When am I going to do it, next year? No, this is the year of the pantry. I'm doing it now." She added, "I'm sure Fitz understands perfectly."

"How about coffee?" Elizabeth suggested.

"I'd love a cup of coffee," Mary said. She picked up the fishing pole and the butterfly net and moved them to the pile of sporting equipment. "Fitz was no fisherman," she said. "That's one thing he wasn't."

Elizabeth made one cup at a time—Mary's Vermont method—slowly pouring boiling water into a cone-shaped filter, which contained a heaping tablespoon of French roast ground to espresso consistency.

"Let's take it outside. The sun's coming up."

They sat at the picnic table. Mary pulled on a navy blue sweater, Harvard emblem on left breast, from the pile of Fitz's clothes. The air was cooler than Elizabeth anticipated, and completely still, the ascending songs of birds amazing, the strong coffee just what the doctor ordered.

"I'm glad you have this place," she said.

Mary nodded. "I still love it, I really do. I want to come back soon."

"I want to ask you something."

"How ominous."

"Just now, inside, you said, I know Fitz understands."

"Did I? And?"

"What did you mean by that? I know Fitz understands perfectly. What do people mean when they say something like that?"

Mary regarded her thoughtfully with clear, intelligent, candid eyes. "I believe Fitz is with me all the time," she said. "He understands what I'm doing."

"You mean, you can imagine how he'd respond to you cleaning out the pantry, you're sure he would understand?"

"No, I mean he does understand. I know he does."

Elizabeth felt her pulse skip with alarm, her hands squeezed the hot mug, and her eyes darted to avoid her sister's blunt gaze. "Well,

I don't understand," she said. "Since when do you have these . . . what do you call them? Beliefs?"

Mary was puzzled. "I feel the same way about Ted. I always have. I can't imagine feeling differently."

"Fitz understands? Ted understands? What kind of talk is that, Mary? They're dead and gone. How do they understand? Who understands? I don't get it. Have you become a born-again or something?"

"Of course not. Is this some kind of revelation? Haven't we ever talked about this?"

"Obviously not. Look at my hands. I'm shaking."

"You're so extreme, Elizabeth. Don't you feel Henry's presence or however you want to put it? Don't you believe Henry understands what's going on?"

"No. Henry no longer exists. He's dead and gone like Fitz and Ted. Henry was cremated. We poured his remains into the Bear River. There's nothing left to Henry, which is unbelievable and unbearable—I can hardly grasp it, Mary—and also undeniable. There is no Henry understanding anything anywhere."

Mary stood up. "No wonder you're miserable."

"Of course I'm miserable that Henry is dead. I can't believe we're having this conversation. I feel like I'm talking to a stranger."

"Calm down. You're so . . . insistent. It doesn't matter what either of us believes."

"What does that mean? Of course it matters."

"My coffee is gone and my feet are getting cold. I'm going inside to finish what I started."

She caught Mary's hand before the woman stood up from the table. "I'm sorry. I'm feeling volatile these days. I miss him," she entreated.

"I know that," Mary said, and her voice had softened. She gently brushed a strand of hair away from Elizabeth's face. "I know how you feel, Betsy, I really do."

No one had called her by that girlhood name since her mother had died. The sound of it, coming from her sister, caused an inward lurch. When she looked up, Mary was smiling at her affectionately. "Betsy Blush," she said, recovering yet another nickname, one that surely hadn't been spoken in thirty years or more. "You were always volatile."

Elizabeth remained at the table after Mary went back inside. A red-gold penumbra of light now defined the hill behind the barn, and the songs of birds intensified, it seemed to her, with the expanding glow. As she looked across the lawn to the woods beneath the brightening sky, she tried to imagine Henry being here on such a morning, alone, with his cup of coffee, taking it all in, but the attempt only made his absence all the more irrevocable. Then she tried to imagine herself gone, as completely gone from the world, as nonexistent, as Henry was, and that only made her presence, as she absorbed the colors and sounds and sensations of the moment, that much more vivid, yes, concentrated, indelible. I'm here, she thought.

Behind her Kelly removed the portable screen in the upstairs window and stuck her head out. "Oh wow," she said. "The light!"

"I know."

"The birds have gone berserk this morning!" She reached her arms out the window as though to embrace the whole morning-in-Vermont scene. "Isn't it incredible here?"

"Yes."

"What are you doing up so early?"

"I was lying in bed wide awake, so I got up. But I'm glad," she added, "I wanted to see it once before we left."

"See what?"

Elizabeth waved her arm in a broad arc. "This," she said.

8 *Mannahatta*

David spent an hour going through the Mackintosh exhibition at the Met, which his mother had recommended earlier at breakfast, and which turned out to be a downer really, the story of an original artist-architect-designer who left his mark, only to end up destitute and pretty much forgotten, wandering around France with his faithful wife, painting watercolors of rocks until he died at sixty. And he couldn't get all that excited about a tearoom, although most people—it was just past noon, Sunday before Christmas, and crowded—seemed pretty psyched to be there. His favorite Mackintosh chair had a flying bird image cut into the tall back of it, maybe a gull, which became a halo, the museum note suggested, above the head of whoever sat in the chair. A magical word: halo. Hello, he thought. Hallow. Hallowed. Haloed, was that a word? He found a present for his mother or maybe Elizabeth, a Mackintosh pin that jumped out at him when he glanced into one of the gift display cases, so his trip to the Met paid off after all. He hadn't started thinking about Christmas yet—tomorrow was plenty of time to start thinking about it—and here he had one present already. Better for Elizabeth, maybe, because she had that half Scottish thing going for her. Scot, Scots, Scotch. He put the small gift box into his shirt pocket under the bulky sweater and tossed the bag into the trash can. Outside he bought a pretzel, squirted some Day-Glo mustard on it, and pitched it after one bite. He tapped the wallet in his left front pocket, just checking. The day was overcast but mild for late December—there were people hanging out on the steps—and he decided to walk downtown, he felt like walking. He went through the park, observing trees, thinking sycamore, buckeye, tulip spontaneously, and he only gradually recalled that naming trees was something he'd done with his father when he was a kid. Yeah, that definitely started with Dad, knowing the trees in the parks. Elm, you got it. How about that specimen still holding some leaves? Oak. You're on a roll, buddy. Ash. You never miss that one, do you?

Past the Plaza the street got busy. He popped up the stairs of St. Patrick's two at a time; he'd only been inside maybe twice before in his life. He walked down the main aisle, past a scattering of people bent forward in pews, some with beads, and turned and walked out again. A memory of his sister playing a Christmas concert in a redbrick church on Madison abruptly intruded: that Corelli his mother had been playing last night when he got in. Remember this piece? she asked. Mom, of course I remember it. Hardly a year and a half since his father's death, and over four years since his sister had died, but to his mother the first loss was like yesterday, over-shadowing and all-consuming, as though her grief didn't have room for the old man. Like she just couldn't let it in, what had happened, at least she didn't let him see it. That was one way. He could jump into Saks and maybe get that new easy-to-remember perfume, Champs-Elysées, which was the only thing she wanted from him, she said, if he wanted to get her something. No, I don't want to get you anything, I've got so many people to shop for, you know. Did you have to say that, David? Today he was sorry he'd said it.

Maybe they'd have Champs-Elysées at a discount in one of the perfume stores farther down.

He'd thought a week would be plenty of time in New York, almost too long, but he'd been mistaken. Tomorrow he had to do his shopping and run errands, drive over to the river and get a small tree for one thing. David, honestly, we don't need to bother with that, do we? Wouldn't a wreath in the front window be plenty this year? Mom, we're not going to start not having a Christmas tree, that's final. Christmas Eve she was having her best friend Susan and her ten-year-old daughter over for bouillabaisse and he had to be there. Christmas day they were going to Connecticut to be with Uncle Jim and some of his kids and some of his wife's kids, along with various boyfriends and spouses, which was always a circus about who seemed to be making it since college, who seemed to have life by the tail, man. Nobody in those families knew anything. Then Thursday he was slated to go to Tenth Street for a quiet dinner, Elizabeth called it, just her friend Lynn, who was definitely a live wire, and Elizabeth wanted him to meet an old friend of hers, who she'd recently connected with again, using that phrase *connected with*. What was someone like Elizabeth supposed to do, turn into a spinster? I'm just surprised, his mother said, and he said, She's full of life, she wants to go out and enjoy herself, what's she supposed to do, sit home and dry up and fade away? I'm just surprised, David, I'm not criticizing Elizabeth. His flight back to San Francisco was first thing Saturday morning, the twenty-eighth. That left Friday for him to meet up with Michael, who was the last longtime New York friend still around that he wanted to see.

So today, his first full day in town, was his only chance to hook up with anyone else while he was here. But then this was the only day she could see him anyway, as it turned out, so maybe it was meant to be. Anticipating the meeting made him walk faster, he didn't know what to expect or how things would go conversation-wise, whether getting together was a good idea or even what the point of it was. She was just someone he wanted to see, that's all he could say. When he contacted her the week before, she sounded surprised, then hesitant—although she was the one who'd suggested he call her in the first place. Finally she said all right, she could do it Sunday, the twenty-second, that was really her only free day, at . . . Why don't we say four. She suggested Bruxelles on Greenwich Avenue, a small quiet place near her neighborhood, and that seemed propitious, he thought, because he knew the restaurant well, a place his father had liked to go for the excellent Belgian beers they served there.

He had on his good boots, clean jeans, the sweater Elizabeth had given him for Christmas last year. He walked with his back straight, his shoulders relaxed, arms at his sides, his stomach firm. You didn't rush, you moved at a steady, comfortable pace that demanded a certain rigor and gathered momentum and could be maintained for hours. That's how you walked, although it wasn't easy to keep your personal rhythm among the teeming masses on Fifth Avenue, man, where everybody sported his or her own walk, inevitably wired into being no one but themselves. It was pretty hard to cruise along in this seething sea of humanity, all right, where everyone had his own walking style whether he knew it or not.

From time to time he tapped his wallet in the front pocket of his jeans. He had about five hundred dollars in cash on him, which was really his entire *personal fortune* at the moment. He'd taken some time off and gone to Yosemite in early November—he'd climbed Sunkist and two different routes on the Needles—and then he had to buy the plane ticket back here, so now he was down to his last five hundred bucks once he paid his January bills, which meant he'd have to work his ass off the minute he got back. He wasn't afraid to work his ass off. What are you going to do, David? You can't live hand to mouth, you need a plan. Mom, please, I just got home. Are you going to apply to Berkeley this year? I haven't been here for two hours yet, have I? Don't worry about me, okay? You don't have to worry about me.

By the time he reached Fourteenth Street he had time to kill, so he continued south. The First Presbyterian Church at Fifth and Twelfth stopped him. One warm summer evening he and his sister and their father had paused here after supper and watched fireflies blinking over the small area of lawn and in the shrubbery against the building. He'd finished his second year at NYU that spring and his sister had finished all the treatment she could possibly receive to combat the ineradicable disease that had dominated her life almost since she'd graduated from college. The fireflies on the small skirt of lawn in the midst of Manhattan that night seemed like a miracle and gave them all a brief, wonderful lift, although of course there was nothing miraculous about that mundane natural occurrence. He stood with both hands on the black iron fence like a man behind bars. He tried the gate, but Sunday services were long over, the gate was locked, and he couldn't see a way into the churchyard.

As he turned right onto Tenth Street, toward Sixth Avenue, he felt tension squeeze his shoulders and he needed a couple of deep breaths. Looking down the narrow street, no one in sight, was like watching his father coming toward him, raising his arm, and then thoughts of his mother and sister and Elizabeth complicated the picture because it was hard to keep them separate. He hadn't been down the street since last July when he'd flown back in order to be with Elizabeth in Vermont for the long July weekend. The Marshall Chess Club, a small sign at a basement door, was a place he'd never set foot in. The street's one pink building was bright even on an overcast day. The wisteria, a twisted, gnarly, leafless tangle, which clung to two of the buildings along this side of the street, was still beautiful—*because you knew it was alive,* he thought. Imagining the profusion of fragrant pendulous blossoms, he was struck by a spasm of emotion. The old man had celebrated this wisteria on Tenth Street as one of the wonders of the world, basically. Each winter he remarked that the pathetic-looking plant was still beautiful because you knew it was alive, because you knew it would bloom and be splendid again, because you knew that all the botanical information necessary to produce the exquisite leaves and flowers was right there dormant and waiting in the dead-looking heap of tangled vines. *Anything alive is beautiful, that's something I've learned.*

He passed his father's building—Elizabeth's building—and crossed the street and started back the other way. Chances were Elizabeth wasn't around, but he had no intention of seeing her today in any case. There wasn't time for that. These emotional flare-ups had to stop, man, he didn't want to look like he'd been crying, for Christ's sake. He continued down Tenth, NYU country, to Broadway. Grace Church, like a little sequestered island of old-worldness, stood directly across the way. For the countless times he had passed the gray stone edifice with its little spires and squat configurations and ornamental trees, it had never occurred to him to visit the place. He crossed Broadway and entered the small churchyard. The main entrance was locked, so he went around to the side, also locked. While open every weekday, according to the posted hours, the building was closed after morning services on Sundays. From within the churchyard, the commotion of Broadway seemed weirdly distant, as though entirely outside Grace Church's sacrosanct pale. He pressed his wallet in the left front pocket. What could have happened to it since the last time he checked? He touched the small box in his shirt pocket through the sweater, then tapped the hard surface of the three-and-a-half-inch computer disk that was in the other pocket of his shirt. No, some monstrous adversary had not taken him by the ankles and shaken him upside down, spilling the precious contents of his pockets onto the street. Interestingly, he'd forgotten about the disk.

Time to kill. He turned west onto Fourth Street, passing the south end of Washington Square Park. Quiet Zone, a sign said. The mottled sycamores were beautiful against the gray sky. Several people lay stretched out on benches. A man with a heaped grocery cart was rummaging through his possessions, maybe rearranging things, taking care of business. He had piles of stuff, man, he had amassed an awful lot of stuff in one impossible lifetime. He looked all right. He was alive. The pink item he was struggling to extricate from the cart just then, David saw, was a rubber hot water bottle. Anything alive is beautiful, he thought, that's something I've learned. That's something you'll learn. Even ugliness, pain, suffering. Do you know what I mean?

His hand went to the wallet. You didn't intentionally make eye contact with people passing you on the street. Eye contact could be dangerous, that was something you learned pretty quick. You got used to passing hundreds and thousands and tens of thousands of people of all shapes and sizes and colors without looking at any of them, basically, you got used to being alone surrounded by hundreds and thousands of people at every moment.

I came to Speedwell, he thought, not a soul in sight, thinking a period of isolation would do me good. Words to that effect. Famous first sentence. Yeah, that did you good, all right. By Twelfth Street, he picked up the pace a little, heading for Seventh Avenue, almost four o'clock. She would be wearing a cranberry-red coat, that's how he'd know her. She had short dark hair. Of course she might not show, they were strangers to start with, the whole convoluted connection between them pretty lame. If she was there, fine, and if not, that would be all right with him too.

Bruxelles was at the narrow end of a short triangular block between Greenwich Avenue and Thirteenth Street. A half dozen men and women walked toward him as he proceeded down the sidewalk toward the restaurant. The candid stare of one woman in a black coat made him glance away. When he looked again, the woman was smiling—at someone behind him, he assumed—and in the next instant, just as he approached the doorway of the restaurant, she stepped directly into his path.

"Hi, David." She extended her hand in a black leather glove. Her smile was unguarded.

"I was psyched for a cranberry coat."

"That's right, I forgot." She added, "I wasn't worried, I knew I'd pick you out immediately."

"Yeah, how did you do that?"

She reached out, startling him, and lightly tapped the side of his face. "Look at you. How could I miss?"

They took a small table by a window. There was another couple at a table behind them and one man seated at the bar.

"So," she said, "isn't this interesting?"

She had a strong face, dark eyes and eyebrows, and full lips. Her makeup style was natural, he thought, and in her off-white shirt, open at the collar, her color was healthy. His father hadn't used words like beautiful to describe *this Helen*, not that he remembered. Maybe his father didn't think she was, compared to Elizabeth. She combed her fingers through short wavy hair. "I wish it would snow."

"I was wondering if you'd show up."

She picked up her gloves, which she'd placed on the table, and put them down again. "I was blown away by your letter," she said, cutting to the heart of the matter. "I wanted to tell you in person—how sorry I am. It's all so crazy and painful."

"I thought maybe you'd want to know what happened."

"Oh yes. I could have lived without it, believe me, but you're right, I'd want to know." She added, "Most people wouldn't have written. That took imagination, David. I was impressed."

"It seems like you were about the last person he spent any time with."

"Was I?"

"I was supposed to go up there and hang out for a while, but I didn't make it. I was too busy screwing around in Italy."

The waitress delivered a tall dark beer for him and white wine for Helen.

"You mean you should have been in Vermont?"

"I don't know." He glanced around the room. "My father used to like Bruxelles. Did you ever see him around here?"

"No, never."

He raised his glass. "What should we drink to?"

"We should drink to Henry."

"Okay." He clinked her glass with his own. "To you, Dad."

"I received a note from him soon after I got back here that summer, but when I didn't hear from him again, I just dropped it. That was that."

"Sure."

"We were just getting to know each other before I left. We had dinner twice, I think. He made something good, I don't remember what."

"And you built the stone wall."

She smiled. "What do you know about that?"

"That came up in the thing he wrote. Fitz's Wall. You know, in the computer."

"I see." She nodded, thinking that over.

He had returned to San Francisco with his father's Mac in July, but he hadn't turned the thing on until one night in October. He'd read the first page of the document entitled *Fitz—I came to Speedwell, population about fifteen hundred . . .* —then turned the machine off. He wasn't ready to read anything then, and he thought maybe he'd never be ready. He couldn't bear the sound of his father's voice, for one thing, coming to him from that summer in Vermont. Maybe *Fitz* was none of his business. In another mood, the first week of November, he double-clicked the *Fitz* icon and read the document through from beginning to end in two days. He felt, he imagined, the way his father must have felt when he first read Fitz's *Vermont*, which he'd incorporated into his own narrative. But more so. Infinitely more so. One result of the reading was that he couldn't get *this Helen* out of his head. The likelihood that the woman didn't know what had happened to his father after she'd returned to New York disturbed him, like an important piece of unfinished business. He wrote her at Pantheon—a stab in the dark really—explaining that he'd come across her name in his father's computer, and he didn't know if she realized there had been an accident, and so forth. Her response was unexpectedly prompt. She was shocked and saddened by his letter, but she was also grateful he'd written her. She enclosed her phone number, saying she'd like to meet him when he was in New York next, if that suited him.

"Fitz's Wall, huh?" She asked, "Did you know Fitz?"

"I met him a couple of times, that's all."

She sat back, leaving her glass on the table before her. "I like your sweater. It looks like one of those Irish seafaring garments."

"Scots or Scottish or whatever. A gift from my stepmother."

"I've forgotten her name."

"Elizabeth."

"Of course. Tell me about Elizabeth. How's she doing?"

"I think she's doing well." He hadn't seen her yet this trip, he explained, he was scheduled to have dinner at her place on Boxing Day. "I didn't know what Boxing Day was until I met Elizabeth. She wants me to meet her new boyfriend, a hot-shit award-winning journalist of some sort."

She laughed. "You sound like you hate him already, David."

"Actually, I hope I like the guy. I want to like him."

"Good for her."

They swapped additional details about their respective holiday plans. Helen was leaving for Chicago in the morning. She posed casual questions about his life in San Francisco. He shared a big apartment on Page, near the Panhandle, with two other guys, who were never there. No, he wasn't with anyone right now, he couldn't deal with the women he'd met lately. He got onto the subject of climbing for ten minutes, the Yosemite trip, prodded by more questions from Helen. Yes, sometimes you were afraid, that was part of it. You did it because it was a pure exhilarating high, just you and this rock, and there was nothing like it. A successful climb that took all you had to give was like a religious experience, he said, a revelation. She listened with her eyes focused thoughtfully as though what he was telling her demanded careful scrutiny. The streetlights had come on outside, people kept coming into the bar, the place grew loud and cozy. They had to lean toward one another to talk. They ordered another round of drinks.

"Let's have an order of these pommes frites," she told the waitress. "I'm hungry." Then she excused herself. She looked trim and sturdy in her plain black pants, he thought, she had a nice body, she looked fine. She was pushing forty or something.

He pulled off his sweater and rolled up the sleeves of his blue cotton shirt. The waitress returned with their drinks, the pommes frites in a silver cup, and said, "Getting warm in here, huh?" She was a pretty young woman in thick-soled black boots, with dark tights under her short black skirt. They were all over the place, there was no end to beautiful young women.

Helen's shirt was a bright spot as she edged her way through standing customers toward their table. "I love it in here tonight," she said. "It's festive. It should be snowing outside." She dipped pommes frites into the creamy homemade mayonnaise. "This is my idea of french fries, David. They're addictive." She sipped her wine. When she spoke again her mood had altered. "This is strange, isn't it? I go to Vermont and meet Henry Ash under extraordinary circumstances, and over a year later I'm sitting in Bruxelles with his son eating pommes frites. You can't invent this stuff, can you? You can't make it up. It's too much. You can't imagine what's going to happen next." She sat back. "What's next?"

He didn't know how to respond. Nodding, he said, "No, you can't imagine what's going to happen next."

She leaned toward him across the table, and when she looked up her eyes were shining, solemn. "I know about your sister. I mean, I realize . . ." She paused. "Fitz," she said. "Now Henry." Shaking her head.

Stupidly he said, "Everything's an accident."

She dabbed at the mayonnaise with a piece of potato and regarded him with pursed lips, as though gauging the propriety of what she was about to say. "Was it an accident? Your father's death? I can't help it, I've had that thought."

He felt his face go hot. "I saw where it happened. No, there's no question. . . ." She was watching him struggle, frowning sympathetically; he felt violent. "That's not a question," he repeated.

"But you never know, do you, with something like that?" She'd decided to drop it. "I guess we'll never know."

His disappointment was greater than his anger; he hated this wrong turn. "Wait, you don't understand. You have no idea. You have it completely wrong." How could he get through to her? "No," he said, looking around the room, motioning to his surroundings, "he loved this. If you knew my dad . . ."

She reached for his hand and brought it down to the table. "Listen, that was stupid of me. I know you're right." She added, "I was speaking from my own jaundiced experience, that's all. Don't be upset, David. I have these dumb ideas, and I blurt them out. I don't know when to keep my mouth shut."

"That's just completely wrong. If you'd read this thing he wrote . . ."

"Look at me," she said. "I know you're right. I believe you. I absolutely mean that."

He sat back and took a breath, as though the woman had come clean, confessed to perpetrating a devastating and unjust lie. She wasn't as blind and stupid as she'd seemed for a minute there. He'd fallen during the Sunkist climb, the rock seemed to fly up before his eyes spectacularly, then the rope caught him. Sitting back at the table just now was like that: dangling in his harness a thousand feet above the ground. He hadn't been wrong about her after all: it was a tremendous relief.

She launched into a story about calling 911 to rescue her neighbor from being strangled one summer night, only to learn that the woman was having sex with her husband. "I'm an alarmist," she said, "I think the worst." They laughed, back on course, the awkward tension behind them. His turn to take a leak. The bar was warm, lively, fun. Returning, he thought she looked great, seated at the table across the room, and the way she combed her fingers through her dark hair. His father had been right about her. Their glasses were empty, the pommes frites were gone.

"Well, what do you think?" he said, afraid this was going to end. He didn't want it to end. "How about one more?"

"I'll be drunk if I have another glass of wine."

"Have whatever you want. Beer," he suggested. "Water."

"You know what we should have? We should have a good scotch. Are you old enough to drink scotch, David?"

"Yeah, I'm old enough."

She ordered two Macallans, neat. "And we'll have another order of pommes frites," she said. "We need our nutrition here."

The whiskey arrived, provoking another inevitable toast, then they became completely quiet for a while, and it was okay. He was comfortable just sitting there, sipping occasionally, nothing to say. Their table was this little island of peace and quiet, he thought, in the midst of the loud, *festive* room. He'd been anxious that she'd want to leave, but she didn't want to leave. She was happy to be there, too. When he looked at her she was sitting back in her chair, the small glass gleaming amber on the table in front of her, hands in her lap, like they had all night. She smiled at him, and her smile was like a wave from his climbing buddy fifty feet below him at the other end of the rope.

She leaned forward to make herself heard. "You look a lot like your father."

He shook his head. "No I don't."

"You have his coloring, and his eyes."

"I don't look anything like him," he said.

"You do to me."

A few minutes later—he had been ambivalent about this until now—he removed the gray disk from his shirt pocket and placed it on the table by her glass. "I made you a copy."

"What is it?"

"That thing my dad wrote in Vermont. Over two hundred pages."

"Oh, David, I don't know," she said. "I don't think I'm comfortable with that. I probably couldn't bring myself to read it even if I wanted to. Did your father intend it for general distribution?"

"I'm not planning to give it to anyone else," he told her. "You're in it."

Smiling, she pushed the disk back toward him. "Put it away. Come on. I have to be frank, David, it's more than I want."

He was determined. "You might read it some day."

Who could he share it with? His mother was not a possibility. He had made up his mind not to mention the document to Elizabeth at all, although she was the person his father had most often addressed directly throughout *the writing*. No, saddling his stepmother with his father's last outpouring would be pointlessly cruel.

"Does it have a title?"

"The disk is labeled *Fitz*."

She picked it up. "That's interesting, isn't it?"

"Yeah, it is."

Helen opened her small black handbag and dropped the disk inside. "Am I required to give a book report?"

"I wanted you to have it, that's all. Do what you want with it."

"No one else has read it, huh?"

"No."

"Why me, David?"

By way of explanation he said, "I think you're the face in the last sentence."

Grinning, she said, "Now I'm thoroughly intrigued."

They'd been sitting there for hours, almost three hours. His scotch was gone and so was hers.

"Let's have one more."

She gave him an amused, skeptical glance. "I really love sitting here," she said, "but I'm afraid this sweet moment has to end."

"How about dinner? We could have dinner."

"David," she said. "I'm going to Chicago in the morning. I've got to get my shit together." She gestured to their waitress to bring the bill.

He didn't want to make a fool of himself. He knew that he'd probably never see *this Helen* again. He already knew that. The whole thing happening here was bizarre to start with. You couldn't make it up.

He took the small gift box from his left shirt pocket and placed it in front of her. "I have something else for you. A token. A little thing."

She sat back, smiling. "That isn't for me. What are you doing?"

"Yeah, it's for you. I went to that Mackintosh thing at the Met today and there it was."

"All right." She opened the box. The large, geometric pin was of a stylized bee, maybe a bumblebee, he thought when he saw it again. "Wow!" she said. She held the pin in the palm of her hand. "What a wonderful bee."

"Yeah," he said, "there was something about it."

She flew the pewter pin across the table in loops and swirls and pressed it against his chest. "A bee his burnished carriage drove boldly to a rose—"

"Who said that?" he asked. The line rang a bell.

Placing their check on the table, the waitress said, "I like that. Boldly to a rose." With a buzzing sound she likewise flew her finger, as it were, against his shoulder.

"That girl has her eye on you," Helen said. She fastened the bee pin onto her shirt collar. "How's that? It's a lovely token, David."

He insisted on getting the bill. The evening was on him, no question. He had it covered. Then he was pulling on his white sweater, helping her with her coat, while she thanked him for contacting her in the first place, the unexpected gifts, the whole thing. She pulled on her black leather gloves. The bar was warm and noisy and wonderful, and they were suddenly outside in the invigorating air of the December night.

"Henry couldn't have imagined this," she said. "Could he?"

"I don't think so."

He was hesitant, awkward, but the good-bye hug they finally drummed up was real. Her body felt smaller than he would have thought, but her embrace, her arms around his back, was emphatically strong.

"This has been good," she said. "It's just been very good, David."

At Seventh Avenue he wanted to break into a run, thinking he couldn't remember when he'd felt so pumped up, happy. He hadn't been this high at Yosemite when he topped Sunkist, you know. Like everything alive is beautiful, he thought, striding fast down the sidewalk, checking out the faces, the countless unique oncoming faces of all kinds. The street was solid with yellow cabs. At Eighteenth Street the cross traffic stopped him and he had to wait for the light. He tapped the left side of his jeans, then plunged his hands into the pockets. His wallet was gone.

His eyes scanned the congested littered sidewalk as he retraced his steps down Seventh Avenue, reciting the crucial contents of his wallet under his breath, but that was just dumb panic. He hadn't lost the wallet out here. He'd insisted on paying the bill, and in the excitement of leaving Bruxelles he'd failed to put the wallet back in his pocket. He'd knocked it onto the floor or left it right on the table. Oh, man. That wallet was gone. Anything mislaid in New York for five minutes was positively gone. Poof. He might as well have dropped it down a subway grid. At Fourteenth Street he fell into a jog, crossing against the light. This was how things happened, he thought, this was how you lost the wallet you carefully kept in your front pocket at all times, conscious of it all day long. This is how you fucked up a good night. Excusing himself, he pressed through people just arriving at the restaurant, getting out of their coats, and others blocking the entrance to the bar. Every table in the room was taken, the holiday mood of the place went on as before. He made his way to the spot by the window where he and Helen had been sitting, and the woman seated there now quailed at his approach. Had they seen a brown leather wallet? he asked, inspecting the table. They'd have to excuse him, he said, and he crouched down on the floor, searching between the legs of the table and chairs, causing the man and woman to come to their feet and step out of the way. Impetuously, he accosted people at the surrounding tables with their Belgian beer and wine and pommes frites, asking them to look at the floor around their chairs. No one had seen a wallet anywhere. Of course not. A wallet mislaid in New York City for thirty seconds disappeared, man, swallowed by the omnivorous thievery of city life. He made his way to the bar, imposing himself between two women on stools, and asked the bartender if anyone had turned in a wallet in the last half hour, a brown leather wallet, and the bartender, raising his hands in the air, slowly shook his head. He'd left the wallet behind, yes, an unforgivable blunder, but then someone had stolen it, he thought, scanning the room for a suspicious face. You can't make this stuff up, he thought, you don't know what's going to happen next.

"David."

He turned to the young woman who had waited on their table. She was almost his height in her quasi-combat boots. Her hair, he saw in this light, was really reddish-brown, auburn, rather than brunette. She had freckles, which he hadn't noticed before. She had a capped front tooth in her frank, pleased smile. She reached into her skimpy black apron, the width of a cummerbund—"I guess you got lucky tonight," she said—and handed him his wallet. Everything was there—the cash, his driver's license, a useless credit card, a short list of phone numbers, and the snapshots, both of them irreplaceable, of his sister and his father. All there.